Sally-Anne Robinso̶ ...
now lives with her ...
Her studies of English Literature as a mature
student inspired her to write, and *Seduction* is her
first novel.

SALLY-ANNE ROBINSON

SEDUCTION

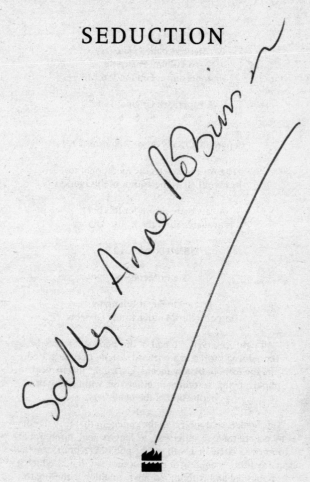

HarperCollins*Publishers*

For Simon

HarperCollins*Publishers*
77–85 Fulham Palace Road,
Hammersmith, London W6 8JB

A Paperback Original 1994
1 3 5 7 9 8 6 4 2

Copyright © Sally-Anne Robinson 1994

The Author asserts the moral right to
be identified as the author of this work

A catalogue record for this book
is available from the British Library

ISBN 0 00 647 319 9

Set in Meridien

Printed in Great Britain by
HarperCollinsManufacturing Glasgow

ONE

Elyssa Berkshire picked up the letter again and reread it. As she did so, a cold, clammy numbness began to spread over her. It couldn't be true; it couldn't possibly be true. Was she really that much in debt?

She swallowed hard, her head pounding as her panic-stricken eyes scanned the typewritten text. She had to force herself to concentrate on the words: 'unfortunately . . . come in and discuss the situation . . . payment by the end of the month'.

She threw the letter to one side. 'Damn! Damn! Damn!'

What the hell did she employ an accountant for if she was in this ungodly mess? More to the point, how the hell was she going to get herself out of it?

She stood up and walked over to the large bay windows, which looked down on the quiet residential square. She had worked so damned hard for everything she had and there was no way some young upstart of a bank manager was going to take it away from her, just because of a little misunderstanding over her finances. There had to be a way out of it.

She turned to one side and caught sight of herself in a glass-fronted bookcase which lined one of the walls. She was still an attractive woman. Tall, slim and elegant, she exuded a carefully cultivated air of rich sophistication. Her years of working as a model in the top couture houses of London and Paris had left her the legacy of graceful deportment which she used to her best advantage. That, and her knowledge of makeup and clothes, gave her all the ammunition she needed to find the men to support her in the lifestyle she had become accustomed to. When she was younger, the men fell at her knees in droves, driven by a frenzied desire to have and hold one of the most beautiful faces in the Western world. Now she was older, it was different. Two husbands had been and gone, their wealth sacrificed on her altar, and she was now left with little to show for her efforts.

She sighed and pushed back her thick red bobbed hair that swung around her neat, elfin face with its high cheekbones, small narrow nose and brown almond-shaped eyes. She still had her beauty and so long as she had that, she would find a way out of this mess.

Having made her resolution, she felt much better. She glanced at her Cartier watch. Ten o'clock in the morning. A bit too early for a drink, but she would have one anyway. After all, it wasn't every day that her life presented her with a new challenge.

She walked over to the drinks cabinet only to find she had run out of whisky.

'Shit.'

She picked up the in-house telephone. It rang twice before being answered. 'Get me another bottle, Aditha,' and she replaced the receiver.

A few minutes later there was a timid knock on the door.

'Yes?'

The door opened and a small dark Filipino maid entered the room, eyes downcast and head slightly bowed. 'Your drink, madam.'

'Pour me one.'

'Yes, madam.'

Elyssa sat down and crossed her long stockinged legs. She was wearing her new Chanel suit as she had a lunch engagement today, one she couldn't afford to miss. Claudia would be there and any opportunity Elyssa had of upstaging that insufferable bitch was more than looked forward to.

They had been models together; the redhead versus the

blonde, said the trade gossip. Each stunningly beautiful and each out to grab as much of the limelight as she could. The rivalry had not lessened over the years. If anything, the hatred was as fierce as ever. Claudia's recent marriage to Rupert Myers had been the society event of the previous summer and oh how she loved rubbing the salt in. Elyssa was determined not to be outdone. She would get her own back.

She smiled. With legs like hers, no one could outdo her, not even Claudia. And whereas Claudia's blonde hair needed to be professionally coloured to maintain its youthful appearance, Elyssa was proud of the fact that hers didn't. Black always looked so good, she thought, on someone with red hair and white flawless skin.

The maid came over with the drink on a silver tray. She handed it to Elyssa who, not looking, promptly dropped it all over herself. She sprang to her feet, the empty crystal tumbler falling to the floor.

'You stupid clumsy bitch!' she yelled at the cowering woman. 'Look what you've done to my new suit!' and before the maid could dive out of the way, Elyssa slapped her hard across the face. 'Stupid cow!'

Aditha burst into tears.

'Clear that fucking mess up and stop snivelling, you idiot, otherwise I'll really give you something to cry about!'

'Yes . . . madam.'

Aditha got to her knees and picked up the tumbler and tray, her eyes fearfully anticipating yet more blows, but Elyssa had gone to pour herself another drink; a large one; one she knocked back in a single gulp.

'I don't know why I employ you damned foreigners. You're all the same. Bloody useless.'

Aditha stood up, trembling.

'Get out of my sight,' snapped her mistress.

'Yes, madam.'

Aditha gone, Elyssa slumped onto the sofa. She felt a momentary surge of self-pity threaten to overwhelm her, but she stopped it. There was no point in wallowing in her misery. So she was penniless? So what? Only she knew that. She still had all the status symbols of a very wealthy woman: a house in Belgravia, a maid, a chauffeur, rooms full of designer clothes and a safety deposit box, admittedly empty at the moment, but still there if she were ever to need it again. And she would.

She picked at her suit and tutted. It was ruined. She would have to change. And then she smiled. Maybe her chauffeur, Kevin, would like to come and help her undress. He had such a rural simplicity about him that she found it hard to resist his vulgar, if somewhat ham-fisted sexuality. She'd go and find him. Half an hour with him and she would forget all her problems and then after lunch she would go through her address book.

She stood up and regarded her reflection in a mirror. She smiled.

'Don't worry, darling,' she told herself, 'there's a man out there somewhere; a rich one, just waiting for you to come and get him. It's just a question of finding him.' With a renewed spring in her step, she left the room.

'Kevin! Kevin!'

It was her smile that he liked most; a warm, engaging curve of her lips and now she was smiling at him.

'I can't believe it. Why me?'

'Why not?'

Claire shrugged, unable to give him an answer and smiled ruefully.

'Well, what are you going to do with it then?'

Alistair waited. It was a pleasant thing for him to do as it gave him ample time to study her beautiful oval face with its soft pink complexion and sprinkling of freckles.

Silence. Her large green eyes reflected the afternoon's dim light. Then she turned her head to one side showing him the profile of her straight aquiline nose and small chin. He watched closely as she thoughtfully ran the tip of her tongue along her bottom lip. It was to his eyes a perfect lip of a perfect pair; very inviting and deliciously kissable. He wanted to kiss her very much; to lean over his desk, pull her gently to him and run his fingers through her long black waves as she yielded to his arms.

But not now. She wouldn't have it. She was always just out of reach.

'Well?'

She stretched out her long jean-clad legs and leant back in the chair.

'Don't know.' Her voice seemed distant.

'Here,' he said, pushing forward a plate of biscuits, 'have another one. I got your favourites.'

She shook her head. 'No thanks.'

'Surely you're not dieting? There's nothing to you as it is.' He ran his eyes down her seated figure ostensibly to show her how concerned he was for her welfare, but they both knew different. When he looked back at her face, her eyes met his with faint good humour. He felt mildly embarrassed.

'No, Ali, I'm not dieting.'

He looked down wistfully at his own waistline. 'Could do with losing a few pounds myself.'

'Less time spent in the rugby club, Ali, and more time spent on the pitch perhaps?'

They smiled at each other.

'Anyway,' he said briskly, 'what are you going to do now that you are one of, if not *the* richest women in town?'

Claire looked bewildered and a little tired. 'I don't know,' she sighed. 'I never really bothered about money before. Matt was the one that . . .' Her voice trailed off. She took a deep breath and started again. 'Of course I've had to do it all since he, well, since the accident, but it's not been easy.' She stopped and gave a nervous laugh and started to pick at one of her nails. She looked up at him again. 'I really couldn't care less about it, Alistair. I'll pay

9

all my outstanding bills, I suppose, and my bank manager will be delighted that I'm finally doing something about my overdraft and mortgage arrears, but apart from that – well, I don't know.'

She fell quiet again and twisted her wedding ring around her finger. She always did that when she mentioned Matt. It had been two years since the accident and she still missed him so much.

'Perhaps,' suggested Alistair gently, 'I can give you some advice. The best thing you could do is to go and see an independent financial adviser. He will be able to give you all the information you need about stocks and shares and where to find the best interest rates. After all, a million pounds, if properly invested, could easily give you a reasonable income for the rest of your life.'

He watched her closely. She didn't seem to be listening to anything he said. He tried another tack.

'What about starting a different business? With that amount of money, you could do almost anything you want.'

'What? I don't know anything about any other business, Ali.' She shook her head emphatically. 'No, I'm more than happy at the farm right now.'

'But you could sell that,' he insisted, 'move into town, move away all together, take a long holiday. The thing is, Claire, now that you have all this money, anything is possible and there's nothing to stop you.'

She looked straight at him and he could feel the full strength of her character. 'And what about Rosie? What would I do about her?'

At the mention of her name, the large black dog, which had been lying quietly next to the table, looked up and cocked her head on one side. Her soft brown eyes were fixed attentively on her mistress's face as her long tail swept across the carpet. Both the man and woman smiled at her; the woman with love and the man because the woman loved her. He wished he was Rosie.

'You know, Claire, I swear that dog looks more and more like you.'

She looked at him with wry amusement. 'Really? Perhaps I ought to make sure my tail is properly tucked in the next time I come to see you.'

'No, no,' he protested laughingly. 'You know what I mean; the same colour hair and what-have-you.'

She held out a lock of her own thick waves. 'Ah, but Rosie has a patch of white under her chin, don't you, girl? And I,' she said looking at him again, 'haven't any grey hairs yet.'

'Yes, I can see that and extremely beautiful your hair is too.'

She blushed; very prettily he thought.

'Ali! You old flatterer.'

'Less of the "old" if you don't mind.'

Claire stroked her dog. 'I can't leave her or any of my animals. It's impossible. I love that farm even if it is backbreaking work, and money or no money, I intend to stay there.'

'Good,' he said quietly. He wanted to tell her how much he would miss her if she were to leave but decided not to. It was not the time for such things. She might take it the wrong way. Once before he had tried to tell her how much he thought of her, but she didn't take him seriously then and he saw no reason why she should now, except of course that she had been a widow for the last two years.

'Look, Ali, this secret benefactor of mine; who is he?'

He hurriedly looked down at the papers in front of him, reorganizing his thoughts. 'Ah yes,' he said at last. 'His name was Harold Carter-Browne.' He read some more before shuffling the papers together and placing them to one side of his enormous red leather-topped desk. 'Well,' he said, leaning back in his deep swivel chair and regarding her with bright blue eyes set deep beneath blond eyebrows, 'it seems that this Carter-Browne chap was distantly related to your mother. He owned and ran a highly

11

successful investment agency in London as well as a large country estate in Oxfordshire where he bred horses. He was unmarried and had no children of his own but he did bring up his sister's children when the parents were killed in an accident. I suppose,' he said, smoothing his gold-coloured moustache, 'that by rights they should have inherited the estate but as we solicitors know only too well, things invariably get unpleasant when there are large sums of money involved and Carter-Browne was no different. It appears that for whatever reason and known only to him, he disinherited all of his relatives and left all of the money, bar the amount you got, to a dogs' home.'

'What!' She smiled incredulously. 'I don't believe it!'

'Yes, it's quite true. Apparently he couldn't stand any of the children he was guardian to and you were the only other beneficiary apart from the dogs' home. Your mother, of course, would have received the money were she still alive, but as she isn't, it goes straight to you.' He smiled at her, glad of her happiness.

'Well,' she said at last, 'if Mum had been around I know what would have happened: a non-stop booze-up down at the pub for her and all her drunken cronies. I suppose I should be relieved she's not here to see it. At least it saves me the embarrassment of taking her home when she's too drunk to walk.'

Alistair looked at his empty teacup. 'Any more?' he asked. Claire's brutally honest assessment of her mother always caught him unprepared.

'You needn't be embarrassed, Ali,' she said, holding out her cup. 'My mother was a drunk. I grew up with it and watched her destroy everything. When she died, I think it was a blessed relief for both of us.' She paused. 'I know it probably sounds terrible to you, Ali, but try to understand what it must have been like for me.'

'Of course, Claire. I'm sorry.'

'Don't be.'

They were quiet for a few moments and then she said, 'It's a pity Matt's not here, though.'

'Yes, it is,' he agreed. 'Mind you, I'm not at all sure he would have made any major changes to his life either. Your husband always struck me as someone who was fairly oblivious to material comforts.'

'True. It didn't matter to him one way or another what other people had. He only ever cared about the farm. Oh, he might have spent a few quid on a new tractor or maybe buy some extra cattle, but other than that,' she shrugged her shoulders, 'I might have got him away for a few days if I were lucky, but trying to persuade him to take a holiday was like trying to prize a limpet off a rock – virtually impossible,' and she gave a soft remembering laugh as the familiar aching welled up inside her. 'So,' she said brightly, forcing it back down again, 'What about Carter-Browne's relatives? They must be angry about all of this.'

'Maybe, but the will was very specific. Everything was done to make sure that everyone knew what they were getting. Nothing was left to chance. I wouldn't worry about them if I were you. No doubt,' he said, smoothing his moustache again, 'they were a little bit peeved – after all, there was a great deal of money involved – but in the end, there was nothing they could do.'

'Oh well, I suppose it doesn't really matter too much then. I mean, it's not as if I'm ever going to meet any of them.' She pulled at her bottom lip. 'I can't help feeling a bit guilty, though.'

'Don't, Claire. They're not poor, believe me. The two sisters have both married well and the brother works in the City or something, so don't imagine they're poverty-stricken.'

Claire stood up and walked over to the window. It was a foul afternoon and very few people were out in the cold blustery rain which threw itself against the windows. She idly watched the figures as they hurried across the square.

She breathed deeply. Beeswax, she thought. Alistair's office always smelt of beeswax. It must be used on all that leather; chair, desk top, leather-bound books all along the walls. Silly, she thought, here I am, one of the richest people in town and all I can think of is beeswax.

She ought to have been happy, ecstatic even, but she wasn't. Instead all she felt was surprised, mutedly happy and quite nonchalant about the whole thing.

Alistair watched her from his chair. It appeared to him that her rear view was every bit as attractive as the front. The way she filled out the seat of her jeans, the way she rested one graceful arm up against the window and the way her long hair fell in silken waves over her shoulders and down her back. She was slim but she curved in all the right places. He could easily imagine what it would be like lying in bed with her and running his hands over her full, round breasts, across her flanks and down along her firm warm thighs and on to her . . .

'Why didn't he like his relatives?' She turned and faced him, fixing him with a look of concentrated puzzlement.

Momentarily caught off guard, he instantly snapped back into his professional persona. 'Carter-Browne, you mean?'

'Yes.'

She waited for him to answer. As usual he had that slightly crumpled look about him. Tall and powerfully built, he filled his oversized chair with ease. His blond hair and red-hued moustache gave him the appearance of a civilized Viking and although he was all smiles now, she could well imagine how his handsome face with its slightly hooked nose and penetrating blue eyes could be quite intimidating under different circumstances.

'Who knows?' he said. 'Family dynamics continually surprise me in this trade.' He paused to look back at the pile of papers on his desk. 'So, what are you going to do with it then? Go on a long luxurious holiday? Personally,

14

I've always fancied a trip to the Pacific. You know, azure seas, white sand beaches, plenty of sun and – '

'Plenty of willing young ladies,' she interjected, 'to keep you company? To play chess with? To discuss philosophy with or maybe,' she teased mischievously, 'to rub sun lotion into your back?'

'Well, there's no denying that the local populace would have certain attractions, but, of course, that wouldn't be the main reason for my visit.'

'Oh no, of course not, Ali,' she agreed, nodding her head sagely.

'I would simply be going there to study local tribal customs and laws. After all, it is the duty of every practising lawyer to keep abreast – '

'Literally or metaphorically?'

'. . . to keep up to date,' he corrected himself, 'with a wide variety of national and international laws so that disputes can be resolved in a reasonable and civilized manner.' He smiled benignly.

'Alistair, you are a fraud.'

He grinned. 'Yes, I know, but a very charming one nonetheless.'

She laughed. She always enjoyed their light-hearted repartee and it was this relationship she supposed that held her back from him. He was too good a friend to get involved with. She wasn't immune to his handsomeness; who could be? But somehow it just didn't work for her. She needed something else; something more intense; something that would give her back the life she had lost after Matt's death.

She looked back at him. The laughter lines around his eyes were now less noticeable. He looked more serious. The time for joking was over. She resumed her seat.

'I've had another letter from Stapletons,' he began slowly. 'They have been instructed by their client Mr Neale to offer you a new set of proposals concerning Orchard Meadow.' He waited. Every time he brought up the subject of Orchard Meadow and especially its prospective buyer, Mr Neale, he knew he might have to face an outburst of her sometimes irrational temper. He hoped that telling her the news of her inheritance first would have softened her.

She rubbed her hands wearily across her forehead. This business with Neale had been going on far too long and she was thoroughly fed up with it.

'Doesn't that bloody man ever take no for an answer?' She glared at him, not expecting a reply. 'Look, Alistair,' she began again with more restraint. 'I don't care if that man offers me the entire gross national product, I am not, nor will I ever, sell him that land.' She paused and breathed deeply, irritated but managing to keep herself under control. 'That land is my land and will stay my land, and if that money-grubbing, greedy little creep thinks he can come down here and just buy up whatever he likes so as to build his executive-style rabbit hutches for the upwardly mobile, then he's got another think coming.' She stopped abruptly, nostrils flaring with indignation.

'Yes, Claire. Of course.' It was at times like this that he relied heavily on his deep mellow voice to calm his more irate clients. Claire was proving to be no exception. 'So I take it you're not really interested then?'

She gave him a cold hard stare. 'Tell him to get stuffed, Ali.'

'Well, perhaps not in those exact words, but I'm sure I can pen a suitable rebuff.'

She leant back in her chair, visibly more relaxed. 'You don't know how close I came to giving in to that man,' she said quietly. 'I've been so worried, what with all the unpaid bills, that I seriously began to reconsider his offer.' She smiled briefly. 'I'm so glad I didn't.' She closed her eyes and rubbed her neck. 'Oh, I'm so tired.'

'I'm not surprised. News like this can do that to some people. I suppose it's the shock of it all. It's not every day that I tell someone about an unexpected inheritance, especially one as big as this.'

He gazed at her. If only she knew how lovely she looked, he thought. Even dressed in dirty jeans and jumper, she still exuded all the charm and femininity that any woman would be proud to have. She, though, seemed unaware of it.

'If it's any consolation,' he added, 'I'm glad you don't have to sell to Mr Neale. I met him once at one of those interminable civic dos I'm always being invited to and he struck me as being a rather loud and vulgar chap. He was wearing the most bizarre waistcoat, if I remember correctly. Still,' he added, 'I don't suppose he means to be rude. Perhaps he just doesn't understand how things are done around here.'

'No, he doesn't. Well, perhaps now he'll disappear down whatever hole he crawled out of and I'll be able to get on with my life.'

'I wouldn't bank on it,' said Alistair. 'Men like Neale are hardly likely to give up when they know they only need a little bit more land and their plans can go ahead. I've heard that maybe one or two of your neighbours might have sold out already.'

'Well, if he comes snooping round my place, I'll send him away with more than a flea in his ear.'

Then she smiled broadly, a dimple appearing in each of her cheeks and her eyes lighting up. 'To tell the truth, I couldn't care less about him. The only things that matter to me are my animals and farm.'

'And your friends, I hope.'

'Yes, and my friends.'

'It's good to see you smile again, Claire. You haven't done nearly enough of it over the last two years.'

She looked away quickly and clasped her hands together. Even an oblique remark like that could instantly peel back the layers of protection she had built around herself. The hollow empty grief she felt was something she preferred not to be reminded of.

Alistair, sensing the sudden change of atmosphere in

17

the room, tried to laugh it off. 'Oh dear,' he said awkwardly. 'Done it again, haven't I?'

She slowly shook her head as if physically pushing away the pain. 'No, no you haven't. It's just that . . . Well, you know what I mean.'

'I'm sorry, Claire.'

She shrugged her shoulders. Another awkward silence.

'Well,' he said at last. 'Perhaps we ought to just leave things here before I really go and cock it up. Look,' making a great play out of looking at his watch, 'I have to see another client in a few minutes. Think about what I've said, especially seeing someone to give you financial advice, and if you have any problems at all then I'll be only too glad to see you. As you know, I'm nearly always here and you don't always have to make an appointment. If you want,' he added, looking at her closely, 'I could come out to the farm sometime and we could discuss it there.'

She barely looked at him when she said no thank you.

They stood up and he guided her out of the office, one hand brushing against her back as they walked to the door. He was so close to her that he could smell the delicate herbaceous scent that came from her hair.

'Alistair,' she said, suddenly stopping in the doorway so that his hand definitely touched her back, sending a small *frisson* of delight up his arm, 'I will get back to you about things, but to tell the truth, I'm so shell-shocked at the moment, I don't know if I'm coming or going.'

He smiled down at her from his six feet two height and wondered once more how it was that she could look so young sometimes. She was twenty-eight but at that moment, her face tilted up to look at him with wide innocent eyes and smooth unlined skin, she looked no more than eighteen. She was all woman, and it irritated him in the most pleasurable way.

'Of course,' he answered. 'You give me a ring whenever

18

you like and we'll have a chat about it, okay?'

They walked into the reception area.

'Heavens, what foul weather,' he said. 'How on earth do you manage up there?'

'With great difficulty sometimes. Last week some of the slates blew off one of the barns and the rendering desperately needs seeing to.' She looked down at her shoes. 'That's why I can't ask you up, Ali. It's a dump at the moment and quite unfit for visitors.' She glanced back at him.

'As if I would notice such things, Claire.'

'Well, I do.'

He helped her on with her waxed jacket and she zipped it up. Rosie sat at her feet.

'I suppose now,' he said, 'you'll be able to do the place up a bit and get things repaired?'

'Yes. My tractor's just about had it and the van is unlikely to pass its MOT.'

'You know, I tried ringing you several times last week and couldn't get through. That's why I had to ask Jack to come over with a message for you. Don't you have one of those exterior bells on your telephone any more?'

'Yes I do, only it doesn't work. As soon as I pay my reconnection charge and outstanding bill, all will be fine.'

'Oh dear, as bad as that, was it?'

'Yes, and worse.'

'You know, you only had to come and ask me, Claire, and I would have been very glad to help you.'

She lay an affectionate hand on his sleeve. 'Thanks, Ali, I know you would, but I have to stand on my own two feet, you know.'

He put his hand on hers. 'Not always, Claire,' he said quietly, looking deep into her eyes.

She smiled briefly and then withdrew her hand. 'I'd better go. The sheep will need seeing to.' She looked out of the window. 'See, the rain's stopped now.'

19

He walked her to the door and held it open while she stepped out onto the top of the short flight of steps leading down into the square. She turned to look at him, her hair blowing around her head.

'Thanks, Ali,' and she held out her hand. He took it in his own, her warm delicate fingers pressed against his and he brushed them against his lips. She said nothing.

'It was a pleasure, Claire, and it couldn't have happened to a nicer person. You will ring me now, won't you?'

'Yes.'

He waved goodbye as she walked across the square, her hands deep inside her pockets as she hunched up against the wind. Rosie walked by her side. She didn't need a lead. Rosie always stayed by her mistress.

Back in his office Alistair slumped in his chair. There were no other clients that afternoon. He had only said that because, as usual, he was so distracted by Claire that he was apt to put his foot in it and ruin any chance that he might have had of getting closer to her.

He sighed deeply. Bloody fool, he told himself. Just because she had turned him down once, and that was years ago now, it didn't mean that she would do it again. He cursed himself for his lack of courage. He didn't have any of these problems with other women.

Right from the day he had met her, he had wanted her. But there was Matt and before he knew what was happening, she was getting married to him, and any hopes he might have had were over before they had even begun.

He pulled open one of the desk drawers and reached under some papers. His hand fell on an antique silver photograph frame. He pulled it out and looked at it. It was a picture of Claire taken without her knowledge at her wedding reception and cherished from that day to this. It was his secret and he always kept it hidden.

Claire went back to her van. She had gone shopping after seeing Alistair and had in her bags a large piece of steak

20

and a good bottle of wine. Tonight she would celebrate. But not yet. First she wanted to go and see Matt. She liked to talk to him. It gave her comfort during times of stress.

'Come on, dog,' she said to Rosie as they climbed into the van. 'Let's go and see the old man.'

She drove off through the late afternoon traffic to the church. Parking next to the gateway in a layby, she and Rosie got out and walked along the wet stone flags covered in ancient green moss until they came to Matt's gravestone. Water dripped disconsolately from the bare branches above Claire's head and the long grass around his plot was sodden. A few rooks called from the spire as the early dusk and murk descended like a heavy woollen blanket.

Rosie stood quietly while Claire leant down and removed some dead flowers from a vase.

Two years; or to be exact two years, three months and one week. To her the loss was far deeper than anything she had ever experienced before. Not even her mother's last few pain-racked months and squalid death could compare with the loss of Matt.

A maths teacher at the local comprehensive, he had stepped into her life soon after her mother had left it. She had been so exhausted by the months of caring for the prematurely aged woman, that she thought herself unable to smile or laugh ever again. Matt changed everything. Where once there was grief, happiness returned; where once there was betrayal and cynicism, optimism replaced it.

Claire had loved him with a strength that sometimes frightened and overwhelmed her. When he asked her to marry him, there was only one answer she could give. By then, he had decided to leave teaching and the pair of them sunk all their money into a run-down small holding called Tor Heights. Now it was the only thing she had left. That and her dog, and nothing seemed to diminish the pain she felt.

21

She unwrapped some fresh flowers and placed them in the vase. They wouldn't last long in this weather and she knew it, but it didn't matter.

'Well, Matt,' she said quietly, 'what do you think of this now? Me, the richest woman in town. It's a joke, isn't it?' She faltered, her eyes filling with tears. 'Oh Matt, I wish you were here to share this with me. What am I going to do?'

But the grave remained silent as the tears rolled unchecked down her cheeks. For several more minutes she stood there contemplating the eerie peace as the sky darkened above her head.

She was so rich and yet so very, very miserable.

Alistair didn't notice how long he had been sitting thinking of Claire until his phone rang. He picked it up. It was his secretary, Julie.

'Elyssa Berkshire on the line, Alistair.'

'Who?' He was tired and not listening too closely.

'A Ms Elyssa Berkshire for you.'

'Oh well, put her through then, please.' Elyssa Berkshire? He hadn't heard from her for months. He replaced Claire's photograph in his drawer. Elyssa. He supposed that if anyone knew how to distract him, she would.

'Elyssa! How lovely to hear from you!'

'Alistair, you so-and-so. Why haven't you rung me? You said you would and like the poor besotted fool that I am, I waited in vain. However, being a resourceful woman, I decided that if Mohammed won't come to the mountain, then the mountain had better come to you.'

'How very nice of you, Elyssa, and it couldn't happen at a more opportune time.'

He wasn't smiling.

TWO

In Devon the lanes are usually set deep between high green hedges, but towards Dartmoor the hedges thin out to pitiful thin knotted scrub, a product of the moor's climatic extremes. The rich Devonshire soil, normally so fecund, disappears too and is replaced by a thin acid topsoil that mainly supports heather and gorse. It is a challenge to all the farmers around to produce anything much on such poor land and Claire, like her neighbours, worked hard for little reward. She had some chickens, some sheep, a few cattle and her horse.

Mostly she was alone, but she wasn't lonely. Eight years of boarding school, the traditional education for an army child, had taught her independence and self-reliance. And she had Rosie. The dog had been a present from Matt just before his accident and Claire knew that she was the one thing that kept her going. During the grief-stricken aftermath of his death, Rosie, then a young bouncy puppy, had stopped her sinking ever lower in despair, until finally she had taken over where he had left off. During the days she was always there beside Claire and at night, when Claire's bed stretched so cold and lonely, Rosie's warming bulk lay next to her, giving her comfort in the dark.

Claire pulled up the handbrake and turned off the ignition. In front of her, blocking the narrow lane with his Land Rover and trailer was her neighbour, Jack Burrows. He climbed out of the cab and came towards her. As usual, he was dressed in blue mud-spattered overalls and wellingtons. Jack was tall, with a wiry build, and his calloused hands were permanently engraved with the dirt and scars of years of farming.

23

He smiled broadly, his face weatherworn and ruddy, his dark eyes twinkling in a mesh of wrinkles. Despite his advanced years, he still walked with a determined energy which came from his lifelong daily routine of hard physical labour. He looked quite comical with his white frizzy hair sticking out at right angles from beneath his woolly hat. Claire liked him very much and always enjoyed their meetings. She got out of her van.

'Good news was it?'

'Mmm, maybe,' she teased.

'I see,' he said, stamping his feet in the cold. 'Not going to tell me then?'

'Well, let's just say it has more to do with my bank manager than anything else, and for once he was pleased to see me.'

'Really?' he grinned. 'Huh! Wish I got messages like that from my solicitor. Anyway, come and see what I've just spent some more of my overdraft on.'

She followed him round to his trailer, trying to bury herself deeper in her jacket out of the squally wind. Jack seemed impervious to the cold. Whatever the weather he always wore the same outfit.

'I've just been to a farm near Exeter,' he said over his shoulder, 'and got myself a prize animal.'

He was tall enough to look in the box but she had to stand on the bumper. She was very impressed with what she saw.

'Heavens! He's enormous!'

'Bloody good bag on 'im as well. Expect to get lots of good calves from 'im.'

'Charolais, isn't he?'

'Yes, and a damned good one. Got a pedigree as long as your arm.'

The bull looked round at them, his eyes showing their whites in the gloom of the box. He was the colour of clotted cream and every muscle under his taut skin seemed to be bursting out of itself. Claire could only stare at him.

24

'A ton or more of prime meat and bone there,' said Jack proudly, close to her ear, 'should improve my stock no end.'

'Where are you going to keep him then?' she asked, knowing full well that bulls were not allowed inside the Park as it was public land.

Jack scratched his chin and characteristically pursed his lips. 'That bottom field of mine that backs on to your place, I thought.' And sensing her reluctance added, 'Don't worry, he's a quiet bugger and I won't have him there for long. Just till he settles down like, and I've got something else arranged.'

They walked back to her van.

'How's your lambing going then?' he asked.

'So-so. Mostly singletons, but I've had a couple of doubles too. Nothing's died on me yet, thank God.'

'Well, I told you they wouldn't. Those Welsh ewes don't look much but they're damned good at lambing.'

They stood next to her van.

'Jack, have you had any more enquiries from that Neale chap, you know, the one who wanted to build on our fields?'

Jack looked away over the gloomy fields, deep frown lines covering his aged skin. He said: 'Yes, I have and I'm sorry, Claire, I know we all agreed and that, but I have a farm to keep going and with all my overheads, it's bloody difficult, I can tell you. Anyway,' he added by way of explanation, 'when I pass on, Robbie will be taking over and I don't want him having to sell because the place is bankrupt.'

'So you sold then?'

'Had to. Only five acres, mind. The rest is still mine. I had no choice.' He looked at her, his eyes pained. 'Sorry, maid. There was nothing I could do.'

'I know, I know,' she sighed, kicking some loose chippings across the road.

'Look, do you think if I had any choice I would willingly

sell to that bloke?' He waited for her to answer. 'No, I didn't think you would. Anyway,' he said more cheerfully, 'I got my pound of flesh from that man and when my heifers see what I've got lined up for them, they'll be queueing up for Bruno's services. I mean, how can a cow enjoy a man from the AI Centre sticking his arm up her you know what?'

'Jack!'

Rosie poked her head out of the van door, her steamy breath ripped away by the strong wind.

'Fine dog you have there,' said Jack, cupping her large head in his hands. 'Fancy selling her, do you?' It was a question he really didn't need to ask as he always knew the answer. He gave Rosie one last pat.

'Well, I'm off now. Missus'll be on at me if I'm not back for milking. Take care and I'll see you around. Bye.'

'Bye, Jack.'

Claire climbed back into her van and reversed into a layby so he could pass. He waved as he went.

She drove back to her farm thinking about the day's events. All that money! A million pounds! She could hardly believe it. She could see at once where some of it would go. There was a huge stack of unpaid bills sitting behind the clock in the kitchen, as well as three months' arrears on the mortgage. It would be wonderful to get cleared of them. Pulling into her yard, she came to a halt. On three sides of her stood the grey granite buildings of her farm. The house stood directly in front of her, square and functional with a barn and stables running down each side. At this time of the year it looked cold and forbidding, but when the summer came back, the swallows returned and her moorland garden blossomed into a plethora of small colours, it was a beautiful place.

She let Rosie out and the pair of them immediately went into the barn, called by the familiar grunting of a ewe in labour. Even before she opened the barn door the pungent smell of ammonia from housed sheep filled her nostrils.

She pulled the stiff door shut behind her and switched on the lights, a couple of bare bulbs festooned with cobwebs and dust.

Between the large communal pen and rows of smaller individual ones, ran a straw walkway. She walked slowly along it, looking closely at her sheep. The few ewes that had already lambed stared blankly at her before turning their attention back to their offspring, skinny bundles of new life that bleated sharply. Some fed hungrily, butting their mothers' teats for more milk, their tails wagging furiously, while others slept.

Claire noticed the water troughs were empty. They would have to be filled tonight, but first she had to see to the ewe.

The animal was at the back of the large pen, lying on her side, her legs stretched out taut, and staring at the ceiling. 'Stargazing' the farmers called it and it was a sure sign that her lamb was coming. Claire told Rosie to sit and then climbed in with the sheep. She moved slowly. The flock watched her warily with their amber eyes, their bellies swollen but still agile enough to run from her grasp.

She moved closer to the ewe. It was so far gone, it couldn't move at all. Claire knelt down beside her and reached over to the ewe's tail. A large opaque water bag was glistening inside her and Claire could just see the lamb's black snout and tips of its forefeet.

She took off her jacket and rolled up her sleeves. With one arm on the ewe's neck, she broke open the water bag, spilling the warm fluid across the straw. Gently she inserted her forefingers into the ewe's pink vagina until she had a firm hold behind the lamb's neck. Pulling it slowly with each contraction, she eased it out until the whole of its hot, yellow-tinged black and white body flopped onto the straw.

She nipped the umbilical cord and wiped clean its face so that it could breathe. Then, seeing that it was okay, she picked it up by its hind legs and swung it backwards and

27

forwards a few times so as to clear the mucus from its airways and lungs. She lay it down in front of the ewe. It clumsily shook itself and blinked in the bright light. The mother started to lick it dry, a deep satisfied purring rumbling up from her throat. The lamb was a fine big one, and a ewe too. It was too big for a twin, but Claire checked, just to make sure.

She stood up and eased back her shoulders. She was very tired. It had been a long hard season and it wasn't over yet. The lambing had a couple of weeks to go but after that she might get some time to rest.

She walked over to the shelf where she kept the iodine. Picking up the new lamb, she dabbed some onto its umbilical stump, leaving a brown-yellow stain. By imitating the lamb's plaintive cry, she encouraged the ewe into a separate pen where they would be more secure. She then checked to see there was milk in both teats and, with a final look at the others, got on with the rest of her chores.

Three hours later, after everything was done, she sat down on the sofa, replete with the steak and chips and raised her glass to herself. Rosie sat next to her.

'Well then, Rosie, now what?'

THREE

James slowly put down the telephone receiver. He was stunned. Even his health club tan couldn't hide his shock as his skin paled.

He stared unseeing at the table top. All that money and not one penny of it coming to him? With one violent sweep of his arm, everything on the table flew onto the floor.

'You bastard! You bloody bastard!' he yelled, his dark, handsome face screwed up with agonized horror. 'How could you do such a thing?'

The lounge door opened and a large pink and white baby-doll, blue-eyed face, topped with a mass of blonde curls, poked around the door.

'Something wrong, sweetie-poos?' said the high-pitched voice.

'Something wrong?' he snarled. 'Something wrong? I'll say there's something fucking wrong! That bastard of an uncle of mine has left his entire fortune to a fucking dogs' home!'

The young woman, dressed in a silk kimono of the most vivid pink, tottered into the room on high-heeled slippers, her ample figure bouncing around under the glossy material.

'What? All of it, sweetie?'

'Yes, all of it. Well,' he added, getting down on the floor to pick up the mess, 'not quite all of it, but most of it. Apparently there's some distant cousin down in Devon who got a bit of it, but that's neither here nor there. The thing is,' he said, scowling at her blank face with furiously angry dark blue eyes, 'he's not left any of it to the family or to me!' and he stabbed his chest with an indignant finger. 'I mean, how the bloody hell am I to survive without that money? Did he expect me to work for the rest of my life? It's sheer lunacy.'

The woman sat down on the leather sofa and examined her long pink nails. 'Well, darling, lots of people have jobs and there's nothing wrong with working in a merchant bank. It's very respectable.'

'Respectable my arse!' he snapped. 'It's still working, isn't it? I mean, what's the point of being brought up in luxury if you're expected to work for a living, for God's sake? Only plebs do that!'

The woman turned her large blonde head to him and regarded him with an indolent face. 'My Daddy works.'

'Your Daddy, Saskia, is a builder. No more, no less. Just a common or garden builder.'

'Property developer actually,' she sniffed.

'Property developer . . . builder. What's the bloody difference? Just because he's floated the company on the Stock Market is crap — doesn't mean anything nowadays. If this present slump keeps up, he'll be joining me down in the dole office.'

'What?' Her face puckered, her large voluptuous lips forming a gaping red hole.

'You heard me. The bank's in trouble. Big trouble. It might not last.'

'But Michelberg & Sons is one of the oldest and most respected merchant banks in London,' she protested.

'They might be, dear Sas, but not for much longer.' He slumped back in his chair and sighed deeply. 'Word's been out for weeks that something might be about to happen. Of course, as a mere member of staff, I don't know any more than the man in the street, but I can bet I'll be the first to know when the place goes down.'

'Well, what will you do?'

He smiled ironically, his voice sneering. 'Oh don't worry

about me, Sas, don't worry at all. Little James will get it all sorted out.'

Saskia looked at him for a few moments before returning to her nails. It would be pointless asking what he meant by that statement. It always was. Any enquiries about his private life were always met with a wall of silence so now she didn't bother asking.

James might have sounded confident, but he wasn't. His fraudulent withdrawals and deposits from customers' accounts were getting perilously close to being discovered. Only last week he had had to do some rapid covering up of his tracks when one of the other managers got too close for comfort.

It was no good, he decided. Gambling debts or no gambling debts, he couldn't afford to go on like this. He had to do something.

He stood up. 'I'm going out,' he announced.

Saskia's face fell. 'What? But you said – '

'Screw it,' he said dismissively. 'I've got things to do.'

'Well, thank you very much,' she retorted huffily as she got up and followed him out of the room. 'And just what am I supposed to tell our dinner host?'

'Tell him what you like, dear girl. I couldn't give a toss.'

'Bastard!' she yelled as he disappeared upstairs.

James smiled. Stupid cow. God knows why he put up with her.

James's night out without Saskia had done nothing to improve his health. He rolled over, rested his forearm against his eyes to shield them from the morning's glare and carefully ran his tongue around his teeth; they felt coated. He wanted very much not to have to move, to breathe or even to think. He just wanted to be held in absolute stillness. A truly unpleasant nausea that started somewhere down in his bowels was rapidly spreading up his torso and threatening to swamp him and he knew, from other such mornings, that if he lay completely still, it might pass over him and subside. It didn't. His guts, despite all his efforts, were twisting and contorting, needle-sharp spasms spiking his flesh. He belched, and with it came the sour rancid taste of bile. It was no good; he had to move. With one supreme effort to defy all his body's pleas to lay down and give in to the imminent peristaltic explosions, he got up and staggered into the bathroom. Moments later, his sphincters capitulated and he vomited all the previous evening's poisons.

He wiped the sweat from his forehead and blinked away the tears. Why, he thought, did your eyes water when you were sick? He looked up from the sink and stared at himself in the large mirror. It was unfortunate that in this bathroom he always looked so pale. It did him no justice at all.

With both hands he smoothed back his straight black hair from where it had fallen over his eyes, running his fingers along his scalp until his muscular shoulders and upper arms were flexed up at their best and then turned slowly from side to side admiring their smooth veined tautness.

He smiled; twenty-eight and pulsating with hormones. He switched on the overhead light and peered closer at himself. His top-up tan from the health club was beginning to fade now but he still had that athletic outdoor look which so suited his square face with its firm lines. Perhaps a couple of sessions with the sun lamp wouldn't go amiss, but not too much; he didn't want to get wrinkles. With his face less than six inches from the mirror, he closely inspected himself. The merest tracery of fine lines were all he could see round the corners of his dark blue eyes. If the light was behind him nobody would notice. But then why should they on a face as handsome as his; a face and a body that both men and women coveted?

He stood back and turned from side to side in front of the mirrored tiles which lined the walls, watching the reflections of his reflection. His stomach was flat and muscular, his legs long and powerful and his genitals hung noticeably awake now that he had got rid of the previous evening's excesses. He made them twitch experimentally. Good, at least they weren't affected by last night. Perhaps Saskia wouldn't mind being woken up now: after all, it was a shame to waste such an opportunity – much as it had been last night when that little blonde at the club had shown such understanding. He smiled to himself as he recalled her young, firm body and insatiable greed. Such excesses of the flesh he couldn't get enough of.

He brushed his teeth and then turned on the shower. Wreathed in soap and hot water he started to feel more human; he even began to hum to himself. He soaped vigorously, enjoying the water's stinging heat and the lightest sensuous caress of the lather. He was fully recovered now, his blood pumping through his body, cleansing the toxicity from within.

After washing, he stepped out of the bath and quickly dried. With one last admiring look, he left the bathroom.

Saskia lay naked, face down, sprawled across the king-sized bed, her blonde hair fanned out haphazardly across the pillow. As she breathed softly, a few stray hairs rose and fell by her nostrils in unison.

The rumpled duvet had been kicked away in the musty warmth of the room and was now lying around her calves and feet. From where he was standing leaning against the doorway, the late morning sun was slanting across the room, lighting up the fine blonde down that ran down the small of her bronzed back, gathering in the hollow above her white buttocks. She might be stupid sometimes, but she had the best and most accommodating body that he knew of.

'Saskia . . . Saskia . . .'

He was going to wake her up the way she liked it best.

It wasn't difficult for him to make love to her. Despite his financial worries, his other women, his hangover, when it came to sex and especially sex with Saskia, he always rose to the occasion.

She lay in his arms, satiated and warm. 'I love you, James.'

He kissed her head, breathing in the perfume of her long blonde hair. 'Love you too.' He put his other arm behind his head and closed his eyes. He could feel her eyelashes brushing against his shoulder.

'James?'

'Mmm?'

'Where were you last night?' She asked it tentatively, unsure of him.

'Working.' He didn't open his eyes and his lips hardly moved. She rolled away from him and he felt her get off the bed, the mattress slightly readjusting as she stood up.

'You're lying,' she said flatly.

He didn't bother to answer. There was no point. He knew exactly what her expression would be; slightly pouting, her full lips in a sullen thick wedge, her cheeks flushed and her eyes quite blank. A day would come, he thought, perhaps in five years' time, when she would stop looking quite so childlike and start looking overblown and fleshy. Women like her, with their Venus-like curves, rarely aged well, especially when they indulged their every addiction as she did. Chocolates, gin or cocaine – it didn't matter. The more the better. Shame really.

'Didn't you hear me?' Oh that voice; so whining.

'Shut up.'

'No, I won't, not until you tell me where you were. I sat up till almost one waiting for you.'

He laughed, a short hollow sort of a laugh. 'Crap! You were so bombed out of your head when I got in you didn't know what month it was, let alone what time, so don't give me that bullshit.'

He rubbed his forehead with his hand. He was beginning to get a headache and just when he thought he'd got over his hangover too. Trust her to start it off again with her damned nagging.

He swung his legs off the bed and looked at her. She was trying to think of something to say, her face slightly puckered with the effort, but as usual nothing happened. Her mind only functioned on one level – the trivial – and he couldn't be bothered with that now.

'Go and shower,' he snapped. 'You look a mess.'

Petulant but compliant, she briefly hesitated and then walked into the bathroom, slamming the door shut. He smiled. So predictable, so stupid; a regular dumb broad. The Americanism seemed apt, if a little jaded, but it suited her exactly.

He reached for a cigarette from the bedside cabinet, knocking over a half-empty wine glass as he did so, sending the stale red-purple contents onto the floor.

'Damn!'

Shattered fragments of glass were strewn across the carpet. He leant down and cautiously gathered them up. A particularly large shard was caught underneath the cabinet. In easing it out he cut his finger badly. Now blood added to the mess.

'Oh shit!' He held up his hand and tried to staunch the flow, but the cut was too deep and blood was running down his hand and dripping onto the carpet. It was making a dreadful mess on the Axminster.

He looked round to find something to put on it – a hanky, a tissue, anything – but in the jumbled chaos he could see nothing except for her mess. Her makeup littered the dressing-table; brushes, compacts and lipsticks strewn around like a modern artwork, decorated here and there with coloured blobs of cotton wool. Clothes hung out of the drawers; silks, cottons, and a lone stocking was hooked over one of the handles. But the bedside cabinet was the worst offender to his eye. Its smeared surface of dust and grease was covered with an assortment of personal effects

– all hers. Nail clippers, emery boards, two bottles of pills – one anti-depressant, one sleeping pills – some jewellery, a half-eaten box of chocolates and in the middle, under a paperback, a small plastic bag of white powder and a silver tube.

He picked it up and looked at it with a cold hard emptiness, the congealing blood on his hand forgotten. He wasn't angry, not any more, he had no right to be really. He had known about her little habit right from the beginning but had assumed, as newly besotted lovers do, that it wouldn't be too difficult to get her off it. He sighed. How wrong he had been about that. No amount of persuasion, cajoling, bribery or finally bullying had worked and she just carried on. Until lately, that was, when she said she had stopped. Only, of course, she hadn't. She was lying; as usual. He clenched his fist around the plastic bag, squeezing it so tight that his fingers were white. The stupid, stupid, bitch!

She was lying full-length in the sea of bubbles, when he returned to the bathroom her thick blonde curls caught up in a loose topknot. She smiled at him sleepily and smoothed the sponge over herself. Seeing his eyes following her hand, she said, 'Want to join me, James? We could have loads more fun.'

He glanced back at her face, saying nothing. He was so tired of this: the pretence, the lies, her soon-to-be pleading for forgiveness.

'Get up.'

She opened her eyes fuller. 'Why?'

'I said get up.'

'No.'

'Get up, Saskia, or this,' and he held up the plastic bag between his bloodied thumb and forefinger, 'will go straight down the pan.'

She was suddenly alert now, her eyes panic-stricken and glancing quickly from his face to the bag. She sat up, the bubbles running over her glistening flesh. She held out her hand. 'Please, James, please don't.'

He smiled without humour, his dark blue eyes hard and brittle. 'And what will little Saskia do if this lot gets flushed away?' He loved to tease her.

Her bottom lip started to tremble and her eyes filled with tears. 'No . . . no, please, James, please don't.'

He opened the bag and held it over the toilet. 'Oh dear, oh dear, just a little bit more and all of this will be gone.'

She stood up slowly, mesmerized by him, her eyes fixed on the bag. She took a step down the bath so that she could almost reach out and grab it. She was openly blubbing now. 'Please . . . please,' she sniffed, holding out her hand, begging him, 'give it to me; please, James, please.'

With his free arm he held her at bay. She was a big woman – strong and powerful, but no match for him. He worked out twice a week at the club.

'Just watch me do it,' he snarled and suddenly he tipped it, the white powder cascading down into the water like a miniature avalanche. 'Wonder if the sewer rats will get high if they eat that stuff?' he commented as he flushed the toilet.

Saskia sank to her knees and howled, her face a mask of utter despair. 'You . . . bloody, bloody bastard!' she said through her anguish, and she chucked the sponge at him.

'Now, now, darling,' he admonished her with malicious glee, 'that's no way for a convent girl to speak,' and he jauntily waltzed out, ignoring her screamed insults.

He lay back down on the bed and lit a cigarette, satisfied but still somehow irritable. Bloody cow, he thought to himself, after all the time and effort, not to mention expense that he'd been through trying to get her off that stuff, and then as soon as his back was turned, she started it again. Why couldn't she leave it alone? Why was she trying to hurt him like this?

He remembered the first time they had met. It was two years ago and Saskia had been escorted by an old friend of James's he had not seen for some time.

'Roddy!'

'Hi, James.'

'How's things then?'

'Better than with you, I think. Who's the old battle-axe tonight?'

James pulled a face. 'Don't ask. Just don't bloody ask.'

He unzipped his fly and began to relieve himself in the urinal. Roddy, finished now, zipped up and went to wash his hands.

'Who's that blonde with you then?' asked James over his shoulder.

Roddy grinned, flicking the excess water off his hands and towelling them dry.

'Saskia Bennet. Twenty-three, ex-convent girl, little enough brains and goes like a scorcher. Her father runs Bennet Construction.'

James did up his fly and joined Roddy by the sink.

'Been seeing her long?'

Roddy pointed to the faint blue rings under his eyes. 'Long enough. I hardly get any sleep these days. Quite frankly, I could do with a break. Sitting in front of those damn computer terminals all day and screwing her all night don't exactly go together too well.'

James gave a small laugh. 'Falling down on the job, eh?'

Roddy smiled wryly. 'No, it's just that even the most red-blooded of us needs some sleep now and then.'

James went to leave and then stopped. 'Tell you what, when you've had enough give me a ring.'

'Bugger off, James. You're too busy with all those yummy mummies of yours. You won't have time for her.'

'Wanna bet?'

Roddy looked at him, working out his profit. 'Hundred quid says you won't get her by this time tomorrow.'

'A hundred pounds! Is that all? Make it five and you're on.'

'Okay.' They shook hands.

James collected his money the following night and by the weekend had moved into Saskia's house in Kensington. Or rather as he found out later, her father's house. She had nothing except what he gave her and as the spoilt only daughter of a wealthy man, it meant she had anything she wanted. Which was all right by him. He gambled, he screwed around and always there was good old faithful Saskia to come home to. He couldn't be happier. Well, he could have been if his miserable old uncle gave him a bigger allowance and he didn't have to work in the bank.

No, she was all he needed now. She had money and looks, but little else. Hopelessly disorganized as well as an addict, not everything had gone well over the last two years. Forgetting to take her contraceptive pill was one of the problems. Recently back from her third abortion, she was now stood over by James every morning with her tablet and a glass of water. She didn't always comply.

Yesterday, for instance, she'd sighed, 'Do I have to, Jamie? We could have a baby, we can afford it. All my friends are getting pregnant.'

He held out her pill. 'Take it, Sas.'

She folded her arms and sulked. 'No.'

'Take it, Sas, or you'll have another black eye to match the one you've already got.'

'Pig!' She took her pill.

'Why can't we have a baby?' she asked later, trying to cuddle him. 'I've got real childbearing hips, you know.'

He pushed her away. 'Forget it, Sas. I like peace and quiet in my life. Christ, it's bad enough trying to look after you, without adding to things.'

And then she had cried.

* * *

Now Saskia appeared, wrapped in a white bathrobe, her face red and blotchy from her tears. She stood in the doorway, reluctant to come in.

James stared at her with indifference. 'Well?'

She looked at him, sulky and defiant. 'You're a shit, James.'

He put out his cigarette. 'Really?' he drawled. 'How observant of you. After all this time you've only just realized it?'

'That was my last supply; the last I had until I see my man again.' Her face crumpled again. 'How could you do that to me, how could you do that?'

He swung his legs off the bed and walked towards her, stopping about a foot from her. She looked down. She never met his gaze when he was really angry.

'Clean this fucking mess up, Sas, or I'm really going to give you something to cry about.'

'No, the cleaner can do it.'

'Clean it!' he shouted.

'Why should I?'

'Because you're getting fat and lazy and it's high time you stopped.'

She glanced defiantly up at him. 'Fuck you, James.'

He hadn't meant to hurt her as much as he did. Once he had grabbed her hair and smacked her across the face, the whole incident took on a momentum all of its own.

'Please, James, please!' she cried, holding her hands up to her hair, a small trickle of scarlet blood oozing from her bottom lip. 'You're hurting me!'

'Shut up, you slut,' and with each word he grabbed her even tighter, pulling her head towards him.

'Now listen to me, Saskia.' His face was so close to hers she could see the fine blood vessels in the whites of his bulging eyes. 'You're going to clean this place up, understand?'

She fell to her knees sobbing. 'I can't . . . I can't!'

He hit her again, leaving another swathe across her distorted face.

'No! Jamie, no!'

'Shut up, Saskia!'

He yanked her to her feet, marched her across the room and threw her onto the bed. He stood staring at her, breathing heavily. At that moment she looked for all the world like some overfat beetle larva that had just wriggled out of its underground lair. She evoked nothing in him except an overwhelming desire to smash her to a bloody pulp.

Suddenly, as quickly as it had come, his anger evaporated, leaving behind a despairing void. It was always like this, violence followed by submission. He hated hitting her, hated reliving all those terrifying childhood scenes of his uncle's senseless rage. He slumped onto the bed, and started to cry, leaning his head in his hands.

'I'm sorry, Sas. I'm so very, very sorry. I won't do it again, I promise, Sas. I won't.'

She lay quietly, not moving, making small sniffing noises. He crawled up the bed towards her. 'Please, Sas, forgive me. I don't mean it.' Desperate now, he needed her comfort.

She rolled towards him and smiled crookedly, running her fingers over his tear-stained face. 'It's all right, Jamie darling. It's all right. Come to me, come to Mama.' Wrapping her maternal arms around his dark head, she pulled open her robe and placed one of her large pink nipples in his mouth. He lay quietly and suckled.

Much later that evening, when just for once he didn't go out, the pair of them were in bed together, languishing over one of their post-coital suppers. An empty champagne bottle was turned upside down in an ice bucket. What was left of the smoked salmon was starting to dry out and curl at the edges while their dirty crockery sat on the floor. Saskia was eating some green stuffed olives and James was peeling an apple. They didn't talk and were staring listlessly at the TV at the end of the bed. The telephone rang. James flipped off the remote control.

'Hello?'

Saskia snatched back the remote control and switched the TV back on.

'James Skerrett?'

He couldn't swallow; his mouth just wouldn't co-operate. Something seemed to be sticking in his throat and suddenly he needed to empty his bowels. The need was almost overwhelming.

'Yes?'

Nothing. The fearful silence was testing him, seeing how he reacted. James knew the speaker would be smiling.

'Skerrett, you owe us a great deal of money.'

James could picture the face with vivid clarity. Eyes like a shark, devoid of emotion, all-seeing; an indolent fleshy mouth and heavy pock-marked cheeks. A big man, but not in height. His was a powerful and muscular physique and nothing, not even the Savile Row suit, could hide the sheer presence and evil menace of the man.

McArdle was his name and James had met him twice; first to ask for money and then for more time to repay it. He was a cold-blooded vicious thug and together with his brother he owned various clubs and pubs, betting shops and other dubious businesses around the West End. He had barely concealed his contempt or, curiously, his attraction to James when they first met and although James was always prepared to accommodate those who were nice to him, this was one character he preferred to stay well clear of. It wasn't just the ever-present violence that hung around the man like an invisible mantle, but also his working-class background. James was a first-class snob.

'Yes,' he replied quietly. It was the only way he could control the terror in his voice.

'Your interest rate has just doubled and if you don't pay

me very soon, then I'm going to get a bit upset and believe me, you wouldn't like it when I'm upset.' He paused. 'Understand?'

The phone went dead. James replaced the receiver slowly, staring at it blankly, vaguely aware of the shivery sweat that now coated him.

'Who was that?' asked Saskia. The olives were now finished and she was deliberating over which chocolate to choose from a large and ornate box. Even though her mouth was violently bruised from their morning's fight, it didn't curtail her appetite.

'McArdle.'

She looked at him, her mouth bulging. He sat quite motionless, hands clasped between his thighs, seemingly unaware of her presence.

She put down the chocolates. 'James, are you all right? You look terrible.'

He threw the apple to one side, reached for a cigarette and drew deeply on the acrid smoke, relishing the transitory comfort it offered. Closing his eyes, he leant back against the headboard.

'We're in trouble, Sas, deep trouble. McArdle wants his money back.'

'What money?'

'The money I've borrowed from them for gambling.'

Saskia knew something of his night-time activities, but was surprised to hear him open up so readily. Usually he made it very plain that it was absolutely nothing to do with her and that she should keep her nose out of it.

'Oh.' She picked up the chocolate box again and started searching. 'How much do you owe?'

His smile was wry and faltering. 'A lot. Do you remember that article in the *Evening Standard* last week?'

She looked at him blankly, masticating like a cow. 'What article?'

'About the restaurant on Brompton Road that was totally gutted by an unexplained fire, and the owner found

43

unconscious with both legs smashed?' He took a sip of his drink. 'Well, McArdle's lot did that. The word is that the owner refused to pay protection money or something, so McArdle sent in two of his hoods, you know, teach the man a lesson. Some lesson.' He inhaled deeply.

'And now he's threatening you?'

He nodded.

'How much do you owe him, James? And this time I want the truth.'

He glanced sideways at her, reluctant, but seeing it was inevitable. 'More than I can afford.'

'How much?' she persisted.

He sighed. 'Sixteen, seventeen thousand. Oh Christ, I don't know!' He was angry now. Admitting to failure of any kind really annoyed him.

'Oh dear.'

James looked at her, his mouth pursed, his eyes penetrating. 'Oh dear,' he said scornfully. 'Is that all you've got to say, "oh dear"?'

She shrugged. 'Well, I don't know what else I can say. I mean, I can lend you some of it, but no way can I pay that much. Daddy would never hear of it and you were, of course,' she added with one of her all-too-infrequent insights, 'looking to me to help?'

James turned away in disgust. The last thing he needed right now was a gloating Saskia.

'It's this recession, you see,' she added. 'Daddy says I have to be more careful, otherwise he might have to get rid of this house and I don't want that.'

'Screw your father!'

She got up from the bed smirking. 'Now now, James, that's no way to talk about someone who pays all your bills here,' and she flounced off towards the bathroom. 'Of course,' she added, stopping in the doorway, 'if you hadn't run over your uncle's little dog, he might have increased your allowance and left you something in his will.' She

44

wagged a finger at him. 'That was very careless of you, Jamie.'

'Fucking bitch!' he shouted, throwing a book at her. It missed, hitting the quickly slammed door.

That remark was typical of her. She just had to get her dig in.

He angrily stubbed out his cigarette. What the hell was he going to do? If only he had kept in with the old man. Damn that stupid dog! Not a bloody penny and all because he'd accidentally run it over. And now this.

Impatiently he got up, sending the cheese board onto the floor. He ignored it and started to get dressed. Saskia reappeared, pulling the belt of her silk kimono around her.

'Going somewhere, James?'

'Downstairs,' he snapped. 'I have to think.'

She went to get dressed too.

'Stay where you are,' he ordered. 'The one thing I don't need right now is you fouling up the works.'

She smiled. 'Oh, I think you've done that yourself, haven't you?' He winced inwardly. Her barbs were getting sharper. He sat down and pulled on his socks, feeling her climb back into bed. Turning round, he cupped one of her beautiful full breasts in his hand and squeezed the nipple hard.

'Ow! James! You're hurting me!'

'Let me remind you, Saskia, that neither of us has any illusions about what you're best at.'

She pouted. 'You're a pig, James, a real pig,' and she brushed his hand away.

His smile was more of a leer when he left her.

Downstairs he made himself some strong black coffee and added a good shot of whisky to it. He lit another cigarette. It didn't go with his athletic image, but right now he wasn't really concerned about that. He just had to think.

45

His sisters were well out of the question; both of them were uptight religious prudes who, although they showed all the dutiful sisterly concern about his wellbeing, didn't stretch as far as lending him money – at least not this much, anyway. He briefly flirted with the idea of trying to bribe Douglas, one of his brothers-in-law, over his affair with his secretary, but then rejected it. There had to be a limit to even his deviousness. The bank was out of the question as well. So far he had got away with it, but he just couldn't risk any more . . .

As Saskia had pointed out, there was no way she could help. Her 'Daddy', whom James had met only once, might indulge his daughter's every whim, but he totally disapproved of James, who got the impression that he regarded him as nothing more than a pimp. In some respects, he wasn't far wrong.

Everything, but everything had been staked on his supposed inheritance. His uncle might not have liked him, but James had never realized quite how much until after his death. Fancy leaving all that money to a dogs' home! He must have been deranged. Damn! There was no one and nowhere he could go to and McArdle was moving in for the kill.

Saskia appeared, her face covered in cold cream. Perhaps her jewellery? No, he couldn't. He did that last time. Got a nice price for it too, but God what a fight they had when she found out. Took all of three days before she would talk to him again, plus a solemn promise on a huge box of hand-made Belgian chocolates that he would never do that again. Just to make sure, though, she now kept her best and most valuable pieces in a safety deposit box.

'Any coffee for me?' she asked, padding across the floor in the pink mink slippers and matching kimono.

'No, it's all gone.'

'Huh! I suppose I'll have to make some tea then.'

He smiled. 'I would have thought that even you could do that.'

She joined him at the table looking like a large pink dolly with a puckered royal icing face.

'Do you have to wear that muck down here?' he asked, grimacing.

'Why not? I have to put up with you clipping your toenails in the bathroom and leaving the bits all over the floor.'

'Bitch!'

'Bastard!'

He sipped his coffee. 'What are we going to do about the money?'

'Don't you mean what am "I" going to do about the money?'

He slowly raised his eyes and looked at her. 'What is it with you, Sas? First of all there's that little dig about your father paying all the bills, then the one about me fouling up and now this.' He paused, glaring at her. 'What the hell's going on?'

She looked away and began fidgeting with one of her nails. 'Nothing.'

'Good.'

They sat quietly for a few minutes, the only noise being the distant drone of the city traffic.

'We could sell something, I suppose,' she said at last.

'What? Sas, I don't think you understand. We're talking about a large sum of money here, which is growing by the week. We haven't got anything worth that much.' The impatience was obvious in his voice.

'Couldn't you go and see that Elyssa Berkshire again?'

'No, Saskia, I couldn't.'

'Why?'

'Because she caught me signing one too many of her cheques and told me if she ever saw me again then she'd have to tell the police.'

'Oh.'

'Yes, exactly, oh.'

Again silence.

'By the way, your sister Charlotte rang last night.'

He distractedly lit another cigarette. 'Oh yes, and what did that sanctimonious old cow want this time?'

'She said she might be getting in touch with some distant branch of the family that lives in Devon; a farmer or something. Apparently he was one of the few beneficiaries of your uncle's will.'

'Yes, I know. The solicitor told me yesterday. Say anything else did she?'

'Well, not really, just something about a grand get-together of the Skerrett family. I don't know, I can't really remember. Too tired, I expect.'

'Too stoned more like. God, I know Charlotte, any party of hers would be dreadful. It would all be best bib and tucker, no decent drink and absolutely no talking about sex, politics or religion.'

He brooded for a while; his dark blue eyes fixed on the middle distance. 'Did she say how much this cousin of ours had inherited?' he asked at last.

Saskia was wiping her face with some cotton wool, peering at herself in a hand-held mirror.

'No, but she seemed to think it was quite a lot.'

He stood up 'Mmm, that's interesting. Maybe I should investigate this cousin a bit more. I'm owed a few weeks' holiday. Maybe I should take it. Well, I'm off. Don't wait up for me now, will you?'

Surprised, Saskia put down her mirror, her face still half smeared in cream. 'But, James, what about our holiday? You said we were going abroad.'

'Forget it. This is more important,' he replied over his shoulder. 'I have some serious work to do tonight,' and he gave her a broad grin. 'Bye.'

She took up her mirror and another ball of cotton wool and angrily wiped her face. 'Stupid shit.'

She phoned Terri about half an hour later. Large gin and tonic in one hand, she was curled up on the sofa watching an old Bette Davis movie. She got the answering machine and left a message.

'You were right, Terri. He's a total bastard and just not worth it. Can we meet soon?'

49

FOUR

'Where have you been?'

'I took the Jag to the garage. It's making a funny plinking noise. Probably the carburettor.'

Elyssa turned away and walked on ahead of him, undoing the buttons of her ivory silk blouse. She pushed open a door and went into a small room. Apart from a small wardrobe, the only major piece of furniture was a single bed. The black sheets were wrinkled, the pillows askew and the duvet half on the floor.

Around the walls were posters of heavy metal groups and a large picture of the West Ham football team. A bottle of Brut aftershave lay on the floor. Elyssa continued undressing. Apart from the blouse and her fawn trousers, she wore no clothes and now stood quite naked. She briskly folded up her garments and left them in a neat pile on the one hard-backed chair.

'I do wish you'd clean this place up now and again, Kevin,' she said, stretching out on the bed.

The young man smiled. Tall, muscular and blond, with gelled spiked hair, the only things she could see wrong with him were minor problems really: his bitten nails for one, and she didn't much approve of his taste in aftershave either. She made a mental note to get him something more appropriate. If she was going to spend her afternoons screwing him then the least he could do was smell nice.

He was watching her, waiting.

'Come here then,' she ordered.

He walked towards her and stood next to the bed.

With long painted nails she deftly undid his jeans, pulling them down over his muscled thighs, taut and well-haired. He kicked them off and then pulled off his sweat shirt. Her face level with his boxer shorts, she eyed him greedily. To her mind this was his one outstanding virtue. Mediocre chauffeur, in bed, he served his mistress well, better than anyone else had done. Certainly better than her two husbands had.

She put her hand over him, feeling his hardness. Always ready to please, he never failed her. She ran her tongue around her moist lips with a ravenous anticipation, her breath already beginning to quicken.

'My God,' she said, smiling slowly and looking up at his smirking face, 'you are something else.' Her voice was low, filled with sex, purring almost.

She slipped her thumbs into the sides of his shorts and pulled them down slowly. He bounced up away from the flimsy material, long and hard. She heard him give a soft moan. Glancing up, she could see his eyes were closed and his lips slightly parted. She cupped his warm heavy balls, lovingly caressing them, feeling them rise to her touch.

'I'm going to eat you,' she whispered and slowly, millimetre by millimetre, she eased him into her wet, soft mouth, pushing down the foreskin with her hand, her teeth cushioned from him by her lips.

He held her head, guiding her downwards, his body taut with excitement. She ran her free hand down his thigh, tenderly stroking, feeling the power of his muscles. Licking and rubbing, she explored the sculptured contours around the head of his penis. He tried to bend down towards her, wanting to touch her, wanting to feel her, but she stopped him.

'Not yet, not yet, you'll get your turn,' and still she excited him, running her fingers over his tight buttocks, stroking and caressing. His moans were louder now, his face grimacing, his hands almost pulling at her hair.

Then she stopped and pushed him away. 'Stand over there.'

Momentarily surprised and pulled back from the brink of exploding, he staggered back.

'Get the box.'

He went to the drawer and took out an oblong cardboard box. Opening it, he removed a long white implement, slightly curved at the end. She held out her hand and took it.

'You can watch,' she said.

He sat on the chair, engorged and staring as she lay back on the bed. Taking the dildo she opened her thighs and slipped it into her wet insides. Slowly she thrusted. Her eyes were tightly shut, completely ignoring him. Her movements quickened. He watched transfixed. From where he sat he could see everything; her ivory-coloured thighs; the white of the dildo; the dark of her insides. She started to moan. Faster and faster she moved, her legs tightly pushed out against the bed.

'Oh God,' she muttered. 'Oh God, I'm coming . . .'

Kevin went over to her.

'Now, Kevin. Now!'

Joined together, they moved in exquisite oneness, their orgasms one simultaneous blur. Her head was thrown back, the blood vessels in her neck straining up under her sweaty skin. As his semen pumped into her, she dug her nails into the small of his back, wanting more and more of him.

But he was spent; an empty force lying exhausted on top of her. In no time at all, he could sense her irritation. She pushed him off and he slid onto the floor. He wanted to sleep. Heavy and relaxed with sexual relief, he crawled up onto the bed and leant back against the wall. He put out his hand to touch her and she slapped it away.

'Don't! You know I don't like it.' Her voice was harsh.

He said nothing. He had worked for her for six months, and she was as nasty now as she had been in the beginning. God knows why he put up with her. He closed his eyes and gave way to his slumber.

Suddenly she sat up and pushed back her red hair. She hated it when it got messed up. She pinched his leg. 'Wake up, there's work for you to do.'

He opened his eyes slightly.

'I've got a friend coming this weekend, a *special* friend,' she emphasized. 'So get everything ready.' She watched him impatiently. 'Well, come on then,' she said, standing up to get dressed. 'Move it. I'm going for a shower.'

Order restored and fully dressed, she looked at her reflection in her large rococo bedroom mirror.

The small tucks around her brown almond-shaped eyes had really improved things. No longer were there any wrinkles. Her face had always been thin, her cheekbones high and her nose straight. Her one disappointment was her lips. Almost nonexistent, they used to require carefully applied lipstick to make anything of them; now she had collagen injections.

She smiled with approval. Forty-six years old and she could easily pass for ten years younger. Her aerobics and personal fitness trainer kept her well trimmed and as she swept her eyes down over her body, she was more than pleased with her size ten. Of course, such slimness had its price. Her breasts, never particularly noticeable, even in her prime, had needed enlarging two years ago, finally giving her a cleavage. Her thighs had also been tucked. However, it was all worth it. A natural, white-skinned redhead, she prided herself on her appearance and a good bout of sex made her look even better.

She went downstairs. If she didn't get Kevin, he would fall asleep again. Elyssa had plucked him from the ranks of the long-term unemployed, tidied him up and got him weight training. His spots had almost gone thanks to his improved diet and he was now quite presentable. In fact, he didn't look too bad at all in his uniform, so long as he kept his mouth shut. He was originally from the Fens, and it gave her a headache to listen to his slovenly accent.

She threw open his door. 'Move it, Kevin, otherwise I might think twice about your pay rise.'

He rose to his feet, eyeing her cautiously. He started to bite his thumbnail.

'And for God's sake don't do that,' she snapped. 'It looks awful.'

She flung his clothes at him and then left the musky-smelling room.

As she walked down the dimly lit corridor, she passed by another door. This was Aditha's room, her Filipino maid. A strict Catholic, Aditha would have locked the room against anyone's encroachment, especially Kevin's, Elyssa knew. She took out her master key.

The room was lighter and bigger than Kevin's. The single bed was neatly made, the pink duvet smoothed out and unwrinkled. On the bedside cabinet was her Bible, daily read, so it seemed, and pictures of a small boy held in the arms of an older woman. It was Aditha's illegitimate son in the arms of his grandmother. So much for religious purity, thought Elyssa. Above the bed on the magnolia-painted wall, was a large wooden crucifix and beneath that a plastic rosary hung by some pins. The dressing-table was practically empty, save for some cheap face creams and makeup, and two suitcases were stacked tidily on top of the closed wardrobe. A pair of sensible brown walking shoes sat under the bed. The only pictures on the wall were some postcards from home.

Elyssa sighed. Her maid was a neat little woman, young and scared, her slanting eyes invariably downcast and disapproving. Her prudish attitude niggled Elyssa. Elyssa would sometimes arrive in the basement fully aware that the maid was sitting quietly in her room, which was barely six feet from Kevin's. Then she made sure she screamed extra loud while she orgasmed. She liked to think it gave Aditha something to be jealous about.

She pulled the door shut and locked it again. At the end of the corridor she climbed the short stairway, stepping through a door into her kitchen. Aditha looked up from her cup of coffee and magazine and then quickly lowered her gaze. Elyssa wasn't at all embarrassed.

'Tea break, Aditha?'

The young woman nodded slightly, her black glossy hair, cut in a short bob, swinging around her heart-shaped face. It was only when she gave one of her infrequent smiles that people saw her huge white teeth, seemingly so prominent in her small jaw.

'Well, finish up and then come and see me in the drawing room.'

'Yes, madam.'

Elyssa strode past, unconcerned, her long legs carrying her tall and proud. In the hallway she glanced briefly at the afternoon post, which sat on a silver plate on the round burnished Regency table. There was nothing of interest except an invitation to view the forthcoming autumn/winter collection of Karl Lagerfeld.

Putting the rest of the letters down, especially the ones in buff envelopes, she clicked over the marble floor to check her gold and diamond watch against the Charles II longcase clock. A small alteration and the watch was on time.

She entered the panelled drawing room and walked over to one of the tall windows which looked down on the private Georgian square. Although the weather was grey and dull, the cream-coloured curtains, matching Chesterfields, and lacquer and gilt Napoleon armchairs gave the room light and warmth. Above the open fireplace was a nineteenth-century oil painting of a lady astride her favourite stallion, the horse rearing up as the woman's black riding habit flowed around her legs. Elyssa had insisted on keeping this in her divorce settlement. It was not particularly valuable – she had other paintings worth far more – but it was the picture's power and grace that appealed to her. She empathized with the figure. Dominance was something she understood.

She poured herself a large Scotch, stopping to admire herself in the large Regency mirror. The silk blouse with its short upright collar, little round buttons and shining luxuriance hung over her pert breasts in a loving caress, showing up each nipple in erect silhouette. She smiled appreciatively.

There was a knock. Elyssa turned away and sat at her table.

'Yes?'

Aditha crept round the door and stood still without closing it as if keeping open her options for escape.

Elyssa put on her glasses, something she did as little as possible, and certainly not in front of anyone but her staff. She flipped idly through one of the glossy magazines, taking no notice of what she saw and sipping her drink.

'I'm expecting a friend to stay this weekend, Aditha, and I expect you to give this place a really good clean. Understand?'

'Yes, madam.'

'The bedroom especially.'

Aditha looked up, the brow furrowed. 'But I've already done that, madam.'

Elyssa stopped. 'Well do it again, Aditha, and this time properly. I've checked it already and it's not good enough.'

The maid looked down at her clasped hands and was silent. 'And another thing, change the sheets on my bed. I want the silk set and make sure they're ironed properly.'

'Yes, madam.' Aditha's voice was so quiet she could barely be heard.

'Well, girl, off you go then.'

'Yes, madam.'

A whole weekend with Alistair: wonderful! She had met him years ago when he was a student at Cambridge studying law. She thought him rather a boring young man, slightly stuffy and a bit too well-mannered, but he did make up for it by being exceptionally handsome. Tall

56

and muscular, he had all the appearance of a young blond bull and she had loved him for it.

The relationship didn't last long; the delights of older, more experienced men were irresistible to Elyssa then. However, there was one thing she never forgot about Alistair: he was filthy, stinking rich, and right now that was the only thing she was interested in. Thank goodness her contacts reminded her about him. Not only that, but the unexpected fact that he was still single.

Elyssa shivered with anticipation. She couldn't wait to see him.

The clock in the hall chimed, breaking her train of thought. Five o'clock. His train arrived at a quarter to six. She had better hurry. She poured herself another drink.

Upstairs in her dressing room she changed her clothes, leaving her other ones in a heap on the floor. Knowing from long experience that men delighted in silken under-wear, she picked out a body stocking of the lightest material. She rarely wore any underclothes and it felt odd to be enclosed like this. Tight black ski pants, a black cashmere cowl-necked sweater, some carefully selected and artfully placed gold jewellery and she was almost ready. She quickly did her makeup, only needing some more blusher to brighten her perfect face and then did her teeth before applying her lipstick. Alistair didn't smoke and although she had cut down to the minimum, she couldn't give up altogether. Quite finished, she came out to inspect the bedroom.

The massive antique four-poster bed dominated every-thing. Draped with the finest Chinese Habutai silk of the purest white, it almost shimmered in the room's dimmed lighting. The rest of the furniture, a tallboy, chaise longue and dressing-table, seemed quite insignificant compared with its magnificence.

Almost virginal in its overall appearance, the bedroom contained, among the few things that gave away the

57

occupant's true character, a collection of erotic prints by Aubrey Beardsley, which covered the walls.

Elyssa looked at herself in the mirror. All she needed now was her full-length silver fox coat with its matching hat. It would offend some delicate feelings, but she had no time for those who didn't appreciate the finer things in life.

Downstairs she called for Kevin on the intercom: 'Fetch the Jag and bring it around to the front.'

She waited impatiently on the elegant steps at the front of her house. The weather was bitter and she was glad of her coat. When Kevin arrived she ordered him out of the car. 'I'll drive myself' she said, taking the keys, 'and I don't want to see you or Aditha for the rest of the evening.'

The traffic was, as she expected, quite appalling. Friday evening and everybody was trying to get home as quickly as possible. Driving through the freezing fog, which now hung over the city like a veil, she felt angry and impatient with all the other motorists. Twenty minutes late, she finally pulled into Paddington. Parking on a double yellow line, she slammed the door shut and raced off across the echoing concrete. She saw Alistair long before he saw her. Standing amid the milling crowds of commuters in his camel overcoat, he looked faintly bemused by all the frenetic activity of the other people. She ran towards him, arms outstretched.

'Alistair!'

He turned around, at first not seeing her, and then he smiled and waved his hand.

'Elyssa, how good to see you. You haven't changed a bit. You're still as beautiful as I remember you.'

They kissed each other on the cheek, their hands clasped together.

'Thank you,' she said. 'And you're still a wonderful flatterer.'

He gave a half-smile.

'How was your journey?'

'Tiring.'

'I'm sorry I'm so late,' she began, 'it's the traffic. It's frightful at this time of day.'

'It doesn't matter,' he assured her. 'I was enjoying watching the crowds.'

She linked her arm through his, he picked up his weekend case and they walked together through the crowd. The foreboding figure of a traffic warden was working his way down the line of parked cars and checking their permits. They got to the car just in time.

'God, you can't park anywhere now,' she laughed as they left the station.

'Well, Alistair, how are you? Long time no see.'

They were driving back, the bright lights of the cars slicing through the murk.

Alistair sighed and lay his head back against the upholstery. 'Tired,' he answered flatly.

She glanced at him. They were waiting at yet another set of lights. 'Oh? You come all this way to see me and you tell me you're tired?'

He smiled briefly. 'Sorry, work I suppose.'

She put her hand on his knee and squeezed it. 'If I know you, you do too much, Ali, you always have. Perhaps you should lighten up a bit, have more fun.'

He patted her hand and then put it back on the steering wheel. 'Yes, maybe I should.'

'Look,' she said, 'we don't have to go out tonight if you don't want to. We could just stay in, have a small supper, listen to some music perhaps.'

Her voice was bright. She didn't want to push things. Aware that she had invited him and that he seemed somewhat distant from her, she wanted him to relax. She breathed deeply. He smelt good; his aftershave filling the car with subtle aromas. It made a change from Kevin's pungent cheapness.

He turned to her. She could see, even in the dim light,

that his eyes were heavy with tiredness. When he spoke, his rich baritone voice was low and beautifully melodic. She had forgotten how seductive he sounded.

'Yes, that's a good idea. I don't feel like doing much tonight.'

She smiled. Food, then sex. Altogether much easier in the privacy of her own home.

After the bustle of the West End, Bayswater Road and Kensington Park Road seemed very quiet when they pulled into the square, the tall Georgian houses forming an elegant frame to the carefully manicured garden in the centre. In the glow of the streetlamps, the bare branches of the trees hung wet and cold over the pavements. She parked the car in front of her house in her reserved space and turned off the purring engine. For a moment they both sat still, unwilling to leave the secluded warmth of the interior.

'I'm so glad you came, Alistair.' Her voice was soft.

'So am I, it's not every weekend I get such a pleasant invitation.'

She glanced at him, her eyes shining like a cat's. 'You know, I didn't think I would ever see you again. It's been such a long time and so much has happened.'

'Why did you phone me?' he asked.

She shrugged. 'I don't know. I'm just fed up with the company here. They're all so . . . so . . . Well, let's just say I needed an old friend to talk to.'

He smiled. 'That's nice.' And taking her small hand, he delicately kissed it, his warm lips dry against her skin.

'Oh Alistair,' her voice wavered, 'I'm so happy.' She touched his bent head. When he looked up, his eyes staring deeply into hers, she knew she had him. She leant forward and they kissed.

Alistair surveyed the fridge shelves.

'How about a soufflé omelette, green salad tossed in my own special recipe dressing and,' he looked playfully over

60

his shoulder, 'slices of thick granary bread with lashings of butter?'

'Yes please.' Elyssa was perched on a stool, drinking another large whisky, her head resting on her hands, watching him. She was enjoying this; rich and he could cook as well. He cracked open some eggs, dividing the yolk from the white. Elyssa admired his skill. 'Where do you learn such things? I never set foot in the kitchen if I can help it. The maid does all this.'

He looked up from beating the yolks. 'I live alone, Elyssa, and a man has to cultivate some skills if he is to manage. I'm a bit of a fraud, though, really.'

'Why?'

He grinned. 'Because this is the only meal I can make. The rest of the time I go to Marks & Spencer in Exeter.'

Elyssa stood up. 'I'll get something to drink. I'm pretty sure I've got a bottle or two of good Bordeaux downstairs.'

They took their supper, which turned out to be delicious, on trays into the lounge. Then Elyssa laid across the Persian rug in front of the crackling fire, the flames dancing up the chimney, and Alistair relaxed on the sofa. Classical Spanish guitar music played softly in the background.

Their trays long discarded on a table, they both drank their wine contentedly.

'Do you remember that party when we first met?'

'Yes. I was still a student at Cambridge and you and some of your modelling friends came up from London.' Alistair smiled, his eyes fixed on the fire.

'You were so handsome, Ali, much more so than any of your friends and infinitely more grown up.'

He sipped his wine. 'I was very young, Elyssa, and inexperienced. I remember gazing at you from a discreet distance and thinking to myself that you would never look at anyone as gauche as me.'

'Rubbish, Ali,' she chided affectionately. 'Of all the men there, you were the only one worth looking at.'

The fire crackled as their memories flooded back.

'Do you remember that walk we had along the river?'

He nodded. 'Half-past three in the morning, a full moon hanging in a velvet sky and both of us gently drunk.'

She moved over to him and leant her head against his knees. 'We were so happy then; so much in love.' She looked up at him. 'It could be like that again, Ali.'

He stroked her gold-flecked hair that shimmered in the firelight. 'That was the past, Elyssa. It's over and done and we can't recapture it.'

'But why not?' she pleaded, her eyes hungrily searching his face. She grabbed his hand and held it tightly. 'Why not?'

He smiled but said nothing. She let go and turned round so that her back rested against his legs.

'You got married soon afterwards, didn't you?'

'Yes. Twice in rapid succession.'

'I never heard anything about them. Tell me what happened.'

'Nothing to tell really. Archie, as you know, was great fun. Far too old, of course, but then so what? If he didn't mind spending his money on me, then I didn't mind bringing some happiness into his life.' She refilled her glass. 'I was very young, only twenty-two, and I thought him the most dashing and handsome man I'd ever met, apart from you, of course. Great fun he was, always wanting to travel.'

The memory warmed her and her smile was soft. Even her eyes lost their characteristic brittleness. 'See those obelisks over there on the side? He collected those. In fact, all things Egyptian were attractive to him. He once tried to ship home some enormous great sarcophagus but the authorities put a stop to it.' She raised her eyebrows. 'God knows where we would have put it. It was all his travelling that finally killed him.'

She sat up and hugged her knees. 'I know his family didn't think so. Insufferable bunch that they were, they fought me tooth and nail over his will, but I won anyhow.' She finished her drink. Withholding on the cigarettes because of Alistair was playing havoc with her nerves. She could really do with one now. She refilled her glass.

'And the other marriage, what about him?'

Unexpectedly she laughed. It sounded hollow and forlorn. 'Dear, dear Bill.' Beginning to get drunk, the tears came easily to her eyes. 'Oh God, Alistair, you can't possibly understand how awful it was.' She looked at him, her eyes swimming.

'Why?'

She tried to straighten her mouth, but couldn't and started to laugh again. 'He . . . he . . . couldn't do it!'

'Do what?'

'Fuck, screw. Call it what you will. He couldn't do it.'

'Ever?' Alistair was surprised. He had heard of William Hansen, one of the country's richest industrialists, he gave every appearance of being a notorious womanizer, his athletic good looks drawing the women to him with little or no effort.

The tears were beginning to fall freely down Elyssa's cheeks, her lips wobbling. 'He tried to,' she sniffed, wiping her nose with a hanky, 'but, you see,' and now she looked embarrassed, 'I've never revealed this to anyone before, Alistair.' Her eyes watched him, flickering across his face through an alcoholic haze.

He held up his hand. 'Gentleman's honour, Elyssa.'

Reassured she continued: 'He didn't have one. Well, not anything you could call a proper one. It was like a baby's,' and she held up her fingers to show him. 'About that long.'

Alistair held his face quite blank. Something in her revelation appalled him.

'We tried, of course, many times, in fact, even went to specialists, but nothing worked. He couldn't and I wanted it. God, how I wanted it.'

Her voice was strangely quiet, the atmosphere laden;

taut with expectation. She was watching him. He knew it, he could feel her eyes disrobing him. He still liked her very, very much. He was convinced of that, but after this . . . it was difficult; awkward. He looked at his watch. It was well past eleven. They had been sitting for almost four hours just talking, and in her case, drinking. He yawned, loudly, so she would notice.

'You're tired, Ali. Why don't we go to bed.'

He glanced at her. 'Yes, I think I will.'

She finished her wine. 'Just a nightcap before we go, I think.'

'No, not for me, Elyssa. I've had quite enough for tonight.'

She walked purposefully over to the drinks cabinet. The whisky she poured was considerably larger than anything that would be served in a pub. She downed it in one.

'Bed,' she said and, giggling slightly, she took Alistair's hand and walked him upstairs. She stopped on the landing and turned to him. 'Alistair.' Her breath was strong with alcohol and she blinked rapidly a few times as she tried to focus on him.

'Yes?'

She stood closer to him, putting her arms around his waist and laying her head on his shoulder. He could feel the wetness of her spent tears through his shirt.

'Don't leave me, Alistair.' Her voice was that of a child; frightened and lost. 'Don't leave me like you did last time.'

He stroked her head, feeling the silkiness of her hair. When he spoke, she could feel his voice resonate through his chest. 'I won't, Elyssa.'

'Promise?'

'Promise.'

They stood gently rocking. Then she pulled back from him.

'Come to bed with me, Ali.' Her eyes searched his face, a mere hair's-breadth from pain, wanting him so much.

He gently removed her hands from around his waist and kissed them.

'Why not?'

'You're drunk, Elyssa, and I'm tired. I don't possibly see how it will work.'

She started to cry, her mascara staying perfectly in place. 'It's not fair, it's not bloody fair.'

Once more her head rested against his chest. He held her close, letting her pain release itself. Poor Elyssa. Wanting to love so much and nobody was there.

'Come on, let's get you in bed.' He picked her up, her light weight nothing for him, and carried her down the corridor to her room.

When he laid her on the vast silken bed, she clasped her hands around his neck and pulled him towards her. 'Please, Alistair, please don't go.'

He removed her hands and patted them. 'Goodnight, Elyssa,' and he kissed her forehead.

For a long while she lay quite still, staring at the canopy above her. Drunk but still aware of what she had done, her embarrassment engulfed her. To stop the noise of her crying from reaching him, she buried her face in her pillow. When it stopped finally she went into her white en-suite bathroom and took down a medicine bottle from the cabinet. Two little pills and she would obliterate everything.

Across the landing in a guest room lay Alistair, just as awake. It had been a mistake, a stupid, stupid mistake. Why on earth had he come here? He might have loved her once years ago, but not now. He didn't need or want to see her again and he knew it. For the first few hours this evening he had really enjoyed himself. He had even considered sex with her because, as they both knew, that was the underlying reason for his visit. But it was no good. Drink and Elyssa never did go together and once she started, she couldn't stop. Before long, her beautiful face would start to crumble as the alcohol made its way through her system and then it was no good at all. However much he needed to have a woman, however deep his frustration, he couldn't take advantage of her drunkenness.

He rolled over to one side, pulling up the duvet, annoyed with himself. When at last he closed his eyes the one recurring image that kept coming into his tired mind was Claire. Hauntingly beautiful, she whispered to him, called to him, never leaving him.

Across London, Saskia and Terri sat in a restaurant having a late supper, the Italian waiters fluttering around the gold and white mirrored room.

'Well, what did you think of the exhibition then?' Terri looked up, her face sharp and inquisitive, her brown eyes sparkling. Saskia had never known a time when her friend didn't exude a shimmering vitality.

'Didn't understand it really.'

Terri's face fell, but only briefly. 'Well, never mind, at least it got you away from that pig James.'

Saskia frowned, her lips slightly pouting and she flipped back some of her blonde hair. 'He's not a pig, Terri.'

'No, of course not, dear, how could I ever suggest such a thing? I mean, it's quite obvious that black eye of yours is a result of you falling into a door, isn't it?' She leant closer as if to emphasize the point.

Saskia looked ashamed. 'Don't, Terri.'

Terri patted her hand. 'Oh, angel, honestly, you do have the most incredibly bad taste when it comes to men.'

'I don't!' she said, her voice childishly indignant.

'What about Roddy then?'

'He was all right.'

Terri drank some of her wine. 'He was the most empty-headed one-dimensional moron I've ever met.'

'That's because he criticized your paintings.'

'Exactly. The man was a Philistine. Anyway,' she added, 'why bother with any of them?' Her voice was quieter now. 'Why not stick to your own kind?'

Saskia shifted uneasily in her chair. 'I couldn't.'

'Why not?'

'Because,' and she glanced up at her friend.

Terri smiled enigmatically, the corners of her small mouth turning up slowly. 'You have no imagination, Sas.'

'So?'

'So what happens when Jack-the-lad has shot his bolt?'

Saskia shrugged. 'He goes to sleep.'

'Exactly,' replied Terri with satisfaction. 'And where does that leave you?'

Saskia was puzzled. 'I sleep too.'

Terri watched her with scepticism. 'Really? You mean you don't ever have those occasions when you're left wanting, when the earth doesn't shake under your feet, when the waves don't come crashing over your shore?'

Saskia pursed her lips.

'I thought so,' said Terri with finality.

Saskia relented. 'Okay, okay, sometimes,' and she held up her finger as if to emphasize the point, 'just sometimes it doesn't work as it should.'

'And then what do you do?'

'Eat.'

'So, he's bad for your figure as well as your mind. Jesus, Sas, don't you see how he's screwing you up?'

'No.'

Terri shook her head with bewilderment. Sometimes she didn't understand Saskia at all.

'I'm going away soon,' she stated after a pause.

'Where?'

'Australia.'

'Oh.'

'Why don't you come too, Sas?'

Saskia grimaced. 'No, I couldn't do that. James wouldn't like it, for a start.'

Terri sat forward again and looked at her earnestly. 'Stuff James, Saskia. You have money and you're beautiful.' She reached up and touched Saskia's face, running her fingers around her chin. 'We could have a great time together.'

Saskia pulled back. She didn't know what to do. In the confusion she knocked over her wine glass. She stumbled to her feet, pulling on her coat. 'I've got to go, Terri.' She turned away. 'I'll ring sometime.'

Terri raised her glass in mock tribute. 'Yeah, you do that.'

Feeling better after his morning walk, Alistair rang the doorbell. Aditha opened the door. He stepped into the hall, taking off his overcoat and handing it to the maid smiling.

'Is she up yet?'

Aditha looked at him, said nothing and lowered her gaze. It was eleven o'clock.

'Oh dear. Well, never mind. Could you make a pot of coffee, please, Aditha, and lay up a tray and then I'll take it up to her.'

The maid smiled. She liked him very much. He was always kind to her. 'Yes, sir.'

'Thank you. I'll be in the drawing room.'

The fire was lit and the room was nicely warm after the sharp cold air of the street. He rubbed his eyes. He hadn't slept well last night. He stood with his back to the fire, warming his hands behind him. As he looked around the room it seemed to him that something was missing. Elyssa had a fine decorative taste; the furniture, paintings and carpet gave the room a subtle elegance, allowing its classical proportions to come through. Along one wall were rows of leather-bound books. He liked browsing through them, but he had never seen Elyssa read. As his eyes roamed over the shelves and the grand piano he suddenly realized what it was: there were no photographs, there was nothing. He wondered about this and realized that despite all the years he had known her, he knew very little of her past. She had simply appeared one day;

beautiful, flirtatious and reasonably wealthy. It was then only a matter of course before someone would marry her and somebody did. Out of sight most of the time because of her travels with Archie, he occasionally heard about her from their mutual acquaintances. If it was a man telling him, the words would be tinged with envy for Archie; if it was a woman, jealousy was rarely kept at bay.

After Archie's unexpected death, Alistair had met her a couple of times and enjoyed her company immensely. He had known only too well as she flirted with him that she could be his for the asking. Except that he didn't ask. That would have been disloyal to Claire.

Alistair pulled himself up, annoyed. He must not think about Claire. Like an addict withdrawing from his drug, if he allowed her image to enter his mind, he would be lost. When she was there she engulfed him, swamping him, overpowering all his resistance.

'Stop it,' he told himself bitterly. 'Stop it!'

Aditha came in, obviously hearing him. She seemed about to ask him something, but instead looked away. Alistair felt embarrassed.

'The tray's ready, sir.'

'Oh . . . good . . . right, well, I'll take it up.' He smiled awkwardly and crossed the room. 'Thank you, Aditha.'

He walked up the stairs with a feeling of mild depression. Despite his solitary walk to the park and a good hour of introspection during which he had tried logically to work through his present emotional turmoil and physical cravings, he was no nearer to any answer. Now he would have to face a hungover Elyssa.

He knocked on her door and waited. Nothing. He knocked again. Still nothing. She must still be asleep, so he entered. The room was warm and dim, the curtains only half drawn, and it smelt of her perfume.

'Elyssa?'

'In here, Alistair.' He turned, her voice coming from the bathroom.

Light shone through the slightly open door. He set down the tray and pushed it open. She lay in a sea of scented bubbles in the vast apple-shaped porcelain bath with its gold-plated fitments. Contrary to his expectations, she looked very well indeed.

'Hi.'

She smiled invitingly and stretched out her hands on either side of the bath's rim. 'Hello. Been out somewhere?'

'Yes. The park. Nice gardens they have there.' He stared at her. He couldn't take his eyes off her. 'I brought you some breakfast.'

He noticed how the bubbles on her breasts slowly slid down over her skin, revealing the shiny white orbs beneath and their pert pink nipples. Seeing his gaze she rubbed one hand over them, caressing them, squeezing her nipples until they were erect. His eyes followed her hand, aware of the heat in his groin.

'Come in, Alistair, there's enough room for two.' Her voice was low and soft.

Without further persuasion he began to strip off, focusing only on her and her beautiful body. Deaf to the screaming voices within, he stood naked before her, the need in him more than obvious. He wanted her now and he wasn't going to listen to any doubts in his mind.

The water was very hot. He didn't notice. He crawled along the bath and her body until he sat astride her legs. Her smile was all-knowing, satisfied and controlled.

'I know what you want, Ali,' she whispered, kissing him lightly. 'I'm anything you want, baby, anything you like. Touch me,' and taking his hand, she placed it on her breast. He gasped. It had been so long; so very, very long. He ached, the heaviness of his waiting rising quickly behind its emotional dam. He ran his fingers around her nipple.

'Harder, Ali,' she whispered, 'harder.'

He glanced up at her. Her face had already begun to close off to him. Soon her excitement would be such that she wouldn't hear him at all.

He squeezed first one, then the other breast. She held him, her light fingers caressing and touching, urging him onwards. He needed no encouragement. He leant down and kissed her, his tongue searching hers, hot, wet and hungry.

Her hands ran over him feeling his strong musculature; the outline of his skin smooth over their surface, except across his chest where the dark gold hair covered him. He pushed against her almost bursting. He couldn't wait. Seeing and sensing his impatience, she gently pushed him back. 'Not here, darling, not here.'

He said nothing. He couldn't. His throat felt constricted. He could hardly breathe. She got up from underneath him and climbed out of the bath, walking down the smooth steps onto the thickly carpeted floor. She beckoned him.

Hypnotized by her inviting flesh, he stood up. If anyone had walked through the door at that moment, he wouldn't have noticed. The pounding in his chest, the excitement in him pulled him onwards. Gasping for his breath, he held her tightly, his fingers digging into her flesh.

'Take me, Alistair, take me.'

Entwined like a marble statue, the steam rising off their hot bodies, he kissed her again and again, clutching her breasts, caressing her buttocks as he pushed against her. By now she was ready for him, her insides pulsating in moisture. Taking one hand she guided him down.

'There, Ali . . . there.'

At once he held back. Delicately restrained, he fingered and stroked her as she arched against him, her head leant backwards, her lips apart as she groaned in his arms. 'So good,' she whispered, her legs almost collapsing. He stared at her, the veins in his powerful neck pumping faster. Bathed in sweat and steam, he could hardly hold her.

She started to move against him, grinding and thrusting, faster and faster, her lips pulled back, revealing her expensive teeth. She ran her pink tongue over them. Sensing her nearness, he picked her up so that she wrapped her legs around his trunk and he walked slowly into the bedroom, lowering her on to him. Unable to hold back any more and with unrestrained passion, they didn't make it to the bed, but took each other as they were, her head thumping rhythmically against the wall. With her nails digging into his shoulders, she held his sweaty head tightly against her neck as he pushed onwards to their orgasms.

'Now, Ali!'

She gripped him powerfully with her thighs as her climax hit her, straining against him, every muscle taut with contractions. He moved with her, watching, waiting. No sooner had she stopped than he started to push; harder this time. With one almighty heave she was pressed against the wall so hard she was almost winded. She climaxed repeatedly, taking every last drop of him. They lay on the unmade bed, she resting her head against his chest, he with one arm around her shoulders, his other over his forehead and his closed eyes.

'You're wonderful, Ali, really wonderful.'

He smiled, his eyes still shut.

'You know, I could easily fall in love with you?'

'Don't, Elyssa. I'm sure you can find plenty of other men for that.'

She wrote her name on his chest hairs, luxuriating in his warm, secure muskiness. 'I'm not so sure.'

He kissed her briefly on the forehead. 'Let's just enjoy each other while we can, okay?'

She fell silent. Things weren't going the way she intended.

Alistair kept his eyes shut because he was ashamed and because he couldn't bear to reveal what he really felt. He knew his eyes would give him away. The minute his orgasm had finished, his feelings for Claire had reasserted themselves with a vengeance; stealing into his heart, his mind and his body. It now inhabited his whole being. His self-disgust was all-encompassing.

72

'Don't you even love me a little bit?'

He held her tightly, wrapping his other arm around her so that her face was buried away from him. 'If you only knew,' he whispered, his eyes squeezed tight. 'If only you knew.'

Elyssa looked up surprised. 'Ali, are you okay?'

He smiled brokenly. 'Yes, yes, I'm fine. You know how these things are sometimes.'

'Oh, baby,' she cooed. 'It's all right. Really it is.' She kissed his cheeks, wiping her face over his. 'You and me . . . we'll be fine together. Just you wait and see. I'll be everything you've always wanted.'

He said nothing, but sat up and helped himself to her coffee.

'I've got to go,' he said.

Elyssa sat up next to him, suddenly alert. 'What? But you only got here last night. Surely you don't have to go now?' Her voice was plaintive, a whine almost. He could barely bring himself to look at her.

'I must. I've got a meeting first thing Monday and I haven't done a minute's preparation for it.' He went to stand up but she held him back, gripping his arm.

'But can't we at least go to lunch first? We could go to a restaurant. Any restaurant. I don't mind. Wherever you like. It's okay by me.' She was sounding desperate.

'I'm sorry, Elyssa, but I can't.' He went into the bathroom. She followed him closely. He climbed into the still-hot water and doused himself.

'But why, Ali? Why do you have to go? Have I said anything? Have I done anything? I mean, we were getting on really well, at least that's what I thought, or maybe all that screwing out there was my imagination.'

Alistair noticed how her lips went very thin when she was angry. He soaped himself. 'You're wrong. I did enjoy what's happened, as did you, but something . . .' He gestured at the futility of it all. 'I don't know.'

73

She sat down next to him and played with the dark strands of wet hair around the nape of his neck, warming to him once more.

'My poor Ali, is it really so hard to understand?'

He looked at her.

'I love you, Alistair, and I want you to stay.'

'You don't know what you're saying, Elyssa . . .' He trailed off. 'You can't possibly love me. Once yes, years ago, but not now. We can't change things.' He took her arm and kissed the inside of her wrist. 'Don't be angry with me.'

She leant forward and kissed his head. 'Of course not, baby,' she lied.

'I think I've got everything.'

Alistair was standing in the hallway. He had rung the station and there was a train leaving in half an hour. He was anxious to go.

'Right then. Kevin will take you if you don't mind, Ali. I've got a bit of a headache coming on and need to rest.'

'Of course, my dear. I understand.'

They held hands and kissed each other's cheek.

'Ring won't you?' she asked brightly. 'Any time. I've got an answering machine.'

'Yes.'

Kevin took his bag and opened the door for him. With a last kiss, Alistair turned and left.

The first thing Elyssa did was pour herself a very large drink and light up a cigarette. It would be the only thing to deaden her disappointment and loneliness.

On the way to Paddington, Alistair steadfastly looked out of the window. His relief at going home was threatening to burst out in a cascade of wide smiles. He knew he mustn't show it, especially as Kevin was watching him with a smug sneer on his face. Alistair wondered why, but only briefly.

Released at last from Elyssa's hold, he sank back into his

74

seat on the train and relaxed. At last he could be himself again. He had enjoyed his visit, but it just wasn't what he wanted. He would be polite, though, and good-mannered about it. Having let Elyssa get the better of him, he couldn't put her down too abruptly. He made up his mind that once he got home he would write a tactful and sensitive letter explaining that although he appreciated her friendship, he knew that there could never be anything else between them. He felt sure she would understand.

He smiled. It was good to be going home, back to Claire. She might not want him yet but some day she would. He just knew it. The train ran on and finally he slept.

FIVE

Deep inside the cocoon-like warmth of the bedclothes, the jarring buzz of the alarm clock finally intruded into Claire's carefree sleep. She normally woke up bright and alert before the clock went off, but last night's visit to the pub for a National Farmers' Union meeting had dulled her senses and waking up was proving to be a drawn-out affair.

She reached out blindly, finally managing to silence the noisy thing by sending it flying onto the floor. It clattered across the polished wooden boards, obviously in pieces. She swore quietly.

Drink always did this to her. Unlike her mother, who could drink the pub dry, she couldn't take it.

She stretched, trying to ease her limbs into readiness. As usual, Rosie's bulk lay comfortingly to one side of her. She never moved. Alarm or no alarm, she liked warmth and lying between the duvet and the blanket was where she stayed until her mistress finally got up. At first, Claire had felt uneasy about Rosie sharing her bed. She knew it was unhygienic and the mass of black dog hairs that clung to the blanket were a testimony to that, but she no longer cared. No one came here and no one stayed. Certainly no man, who would probably keep her awake half the night and pinch all the covers. At least Rosie let her sleep in peace.

Claire tried to stay awake by forcing her eyelids up slowly but the pull of sleep was overwhelming. She had almost given in again to the deep warmth when the cow started bellowing. It was no good; she had to move.

She boldly threw back the covers, the cold air making

her hold her breath. As she sat up her head began to pound and her legs felt quite dead. She consoled herself with the thought that at least she didn't feel sick.

She pulled on her cold clothes, irritated. Normally she left them over the hot water tank so they would be nice and warm for her but last night she couldn't be bothered and their penetrating dampness made her even more annoyed with herself.

At last, her multiple layers on, she padded silently across the floor in her thick outer socks, her breath coming in wisps of steam and pulled back the thin flowery curtains. The light shone unusually bright through the glass and even before she had rubbed away the thin layer of ice that formed delicate opaque patterns on the uneven surface, she could see why: snow had fallen. Overnight, like an unseen and unheard burglar, it had drifted down, covering the landscape in an undulating blanket of cottonwool, now sparkling crisply in the cold winter sunshine. About six inches, she thought; not much, but enough to make life difficult. The pipes would be frozen, the stock would have to be watered by hand and she would have to get some hay out to the cattle. All this and lambing now at its height.

'Damn!' She turned to Rosie. 'Come on, you, time to move.'

The pair of them went down the steep wooden stairs, lit by a single bulb. As she opened the door at the bottom the warmth of the Rayburn welcomed her. Thank God for that, she thought. If there were going to be power cuts at least she would have one warm room and something to cook on. She thought about breakfast, her stomach rumbling hollowly, but the cow was insistent.

'All right, all right, I'm coming.'

Donning her wellies and mud-ingrained waxed jacket, pulling on gloves and a woolly hat, she picked up a stainless-steel bucket and opened the door. Rosie ran out before her, head down, nosing the crisp white powder,

77

sending showers of it up into the air. Claire smiled fondly. Every time the snow came she behaved like that, gambolling and jumping about, almost human in her wild excitement. They crossed the dampened yard, their feet muffled in the strangely quiet air, the snow squeaking underfoot like newly broken hazel twigs.

She opened the barn door. Inside stood Jacky, her cow. A ten-year-old Friesian, hugely pregnant with her next calf, she was a pretty beast as cows go. She stood four-square, black and white, her belly distended, her udder swollen.

The cow eyed her expectantly, her large orbs graced with the most elegant of long black lashes, set each side of a dainty dish-shaped face with clean wide nostrils below. A stream of glutinous saliva dribbled from her jaw, but her long pink tongue, stained green from silage, gathered it up.

Claire put down the bucket and set to work mixing some feed. She filled up the trough and the cow bent down to eat. Inside another pen stood two young bullocks. About two months old, they were soon to be weaned and came greedily as soon as Claire took them their feed.

'Come on, you buggers, move it.' As their strength grew, it was getting harder by the day to move them out of her way. One had inadvertently trodden on her foot and she knew she would have a vicious bruise by the time she got in.

Now it was her turn to milk. She pulled up an old feed bucket that was minus its handle and, turning it upside down, sat down to milk the cow.

At first the teats were covered with the calves' sticky saliva. She soon worked them dry. Claire milked expertly, pulling and squeezing the sausage-like teats, letting the warm milk spurt into the bucket as a white frothy liquid. Her face was pressed up against the cow's warm flank, which was covered with dried cracked dung, but she didn't notice things like this any more. If anything, milking Jacky

78

was a time of such peace and quiet that she looked forward to it.

The quarters were empty now, hanging deflated, like days-old party balloons. Claire stood up, taking the bucket with her. She unchained the cow and left her peacefully munching her hay.

On her way out she tested one of the water pipes. It was, as she expected, quite frozen. That meant a miserable day cracking the ice on the water butt and heaving buckets full around until all the animals were done. She wasn't looking forward to it at all.

Out in the sunshine of the yard, she let out the chickens. She had already thrown down some corn for them and in a flurry of feathers, they ran over to peck.

In the third outhouse was her horse, Bonny. Of no genetic distinction, she greeted Claire warmly, rumbling softly as her forehead was patted.

'Hello, girl, how are you this morning? Want to go out to the field, do you?' The horse breathed warm breath into Claire's face.

Claire then went into another loosebox and picked up some hay. She led Bonny over the yard to the field, cracked the ice on the water trough and then stood watching as the horse rolled about, her legs flaying the air as the sparkling ice and snow crystals flew about her. She too was enjoying the snow.

'Silly girl.'

She shut the gate and headed back to the house.

After straining the milk, she washed the bucket and put it away. She made herself some porridge and gave Rosie her biscuits and tea. Seated at the old wooden table, she eyed the pile of bills stacked up behind the clock on the shelf over the Rayburn. She hadn't realized how worried she was about them until now. The news from yesterday made her feel quite magnanimous towards those who sent them. Even the ones printed in red with dire warnings of disconnection made her smile. Well, she couldn't do much about them today, the lane would be blocked off with drifting snow. They would have to wait for the mild southwesterlies to melt it. Anyway, it wouldn't matter. A few more days was neither here nor there when it came to bills.

After breakfast came the sheep. During the night two more ewes of her flock of thirty had lambed successfully, their newborns standing firm and quite oblivious to the other ewes' curiosity. She lifted them out, saw to their navels, and put them in with their mothers in separate pens. Using her penknife, she cut the twine on a bale and spread the fresh straw about the pens, breaking it up with vigorous kicks, sending the yellow crisp stalks flying around her.

While doing so she noticed a dark form lying quite still at the back of the pens. The first time she had seen a dead lamb like that it had made her feel quite sick. Dead for possibly two weeks inside the mother, it had begun to putrefy before finally being expelled, so that now it was limp and black. It was hard to tell which ewe it had come from. The rest of the flock looked healthy enough, watching her suspiciously from the other side of the pen. She chastised herself. Had she been up and awake sometime during the night, as she usually did when lambing was on, she might have seen it happening.

She picked up the cold damp body by its back legs and took it outside. Any dead sheep must be burnt.

The water butt stood by the barn door. Ice about an inch thick covered the top. She smashed it with a hammer, throwing the broken pieces to one side and slowly let the bucket fill. Heaving it out was back-breaking and several times it spilt down her jacket, freezing on contact. A stiff northerly breeze was blowing now, turning her cheeks even pinker, the cold air catching in her throat and her fingers were going numb. It was at times like this that she thought back to her comfortable, centrally heated office, doing a job that required enough effort to push a pen and no more. She knew, though, that her nostalgia was only fleeting and that when the spring came, she would be only too pleased to be on her farm with nature all around her.

For an hour she struggled with the water. Every animal needed its share and by the time she had finished, she could feel the sweat on her back already cooling. She put the bucket down and leant against the wall panting slightly. Squinting through tired eyes at the reflected glare of the snow, she contemplated her next move — food for her cattle.

They were a motley bunch of sucklers, mongrels all, that eked out their meagre existence between the rocky outcrops and gorse bushes on the moor. From where she stood, Claire could see the chiselled outline of the tors that were their home looming up towards the blue sky like a line of regimented whale backs. Somewhere up there were her cattle and she had to find them. With a bit of luck they would be sheltering low down, out of the bitter weather and not too far from the road.

Her stomach rumbled and for a moment she stood poised with indecision, but then, too cold to carry on, she headed back towards the kitchen's beckoning warmth. Tea and cakes first. Rosie came too and the pair of them gathered in next to the Rayburn, chilled to the marrow. Claire sat on her chair, her stockinged feet propped up against the towel rail, her left one throbbing painfully from being stepped on by the calf. She opened the oven door so that its heat gradually thawed her while a mug of hot tea warmed her hands. On the table next to her sat the cake tin which Rosie watched intently, saliva drooling from her jaw. Claire looked at her.

'You really are a pig, do you know that?'

Rosie's tail wagged furiously but she stopped when she realized the cake still wasn't forthcoming.

'You're a four-legged garbage disposal unit.'

Again the tail swished, knocking out long-forgotten crumbs from beside the Rayburn. Claire took a piece of cake and waved it slowly across the dog's line of vision. Rosie followed it, mesmerized, occasionally glancing at Claire, pleading to be put out of her misery.

'Lie down.' The dog lowered herself slowly, transfixed by the morsel lying on Claire's leg. 'Good girl. Now don't snatch,' and she offered the titbit that vanished instantly, only to be replaced by more begging. 'Honestly, Rosie, anyone would think I didn't feed you. If you were human, you'd be the size of a house. Here you are then,' and she gave her the rest of the bun.

It took half an hour of fiddling with the van before it finally consented to start. The intricacies of the internal combustion engine never had been one of Claire's strong points, and Matt had always seen to that side of things. If it went wrong, she blindly used what rudimentary knowledge she had and hoped it worked. The van was old and needed a thorough service, something that up until now was out of the question.

She backed into the yard and let it idle while she loaded it up with hay, potatoes and a few turnips. After that there was the slow climb up onto the moor, along tracks that at any other time she knew well. Now they had disappeared into a uniform blanket of white and she drove with more care, the ruts and bumps jolting her and Rosie about.

Her cattle were more or less where she expected, sharing what shelter they had found with some ponies, short barrel-shaped beasts with long shaggy coats. She spread the food about, looking at them closely. A real farmer, Jack had informed her, spent a good deal of his time watching his stock. They ambled slowly towards her like some bovine JCBs, leaving deep trenches in the snow with their hooves. Soon they were all eating, pulling out tendrils of hay by shaking their heads up and down and wrapping their long prehensile tongues round each mouthful.

Claire didn't mind the ponies taking their share. Strictly speaking, their owners should be feeding them, especially

82

in this cold weather. Like everything else, they were a crop to be harvested once a year and those left to fend for themselves sometimes didn't survive. There had been a terrible row in Plymouth the year before when a lady out walking her dog had found the frozen remains of some yearlings and local farmers had been accused of neglect. In the empty expanse of the moor, Claire thought, it was bound to happen sometimes.

Content that her animals were well, she left them and drove back to the farm. By now it was lunchtime. In the afternoon she would collect the eggs, if there were any, see to the sheep, water everything again and then finally, slump exhausted, with hardly enough energy to make her tea.

Two weeks later and the thaw was complete. Snow never stayed long in Devon. Its proximity to the warm Atlantic, and the prevailing southwesterlies, saw to that. It even began to smell like spring. Instead of the steel grey which generally blanketed the sky, patches of forgotten blue began to appear and when the sun did shine, it felt warmer.

Below the farm, in a steep valley, stood some ancient stunted oaks near a stream, their branches gnarled and moss-covered. Every year rooks nested there, calling raucously to each other when spring came, fighting over nest material and squabbling with their neighbours. Their activities were one of the beacons of the year's turning for Claire: calendars meant nothing.

Lambing was over and all the flock, bar two little ones whose mother had died, were out in the field relishing the fresh green grass. While the ewes grazed, the lambs would play king of the castle, racing up the field in fast tight-knit groups and mock fighting over a hillock, taking it in turns to butt the others off.

The sheds now empty, Claire needed to clear the dung and straw. It was a chore she didn't look forward to, but she could now afford to hire someone to do it for her. Maybe Jack would know who to ask. She was about to phone him, when it rang for her.

'Hello, 285.'

'Claire!'

'Ange! How are you?'

'Still alive, just. 'Scuse me. Matthew get down from there.'

The phone was put down while Ange saw to one of her twin sons. Claire could hear the two-year-old's cries of protest as his mother sorted him out.

'Sorry about that. Dear little darling that he is. Now where was I? How are you and how's the farm? I was worried about you during the New Year. I tried to ring you but couldn't get your number.'

'I was disconnected.'

'Oh dear! Well anyway, you're back amongst the living now. How was your lambing?'

'All right. I didn't lose many, just one ewe who was getting on a bit and a couple of lambs. What about you, though? How are you doing?'

'Fine, just fine. I'm only working part-time at the moment and I can't tell you what bliss it is.'

'I bet, sitting at one of those word processors all day can be a real strain.'

'Yes, I've just been told I'll probably have to wear glasses.' A short pause and then: 'Hang on a minute, dear, disaster is about to strike.'

Again the phone was put down. Claire smiled to herself imagining the scene at Ange's house: toys littering the floor while the twins ran riot. Eventually Ange came back slightly breathless.

'Honestly, dear, how these two are ever going to see adulthood is a mystery to me. They were only trying to put the cat in the spin dryer.'

Claire laughed.

'Are you sure I can't persuade you to borrow one from me? I'll pay you if you like.'

'No thanks, Ange. Believe me, your two are little angels, but I'm sure they would behave much better with you than with me.'

'Nonsense, dear, all you need is a bit of practice. If you'd had one of your own . . . Oh dear, sorry, I didn't mean to say that.'

Claire smiled ruefully. Matt's infertility was something she had had to accept.

'Don't worry, Ange, I'm not bothered, honestly I'm not.'

'Well, so long as you're sure . . . Right, changing the subject, I rang up to tell you about the absolutely scrumptious knockout that's taken over Briar Cottage, you know, the house between you and Jack.' Ange was excited and spoke in a hushed conspiratorial tone. 'He's really yummy, well at least from about ten feet he is. I saw him the other day with Jack, and later Jack told me he was renting the cottage. Seems he's a broker or something. Anyway, dear, he's the sort of man that positively oozes it from his hair roots down to his toenails.'

'Well, why should I be interested? I mean, what's he like?'

'Tall, dark and handsome, Claire, tall dark and handsome. You know, your regular Byron.'

'But what's it got to do with me?'

'Oh, Claire, how can you be so dense? There he is, all alone, no lady of any description anywhere, ripe for the picking and there are you, lovely and lonesome! I'm sure you'd make a beautiful couple as they say. So what d'you think?'

Claire sighed. Ange was a dear friend but her nonstop efforts to get her hitched were sometimes quite irritating.

'Ange, I don't need anyone, really I don't. I'm quite happy as I am, especially now things are financially more secure.'

'Oh? Do tell.'

'Well, actually I've just inherited some money from a long-lost relative.'

'God, you lucky thing!' exclaimed Ange. 'How much?'

Claire faltered, her natural reticence coming through. 'Enough,' she said at last, 'for a few years, plus some goodies for the house.' She paused and then added more thoughtfully, 'Honestly, Ange, I was beginning to think I might have to sell up, things were getting so bad, but not any more. Now I can go and tell that Neale chap to get stuffed.'

'Oh, Claire, I'm so happy for you. I really am. It's about time something good happened to you. So when are you going to contribute to the Angeela Wilkinson Benevolent Fund then?'

Claire laughed. 'Will a pint and a packet of crisps do instead?'

The smile was wide in Ange's voice. 'Yes, of course it will. Now back to the main topic. How would you like it if I planned a little evening get-together, you know a few old friends having a nice meal, mellow wine, candlelight, et cetera, et cetera? Does that meet with your approval?'

'Oh look, Ange, I don't want to sound ungrateful or anything, but please don't. If I'm going to meet him, I'd much prefer it if it was on my own terms when I feel a bit more comfortable. Anyway, I hate dressing up, I always feel such a wally.'

'Rubbish, dear! You looked lovely at that dinner a couple of years back, your hair up, your makeup done. Honestly, I really think you sell yourself short.'

Claire remembered that dinner. It was the last time Matt and she celebrated together. Soon after that had been the accident. Her eyes began to swim. How odd she should start crying now.

'Claire . . . Claire, are you still there?'

'Yes, yes, just thinking, that's all. Look,' she said brightly, blinking away her tears, 'I'll ring you soon and let you know about that dinner, okay? I must go now, I've got to see to the sheep.'

'All right, but promise you'll ring, won't you, and once again congratulations about your windfall. I'll just go away now and throw up and then see if I can find some makeup that will hide my green complexion.'

Claire laughed. She could always count on Ange to cheer her up. 'Thanks, and yes I will ring. Bye.'

Standing on the small table beside the telephone was a picture of Matt leaning against their van. She picked it up and stared at it. He hadn't been a conventionally good-looking man, very ordinary really. About five feet ten inches with brown hair and hazel eyes. It was much more his manner that won her over. His shy smile and twinkling eyes warmed their way into her, taking hold of her heart and refusing to let go. His goodness was almost palpable and she still missed him.

The tears started again, running down her cheeks and dripping off her chin. She replaced the picture and sat down heavily on the chair. It always happened like this. Just when she thought she had finally got over it, something, sometimes so trivial it was almost insignificant, started her off again. She reached for her hanky and cried softly.

Rosie, who had been sitting in the kitchen, came out and tried to poke her nose into Claire's hand, whining and licking her clenched fingers. Getting no response, she used a paw, her hard black nails pulling at Claire's skin.

'All right, all right,' Claire sniffed. 'I'm okay.' She stroked the dog's large head and then, putting her arms round her neck, cuddled her, burying her face in the thick black coat. 'Just thinking about the old man, that's all,' she whispered. Rosie stood patiently. 'Come on then, let's go out.'

Walking across the moor had always been a delight for Claire; grey, wet or windy like today, it made no difference. Its rocky barrenness, bleak windswept hills and ancient tors standing like so many grey sentinels calmed and placated her. She knew that an hour or so of tramping across the tussocky landscape, breathless and warm from the sheer physical effort, would leave her tired but rejuvenated. It was enough simply to stop thinking and allow the senses to be bombarded by the richness of the topography.

Few people were around at this time of the year. In the summer, when the tourists came, it sometimes got quite crowded in the lanes near her farm, cars parked on the verges, their occupants sleeping inside or sitting on deckchairs nearby, their picnicking utensils strewn about. Relatively few people were prepared to walk over the hills and for that reason she was grateful. She felt a kind of jealous proprietorial ownership of the land which made her resent outsiders' intrusions and quick to anger if she saw someone dropping litter or frightening the stock. It wasn't her land, but time and proximity had welded her to it.

The pair of them climbed over a stile and walked up a rocky, puddled track. Winter's grip still held the land, despite the warming days. Up here, it was slow to thaw and the grasslands still had that yellowing deadness left by the hard frost and snow.

Lost in her own thoughts, Claire was unaware of the direction she was taking. It was Rosie's sudden barking that made her look up.

A tall figure, dressed in a long black coat, his face half buried in its high collar, a scarf flapping wildly in the wind, was walking towards her.

He wasn't local – she knew all of them – and he was no hill climber either; his dress was all wrong, without the regulation red or blue waterproofs and bulging rucksacks. Skewers of unreasonable panic stabbed her insides and she stopped. Rosie ran towards him, barking dementedly, prancing and jumping, her head up and tail down. She too was frightened.

'Rosie! Rosie! Come here, dog!' The animal ignored her. Claire ran after her, her feet heavy with clogged wellingtons, her arms restricted by her waxed jacket and gale-blown drizzle lashing her face. 'Come here, dog!' She wanted to get hold of her and run away, but now of all times, Rosie ignored her.

The man stopped. Claire halted about ten feet away, her dog now obediently at her heels, firmly held by the collar. She still rumbled with anxiety, deep barely audible growls issuing from between clenched teeth, her lips curled.

'I'm so sorry, she doesn't normally behave like this.' Claire felt embarrassed; hot and awkward.

At first no reply; the man just kept on staring at her. Then slowly he smiled. A hand, manicured she noticed, extended from a pocket.

'James Lamont.'

She hesitated. 'Claire Bromage.'

His grip was firm and cold and he didn't let go. Instead, those deep blue eyes kept looking at her. She tried to smile, but her face wouldn't co-operate. She felt sure that her attempts produced more of a grimace than anything else. He released her hand. It tingled. Seeing her discomfort he said: 'I've just taken over Briar Cottage. A spring let.' His voice was muffled and he unwrapped his scarf from around his neck, fully revealing himself.

That face.

'Escape from the rat race at weekends,' he explained when she said nothing more. 'I thought a bit of rural peace and quiet might do me good.' He smiled encouragingly.

Claire didn't hear any of it. She was five feet nine, so he must be at least six feet one.

'There's something about this lonely place, don't you think?'

'Well . . . yes, actually I live here. Rosie, be quiet!' The dog still growled.

'Oh yes, where?'

Claire pointed. 'That's my farm, Tor Heights.'

'Oh, so we're neighbours then?'

'Well, I suppose so. As the crow flies it's about two miles between the two places, but by road, it's easily five.' Rosie still complained. 'Be quiet, girl.' Claire looked up, flustered. 'I'm sorry about this, she's not normally so . . . so . . .'

'Vocal?' he volunteered.

'Yes, exactly.'

'That's all right.' He walked forward and leant down towards Rosie, extending his hand and so close that Claire could smell his expensive aftershave. Rosie ignored him, turning her head away, still growling.

He straightened. 'Very particular, your dog, isn't she? But very beautiful, rather like her owner,' he added. 'Anyway, I mustn't keep you. Goodbye.'

Abruptly he strode off.

Claire watched him for some time until he disappeared into the mist, and then laughed out loud. She had never heard such rubbish! He couldn't possibly expect her to believe that nonsense. Oh well, she thought, he won't be around for long so at least she would be spared any more of his flattery. Still, insincerity aside, there was no doubting his good looks. On that point at least she agreed with Ange.

SIX

'Alistair, Mr Brockman is on the line. He wants to discuss the sale of his house with you.'

'All right, put him through.'

He reluctantly turned away from his window. He had been looking out for Claire. It was Wednesday, market day, and the square was packed with stalls and people. He knew it would be the one day she came to town. He picked up his phone.

'Good morning, Mr Brockman, what can I do for you?'

Once a week Claire liked to come down to do some shopping. It was her little treat when she could briefly forego the constant demands of her farm and start relating to humans again.

She didn't waste time – a quick dash around the shops, a visit to the library, followed by a currant bun and a coffee in one of the High Street tea shoppes.

The market was in full swing when she arrived, adding barber shop colouring to the spring sunshine. Everyone it seemed came to town on market day. Not so much to shop, although plenty of that went on, but more to stand and gossip.

To an outsider, it would seem that Devonians are basically of one shape: short and square, great bulging haunches and thick-set midriffs encased in utility clothes, practical and long-lasting.

Claire stood out. With her height and good looks, furtive and sometimes envious eyes would follow her progress through the mêlée.

She sat in the tea shop nursing a coffee, watching the

passers-by. She was enjoying the colourful spectacle.

'May I?'

She looked up, momentarily startled. It was him, the man from the moor. He smiled briefly at her, his eyes friendly.

'Yes, of course.'

He took off his tan leather jacket, revealing a dark blue sweater. Pulling gently at the knees of his jeans he sat down. Again that aftershave; a subtle musky undertone that hinted of excitement and danger.

'Well,' he said, leaning forward, 'how are you? I haven't seen you around for the last few days.'

'I've been busy.'

She tried to look at him but found it difficult. For so long she had only dealt with the local men whose lack of social skills never intimidated her. He was different. Unsure about him and feeling vulnerable, she debated whether she should leave, but curiosity stopped her. He was intriguing. And very handsome. She felt herself warming to him.

'A farmer, you said?'

'Yes,' she replied, 'it was my husband's. Now it's mine.'

'Oh. Did he . . .?' The question hung in the air.

'He died. Two years ago.'

'I'm sorry.'

She smiled bleakly. 'Don't be. You weren't to know.' She idly looked down at her cup. A congealed skin of cold milk was beginning to form on the surface. It looked unsavoury. She tilted it up towards her and the thin layer hung on to the smooth white china.

'Would you like another cup?' he asked. 'I was just about to have one.'

'Yes, please.'

He beckoned the waitress, a mature woman whose black skirt was too tight and white blouse vast over a mountainous bustline. Smiling and bobbing, her eyes twinkling and her face quite flushed, she came over to them.

'Two coffees, please.'

'Yes, sir. Anything else?'

He looked at Claire. 'Would you like anything to eat?'

'Oh no, no thank you.'

'That will be all then, please.'

The waitress took away Claire's cup, smiling through her dark rouged hole of a mouth.

'So, what's it like being a farmer?'

'Hard work. All hours, all weathers, no time off.'

'Sounds dreadful. I don't think I could cope. I suppose you spend a lot of time by yourself as well? You must get terribly lonely sometimes.'

Claire sighed. 'Occasionally, but mostly I'm too busy,' she said quietly.

Their coffees arrived, interrupting them. Claire noticed how the waitress lingered by, reluctant to move away, her eyes openly appreciative of James.

'What do you do with yourself when you're not farming?' he asked, fixing Claire with his unwavering gaze, probing and searching.

She looked down at his hands, which lay linked together on the white tablecloth. Long capable fingers, she thought. Each one dusted with a covering of fine black hairs behind the knuckles which continued up to his wrists. He wore a heavy gold signet ring on the little finger of his left hand.

'Nothing much. I'm usually too tired for anything else except to collapse in front of the fire.'

Careful, she told herself, he's pulling away at the layers.

'Well,' he said, taking a sip of his coffee, 'I've been trying to find something to do during the evenings around here and I have to say that so far I've been disappointed.'

She glanced at him. She had started to pick at a loose thread on the tablecloth. 'Well, there's always the pubs and there's whist drives or meat bingo if you like that sort of thing.' The thread snapped.

'Oh dear,' he said, slowly covering her hand with his. 'Now look what you've done.' His voice was suddenly so

93

quiet, the words nothing to do with the true message he was conveying. Claire felt it, though. The sensations running along her skin, up her arm and into her body were piercingly obvious to her. She shifted in her seat and gently pulled her hand away out of sight under the table.

'Do you think I would enjoy these activities?'

She looked up and, seeing his easy smile, smiled too, relieved almost. 'No, I don't suppose so. I've never been to a meat bingo and I live here.'

'But you don't sound like your neighbours. When I was speaking to Mr Burrows the other day I could barely follow a word he said.'

'Well, he's lived here all his life. I only came down about ten years ago.'

'Where were you before that then?'

'Oh, all over the place. My father was in the army.' She paused. 'What about you?'

He shrugged. 'Home Counties mainly, and then boarding school and now London. I used to work for a bank in the City. Now I'm a commodity broker.'

Claire frowned. 'But why come here?'

'London can be unbearable. Polluted, crowded and far too distracting, especially at the weekend. I need to get away from it all.'

She smiled, comfortable at last. 'You'll like it here, it's so beautiful.'

He finished his coffee. 'Mmm. So I've noticed. The moor especially.'

'And in summer, it's so much better. You'll love it then.'

'I can't wait. Well,' he added, 'now that we've discussed the nonexistent nightlife, I wonder if you would like to come to dinner some evening? I've been told I'm a fairly reasonable cook. At least no one's died on me recently.'

She gave a small laugh. This was unexpected. 'I don't know.' She turned away and stared thoughtfully at the passing crowds. She could see Jack with some of his cronies standing outside a pub nearby, his head thrown back in hearty amusement. 'I don't know,' she repeated. 'I've got too much to do on the farm at the moment.'

'But surely you do that during the day. I'm talking about dinner. You know, that meal we eat at about nine o'clock.'

She shook her head. 'Five thirty, you mean. We only eat at that time during the harvest.'

'Okay, then,' he acquiesced. 'Make it . . . six thirty? And I solemnly promise not to put any belladonna or toadstools in the gravy. Scouts' honour.'

She wavered. It was such an attractive invitation.

'Look,' he said patiently. 'It's only dinner.'

She bit her bottom lip and finally said: 'Okay, I'll be there.'

His face broke into a wide smile. 'Good.'

The clock tower chimed two. Claire started.

'Oh no, I've left Rosie in the van and if I don't get back she'll start howling.'

She stood up, James helping her on with her waxed jacket. He left a five-pound note on the table, much to Claire's surprise, and they left the café.

'Here,' he offered, 'let me take your bags.'

'No, that's okay, I can manage.'

He smiled. They pushed on through the crowds that were still thronging the pavements, islands of old ladies blocking the flow of human traffic and errant toddlers being called to heel by harassed parents. James had difficulty in keeping up with her.

'Hang on a bit,' he said, knocking into a pushchair. 'I am sorry,' he apologized to the comely woman who tutted at him. 'Goodness, you walk fast.'

Claire stopped. 'I'm sorry. I suppose it's all that tramping over the fields. I have to go this way now. Thanks for the coffee and I'll be with you about six thirty on Saturday.'

'Can't I see you before then?'

Tempted, she said, 'No, I don't think so. I really am very busy.'

'Right, six thirty it is,' and before she could say anything he held her gently by the shoulders and kissed both her cheeks. 'I can't tell you how much I'm looking forward to it.'

'Yes,' she murmured. 'Goodbye.'

He left her surprised and delighted.

Jealousy; tearing, ripping, searing jealousy. Why couldn't he get used to it? First Matt and now that bloody man.

Alistair stood at his office window watching Claire. He had seen everything – the way she smiled, and the way she laughed and it was all directed at that tall dark man who even had the nerve to kiss her, and in the middle of the bloody market as well. Damn him!

The telephone went. He grabbed it.

'Yes?' he snapped.

Julie hesitated. 'Mr Tucker rang. Can you go and see him at Mole Avon?'

'What, now?'

'Well, if you can,' she replied gingerly.

He sighed. 'If I must, then. Get his file out, please, and I'll go right over.'

He slammed the receiver down and sat in his chair. Just who the hell was that man?

Rosie. Walking as fast as she could, hot and flustered, Claire marched across the car park. As usual, she had left the van under the trees which, even though they were bare, kept off most of the sun.

Nearing the vehicle, she could hear the familiar low-pitched mournful howl, which seemed so out of place in the spring sunshine. As soon as she opened the door, Rosie flung herself at Claire, her whole body gyrating with happiness, her wet tongue licking Claire's face and her tail flaying the dashboard.

'All right, all right, I'm back now so calm down. Shh, shh, shh, calm down.' The dog's whining stopped and at last her excitement abated. 'Come on then, out you get.'

96

Rosie jumped down and immediately started to poke her nose into the shopping bags, sniffing and snuffling at each new smell.

'Here you, get out!' Claire pushed her to one side and put the bags into the van. 'Right, let's go and get some milk for the lambs and then all will be done.'

Normally she would have driven round to the suppliers, but today, feeling unusually happy, she wanted to walk; slowly.

When she got to the park Rosie bounded off and Claire watched her investigate the new and interesting smells. Then, with her hands in her pockets, she meandered along the path which bordered the riverside.

Although the land was still gestating its springtime colours and last year's growth of reeds stood brown and faded along the bank, other hints that spring was here were abundant. Mallards swam in couples, their iridescent heads glinting purple and green. The air was full of birdsong, a hubbub of shrieks and trills overladen with the ubiquitous call of rooks. Across the river on the other bank, yellow strings of catkins swung from the bare branches, shaking out their pollen on the breeze.

It had been a strange and exciting day for Claire and had left her curiously elated. The last thing she had been expecting was a meeting with James and she certainly hadn't anticipated liking him so much. She had firmly decided that he was a nice man, although as soon as she heard that word in her mind, she altered it to attractive, but then even that seemed inadequate. One thing was for sure: he was definitely the most handsome man she had met for years. He was everything Ange said he was: tall and dark, although his cobalt-blue eyes gave away some Anglo-Saxon inheritance. And physical too. Not too muscular, but just right. He filled out his expensive clothes very well and it gave him presence. Yes, she thought, that was it, he had presence. An overwhelming animal instinct, a danger almost, that hung around him like an invisible aura. It was hard to remain indifferent to him. She reached the end of the park and called Rosie to her so that they could cross the road.

The farm suppliers was a utilitarian grey building with its name in large green letters across the top. Farm machinery lay around it like a collection of modern-day torture instruments, their sharp blades glinting in the sun. Claire walked past a heap of fertilizer bags and entered the shop. Alistair was there.

'Hello, Claire, how are you?' he hailed, smiling. He kissed her on the cheek and stood back. He seemed inordinately pleased to see her.

'Why didn't you ring or something?' he asked. 'We could have had lunch together.'

She shrugged. 'Wednesday is shopping day, Alistair. Anyway, I just assumed you would be too busy.'

'Never too busy to see you, Claire. And how are you, Rosie?' Rosie wagged her tail effusively while Alistair stroked her and she then rolled over on to her back, showing the smooth pink skin of her stomach.

'Pathetic creature,' muttered Claire proudly.

'Nonsense!' he exclaimed. 'She's an extremely beautiful and devoted pet to someone who looks after her very well.' He stood up. 'Well, how's things going now that you're in the financial big time?'

'Fine. I've paid off all my bills, got the repairs to the barn roof sorted out and am now deciding what to do next. You know,' she added thoughtfully, 'it's really strange having all this money. When I was dirt-poor I used to daydream about going on huge spending sprees, but now I'm rich, I couldn't care less about it. All my past plans about shopping have come to nothing.'

'I'm not surprised,' he said, smiling warmly. 'Having known you as long as I have, I think I can honestly say that you are one of the least materialistic people I know. It's something to be proud of, Claire. Most of the people I meet in my profession are absolute vultures and it makes a pleasant change to deal with someone as nice as you.'

'Thanks, Ali,' and she blushed.

'By the way, how about seeing Peter Collier, you know, the financial adviser who has a place in the High Street? The other day I bumped into him and hinted, in a very roundabout way, you understand, that you might be requiring his services.'

'Oh, right. Well, to tell the truth, Ali, I hadn't really thought about that yet.' She looked guilty, a slight frown puckering her forehead.

'That's no problem. I've got to know him quite well and he said he might come over on Saturday evening. Why don't you come round too and perhaps you could speak to him then. What d'you say?'

'Can't,' she said, the word barely escaping her lips. 'I'm sorry, Ali, but I've already accepted an invitation to go out on Saturday.'

Just for an instant, his eyes clouded over, the sparkle gone. She had snuffed it out.

'Oh well, that's okay,' he laughed. 'Are you doing anything nice?'

She smiled secretively, her full lips pressed together as she tried to suppress a wild grin. 'Maybe,' she said.

Alistair stared intently at some point past her left shoulder. 'Oh I see. Like that, eh? Sounds interesting.'

'If you must know, I'm going to have dinner with a chap called James Lamont.' She knew she had a silly grin on her face but she couldn't repress it any longer. Just the mention of his name made her feel a teenager again. 'Do you know him?'

'Mmm, yes,' he replied deliberately. 'Let me just say that I have heard mention of him via my secretary. A man of extraordinary handsomeness so it seems. She was quite besotted and by the look on your face, I can see he's having much the same effect on you.'

Claire looked down at her feet, embarrassed that she was so obvious.

'Still,' he continued gently, 'at least you're happy and that's the main thing.'

'I can't help it,' she replied. 'I met him today at the market.'

'Ah, so that's who you were talking to.'

'You saw us?'

'Only briefly,' he said lightly. 'I was on the phone at the time. I often look out of the window for a diversion. I see what Julie means about his handsomeness. God help the rest of us mere mortals now this Adonis has arrived.'

She looked at him playfully. 'What rot, Ali. If you lost a little weight and smartened yourself up a bit, the women of Torhampton would be clamouring after you. Mind you, from what I hear, they already are.'

'Would that include you too?'

She pursed her mouth and looked away. 'Well now, that would be telling, wouldn't it?' They both smiled good-humouredly. 'Well, I must be going. I've got two hungry lambs to feed at home as well as everything else.'

'Have fun on Saturday, Claire, and take care, won't you?'

She looked at him quizzically. 'Of course. Why?'

He shrugged. 'I don't know. I don't mean anything really, and ring Peter Collier, won't you?'

Back at his office Alistair phoned Elyssa. He felt numb after his conversation with Claire; numb and hopelessly inadequate. The idea of Claire with that man wrenched at his insides and he couldn't face the weekend alone.

He hadn't expected to see Peter Collier on Saturday. That was just his way of getting Claire to come over without suspecting anything. He thought that if she had accepted his invitation, he could have taken her out somewhere really nice and then maybe, take her back to his house for a nightcap or whatever else might happen. His disappointment was crushing. It was, in fact, his birthday, and Claire had evidently completely forgotten.

'Hello?'

'Elyssa, it's Alistair.'

'My goodness. What a surprise.' There was a slight tone of irony in her voice. 'I thought we weren't going to see each other again.'

'Well, in these days of equal opportunities, Elyssa, I've changed my mind. Are you doing anything this weekend?'

He took out the letter he had written to her that was in his pocket waiting to be posted and tore it up, scattering the pieces into the rubbish bin.

'Well, now you come to mention it, Ali, I was thinking of entertaining a tall, blue-eyed blond. What d'you think?'

'Sounds okay to me.' He tried to sound happy.

SEVEN

'Well, well, well. Didn't expect to see you for a while.'

'Don't gloat, Terri. I need a drink.'

Terri pulled back the door and let in her friend.

Saskia took two steps into the flat and then started to cry, her shoulders hunched up as the tears flowed.

'The bloody bastard has gone,' she sniffed. 'Just pissed off.'

'Here, wipe your face,' Terri held out a tissue, 'and tell Auntie Terri all about it.' She put her arm round Saskia's shoulders and led her over to the sofa. Saskia sat down heavily and blew her nose.

'The pig! He just took off. I've no idea where and he wouldn't tell me. We were supposed to be going on holiday together.'

Terri poured her a large gin and tonic. 'Drink that, it'll make you feel better.'

'Thanks.' Saskia's smile was brief.

'So what happened then? You two row or something?'

Saskia lit a cigarette. 'No, not really. Oh Christ!' she wailed, her tears renewing. 'I don't know what's going on.'

A door opened. A young man looked round, naked from the waist up and obviously irritated.

'You going to be long, Terri? I'm bloody freezing in here!'

'Oh sorry, Pete.' She nodded towards Saskia. 'Something's come up. Look, sweetie,' she got up and walked over to the man, 'get dressed and come back tomorrow. We'll finish it off then, okay?'

He withdrew, giving Saskia a loaded glance.

Terri turned round to Saskia. 'Models,' she explained apologetically, 'they don't like being ignored.'

'Who is he?'

Terri got up and refilled her glass. 'Just a friend. He's an unemployed actor and does this sort of thing to supplement his dole money. If I wasn't so indifferent to men, I'd say he was damned good-looking.'

Saskia smiled, her interest aroused. 'Mmm, I agree with you there.'

The man entered the room again, putting on his jacket. 'Tomorrow then,' he said sullenly, 'and perhaps this time we won't get interrupted.' With a last glance at Saskia, he left.

'Bloody temperamental little shit,' said Terri. 'One small part at the Shaftesbury Theatre and he thinks he's God Almighty.'

She sat down again taking a small foil package from her trouser pocket. She picked up a packet of cigarette papers from the coffee table and very carefully began to roll herself a joint, skilfully joining the papers together until eventually she had a large cigarette.

'Going to leave the bastard then?' she asked, lighting it and inhaling, holding the pungent smoke deep in her lungs. She closed her eyes and leant back, the smoke escaping from her flared nostrils. After a couple of puffs she passed the joint to Saskia, who also inhaled deeply.

'Screw him!' exclaimed Saskia angrily. 'I don't give a damn for him any more. He's up to his eyeballs in debt and in all kinds of trouble at the club. As far as I'm concerned, he can just bugger off.'

Terri smiled. 'That's my girl.' She took another puff at the joint. 'And now that you've made that decision, what are you going to do with yourself?'

Saskia shrugged. 'God, I don't know. Kick him out, start afresh somewhere else.' Her voice began to break. 'I . . .

don't . . . know. Terri, I just don't know. I love him so much. I don't know what to do.' She put her face in her hands.

Terri sat down on the sofa and put her arm round Saskia's shoulders. 'Oh, baby, don't cry. Here, have some more,' and she offered her the joint.

'It's just that I love him, Terri, he can be so sweet when he wants to be.'

'Yes, babe, I know. Men can be like that sometimes, although, thank God, I've never had the misfortune to be mixed up with one.'

Saskia still cried. 'You don't understand, he's not like other men. He's different. He's exciting, he's . . . he's, oh God . . .' and her voice trailed off into sobbing.

'There, there, Saskia, let it all out. I'm here to take care of you,' and she gently rocked her friend to and fro.

'Do you remember Sister Agnes?' said Saskia, some time later.

Terri laughed, a small hoot. She was laid out on the sofa, her head resting on Saskia's lap.

'God, she was such a bitch! I remember that time she caught me smoking in the walled garden. She gave me such a thrashing and on top of that she made me clean all the dining-room tables. It was half-past eleven before I'd finished. Old cow!'

'Yes, she was a monster, but Frances was nice, though.'

They both smiled. Little Sister Frances, petite, bubbly and young enough to want to be the girls' friend.

'You know, in all the years I was there, she never once told anyone off.'

'Yes,' Saskia giggled. She was getting drunk now, and the joint had made her feel light-headed. 'Do you remember that time in church when you and I were sitting up in the gallery and dropping little bits of paper onto that bald man underneath? Christ! We got such a bollocking for that!' Their giggling became louder.

Terri reached for the gin bottle and tipped it up clumsily. 'Oh dear, all gone. Must get more.' She staggered to her feet, seemingly drunk, and waved a finger at Saskia. 'I know what,' she said, 'to hell with this. Let's have some real fun.'

Saskia grinned. 'What?'

Terri held her arm. 'This way and you'll find out.'

Saskia followed her, led along by the arm, the room gently swaying before her. 'Where are we going?'

Terri held her finger to her lips. 'Shh, you'll find out.'

Saskia stopped. 'Don't want to,' she announced petulantly.

'Oh come along, baby, I'm not going to eat you.' Terri's face was gentle. She held Saskia by the shoulders. 'Mummy's not going to harm her little girl.'

Saskia's grin was lopsided. 'Okay.'

Terri led her through her studio, a crowded room smelling of turpentine and a mass of canvases, paints, brushes, palettes and impedimenta of her craft. On a small stage was a chaise longue draped with red velvet. To one side was a large ornamental vase full of dried flowers and grasses.

'Pete,' explained Terri, seeing Saskia look at the rough charcoal drawing on a canvas sitting on the easel. 'What d'you think?'

Saskia tilted her head to one side as if to study him better. 'Not very big, is he?'

Terri threw back her head and laughed. 'God! Trust you to notice something like that!'

Saskia pointed. 'Well, he isn't. Perhaps if you warmed things up a bit in here, it might get bigger.'

'You're supposed to appreciate the fine lines of his classical body, the overall composition, not the length of his bloody prick!'

Saskia waved her hand dismissively. 'Oh well, I never did appreciate art.'

105

'Damn right you didn't.' Terri took her hand. 'Now this way, sweetie.'

Saskia followed, mellowed by the drink and joint, relaxed and unprotesting. She was enjoying herself.

They went through a door at the back of the studio, leaving behind the clutter and smell of paint. The room they entered was at first dark until Terri turned on the light. A diffuse glow of maternal pink filled the room, lighting up a high couch and a small table with a collection of tiny bottles.

Saskia stopped, suddenly wary. 'What are you going to do?' she asked, looking from the couch to her friend.

'Massage.'

'But I don't want a massage.'

'Oh yes you do, you're all uptight and anxious and the best thing for that is a massage.' She walked over to the table and started to wash her hands at the basin. 'Undress,' she said, smiling over her shoulder, 'and stop looking so worried. Believe me, I'm very good at it. I do it for lots of my friends and it's the best thing I know for getting rid of stress.'

Saskia didn't move. 'I don't know,' she faltered. 'I mean, I'm not sure about this.' She looked pensive. 'Can't we just talk and have another drink?'

Terri came over to her and took her hands, looking intently into her eyes. She said: 'I'm gay, you're not. End of story really, and I'm not going to do anything you don't like so you can stop worrying. Okay?' She squeezed Saskia's hands reassuringly.

Saskia smiled ruefully; she was embarrassed at being so obvious.

'I'm sorry,' she mumbled. 'I didn't mean to sound . . . well, you know what I mean.'

'Yes I do, and don't worry, no offence was taken. Now get undressed. You can keep your undies on if you like.'

'No,' she replied laughing. 'I trust you.'

106

Terri went to put some music on while Saskia undressed and lay down on the couch. Then Terri opened a selection of the bottles on the table.

'What are you doing now?'

'Mixing the oils. Essential oils are so concentrated that they need to be mixed with a carrier oil so that I can spread them easily and the curative effects can get through to your bloodstream.'

'What oils are you mixing then?'

'Grapeseed and bergamot.'

'Mmm, smells delicious.' She turned her head away. 'What's that music?'

'Charlie Parker. Now shh and relax.'

Terri's warm oiled hands ran all over Saskia's back with wide sweeping movements. Saskia smiled contentedly and closed her eyes. 'That's lovely.'

'Good. Breathe out, Saskia, whenever I apply pressure.'

Quietly, against the background of low music, Terri's hands worked over Saskia's firm bronzed flesh, pushing and stroking, kneading and easing the spine and shoulders, the neck and back.

'How's that?'

Saskia didn't reply, only smiled. There was a small towel lying across her buttocks.

'I'm going to take off this towel, Sas, as I need to get to your thighs, okay?'

'Mmm.'

With the towel deftly flung to one side, Terri stared, her mouth slightly open as she tried to control her faster breathing. She must not frighten Saskia. She poured some more oil onto her shaking hands from the blending bottle, rubbing her fingers over the palms, conscious of how much she wanted to touch her friend. Two perfect mounds of white firm flesh lay before her. She reached out tentatively, watching her friend's response. Delicately, gently; she must be gentle.

'We have lines of force running along our bodies.' Her

voice sounded strange to her, but Saskia didn't seem to notice. 'They're called meridian lines and they run from your feet to your head. Each one has pressure points along it which correspond to parts of your body. By massaging them, I can release tension in you.'

Two slits of pale blue shone from Saskia's eyes and then vanished. 'Okay.'

Terri put a hand on the back of each of Saskia's thighs and started with slow stroking movements to massage. The flesh beneath her fingers felt smooth and hot and Saskia's crotch was clearly visible. Terri's heart pounded as the thumbs eased upwards towards Saskia's buttocks.

'Is that nice?'

Saskia nodded slightly.

Terri wanted to kiss her. She was finding it difficult to hold back. 'You're beautiful, Sas,' she whispered. 'Really beautiful. Open your thighs.'

Saskia obeyed and when Terri looked at her face she saw with surprise how Saskia's lips had parted, revealing her pink tongue.

Terri held her hands up in front of her eyes. They were still shaking. Her whole body was. The drinks, the joint, the smell of Saskia; it was all affecting her. She replaced her hands, the sudden impulse to squeeze Saskia's flesh nearly overwhelming her.

'You have cellulite,' she admonished gently, 'but I can help with that.'

She massaged Saskia's inner thighs one at a time, the heat and oil fusing their flesh together. She leant forward, the bronzed flesh filling her eyes and her mind, and inhaled the aroma of woman.

'Oh Saskia,' and she kissed her.

Saskia flew off the couch, her face a mask of indignation. She picked up the small towel from the floor and tried, unsuccessfully, to cover herself.

'You . . . you said,' she spluttered, 'you said I could trust you!'

Terri held out her hands. 'Saskia, I'm sorry . . . I didn't mean it. Please . . . I'm sorry.'

'Like hell you are, you bloody pervert! Leave me alone!' And crying hot bitter tears, she hurriedly dressed.

Terri stood motionless. There was nothing she could say. Saskia was livid.

Dressed and still fuming, Saskia stumbled to the door. She stopped and turned, her face heavy, her eyes pained. She held up a finger.

'You're my friend,' she cried, 'my friend. And you . . . you do this to me? How could you?'

Terri was crying too. It was all such a ghastly mistake. How had she let it happen? 'I'm sorry, Sas,' she mumbled, wiping the tears away with her hand. 'Please believe me.'

'Believe you! I wouldn't believe anything you ever said ever again, you bitch!' and with that she flew out of the flat, slamming the door behind her.

Terri spent the rest of the night listening to her saddest and most evocative music and getting hopelessly drunk.

'Alistair, I'm so glad you're here.' They embraced. 'We're going to have a wonderful weekend.' Elyssa stood back and looked at him, her face shining. 'So where do you want to go?'

'For a walk,' he replied, picking up his luggage. 'Two and a half hours on that train and I'm fit for nothing.' He smiled, putting his arm around her shoulder. 'Let's go to Hyde Park and walk across to the Serpentine.'

Kevin took Alistair's bag and put it in the boot of the car while they sat in the back, hands clasped together like young lovers. Alistair leant over and kissed her.

'You smell wonderful, Elyssa, and that suit looks fabulous.'

'Thank you, darling.' She crossed her long legs, the faint swish of silk attracting him as her stockings rubbed against each other. He squeezed her hand tighter. She watched him through placid eyes, smiling.

Kevin got in and looked at them in the rear-view mirror.

'Edgware Road, Kevin, near Marble Arch.'

He started the engine.

'It's so good to see you, Ali. What made you change your mind?'

He looked up at her, his face happy but his eyes sad. 'It's my birthday and I didn't want to spend it alone.'

'Oh, Ali! Why didn't you tell me before? I must get you something.'

He chuckled. 'No need, Elyssa. I've got everything I need already. Your company is quite enough as it is.'

From Paddington to the Edgware Road they crawled through the traffic. Kevin parked the car and got out to open the door.

'Where shall I pick you up?' Kevin sounded sulky.

'Don't,' replied Alistair. 'We'll get a taxi.'

Elyssa wrapped her mid-length fur coat around her. Alistair took her hand and walked her towards the subway.

'What's wrong with him?' he asked.

'Who, Kevin?' Elyssa shrugged. 'In a huff because I wouldn't give him a pay rise.'

'Surely you don't need him? I mean, it's not as if you ever leave London.'

'Oh I do sometimes. Anyway, it's not so much his driving I need as his presence. I have many valuable items in the house and it's good to know there's a man on the premises, you know, just in case anybody felt like breaking in. Of course,' she added, glancing at him, 'I wouldn't need him if I were to remarry.'

Alistair smiled. 'No, I don't suppose you would.'

She squeezed his hand.

In the dank subway they passed a drunk pushing his worldly goods in a shopping trolley, his many-layered dirty clothes buttoned up against the cold.

'Got some coppers for a cup of tea then?' he asked, his dead eyes looking out of his grimy face.

Elyssa grimaced and pulled away, ignoring him as if his presence affronted her.

Alistair reached into his pocket and, without looking, gave him his loose change. The man grinned, his face a rumpled, broken-veined mess.

'Come on, Elyssa. Give the man something.'

She hesitated. It was hard for her to hide her utter disgust at the dirty figure in front of her. Her nostrils twitched and the corners of her mouth were pulling in on themselves, but then seeing Alistair's smiling face, she capitulated. 'Oh, all right.'

She reached into her bag and took out a ten-pound note. 'Will that do?' she said, holding it out to the derelict at arm's-length, just in case she came into contact with his leprous flesh.

'Cor, thanks, miss. You're proper generous.'

'You're quite welcome,' she answered tightly. They walked on.

'That was very generous of you,' said Alistair.

'Well, what's a few pounds? Anyway,' she added, 'one must do what one can for the less fortunate members of society, mustn't one?'

While Alistair was momentarily distracted by a police car racing past, its siren blaring, Elyssa threw her expensive calfskin gloves into a rubbish bin. She couldn't wear those again. That awful stinking man had touched them. She shuddered with horror, but composed herself when Alistair turned back to her.

'Anything wrong, Elyssa?'

'No . . . why should there be?'

He smiled. 'Give me your hand. Let's walk.' He didn't notice she wasn't wearing her gloves.

Out in the flat expanse of the park, away from the busy intersection, Alistair stopped and breathed deeply. The cold wind had brought colour to his cheeks, making his eyes more blue.

'Not the same,' he said at last.

111

'What is?'

'The air.' He started walking again. 'On a windy day on Dartmoor the only thing you can smell is the vegetation and animals.'

Elyssa pushed back her windblown hair and looked up at him, squinting in the icy wind. 'Why do you want that when London has so much else to offer? I mean, on the few occasions I've been to the Southwest, the place seems absolutely dead, a kind of living graveyard where people go to retire. I can't imagine what you do down there for entertainment.' Her voice was dismissive.

'I don't think you understand,' he said, moving to one side to make way for a Walkman-clad jogger. 'There's more to life than just a constant round of social engagements.'

'Yes, I know that, Ali. Of course I do. I just meant that London can offer you, us, many opportunities, as well as getting married, having children, working for a future.'

He looked surprised. 'Heavens, I never thought I'd ever hear you say that.'

She held his arm tightly. 'I've changed, Alistair,' she said quietly, resting her head on his shoulder. 'I'm not the hedonistic and superficial person that you think I am.'

He went to say something, but thought better of it.

She continued: 'I'm getting older and I can't keep pretending otherwise. I know this might sound odd to you, but I want a family before it's too late.'

He glanced down at her.

'Really, Alistair.' She looked away towards the line of trees where some people were out riding.

'It isn't too late, you know. Plenty of women my age are having children and there's absolutely no reason why I can't. Look at Jane Fonda. She's trying to have a baby at her age. I'd like it to happen before long too.'

He didn't reply and they walked on.

'Let's go and sit down,' he suggested.

The metal bench, exposed and freezing, seemed a peculiar place to be for Elyssa on such a cold day. Parties of joggers went by them, dressed in their multicoloured tracksuits, their faces red with effort. A large flock of geese and seagulls noisily squawked as they made way for them.

'If you came to live up here,' she said at last, 'life could be much more interesting for both of us.'

He patted her hand and then kissed it. 'Yes, I know and I would certainly enjoy myself, every bit as much as you do but . . .'

'But what, Ali?'

'I don't know if it's what I want, if I can cope with all this now,' and he waved his hand around. 'The noise, the traffic, the pace of life. I've got used to things the way they are in Devon.'

'But we could always go and stay there for holidays and things.'

'Oh really?' His voice was disbelieving. 'You mean you'd give up the Caribbean and skiing in Aspen for Devon?'

'We could.'

'I don't believe it,' he said laughingly. 'You'd never do that.'

She pursed her lips and then said, 'I would, Alistair – if it was for you.'

He pulled her to him and held her close, kissing the top of her fragrant head.

'I love being held by you, Ali. I feel so warm and safe.'

'And I love holding you, Elyssa.'

She looked up and smiled, and Alistair let himself be drawn to her.

'Let's go and have some tea,' she suggested. 'I'm freezing.'

'Have you decided, madam?'

The liveried waiter hung over her obsequiously.

She handed him the menu. 'Earl Grey.'

He turned to Alistair.

'The same, please.'

When the waiter had gone, Alistair crossed his legs and looked at her, his smile mischievous. 'Well, Elyssa, do you come here often?'

She slightly tugged at the hem of her short black skirt, aware of his gaze, and slowly crossed her sculptured ankles.

'Only in the best company.' Her voice was low.

'Are you warmer now?' he asked.

'Yes, much. In fact, I'm getting warmer all the time.'

They were sitting at a small table in the huge foyer of a hotel, other guests mingling about them, expensively dressed and coiffured. Some sat like they did, having afternoon tea.

'Really? Any ideas on how to cool down again?'

But before she could reply, the waiter returned. He placed the bone china on the table and left them.

Elyssa sat forward, her short skirt pulled tight across her legs. Alistair glanced at the dark area between her thighs. It seemed to be pulling him forward.

'Shall I pour?' Elyssa asked.

He nodded.

'And is there anything else you would like me to do?' She looked at him sideways, holding the teapot poised above the cup. Alistair moved forward and took his tea.

'Why don't we stay here tonight?' He held her wrist. 'I can't think of any reason to go back to your house, can you?' He put down his cup and stood up. 'I'll go and book us a room.'

With a door card in his hand, he led Elyssa to the lift.

'Which floor, sir?'

'Room 205.'

'Yes, sir.'

Standing behind the professionally unseeing liftboy, Alistair, whose hand was round Elyssa's waist, let it slide down until it was cupping one buttock. Without any change of expression from either of them, he moved it

114

slowly down until it was at the hem of her skirt.

Underneath he went, silencing the small sound that escaped him, which he changed into a cough.

The liftboy turned around. 'Nasty weather for colds, sir.'

'Yes, it is indeed.'

Elyssa smiled with satisfaction. She opened her thighs, her hands still clasped modestly in front of her, holding her clutch bag, and the lift raced on. When it stopped, Alistair hurriedly removed his hand and pulled down her skirt.

'Room 205 is along the corridor to the right.'

They walked briskly to their room. They were both hungry. As soon as Alistair had opened the door, they spilled in, pushing the door shut with their feet and embraced. Kissing and panting, they tore at each other, their tongues tasting each other's mouth. By the sofa, Alistair pulled back, turned her around and pushed her forward. She pulled up her skirt and spread her thighs. He caressed each buttock, words superfluous.

She was soaking. He touched her and teased, her hardness rising beneath his fingers, the whole area dark red with pulsating blood. Elyssa moaned, moving against him. He couldn't wait any longer.

As he entered her she shuddered and slowly they moved together. He saw her take her hand and start to masturbate. The eroticism of her actions left him breathless.

Harder and harder they went, the sofa beginning to move beneath them. Gripping her shoulders, his orgasm rising, he felt her shuddering beneath him, her animal sounds muffled by the cushions. He exploded, biting his lips, his head up, staring at the ceiling. Elyssa didn't stop until she had had enough, taking every last bit of him.

He moved away from her, exhausted, and slumped on to the sofa, too tired to say anything.

Elyssa got to her feet and pulled down her skirt. 'I'll just go to the bathroom,' she said. 'I won't be a minute.'

As he watched her retreating back, he felt his lip where

he had bitten it. It was beginning to swell. It was the only way he could stop calling out Claire's name and Elyssa would never understand that.

'Happy birthday, Alistair,' he whispered to himself.

'Hello, Jack,' said Claire.

He nodded. The old farmer was standing against a rusty gate, one foot up on the bottom rung. 'Come and see Bruno.'

Claire stood next to him. The Charolais bull was grazing quietly in the field, unperturbed by their presence, his massive frame dwarfing anything Claire had seen before.

'Heavens, he's huge!'

'Yes, he certainly is. Lots of air between his legs and he can run as well. Took me and Robbie half an hour to get him in the trailer this morning. Bloody bugger.'

'He's a fine animal, Jack. You must be very proud to have him.'

'Certainly am. My heifers should produce much better stock now I've got him.' Jack rattled the gate. 'And I've checked all the fencing and repaired this gate so you needn't worry either.'

Claire smiled. 'Of course not, Jack. I'll make sure none of my animals comes near him.'

They were silent, Jack chewing a piece of grass, like one of his beasts.

Claire really did admire the animal. In every way he was hugely proportioned, his lengthened scrotum hanging between his rear legs. Ordinarily she ignored such things, and it surprised her to be noticing it now. She shifted her feet.

'I have to go now, Jack. I'm going out tonight.'

He looked at her and smiled. 'Anyone I know?'

'Your new lodger at Briar Cottage.'

Jack looked back at his bull. 'Oh well, have a nice time then. Goodbye.'

'Bye.'

Claire turned round and walked back to her farm. She wondered why Jack was so indifferent. Normally he couldn't wait to hear all the details of her social life. But she didn't have time to mull over it now. The two orphaned lambs were bleating noisily for their bottles.

EIGHT

What to wear? Claire stood in front of her open wardrobe and looked dejectedly along the rail of hanging clothes. Nothing; not one decent outfit.

Damn! If only she had thought about it sooner then she would have had time to go to Exeter or Plymouth and buy herself something special. She wanted to look really good tonight but what she saw depressed her. A meagre row of worn-out unfashionable tops and skirts with a couple of faded cotton dresses, bereft of colour, excitement or allure. She was really disappointed. She could kick herself for being so boring.

During the few days since she had seen James, she had found herself constantly thinking of him, his image flitting in and out of her mind without conscious effort. He had even entered her dreams and left her wet and wakeful, shamefaced and embarrassed that she should react to him in such a physical way. Tonight of all nights, she wanted to impress, or if not that, then at least leave an attractive impression. She slammed the wardrobe door shut and sat down heavily on the bed.

'Blast!'

She recalled the last time she had really dressed up. It had been the night of her fifth wedding anniversary and, as she and Matt had made a bit of extra money on that season's bullocks, they had hired the church hall and laid on a band and buffet for some of their friends. For Matt, generally being an unsociable man, it had been quite an occasion. That night she had worn a long red velvet dress, one that she had had especially made by a local seamstress. She remembered it now because many people had complimented her – even the usually taciturn Matt had been moved to tell her how beautiful she was – and she had really enjoyed herself.

Shortly afterwards had been the accident, a dark period of grief and solitude. She had cleared out a great deal of stuff after that but she couldn't now remember if the dress was amongst it. It could still be somewhere in the house.

She looked around the room, her excitement returning. It was just the sort of dress for an evening like this. The shelf on top of the wardrobe was covered in old sweaters so it wasn't there. It wasn't under the bed, although she did find a missing slipper. She sat back on the bed again to think. She vaguely remembered getting it cleaned and packing it in a box, but then she did that with quite a bit of stuff. Perhaps it was in one of the other bedrooms.

She went into the dimly lit corridor. It was cold upstairs, the only rooms in the house that were properly heated being the kitchen and, on the infrequent occasions she was in there, the small sitting room.

The door to the first bedroom creaked when Claire opened it, and she switched on the light. It was going to be the nursery and was the one room in the house that she had decorated properly. A white dropsided cot sat against the wall with unwrapped blankets and sheets sitting on the mattress. The pine furniture, a wardrobe and dressing-table, stood empty next to the other wall. Even the light shade was new, covered in pictures from nursery rhymes.

She pulled the door shut, closing off her maternal disappointment.

The door to the other room opened more easily. It was always musty-smelling and felt especially cold at this time of year.

Like an opened tomb of memories, it contained all that was left of Matt's things. A box of books and other odds and ends sat on the bare bed. Some furniture they had never found any use for was stacked up in the corner

119

gathering layers of fine white dust. It looked awful and instantly Claire resolved to do something about it. It couldn't go on like this, slowly decaying. The time had come to clear out her past and start afresh.

She got down on her knees and looked under the bed. The dress box was there. Slowly she pulled it out from its wrapping of cobwebs, festooned like a gossamer curtain around it.

Clutching it tightly, she excitedly went downstairs. She placed the box on the kitchen table and opened it. She peeled back the layers of tissue paper and there was the dress, a small spray of lavender, faded but still fragrant, lying across it.

Holding it by the shoulders she pulled it out. It was every bit as beautiful as she remembered and would be ideal for tonight. A good pressing and no one would know that it had been hidden away for the last two years. She looked at the clock; she had two hours to get ready.

Rosie, aware that something out of the ordinary was happening, was following her everywhere. When Claire went up for her bath the dog lay on the carpet outside the open door watching her mistress intently. At one point she even came in and lay her silky head on the side of the enamel, sniffing the unfamiliar bubbles.

'What do you want, girl?'

The dog's tail thumped the floor.

'No, you can't come tonight.' Claire stroked her, leaving a trail of bubbles across her head which Rosie rubbed off by rolling on the carpet.

After bathing, Claire walked back to her bedroom, her legs pink from the hot water, tendrils of her long black hair clinging to her damp forehead and neck.

She sat down in front of her dressing-table and undid the white towel so that her full nakedness was staring back at her. It evoked little response in her. For more than two years her body had simply been the instrument by which she had worked. Its shape and overall welfare wasn't something that she bothered about. So long as it functioned properly was all that mattered. Now she looked more critically at it. Strong shoulders from hard physical work had their masculinity softened by the fullness of her large white breasts and the tapering of her narrow waist. Ange was always talking about her 'cellulite', but when Claire tried to find hers, there was nothing. Her legs ran long and smooth.

She stood up and dried herself while her audience of one watched from the bed, trying to catch her eye.

'It's no good, Rosie, I'm not taking you so stop looking at me like that.'

Rosie's tail wagged a couple of times and then stopped, all hope receding.

Claire didn't know what to do with her hair. Hanging down to her waist, it was normally plaited, but tonight she wanted something special. Squeaky clean and heavy it refused to do anything much without causing her arms to ache and eventually she gave up. Instead she bent down and brushed it vigorously before flinging it backwards so that it cascaded around her head and shoulders like a veil of black crushed silk, lustrous and shiny, its slight wave thickening it. She looked at her reflection; it would do.

The dress slipped on as though she had purchased it that day. The tight bodice with its scalloped neck fitted perfectly, giving her a more than noticeable cleavage. The full skirt hung down to her mid-calves, showing off her usually hidden dainty ankles and the long sleeves wrapped themselves around her arms snugly. She pulled up the zip and then twirled around in front of the mirror. She felt so different; so alive and exhilarated. She had quite forgotten how exciting it felt to look so feminine. Having cast off the drudgery of her everyday wear, she marvelled at the butterfly which had emerged from the drab chrysalis. It even showed in her face; her eyes green and sparkling, her cheeks faintly flushed pink and her mouth permanently smiling as if she were laughing at some secret joke.

She picked up her handbag and, followed by Rosie, went downstairs.

'Right then, girl, in your basket.'

The dog lay down obediently on an old sheepskin rug which had long replaced the original basket after it had been chewed up. Her whole demeanour was one of accusation and sulkiness, her liquid brown eyes pained and hurt, never leaving Claire.

'Stop looking at me like that, Rosie. I'm going out and you're not, so forget it.' Claire was putting on her lipstick in front of a small round mirror and could see Rosie's reflection in it.

Dressed and ready, a final dab of perfume behind each ear, Claire prepared to go. She went to the cupboard and got a handful of biscuits which she put on the floor in front of the dog. As Rosie ate them Claire stroked her head and said, 'Right, you guard the house and I'll see you later, okay?'

The biscuits finished, Rosie sat down and looked at Claire, pleading with her. She even lifted one of her paws and tried to hook it round Claire's arm.

'No, no, no, Rosie,' said Claire gently. 'Just sit down and be a good girl.' She gave her pet one last kiss and stood up. 'Now stay,' she instructed.

After she had left, Rosie jumped up onto a chair by the kitchen window and watched the van drive away until its lights disappeared into the night. She then nosed open the kitchen door and ran upstairs to the bedroom where she settled down to sleep, her head on Claire's pillow.

Claire felt conspicuous dressed up to the nines in her party frock while her surroundings were so shabby. Bits of hay clung to the van's upholstery, empty feed bags lay on the floor, binder twine tumbled out of the glove compartment and some rotten vegetables were giving off a noxious smell from behind her. Heaven knows what any of her neighbours would say if they met her now. But it was only a passing thought; she was really far too excited to think of anything. Since leaving the house, her stomach had been in a tight knot of nervous apprehension, completely banishing any hunger pangs.

She drove along the narrow lane, her headlights bouncing off the occasional gorse bush and large grey rocks which stuck up through the thin topsoil.

She reached Briar Cottage by driving down the short hedge-lined drive. Stopping the van, she looked at the house where she could see the warm glow of lamplight shining between the curtains. When she opened the van door to the crisp night air, faint sounds of orchestral music could be heard in the stillness.

She shivered. She was cold, but it was more a shiver of nerves than anything else. She pulled her coat tighter around herself and then crunched across the gravel on unfamiliar heels to the front door. Before she could knock, it opened.

'Claire! How lovely to see you. Come in, come in.' James, tall and handsome in a white polo-necked sweater and black trousers, held open the door and gestured her in.

'Hello.'

He kissed her on both cheeks. 'Let me take your coat,' and standing behind her with his hands at her shoulders, he removed it. In front of them was a full-length mirror. Their eyes met as they looked at their reflections; a slight smile on her face; open appreciation on his.

'You look very beautiful,' he said quietly, his breath warm against her neck.

'Thank you.'

'Well, we can't stand here. Come this way and drinks will be served.'

He guided her into the sitting room. 'Our meal is nearly ready, but until then we'll have some wine, shall we?'

She sat down on a deep chintz sofa, her legs warmed by a log fire which spat and hissed, the damp applewood giving off an autumnal aroma of burnt leaves.

He handed her a glass. 'To you,' he said, and she blushed. He raised his glass and sipped. 'I hope you like it. I found it in a small wine store along that side street off the market. It's rather nice, don't you think?'

Claire agreed. She didn't know anything much about wine, but it did taste pleasant. She made a mental note not to drink too much.

He sat down next to her and lounged back, comfortably relaxed. 'You look much prettier than when I last saw you,' and he took her hand and kissed it.

'I haven't been here for ages,' she said quickly. 'I had no idea Jack had cleaned it up so much. It looks much better now than it used to.'

'You know, you have a wonderful way of changing the subject.'

She looked at him puzzled. 'How do you mean?'

'Well,' he said, taking a sip of wine and placing the glass on a small table next to the sofa, 'I compliment you and all you can do is comment on the room. Don't you like men complimenting you? Perhaps you would prefer it if I insulted you; made up a pack of lies and called you the ugliest thing I'd ever seen?'

She smiled nervously. 'Of course not. It's just . . . you wouldn't understand.'

'Try me.'

She glanced at him quickly and then said, 'I've been a widow for over two years now.' She shrugged, introspection wasn't something she cared to indulge in, seeing it as selfish. 'And, well, I'm just not used to it, that's all.'

'Why?' Now he was puzzled. 'You are, if you don't mind me saying so, a very attractive woman. There must be many men who would like to get to know you better.'

'Hardly. I think the problem is that I'm not local so the men round here tend to overlook me, but then I'm a well-established newcomer who lives like a local, so the newcomers ignore me. Either way, I don't fit.'

'Poor you,' he said gently teasing her. 'All on your own and no one to love you.'

'No, no,' she shook her head, smiling brightly — too brightly, he thought. 'I have Rosie and I do have some friends and, well, my life is fine as it is.' She stopped, aware of his gaze. He instinctively knew too much and she found him unnerving. He seemed to be waiting for something. 'I'm all right,' she assured him. 'Really I am.'

'Good,' he said at last. 'Time for food, I think, so come with me.'

Holding her hand, he led her to the kitchen. Steam rose from a couple of saucepans. She stood by the sink and watched him as he donned an apron and set to work.

'I got us two prime steaks,' he said, removing the plates from under the grill. 'We're having them with white wine and mushroom sauce and with carrots, peas and some horrendously expensive new potatoes.'

'Sounds nice.'

'I hope so. I'm afraid I'm not much of a chef, so let's hope I haven't ruined it.'

Their food ready, he took off his apron and put on his jacket. She thought she had never seen anyone look as handsome as he did.

'You look very nice,' she said hesitantly.

'Thank you.' He picked up the plates. 'This way then.'

They went back through to the dining room, where he placed the plates on the table. He helped her to her chair, the candlelight flickering across her radiant face. Before sitting down, he refilled both their glasses.

'A toast,' he said, holding up his glass.

'To whom?' she asked.

His eyes met hers in a soft, lingering gaze. 'Us,' he replied quietly.

Her stomach lurched. Every word, every glance, drew her to him. She could no more resist him than a moth could a candle flame.

'To us,' she echoed and they sipped their wine.

Under the circumstances, she found it difficult to eat. Nerves always affected her like this and although she had been looking forward to the meal so much, she really did no more than push the food around her plate. James watched her.

'Not hungry?' he asked, laying down his cutlery and taking a sip of wine.

Claire went to say something but didn't. She smiled nervously.

'It doesn't matter,' he assured her. 'I don't mind.'

'It's just that . . .' she began. 'Well, it's just that I find it difficult to eat sometimes when I'm nervous,' and she glanced at him.

'You're nervous? Why?'

She sipped her wine, knowing full well that a deep crimson flush was threatening to envelop her face. She suddenly felt very hot. 'I just do sometimes.'

'But why? You've got nothing to feel nervous about here. We're only having dinner.'

She shrugged. 'I just do, that's all.'

He smiled indulgently. 'How long has it been since you last went out?' he asked.

'Oh . . . I don't really know. Months, I suppose.'

'Well, that's it then,' he said matter-of-factly. 'You're nervous because you've forgotten how to enjoy yourself. Simple really.'

She sat with her hands in her lap and her eyes downcast. What he said made so much sense.

'Claire?'

'Yes?'

'I've got some proper Italian ice cream for sweet. Would that improve your appetite?'

She smiled broadly, feeling silly. 'I'm being an idiot,' she said, picking up her knife and fork.

'No, no, no,' he chuckled. 'Of course you're not. Look, it doesn't bother me if you eat or not. At least you're here and that's really all that matters.'

'It is. Why?'

He threw up his hands in mock exasperation, stood up and walked around the table to her.

'Claire,' he said, putting his arms around her shoulders and squeezing her affectionately. 'Has it really been so long since any man told you how attractive you are?' He straightened up and pulled her gently to her feet so that they stood face to face. She was unable to resist. At that moment he could have done anything with her.

'Look at you,' he said softly. He held out her hands. 'You look as beautiful as any top London model. Honestly,' he added, seeing her sceptical glance and embarrassed half-smile. 'How can you not see that?'

She bit her lip when she smiled. 'I don't know.'

He stepped forward again, raised her chin and kissed her. It was as if a beam of powerful sunlight had passed through her.

'Don't ever let anyone say any different,' he said. 'You are quite, quite stunning.' He sat down again. She watched him closely until he had regained his seat. 'Now eat,' he commanded with a smile.

He proved to be a wonderful host. A fund of stories and amusing anecdotes meant the candle had burnt very low before they left the table.

James stood up. 'Well, as we've finished eating and swapped life stories, shall we go back into the sitting room?'

He took her by the hand. 'What music do you like?'

'What was that you were playing when I arrived?'

'Debussy.'

'It was lovely. Can we have some more of that?'

'Yes, of course.'

She put another log on the fire and sat down, watching the sparks fly up the chimney.

He joined her and they listened quietly. He searched out her hand and held it softly.

'You know,' he said after a while, his head leant back

against the sofa, eyes closed in the warmth of the room, 'I wasn't absolutely sure you would come tonight.'

'Why?'

He smiled. 'The other day,' he said, delicately stroking the back of her hand, 'you seemed so . . . so . . . apprehensive. I thought maybe you would change your mind.'

'No.' Her answer was firm. 'I wouldn't do that. If I didn't want to come, I would have said so there and then.'

'Good, you're honest. I like that. Not many people are, you know.' He took another sip of his wine. 'What was it exactly that made you say yes?'

She stared unblinkingly into the fire. 'I don't know really. Maybe it's because I've only just realized that I have to start living again. I mean, I can't spend all of my life cooped up on the farm, never going anywhere or seeing anyone.' She looked back round at him. 'I guess you just happened to come along at the right time.'

He held her gaze and it was now that the inevitable happened, the moment that she had unconsciously been waiting for. When his lips touched hers, a ripple of long-forgotten feelings began to flow through her being, a sensation that she had never thought to relive.

When he pulled away her hand went to her mouth and touched her kiss-scorched lips.

'Why . . . ?'

'Because it was meant to be,' he whispered. 'You . . . me . . . It's fate and it's no good denying it.'

She turned away bewildered by her emotions.

'Look at me, Claire.'

Her huge bewildered eyes met his.

'We're two single people,' he began slowly. 'We have only ourselves to think of. I don't know about you, but something tells me we might be about to rediscover what it's like . . . well,' he smiled awkwardly, '. . . to trust again.' He paused, stroking the side of her face. 'You never know,' he continued, 'you might even get to like me eventually,' and with that she smiled.

'Good,' he said, and they held each other close.

'Shall we dance?' he said after a few minutes.

She frowned. 'To this?'

'No, I have something else which I think you might like.'

He got up and replaced the Debussy tape with Alexander O'Neal. He returned to her, holding out his hands.

'This we can dance to,' he said, lifting her up from the floor.

It felt so good to be in a man's arms again. She had quite forgotten the way she felt protected and warm. So used to having to rely on only herself, it was a relief to relax with him.

They swayed backwards and forwards to the soulful sounds, the music weaving its own particular brand of magic around them. He held her close, in a full embrace. After a while he started to kiss her. Her head, her neck, her cheeks and finally her mouth. At first he was gentle and so was she. His kisses only hinted at a hunger, but then it changed. The tempo of his breathing began to quicken, his hands began to press her to him and she felt the unmistakable tightening of his hold.

It changed for her too. All her instincts, all her primitive drives; everything that for two years she had sublimated into her farm roared up from the depths of her soul, rekindled by this man's touch. Her whole body ached for him, every sinew and every nerve straining towards him, ravenous for him.

'I want you, Claire,' he whispered, his voice urgent against her cheek. He kissed her again.

'I can't,' she replied, breathless. 'I must get back to the farm.'

'No, please don't go, don't go.'

'I must.'

They kissed again.

'I want you; stay, just for tonight.'

'James . . . I can't . . .'

More kisses.

'Please, Claire . . .'

They kissed, violently now.

'Please, darling.'

'Don't, James . . . please.'

'You can leave later.'

'I . . . don't . . . know.'

'I need you, Claire.'

'Oh James.'

Still kissing her, he walked her backwards to the door and then, picking her up in his strong arms, he took her upstairs. She had finally acquiesced to her body's demands which for so long had lain dormant.

The bedroom was warm; pleasantly so. The duvet was pulled back ready for them. Bright moonlight filtered through the half-closed curtains, bathing everything in a diffuse silvery glow.

He silently led her by the hand to the window and pulled back the curtains so that the light shone fully on her face. He looked at her, his eyes devouring her.

'Do you know what this means to me, Claire?'

'No.'

He kissed her hands, the backs and then the palms.

'This is the first time anything like this has happened to me. I feel . . . I feel so excited being with you. It's extraordinary. Don't you feel it too?'

'Yes. Oh yes.' She stepped forward and embraced him. 'Love me, James.'

His hand found the zip of her dress and undid it slowly. The garment slipped down her body and fell at her feet in a dark red rosette. He cupped her breasts in his hands, feeling her erect nipples in his fingers.

She undressed him. All her nervousness had gone now. It was her instincts that drove her onwards; to find and explore, to taste and touch.

He stood her at arm's-length, his eyes sweeping over

her body. She wasn't at all embarrassed. 'You're exquisite,' he whispered, and pulled her to him once more. They kissed again; a slow, deep and passionate kiss that sent shivers of desire right down to her soul. He moved her towards the bed and lay her down. He looked at her, bathed in moonlight, and smiled.

'If anyone had told me,' he said, 'that this night I would have one of the most beautiful women I have ever met in my arms, I wouldn't have believed them.'

She smiled, the light from the windows reflected in her eyes. 'Oh James.'

It was then she began to realize just how empty her life had been.

Lying on top of her, each of his powerful arms encircling her head, he began to love her. He kissed her eyes, her nose, her ears, her cheeks. Then he kissed her lips. Down and down he went. Her neck, her shoulders, her breasts.

As the heat rose in her, she pressed his head against her. She wanted him so much.

Taking each nipple in turn, he teased it and kissed it, running his hands over her breasts.

'You're so beautiful,' he murmured. 'So beautiful.'

And still he went down.

She kept her eyes tightly shut. No man had done this before. No man had made her want so much. She was burning, a white hot heat searing her insides. Her stomach, her navel, his kisses were like hot little stabs, a hundred needles scratching her skin. She held his head in her hands. She was breathless, sweat beginning to cover her.

'James . . . James!'

She tossed her head from side to side, finding no solace in the pillow. And still he didn't stop. When would she find relief? Would the end never come?

He kissed her, his mouth against a place where no mouth had been before and she cried out. The animal inside her had come alive.

Slowly, he took her, her flesh trembling against him as he expertly, and with each of his kisses, increased her agony.

Soon . . . so . . . soon . . .

Unaware of what was happening to her, she screamed into the dark when her orgasm, the first she had ever had, finally hit her.

'James!'

With her legs wrapped around his shoulders, her powerful muscles gripped him with an iron embrace.

'Oh . . . James!'

The second one hit her almost as powerfully as the first, dissolving what little was left of her insides. In the end, exhausted and replete, she could give no more.

She lay outstretched, panting and covered with a sheen of perspiration, her breasts rising and falling.

'Oh James, that was so . . . so wonderful!'

He lay beside her, holding her close and stroking her hair. 'Good,' he whispered.

When she had recovered, he started to kiss her again. This time she had no hesitation. She wanted him again . . . and again . . . and again.

Their consummation was every bit as wonderful as she expected. His powerful body held her down as she willingly succumbed to him. Together, as one, they moved towards their final destination.

Their primitive cries filled the room, echoing into the moonlit night like a couple of beasts locked in battle. She took him as he took her – totally. There were no secrets now. Then, lying in each other's fulfilled arms, they slept their deepest.

Both of them slept peacefully, their brows smoothed, their breathing calm, wrapped in each other's arms as if even in sleep they couldn't bear to be apart.

Suddenly she started, half sitting up, blinking from a deep comforting sleep. 'Did you say something, James?'

He grunted and then rolled over. Obviously it wasn't

him. She must have been dreaming. She lay back again, puzzled. She could have sworn that something had woken her, some half-heard vaguely familiar voice had been talking to her. But however hard she tried to recall it, it had escaped her back into her subconscious, only its shadow remaining in her mind. She wondered what it had been saying.

She yawned and got out of bed. She padded across to the silvery light that fell through the window. Outside, across the moor, dark shadows of the clouds raced over the glittering land, the high tors lonely and grey against the ragged sky.

A few miles away, almost hidden in the valley, was Torhampton, its lights offering warmth and comfort in the dark. Claire wondered how many of the good residents of the parish had enjoyed themselves the same way she had done that night. Not many, she thought, or was that just conceit?

She heard a noise. James was awake. He got up and came over to the window. Standing behind her he put his arms around her waist and nuzzled her neck.

'Can't sleep,' she offered by way of explanation.

'Doesn't matter, neither can I. Watching you from the bed silhouetted against the light made you look ... ethereal.'

'Thank you.' She paused and then said, 'It's beautiful, isn't it?'

He looked out up at the moor. 'Yes. Just like you. Quite perfect.'

She turned and kissed him, the urgency returning. She needed him and she needed him now. He took her back to the bed and loved her again and again.

NINE

She felt wonderful but thirsty. She needed a drink. She opened her eyes slowly. Gradually in the pale orange light, she focused on the sleeping form of James. He was lying flat on his back, one arm flung carelessly up above his head, his dark hair tousled. His long black lashes lay against an almost boyish cheek, smooth and untroubled as he slept. With one finger she caressed his arm with the merest touch while filled with the tenderest warmth and love for him.

He was such a paradox. So commanding in his animality; so strong and muscular and yet now so vulnerable. The emotion she felt for him was at once strong and direct but tinged with aching sadness, a sadness that came from disbelief that he was so perfect – and hers. It was like looking at something of infinite beauty and delicacy; she wanted to cherish and protect him because somehow she knew it would not last.

Aside from her need for a drink, the deeper and more basic layers of her femininity that had been wrenched awake from their slumber were starting to ache in her once more. Indifferent to sex for so long, and simply accepting it as her lot, her experiences of the night before now coloured her entire outlook. Unprepared ever again to tolerate a halfway state of sexual frustration and its all-too-inevitable irritability which she saw was clearly a result of her previous sex-life, she knew James had connected her to her innermost drives and a powerful, almost euphoric desire was welling up within her. She could almost eat him.

She slid out of the warm musky bed and crept towards

the door. James rolled over towards the empty space, but remained asleep. Downstairs, she poured herself a glass of cold water. As she stood at the sink, weary but satisfied, she looked out over the dampened landscape. It was not yet fully awakened by the sun, its colours still grey in the mist. Only the highest tors were painted orange. From a nearby bush a robin sang out, every note clearly heard on the calm spring air, followed by a blackbird's alarm-call trill as it flew low across the back lawn, landing alert and indignant a few feet from the window. She smiled.

She drank thirstily and then returned to the bedroom. He was still asleep, undisturbed by her absence. She climbed in beside him, waking him with her cold feet.

'I'm sorry,' she whispered. 'I had to go downstairs for a drink.'

He blinked sleepily and yawned. 'Doesn't matter. How are you this morning?'

She snuggled up close to him. 'Wonderful, just wonderful.' She kissed him.

They lay together, she wide awake, impatiently waiting for him, but in the quiet that followed she could see that he had fallen asleep again.

She wondered what the time was. Her watch lay on the dressing-table, which was over by the window. There was a small travelling clock on the table by James's side of the bed and easing herself out of his arms, she leant over him.

Half-past six! There was the milking to do and the lambs needed feeding. And Rosie! Poor Rosie, on her own all night.

'Oh my God!' She flung back the duvet and began gathering up her clothes from where she had carelessly left them. She couldn't find her panties anywhere. She was looking under the end of the bed for them when she realized James was awake and watching her. He seemed amused by her behaviour.

'Claire, what are you doing?'

She leant over and kissed him, still naked.

'Trying to find my things. I must go. I'm late as it is. I've got to milk the cow, see to the sheep, not to mention poor Rosie.' He was still smiling. 'If I don't go, all hell will break loose.'

His eyes swept down her naked body, taking in the full rounded beauty of her breasts and the supple line of her thighs.

'What if I said I didn't want you to go?'

'Can't, James. Not this time.'

She tried to move away from him, but he held her by the arms. 'I want you to stay, Claire, and you want to stay too.' He pulled her to him and kissed her. 'See, I can feel it.'

She stared at him. How could he read her so easily?

'I can't stay,' she protested, easing off his grip. 'I really have to go.'

'No. Not yet.' Holding her hand, he pulled her gently to him and then with a strength that she couldn't resist and didn't want to, kissed her fervently, pressing himself to her.

At last she broke free and stood up, breathless. 'It's no good, James, I've got to go.' His face was impassive. 'I'll come back when it's all done, okay? I won't be long.'

'If you must,' he said. He got out of bed, wrapped a towelling robe around himself and left the room, ignoring her.

'James!' She ran after him, down the stairs, still naked. He was filling the kettle and didn't acknowledge her. She stood in the doorway looking at his back. 'James, please, let's not argue over this.' He didn't move. 'James.' She walked up behind him and put her arms round his waist, feeling the warmth of his body. 'I'm sorry, James,' she whispered. 'Please, I'm sorry.'

'I need you now, Claire, and I'm only put out because you don't seem to want me as much as I want you. You say you'll come back later, but love isn't like that, is it?

We need to make the most of the moment and that is now.'

She stood mesmerized before him. She saw his face, she heard his words and her resolve disappeared.

'I've never been so happy in my life, James. I love you more than anyone else. You've ... brought me back to life.'

'Then let's go back to bed,' he said smiling, his voice so deep.

They kissed and she knew she was lost. Obediently she followed him upstairs, deliberately pushing to one side all thoughts of the farm. Just for once, it wouldn't matter.

Their love-making was fierce, with a renewed intensity as if they were discovering each other for the first time. Yet again, he led her along new paths of enjoyment, kissing, and tasting her until she hung precariously balanced. Her heightened pitch of desire led her inexorably onwards and upwards until finally she slid down the roller coaster of delight, rising and falling, her whole body rigid with shuddering intensity.

Afterwards, she lingered quietly utterly replete. Eyes closed, she reached for his hand and squeezed it. She marvelled at his self-control, only allowing himself to let go when she begged him to stop.

'You know, I never thought it could be like this.'

He lay on his front, face turned towards her, half hidden by his upper arms and breathing deeply.

'Mmm, I know. I think it must come as a bit of a surprise to some women when they realize what they've been missing all these years. I wonder sometimes if it doesn't make them look at their husbands in a new light.'

'How do you mean?'

'Well, I suppose dear hubby is all right for a quick five minutes once a week, but real lovemaking, that's a skill and very few people have it.'

She fell silent. His words had an all-too-familiar truth-

137

fulness to them which she tried to ignore. The memories, however, still came flooding back.

Matt: reliable, hardworking, reticent Matt. She could only remember the one time during their marriage when he had complimented her and that was their fifth wedding anniversary party. He was never rude to her, but he never made her feel special either. Claire accepted his ways because she loved him, but she had to be honest with herself: his failure really to appreciate her hurt very much.

His life was entirely without adornment and in bed he was just as unfrilled and straightforward. Normally so predictable, he usually read a book each night before settling down to sleep.

But on Sunday it was different. They would have their baths and then clad in their warm practical nightwear – she in a neck-to-toe nightie and he in his striped cotton pyjamas with their cord sash – they would climb into the cold bed, the light being switched off immediately. It was their sign; he wanted her instead of his book. He would turn towards her and hold her close, their body heat warming the bed. Then he would begin to kiss her and run his hands gently up and down her back. Soon she would feel him against her thighs.

With the minimum of preamble, he would pull up her nightie and reach inside, his cold, rough hands exploring her body. Just as she was beginning to want him, he would stop and climb on top of her, enter and climax. It took all of five minutes and left her very wakeful and frustrated. Her complaints went unspoken. Inexperienced, she had no idea what to say.

And now James: everything Matt wasn't and so much more. How he knew her! He knew where to touch her, where to caress her, how to caress her. It seemed as though her entire sexuality had been switched on by him. Before she was living a half-life: now she was completely awakened.

'Claire . . . Claire?'

'Oh sorry, I was miles away.'

'I could see that.'

'About what you were saying,' she began slowly, 'you know, about most people's sex lives, can it really be so boring?'

He shrugged. 'I don't know. I only know from my own experience that for some people, especially women, it's dreadful.' He kissed her arm. 'You know, a rich woman in London could buy herself absolutely anything; man, boy or girl, it wouldn't matter. I've heard that some of them do that, especially the ones who're hitched up to some boring old sod who can't get it up any more. Can't say I like the idea too much myself.'

Claire pulled a disgusted face. 'Oh yuk! That's awful! How could anyone do that?'

He leant on his elbows, his face in his hands. 'Maybe if you were married to some pillar of the community for thirty years, your children all grown up and you were still an attractive, financially independent woman with time and libido on your hands, you might. Society women have always behaved to a completely different set of sexual mores. They just keep quiet about it, that's all.'

Claire pulled the duvet up around herself as if it were some kind of protection. 'I don't know,' she said. 'I still find it so peculiar that people could do that.'

'Why? Men have been buying sex since time immemorial. Why should women be any different?'

She sighed. 'I'm not saying that women should behave differently, I just think it's rather pathetic that anyone should do it. I never could. It wouldn't matter how broke I was, I could never sleep with someone just for money.' She put her arm round him. 'I'm glad we're not like that. I could only make love to someone I really loved.'

He smiled back at her, all the cynicism gone from his face. 'You're very sweet, Claire.'

She moved over and cuddled up to him. 'I don't want to talk about those horrible things any more. I want to talk about us.'

'What about us?' he asked, stroking her hair.

She didn't answer at first, but then said, 'Nothing really, except that I love you.'

He kissed her head. 'And I do too.'

The sky was brighter now and however hard she tried, Claire couldn't put off the fateful moment any more.

'I've got to go,' she whispered.

'Yes, I know.'

With a last lingering kiss she got up and dressed. He accompanied her down to the hallway and helped her on with her coat. He opened the door.

'When will I see you again?' she asked, shivering. The wind was cold, a northeasterly breeze that cut straight through her, whipping her bare ankles and lashing her hair across her face.

He looked out past her, one arm round her shoulders. 'I'll come round later, I expect.' He smiled briefly.

'We had a lovely time last night, didn't we?' She wanted to possess him, hold and not let him go.

'Yes, we did. It was fun.'

'Fun?'

He shrugged. 'Well, don't you think so?'

She looked away to hide her disappointment. 'Yes,' she answered slowly. 'I suppose it was "fun", but more importantly . . .'

He gently interrupted her, pulling her to him and kissing her, 'Well, that's all that matters then, isn't it?'

She tried to explain. 'But it was more than that, wasn't it? I mean, I feel . . . incredible. I . . .' She sensed his attention had been distracted. She turned to see what it was.

'Look.' He pointed. A fox, nothing more than a brownish-red streak ran across the rutted drive and disappeared into the hedge. 'Damn pest!' he said with venom.

'I've always rather admired them,' she replied. 'They're such survivors, totally at one with their environment, able to eat virtually anything. I like them.'

'Well, I don't.' He pulled his robe tighter around him and yanked angrily at the sash. 'My uncle used to shoot them when they came anywhere near his farm. On one occasion he was rearing some ducks for the season when a fox got in with them. Forty were killed in one night. Terrible mess it was, feathers everywhere.'

'What happened?'

'Well, a couple of carcasses were laced with poison and placed outside the den. We never saw that fox again. Strictly illegal, of course, but it was only a fox, after all.'

Claire turned away and said nothing.

James shivered. 'God, it's cold. Look, Claire. I'll ring you later, or probably drop by. I don't know what time yet because I have to make some phone calls.'

'Oh.' She looked downcast.

'Listen, darling, we did have a wonderful time last night and I am sorry if I sounded a bit offhand just now. I have some worries at the moment – nothing I can't handle – but sometimes they get to me.' He looked at her intently. 'I'm sorry if I inadvertently hurt you. You know, I'm apt to be a bit tactless sometimes.'

She kissed him. 'That's okay.'

'Good. Now off you go before I make you stay again.' He patted her on the backside and she walked to her van.

She watched him in her rear-view mirror as she drove away. He went in before she was out of sight.

Once out in the lane she drove quickly. It was well past seven and Rosie would be very anxious by now. She tried not to think about her dog's lonely vigil through the night and how upset she would be.

Familiar with the route, she increased her speed and was going far too fast on the damp road when a milk tanker came round the corner. She slammed on her brakes and slithered across the tarmac, stones and leaves being

141

thrown up in all directions until she finally came to a halt. She had ended up sideways on to the tanker, her left-hand front wheel in a shallow ditch. Slightly winded but otherwise relieved that she was all right, she looked up at the tanker driver. Her heart was thumping and she felt flustered and embarrassed. It had very definitely been her fault.

The driver watched her balefully from his cab, a look of utter resignation on his face. She could see that he was thinking something derogatory about women drivers and just for once, she was inclined to agree with him. It was unlike her to be so reckless.

The engine had stalled. In her blind panic to avoid a crash, she had missed the clutch. She switched it on and it started first time, but when she put it into reverse and let down the handbrake, nothing happened. The front wheel was stuck, spinning out of control and digging itself into a deeper hole.

'Damn!' She slammed her fists onto the steering wheel. This was all she needed. The tanker driver was smirking.

She tried again, but it still wouldn't move. If anything, the angle at which the van was resting became more acute. She was getting into a real mess and needed help. She looked up at the driver and shrugged. He didn't move. She got out and went over to him, feeling self-conscious in her red evening dress. The man opened the door of his cab and got down.

'Going a bit fast, weren't you, my lover? Could have had a nasty accident there.' He looked her over appreciatively. He was big, fat and virtually bald, like some scaled-down version of a Sumo wrestler. To pamper his ego he had scraped over his shining head his last few remaining wispy hairs so that his parting was just above his ear. In the strong breeze they uncovered his pate immediately.

Claire instinctively disliked him. He was the sort of man that drank too much, bit his fingernails and smelt. His grubby clothes stretched themselves around his vast girth;

142

the collar particularly tight round his nonexistent neck. He stood with both hands in his blue overall pockets, kneading his crotch and gently rocking to and fro on the balls of his feet. He disgusted her.

She smiled. 'Please will you help me? I seem to have got stuck.'

He leered closer, his small eyes fixed on her cleavage. She self-consciously did up her coat buttons.

'All right, love, guess we won't be going anywhere until I do.' She followed him to her van, marvelling at the huge width of his backside. It looked like a shire horse.

'Here, you hop in and switch on and I'll see if I can shift it.' He positioned himself by the front bumper, one foot braced on the road and one in the ditch, hands against the bonnet.

'Right oh, turn her on and let down the handbrake. Don't give her too much welly!' he shouted.

She put the van into reverse and gradually pressed down on the accelerator. All she could see of the driver was the top of his sweaty head as he heaved and swore.

Nothing happened.

He stood up, breathing heavily, his round smooth face red and perspiring. 'It's no good,' he announced, leaning on the bonnet. 'You'll have to get out and help me. It weighs too much.'

Claire looked down despairingly at her dress and court shoes. Her one good outfit and she had to push a muddy van. Typical! She reluctantly leant against the van.

When it did finally move, it happened so fast that she fell forward onto her knees, grazing herself. 'Ow!' She stood up and began picking out bits of gravel from her torn flesh.

'Nasty graze you've got there,' observed the driver.

'I'll soon clean it up. Sorry about all this and thanks for helping me.'

He smiled, a bit sheepishly, she thought. 'That's all right, only next time don't get so dressed up. A pretty woman like you can put a man off his stride and believe me, if it had been any of my mates instead of me . . . well, they're no gentlemen, I can tell you.' He winked, tapping her on the behind as he walked past her.

When Claire got to the farm all was quiet. No howling, no bellowing, nothing, but as soon as Rosie heard her footsteps, the yelping started.

She ran as fast as her high heels would allow her to the kitchen door. Rosie's first reaction was uncontrollable delight. She leant back against Claire's leg, her face joyously grinning, her stomach exposed to be rubbed and her tail thumping the floor.

'Hello, my darling!' As Claire stroked and patted her dog, she kept up a nonstop stream of endearments. 'Have you missed me then, sweetie, eh? All right, Rosie, yes, yes, I'm home to see you. I didn't mean to leave you. Yes, yes, my beauty. I missed you too. Shh, shh, I'm home now.'

Rosie made little whining noises as she tried to get as close as possible to Claire. She jumped up on her back legs and licked Claire's face.

'Down, silly. Get down before you ruin my dress,' and she pushed her off. 'Now that's enough. Calm down will you? Shh, shh, it's all right.'

Gradually the dog relaxed and Claire let her outside. 'Go on, garden.' But Rosie wouldn't go. In the end Claire had to take her out and stand sentinel until the dog had seen to the call of nature. Back in the kitchen it was obvious why Rosie was reluctant to go out: the back door mat was sodden. Claire hadn't noticed at first, but obviously the long wait had been too much.

'Oh, Rosie!' exclaimed Claire tiredly, holding up the mat. 'What have you done, girl?' Rosie slunk onto her rug and lay down.

Claire threw the mat out of the door and knelt down beside her dog. 'It's not your fault, no it's not,' and the pair of them cuddled, their heads together, Claire sitting on the floor, her arm around Rosie's shoulders. 'Silly girl,' she murmured.

It was warm sitting next to the Rayburn and Claire began to wish she didn't have to move. She could only have had about four hours' sleep last night and although she felt exhilarated by it all, she was also beginning to feel tired. She had to move.

'Come on, girl, breakfast.' At the mention of food, Rosie leapt to her feet and began to bound around.

Then Claire made herself some tea and toast, but it remained untouched. The excitement of the night kept coming back to her, infusing her stomach with a heady mixture of excitement and love every time she thought about him.

Feeling as if she had been through some seminal rite of passage, the afterglow lingered on. She could also see how entrenched she had become in accepting the preferred limits of sexual behaviour. But not any more. James's unusual and open-minded approach, surprising though it was at first, had pushed her through the rigid walls of convention. Even if nothing else came of their relationship, and at that moment she wasn't prepared to think too far ahead, at least she now knew what it felt like really to enjoy herself.

She picked at her toast. It had gone cold now and blobs of butter sat congealed on its surface. She pushed it away. Rosie was watching her, ever hopeful. 'All right then, you have it.' She put it on the floor and it vanished instantly.

Upstairs she undressed; she needed a wash. On her way to the bathroom she stood in front of the full-length mirror on the landing and smiled at her reflection. Perhaps it was just her imagination, perhaps not, but it seemed to her that her body was fuller, more rounded, more aware of itself. The skin of her throat and chest was still flushed pink with the exertions of their lovemaking, her nipples standing up hard and deep red.

She ran her hands gently down her body, feeling the

145

contours of her flesh, much as he had done. Then she cupped her breasts in each hand and squeezed them. She watched herself steadily. Her eyelids lowered with the returned desire, her lips fleshy and moist. The animal in her only dozed now and could be awakened with little stimulation.

She touched herself intimately; she was soaking. Running her hands over herself, she felt her desire increasing. Her quick fingers explored her insides, feeling the softness and heat. She had never done this before, never known what it felt like.

The need in her increased. She opened her eyes fully. It seemed to her that the person she saw reflected was not her. Someone else, a new someone, who knew and expected all those things a real woman felt, stared back at her and still she didn't stop. On and on she went, the excitement buckling her knees until she sank to the floor. She lay on her back, fully stretched out along the carpet and began to enjoy herself. Somewhere, on the edge of her consciousness, just as her first orgasm hit her, she heard the telephone but she ignored it. Her instincts and desires were now so strong, nothing mattered any more.

She stopped long after the phone had stopped. Bewildered almost by her unfamiliar and insatiable appetite, she lay exhausted, spread-eagled across the carpet, aware only of her thudding heartbeat, which gradually slowed. With one final effort, she used her last remaining energy to sit up. The face that looked back at her was damp with sweat, hair stuck to her forehead. She could barely keep her eyes open.

Bathed, dressed and after a second breakfast, she went to see to her animals. On entering the barn she could see at once Jacky's barrel-like shape. Claire ran her hand down the cow's belly and Jacky looked round at her and slowly blinked her large brown eyes. She seemed quite unconcerned at her condition and not at all uncomfortable.

146

She was vast, the black of her coat stretched like glossy paint over her sides. Claire looked at her thoughtfully. Last time Jacky had calved there had been no problems. The cow had been out in the field and had simply dropped her offspring with no more than minimum effort. Claire hadn't even realized it had happened until she had gone to fetch her in and had found the still-wet youngster trying to stand on its wobbly legs. She had hoped that this pregnancy would be just as trouble free, but she was beginning to have her doubts. Jacky was getting old and she looked huge this time. For the first time in months, she wished someone was here to help her. Perhaps James would; he certainly had the build for it.

She mixed some feed for the cow and left her to it.

Throughout the day she did her chores, one ear strained for the sound of his car pulling into the yard or for the telephone. Whoever had rung that morning hadn't got back to her and she began to be angry with herself. Maybe it had been James.

Each time she went into the house she would walk into the hallway and glare accusingly at the damned thing, willing it to ring. But it didn't. Her appetite had disappeared again – nerves she supposed – but she forced herself to eat a sandwich, each mouthful masticated thoroughly as she summoned up the will to swallow it without retching. And still the telephone sat silently. Alternate waves of anger and foolishness swept over her when she realized how much power this thing had over her. One small ring, just one, and her whole life would be so much happier. Its silence would condemn her to misery.

After lunch she found all kinds of excuses to stay in the house. The dining room curtains that needed altering finally got done after sitting half-finished in her work basket for weeks. She even did some baking. As she usually spent the minimum time possible in the kitchen, preferring to open a can of beans rather than preparing proper meals, she wasn't at all surprised when the cake

147

appeared from the Rayburn sunk in the middle.

She left it cooling on a rack and decided to go outside. She had spent enough time waiting for his call and if he wasn't going to ring, she was going out. Her increasing agitation needed some form of release. A good gallop would do it.

Bonny was filthy. It took Claire three-quarters of an hour to clean the mud off her long winter coat. As usual, she blew up when Claire put the saddle on, but quickly got back to normal when she had been walked round the yard a couple of times. Claire mounted.

'Come on, Rosie,' she called. 'Walkies!'

Woman, horse and dog took off across the moor up the track where she had first seen James that cold, wet blustery day. Now the sun was shining but the wind was still very cold, the air catching in her throat.

She rode along, quietly angry at his silence. It wasn't fair, she thought, it was well into the afternoon and he still hadn't rung. Making her worry like this just wasn't on. Damn you, James Lamont!

She kicked Bonny into a canter and hacked over the open grassland, Rosie running alongside her. The horse hadn't had much exercise recently and was full of energy. She responded immediately and Claire had difficulty in keeping her under control. When they came to a flat open expanse of ground between the tors, Claire gave her her head and the horse took off, fully stretched out, galloping as fast as she could. Exhilarated and excited, the cold wind lashing her face and coursing down into her lungs, Claire leaned forward in the saddle, shortening the reins, her fingers wrapping around the long black strands of Bonny's mane.

After a while the ground became more uneven and Claire pulled back to a walk. She felt much better now, her back prickly with sweat and damp curls of hair sticking to her forehead underneath her hat. She turned back for home, tired but happy.

With Bonny unsaddled, fed and watered, she was ambling across the yard in the twilight when the phone went. She raced for the door, practically taking it off its hinges as she crashed through it. Breathless and excited, she picked up the receiver.

'Hello?'

'Hi, Claire, it's me, how are you?'

'Oh . . . Ange . . . fine, just fine.'

'Well, don't sound so pleased to hear me, will you?'

'I'm sorry, it's just that I . . . well, I'm expecting a call from someone else.' She tried to hide the disappointment in her voice. 'You didn't ring earlier did you, about seven-thirty this morning?'

'God no, I'd be up to my eyeballs with the horrors at that time of day. Anyway, the reason I rang is that Colin's taking the little perishers over to visit his mother tomorrow and I thought you and I could meet up for a coffee somewhere, or maybe lunch. What do you think?'

'I don't know.' She wanted to see Ange very much, but if she were out most of the day and James rang . . . 'Look, Ange, can I get back to you about this?' She was trying hard not to hurt her friend's feelings.

Ange sounded puzzled. 'Why, what's up, Claire?'

'Nothing.' She had answered too quickly and Ange knew her too well to be deceived.

'Oh come on, Claire, this is me you're talking to, not some stranger and I've known you long enough to realize when you're not being, how shall we say, altogether truthful. So come on, out with it.'

She waited. Claire said nothing. It was impossible to hide anything from Ange.

'I've got involved with someone.'

'Oh, Claire!' screeched Ange. 'That's marvellous! Who is he? What is he? When can I meet him?'

Claire sighed. 'I'll tell you when I see you, okay? Now where shall we meet?'

'You ratbag, Claire Bromage, fancy giving me a jewel of

149

a snippet like that and then expecting me to wait until tomorrow.'

Claire smiled to herself. Ange's enthusiasm was infectious. 'I know, dreadful, aren't I?'

'Well at least you're happy and that's the main thing. So, where shall we meet? How about the Seven Stars?'

'The Seven Stars! What on earth do you want to go there for? It's a real dump. All the bikers go there. Can't we go somewhere else? How about the Tannery or the Crown?'

'Surely, Claire, you know I like a bit of rough now and then, and given that Colin has become every bit the Establishment image, an afternoon of lusting after a piece of leather-clad, grease-smelling grunt with muscles like a neanderthal won't go amiss. Might help remind me that I'm a *femme fatale* after all.'

'Ange! I'm shocked! And you a married woman too!'

'Yes, it's terrible, isn't it? I can see you're deeply offended. Oh well, maybe you're right; perhaps it isn't done for a deputy head teacher's wife to have any life at all from the waist downwards. Perhaps I ought to organize a coffee morning for the WI instead.' They both laughed. 'Anyway,' continued Ange, 'where shall we meet so that you can give me all the juicy gossip?'

'Kate's Coffee Shop. I'll see you there at about eleven. Okay?'

'Fine. And remember, come prepared. I want a full action replay of all events with relevant sound effects.'

'I'm not sure that would be allowed.'

'Mmm, that juicy eh?'

'Well . . .'

'Goodness, this chap sounds more and more intriguing and I can't wait to hear about him.'

When Ange had rung off, Claire put down the phone and rubbed the muscles of her neck. She hadn't realized how uptight she had been until Ange phoned and made her relax and release some of the tension. She looked at her watch: 5.30. Plenty of time for James to ring yet.

She went out to check over her sheep, and then collect a few eggs. After that she made herself some tea, followed by a slump on the sofa with Rosie in front of the television. Now that she had a new remote control set, it made watching even easier. She flicked disinterestedly through the channels.

The clock on the mantelpiece inexorably ticked onwards and by ten o'clock he still hadn't rung. What was he doing, she thought. He was only two miles away, surely he could pick up the phone or even come over. Maybe there had been an accident or something. The thought was too awful to contemplate and made her feel sick. She hurriedly switched on the news but there was nothing about an accident. Her relief was enormous.

By 10.30, after she had taken Rosie out for her last amble round the garden, she decided that she had to do something. There was no way she was going to be able to sleep tonight unless she did something positive. She went to call him.

She shook as her finger dialled the number. Her action was quite against everything she had been brought up to do.

'Don't chase men,' was her mother's firm instruction. 'Let them do it. If they want you, they'll come running, believe me.' So she didn't and neither did they. Instead Claire, with her spots and her brace, would cry silently upstairs in her bedroom.

This was different, though. James had said he loved her; he had said he would ring. There had to be a reason for his silence. His phone began to ring.

'Come on,' she urged. 'Answer it, please answer it.'

Nothing. At first disappointed, she then cheered herself up by reasoning that he must be on his way over.

Half an hour later and the icy pit in her stomach told her she was wrong. Unable to sit, sleep, eat or stop fidgeting, she picked up the van keys and put on her coat.

If he wasn't coming to see her then she would damn well go and see him. She had to find out what was going on.

It was a cold crisp night with dark clouds scuttling across the star-laden sky, promising rain as she drove to Briar Cottage. Nervous and excited she bumped her way down the drive and pulled to a stop in front of the house. His car wasn't there and the house was dark.

'No, please, this isn't true.' She couldn't believe it. He said he would ring, he said he would. Hot tears began to fill her eyes.

She got out and walked up to the front door. Maybe he was just asleep. Biting on her bottom lip in an effort to stop it wobbling, she knocked on the door. 'Answer it, damn you.' She knocked again, harder and harder until she was pummelling with both fists and shouting out her pain.

'You bastard! You bloody bastard!'

She sunk to her knees on the cold doormat. 'Welcome', it said. She smiled tearfully at its irony.

She stood up and stepped out in front of the house, looking up at the bedroom window. This time last night she had lain up there in the arms of a man who had told her he loved her and she had given him all that she had.

The memory of his touch dug into her mind, the images tormenting her. She had given him everything; all the parts of her body that no one had ever explored had been his. He in his turn had awakened her, the smouldering fires of her primitive instincts being wrenched alive from their dormancy. It wasn't fair. It was so bloody unfair! What was she going to do now? How would she cope? How could he do this to her?

She turned away. The small seedling that had shot up within the last twenty-four hours, withered and died.

James was in London. Soon after Claire had left that morning, his telephone had rung. When he heard the voice, the deep, threatening, Scottish voice, he had felt sick. McArdle had hunted him down.

'Well, Jamie boy, and how are we this fine morning? Enjoying your stay in Devon, are you?'

'How did you get this number?'

McArdle ignored his question. 'Well now, isn't that nice. However, unless you get back here and do something about your little standing problem you won't be on holiday much longer. Understand?' and the line clicked dead.

James stared hard at the receiver. How the bloody hell had McArdle found him? James had found out about Claire from his sister, but she didn't know he'd come down to Devon. No one knew about this place. No one.

He blinked rapidly, his heart pounding, trying to think, but unable to. His mind simply couldn't focus.

McArdle; McArdle; McArdle, said the voice in his head. How did he know? Who had told him? And what about Claire? Oh Christ! Just as he was getting things sorted out and now this! He would have to go back immediately.

He picked up the phone and dialled Claire's number. It rang for well over a minute with no answer, his impatience and frustration increasing all the while.

'Stupid woman!' he cursed as he slammed down the receiver. Oh well, if she wouldn't answer, there was nothing he could do about it now. He had other things to worry about: McArdle.

TEN

Back in London, James put his bags down on the kitchen table. It was filthy; littered with dirty crockery and glasses, the ashtray piled high with cigarette butts. He picked one up; it had Saskia's familiar coloured lipstick around the filter; some of the others didn't and weren't her usual brand. Alert and suspicious, he put the butt back and looked around the room. Three different bowls of cat food sat on the floor, the food that was left in them hard and dry and stuck to the edges. The sink was full of dirty grey water, a casserole dish half submerged, pieces of soggy food floating around the grease-covered surface. It revolted him.

He wanted a drink. The journey from Devon had been long and tedious. He was not in a good mood. He had to do something about McArdle. And soon. He still wondered how he had found out where he was.

He opened the fridge. Every shelf was full; half-empty pots, tubs and plates of food, piled on top of each other. Some of it had a faint coating of green fur. It smelt bad. A bottle of French dressing had fallen over, spilling its contents onto the two shelves underneath, forming a puddle of congealed opaque green slime on the salad tray. He slammed the door shut, the milk bottles rattling in the door.

He had made himself a strong black coffee, then went into the sitting room. The curtains were still drawn, although it was now well after lunch. There was a sour smell of cigarettes and alcohol like a pub the morning after a riotous party. The coffee table was covered in more dirty wine glasses and the ashtray was full. He looked down and

154

saw that someone had stubbed out their cigarette in one of the pot plants.

He angrily strode over to the curtains and pulled them back. It was then he saw a pile of cold vomit by the side of the sofa, the liquid soaked into the carpet, trails of the stuff dried on to the side of the chair.

'Jesus Christ!'

He just couldn't leave her alone for a minute without this happening. It disgusted him. She was such a slut.

He heard a noise. She had obviously just woken up. Resigned more than angry, he went upstairs to face her. As he did so, he undid his belt and removed it from his trousers, wrapping one end of it around his right hand for a good grip. He opened the door and was just in time to see her naked body running into the bathroom and slamming the door behind her. She would lock it and then plead with him tearfully not to hit her. It rarely worked.

He stood by the door waiting. 'Saskia, don't do this,' he said quietly. 'Come on out and then you and I can talk it through like two sensible adults and get this problem resolved.'

He could hear her muffled whimpering. Last time this happened, she didn't lock the door properly and with one good shove he had pushed it open. He had found her hiding beneath a towel behind the door, her whole body shaking in fearful apprehension. He had helped her up, taken her into the bedroom holding her close, calming down her near hysteria, and then thrown her over his knee and belted her. If he hadn't been so tired that time, he would have screwed her as well, since violence invariably excited him. Even she seemed disappointed when he didn't.

'Saskia, I have a little present for you.' She still sniffed. 'A nice little present, Sas. A pair of silk stockings that we can put on, rolling them up your thighs in the way we like.' His voice was soft and persuasive. 'Come on, Sas, if you come out here, I promise I won't hit you.'

155

She loved presents. Not big ones necessarily, just little intimate ones. Presents that could be offered to her prior to sex was what she liked best, especially stockings. After he had rolled each one up her legs, he would get down on his knees before her spread-eagled flesh, his fingers massaging her thighs, exciting and teasing her. By then, he too would be straining to have her, but they each resisted it, doing nothing else until the point came where they could hold back no more. He would always take her violently. It was a game they both liked.

He heard her padding towards the door across the cork floor tiles. He put his hands behind his back, concealing the belt. The lock turned and slowly the door opened. She stood behind it, hiding from him. Experience had taught her to be circumspect.

'Come on, Saskia,' he urged. 'Come out. Stop hiding behind the door. We're adults,' he reasoned, 'and you're behaving like a child.'

'You won't hit me?' Her voice was small and childlike. Odd really, considering her bulk.

'No.' He was all gentleness.

First her head appeared, heaped up with golden curls, and then her eyes, red and swollen.

'I'm sorry, Jamie.' She walked to him, arms outstretched and cuddled him, pressing her wet face against his chest, 'I'm really, really sorry. It won't happen again, I promise you.' She smiled up at him. 'Anyway, the cleaner will be in tomorrow, so it doesn't really matter.'

He kept the belt held tightly in his fist behind his back and stroked her hair with his other hand. 'Of course not, darling, but just in case you ever do behave like that again, I want you to remember something.'

She looked up at him again. 'Yes?'

He smiled slowly, looking like a viper before it strikes. 'This,' and he grabbed her hair, pulling it tighter and tighter. 'I'm going to teach you a lesson so you will never forget.'

'No! Jamie, no!' Her eyes, a moment ago so relaxed, now filled with fear. She put both hands up to her head desperately trying to free herself from his rigid grip. She started to sob, her face screwed up in pain. 'No, Jamie . . . no!'

'Oh yes, Jamie, yes,' he hissed through his clenched teeth. He grabbed her arm and threw her onto the floor. He then started to thrash her, the leather belt stinging the plump white flesh, leaving long red weals across her buttocks and thighs.

She tried to crawl away, crouched like a beetle, her hands protecting her head, while she screamed, her voice rising with each blow. 'No . . . no . . . James, please . . . no!'

He heard none of it. Filled with a white-hot fury which unleashed enormous, uncontrolled anger, an unstoppable force sweeping through his body, he hit her again and again.

'You fucking . . . fucking . . . stupid . . . dumb . . . bitch! I hate you! You told McArdle, didn't you? You told him!'

She didn't answer, but only screamed.

At last he stopped, quite breathless, his arm hanging limply by his side. He was so hot that sweat was beginning to run down his temples. He wiped it away. As he did so, Saskia took the opportunity to crawl away from him and hide herself under the bed.

He sat down on the bed and looked malevolently at her foot, which stuck out. He kicked it viciously. She yelped and withdrew it.

'Bitch!'

She continued sniffing.

'Who was here last night?' he demanded. 'One of your lover boys?'

She didn't answer.

He bounced up and down, squashing her. 'Who was here, Saskia? I know someone was, so tell me.'

'Ow, you're hurting me. Please stop.'

He stood up. 'Get out of there, Saskia, before I really lose my temper.' Nothing. 'Get out, bitch!' he shouted.

She inched her way out slowly, her body, red and white, crisscrossed with weals, and stood up awkwardly, avoiding his gaze. Cowed and frightened, she still cried, but quietly now. She shifted from foot to foot.

'Who was here last night? I want to know because if there's been another man, you're really going to pay for it. Are you listening to me?'

He held her jaw in his hands and forced her to look at him. 'I don't like it when other men play with my toys, Saskia, so you'd better have a good excuse.'

She didn't answer him but shook her head, emotion and pain overwhelming her, arms held crossed in front of her breasts.

'You snivelling, wretched human being.' He walked around her, sneering at her, his face so close to hers that she flinched every time he said something. 'How I got involved with somebody like you I'll never know. You are without doubt the most pathetic creature I've ever had the misfortune to meet.'

He raised his hand and she instantly dropped to her knees, shielding herself, waiting for the blow. It didn't come. He liked to tease her like that. When she realized what was happening, she gingerly looked up, her face streaked with tears, a line of runny snot coming out of one nostril.

'No man was here,' she said quietly. 'Anyway, where have you been?'

'None of your fucking business, bitch!'

She looked away. 'A friend was here.'

'Really? I didn't think you had any.'

'You bastard!' she snarled. 'You bloody rotten bastard! You piss off without so much as a word of explanation and then accuse me of all sorts!'

Her eyes blazed with anger at his smirking face and

quite suddenly she stood up and slapped him. He had gone too far. He stepped back holding a hand to his face with shocked surprise. Too enraged to care what she did, she came at him again, her outstretched arms a blur of movement as her blows rained down on him.

'You . . . shit!' she screamed. 'You bloody, bloody shit!' He moved swiftly away from her as she chased him, her white breasts bobbing up and down on her chest like plates of blancmange. 'I don't know where you've been or who with and you have the gall to criticize me? I can't believe it!' She kicked him, her foot dangerously close to his upper thigh and instinctively he curled away from her, his hands crossed in front of him. 'You bastard!'

Her fists pummelled him, doing no real damage. When he had had enough, he stood up straight and grabbed her wrists. She was still full of energy.

'Want to fight me then, Sas?'

She glared at him, nostrils flaring. He pulled her closer, pinning her arms behind her back. He was smiling now. She spat at him, but he simply wiped his face on her hair.

'Tut, tut. You're just such a peasant sometimes, aren't you?'

She began to struggle. 'Let me go, James, let . . . me . . . go!'

He held her fast. 'No way. McArdle's been here, has he? Did he ring you?'

'No! I told you, a friend was here, that's all.'

Using his much greater strength, he picked her up, walked towards the bed and flung her down. She lay on her back staring up at him, her breasts heaving, her legs outstretched.

He stood between her thighs, his hands on his hips. 'You're not going anywhere yet. I haven't finished with you.'

'Fuck you, James Lamont Skerrett!'

She tried to wriggle away from him but she wasn't quick

enough. Using his full weight to pin her down, her calves hanging over the end of the bed and him kneeling on the floor, he tried to kiss her.

She violently turned her head, pressing her lips tightly together, her loose fists pummelling his back. When he couldn't get her to keep still, he slapped her.

'I'm going to have you, Sas, so pack it in.'

'Piss off, you bastard, leave me alone!'

'Oh, Sas, you don't mean that; you want it really, I can tell.'

He kissed her. Again she struggled, but he took no notice. Using one hand to hold her down, he began to undo his flies. At times like this he saw no reason for preamble. She wanted it and so did he. It was hard work, though, Saskia, bigger and stronger than the average woman, fought him determinedly, biting, kicking and scratching whenever and wherever she could. Occasionally he felt one of her nails digging into the flesh of his back, but mainly he just ignored her. She couldn't overpower him and that was all that mattered.

'Lie still!' he commanded. 'You bloody whore!'

'No . . . leave me alone . . . leave me alone!'

Her face was red with exertion, her golden waves curling around her head and spread out against the duvet. As he looked at her, his body suffused with desire, his hot breath bathing her face, he knew he couldn't wait.

His fingers pushed inside her, forcing her open, just as her legs curled round his back and crossed over, holding him tightly. He noticed that she was breathing just as heavily as he was.

'You wanted this, didn't you?'

She didn't reply, her eyes heavy.

'God, you're so good,' he moaned.

Her fighting stopped and as he entered her, she rose to meet him, her back arching off the bed.

He rode her quickly. This was no time to be gentle. She writhed beneath him, moaning aloud. When she came, she dug her nails so hard into his buttocks he screamed with her before biting her shoulder. When he came soon afterwards, he pushed so hard he actually hurt her.

Afterwards they lay together, their perspiration mixing, body on body. His face was lying on her wet breasts; her arms wrapped around his head.

'I missed you,' she whispered.

'I missed you too.' He paused. 'You won't leave me, darling, will you?' He spoke awkwardly, the sentence disjointed as he struggled to admit his need.

'Whatever made you say that?'

He wouldn't look at her. 'Don't know, just don't, that's all.'

In a wave of tenderness she squeezed him closer. 'I wouldn't leave you, baby,' and she kissed his head.

He kissed one of her large pink nipples. 'By the way, who was here last night?'

'Oh, only Terri.'

'What's she like then, this Claire whatever-her-name-is?'

'Nothing like the rest of the family. You wouldn't think she was related to the Skerretts at all.'

'And you say she's your cousin?'

'Second or third. I'm not sure exactly.'

They lay on the bed smoking, the blue wisps curling up into the musky air.

'So how come she's got all this money then?' asked Saskia.

'Don't know, but I can tell you one thing, I intend to get the whole bloody lot back.'

'How?'

He didn't answer.

'How, James?'

'Just leave it to me, Sas, okay? There's no need for you to get involved.'

'Oh I see,' she sneered, sitting up and staring balefully at him. 'You're poking her, aren't you? And you expect

161

me to just sit here and take it? Well, you can get stuffed!'

She went to get off the bed when he grabbed her. 'Look, Sas, she's a semi-literate, badly bred yokel and if you think I'd go to bed with something like that, well . . .' and he chuckled. 'No way! I like women like you, blonde, blue-eyed and sexy. Not country bumpkins.'

She smiled, a small tired one. 'Okay,' she relented, getting back down beside him. 'I believe you, though thousands wouldn't. But why didn't you tell me about her instead of just disappearing?'

He stubbed out his cigarette. 'I couldn't. I wasn't sure if I'd find her to start with and it took a great deal of careful questioning before I got any joy out of my sister.' He faltered. 'That's how McArdle must have found me.'

'McArdle?'

'Yes,' he said, looking at her. 'That bastard rang me at the cottage. That's why I came home. He must have got the information from my sister.'

'But surely not. She'd never speak to someone like him. You know what a snob she is.'

'She might not,' emphasized James, 'but you don't know what McArdle's like. He could charm the birds out of the trees if he wanted to.'

They both lay quietly.

'So what are you going to do?' asked Saskia.

'I have to get the money from Claire. But don't you worry about that, darling. I'll see to everything,' and he leant back, his head resting on his hands, another cigarette in his mouth.

'Promise me you're not going to sleep with her, James.'

He glanced at her, his face not changing at all.

'Please don't, James. I couldn't bear it if you did.'

'Of course not, Sas. Would your little Jamie do anything like that?'

'Oh good,' she said, snuggling up to him. 'Is she young, this Claire?'

He pulled on his towelling robe. 'No, not really. Thirty odd, a few grey hairs, some wrinkles. Nothing to write home about.'

'She's not beautiful then?'

'No, not at all.' He stopped in front of the mirror and looked at himself. As he peered closer at some imagined blemish, he pulled a face. He liked his complexion to be flawless.

'Not as beautiful as me then?' she asked, and she got off the bed. She encircled his waist with her arms and pressed herself against him, rubbing against his back. She put her hands inside his robe exploring his body.

He pushed her away. 'Not now, Sas. Can't you see I'm busy. Christ, you're like a bitch on heat sometimes.' He finished checking his face and stood up straight.

She was pouting. 'Can't we go back to bed, James?' She moved towards him again and started to kiss him. 'I'm hungry,' she whispered, 'and I've missed you.'

'No.' He stepped to one side. 'Now get dressed and go downstairs and clean up that mess.'

'But why? Maureen can do it tomorrow. God, I pay her enough.' She slumped onto the bed. He pulled her to her feet.

'Don't be such a slut. It's awful downstairs, really filthy, and it's all your mess. I am not going to stay here if you don't do something about it and I don't want to have to get angry again.'

'Why not?' she teased, her fingers moving down his chest, 'you liked it last time.'

'Move it, Sas. I'm in no bloody mood for it.'

'Oh all right, if I have to.'

The coffee she made was too strong, but at least it was hot, which was an improvement on her usual efforts. Order of a sort had returned to the house and he could now sit at a cleared kitchen table and not be offended by the mess in the sink. She had even scrubbed the carpet and upholstery in the sitting room. Now she was upstairs hoovering. James couldn't remember the last time she had done that.

He put down his cup and grimaced. He poured it down the sink and made himself a fresh cup, putting a good tot of whisky in it this time. He rubbed his shoulder. It was smarting painfully from where she had bitten him and she had left a series of red nail marks on his buttocks. He smiled to himself. That was one thing she was really good at. What a pity he didn't feel any better.

He was really worried. Time was running out and if he didn't get the money to McArdle before long, his interest rate would be going up again. He had to move, and soon, or he might be paying back double what he owed. Perhaps an evening at the club would do it. A little blackjack; a little chemmy. Something was bound to go right for him eventually.

Saskia's fat Persian cat came through the flap in the door and meandered hairily towards him. It started to wrap itself around his legs, purring loudly. He kicked it to one side and it skidded across the floor, miaowing in protest. Without looking at him it glided haughtily out of the room.

James hated animals. Their fawning and general slobbering nauseated him. It brought to mind Claire's dog. Bloody mongrel, he thought to himself, yapping at him like that. If it went for him again, he might have to show it who was boss.

And then he thought of Claire. Not too bad really. A bit skinny; he liked his women big and fleshy, with plenty to get hold of, to knead and squeeze. Still, she would do for the time being. Promising and enthusiastic, if nothing else. He thought of their night together and the way she had given herself to him and it made him smile. He generally steered clear of innocents, feeling in his experienced opinion that they were easily misled, getting all emotional over trivialities and ending up causing too much hassle.

164

He really ought to ring her. An old-fashioned girl like her would only get upset if he didn't keep up the attention.

He glanced at his watch. He would do it later, from the club. That way Saskia wouldn't overhear anything.

Saskia appeared dressed in a silk kaftan, nuzzling her cat close to her face. It made him sick the way she fussed over it.

'Does Susie want some din-dins then?' she cooed, stroking its long peach-coloured hair, caressing it and rubbing her face in its fur. 'Will Mummy get you something to eat then, darling.'

The cat stared at her, its amber eyes blank and expressionless and its tail twitching. They made a wonderful couple, thought James – entirely selfish, egocentric and hedonistic.

Saskia put the cat down and then fixed its dinner. She then sat down at the table and began to brush her hair.

'Do you have to do that over the table?' James protested. 'Look at this,' and he picked up a stray hair and threw it fastidiously to one side.

'You know what you said about McArdle, James? Well, he did phone, I remember now.'

He almost choked on his coffee. 'What! When? But I thought you said he didn't!'

She pouted. 'Well, if you hadn't been so angry with me and given me time to explain, I would have told you earlier. Anyway, I can't be expected to remember everything. I'm not your bloody secretary.'

He sighed. 'Okay, I'm sorry. Now when did he ring?'

'Last night? The night before? I can't quite remember.'

'You mean you were too drunk to remember.'

'No I wasn't,' she whined.

'Too stoned then.' He glowered at her while she avoided his gaze.

She stood up and started to fill the kettle. 'If you're going to be nasty, James, then I won't tell you what he said.'

'And if you're going to be awkward, Sas, then I can always get nastier. So what did he say?' He glared at her.

She put down the kettle. 'He said to warn you that time was nearly up.' She got a mug out of the cupboard. 'Awfully common little oik, isn't he?'

'Yes, his father was a builder too, so I've been told.'

Saskia started to protest but James wasn't listening. 'James, are you all right?'

'Yes, yes.' God, he was tired. 'Oh shit! shit! shit!' and he pounded the table top with his fist.

'What is it, James, what's the matter?'

Ignoring her, he went out of the room. When he came back he had his wallet and her purse. He emptied both on the table. There was roughly five hundred pounds. He looked at her.

'Where's the rest?'

'I haven't got any.'

'Don't give me that, Sas, where is it?'

He walked towards her. She could see he meant trouble. She backed off; there was no option.

'Upstairs, in my vanity case.'

He smiled. 'Good. I like it when you co-operate.'

He came down with a thick roll, unfurled it and counted it. There was over a thousand pounds; enough for him to put up a reasonable stake. If he could just get it right tonight then he might be able to fend off McArdle. He folded up the money and put it in his pocket. Glancing at his watch, he decided it was time to get ready. He would have a long evening ahead of him.

Saskia followed him upstairs. She had been quietly watching him in the kitchen, but not any more.

'Please don't take it all, James.'

He didn't answer her but started going through his wardrobe. It didn't pay to look scruffy.

'Please, James,' she said, pulling at his arm. 'I need some money, please.'

He ignored her. She was about to grab him again when

he rounded on her. 'For Christ's sake, stop pawing me!' he snarled. 'I've got work to do tonight and you're being a real pain in the arse, so push off!' and he swept her aside.

She fell against the bed. He went into the bathroom and locked the door after him.

She stood outside. 'But I need some money, James, please let me have some. If I don't get . . . some . . .'

'What?' he shouted. 'Your bloody precious powder?'

'But I won't be able to sleep,' she wailed.

'Try counting sheep,' he retorted.

He splashed some aftershave around his face and smiled. He loved this stuff, it was very expensive.

Saskia started to cry. 'Please, James, let me have some money, please.' She was sobbing like a little child whose favourite toy had been confiscated. 'Please, James!' Getting no response she started to bang her fists against the door, driven by panic. She had to have her stuff. She and Terri had finished it all last night after they had made up and she must buy some more. 'Give me some money, you bastard!'

James finished brushing his teeth and then carefully combed his hair.

'You fucking bastard, give me some money!'

He was amused at her. All that expensive schooling and impeccable upbringing and the minute she couldn't get what she wanted she gave away her humble origins. Suddenly he slammed his fist against the sink. God, how he despised her and her habit! Why couldn't she stop? If she loved him she would! But would she?

She was kicking the door, her feet pummelling the wood. 'Shit!'

Cigarettes and alcohol didn't count to his way of thinking, but cocaine . . . that was different.

He opened the door quickly. Saskia was lying on her back about to lash out at the door again. Her kaftan was up around her bottom, revealing her large dimpled thighs. She momentarily disgusted him.

Standing over her, he took out the roll of money and peeled off a note. He let it go and it fluttered down to her, landing on her chest. She grabbed it like a drowning man to a lifeline.

'Don't spend it all at once, will you?' he said and walked away, her curses and shouts following him down the stairs.

'Well, well, well, aren't we the glamorous one then?'

Ange put her coat on the empty chair and sat down heavily opposite Claire, her red hair curling round her plump face. 'Come on then, stand up,' she urged. 'It's not every day I get the opportunity to see you looking so smart. Give us a twirl.'

Claire hesitated.

'Oh come on, Claire, nobody's looking,' urged Ange. She smiled encouragingly, showing the two dimples in her cheeks.

Claire self-conscious and shy, slowly got to her feet, gave a quick half-hearted turn and quickly sat down again.

'Very nice,' approved Ange, smiling, her blue eyes twinkling. 'Cotton, isn't it? Where did you get it.'

'That shop in the Piazza.'

'What. Cromwells? Well, I must say it looks good. I never thought I'd see you wearing something like that. Very Laura Ashley, with all those little flowers.' She paused. 'Expensive, was it?'

'Not really.'

'Still, I don't suppose you have to worry about such things now with your new-found wealth.' Her teasing was gentle and Claire smiled in return.

'Just how much did you get then?'

Claire looked down and said nothing.

'Oh come on, Claire, I've known you for ages. Don't you trust me?'

Claire glanced round the room then sat forward, her

clasped hands in front of her mouth. 'Enough to pay my mortgage, your mortgage and maybe a few others,' she mumbled.

Ange's mouth fell open. She looked very shocked. 'What!'

Claire nodded.

'Good God! As much as that? And it's all yours?'

Claire smiled. 'Yes.'

'Christ!' She slumped back in her chair. She looked flushed. 'I can't believe it,' she said at last. 'What are you going to do with it?'

Claire shrugged. 'Don't know. I've got nothing planned at the moment.'

'Well, dear girl, I think this calls for a bit of a celebration.' She looked towards the laden counter, groaning under the weight of gateaux and cream buns. 'How about an extra special little something to eat? It certainly won't do a svelte lovely like you any harm and I think just this once I'll postpone my diet.'

Claire watched her fondly as Ange went up to the counter and stood undecided, drooling over the goodies. She had met her not long after she had arrived in town and for the first couple of years they were good friends. Then Ange had gone away to university and their friendship didn't really take up again until Ange's marriage. Whenever she had a problem, it was to Ange she turned. On reflection, she realized she didn't really have anyone else. There was Ange and that was it. Happy, smiling, humorous Ange, married with twins and every bit the busy young housewife.

'Here you are, dear,' Ange placed the coffees and slices of rich chocolate cake on the table, then handed Claire a fork. 'Get your teeth into that. I must say it looks absolutely yummy.' She sat down and unrolled her fork from its paper napkin. 'Talking of yummy things, just who is this new man of yours then?'

Claire took a mouthful of cake. 'Well,' she said slowly, 'he's the one that oozes it from his hair roots down to his toenails.'

For a second time that morning Ange looked at her, eyes wide with disbelief. 'What!'

'It's him, the lodger at Briar Cottage.'

Claire couldn't help smiling. The mere mention of him was enough to do it. Last night's crushing disappointment had been forgotten. It was quite obvious James had gone back to London and if she hadn't been so preoccupied when he rang, she would have been able to speak to him. Therefore, it was all her fault he was not there.

She didn't sleep too well either. Restless and disturbed, sleep came late into the night and was filled with terrible dreams. She couldn't recall them now and was grateful for it.

'You absolute bloody so-and-so!' exclaimed Ange, her face animated and shining. 'I can't believe it! He's only been here two minutes and you're going out with him!' She shook her head. 'And you, the little hermit! I was beginning to think that you were never going to socialize again and then you go and do this! Astonishing!' She started to eat her cake again. 'Well, let's hear all about it then.'

She listened closely as Claire told her about the meeting in the café and the subsequent invitation to dinner.

'What did you wear?'

'That red dress I wore to our party in the church hall.' Ange looked puzzled. 'You remember. It was our fifth wedding anniversary and I got that lady to make me that beautiful red velvet dress.'

'Oh yes!' recognition hit Ange. 'Yes, I remember. You looked gorgeous that night, really slim.' She grabbed the rolls of extra flab around her own waist and smiled ruefully. 'Unlike me. Anyway, carry on, what else happened?'

'Well,' said Claire evasively, avoiding Ange's stare.

'Come on, tell all,' urged Ange.

'Well . . .' and she looked at her friend, her cheeks pink with delight.

Ange looked at her and clapped her hands. 'Ha! You didn't, did you? Well, I say, what a turnabout! And was it worth it then?'

Claire blushed. 'Ange!'

Her friend playfully punched her on the arm. 'Don't be embarrassed, Claire, we're only human after all, and even someone like you needs to find a man occasionally.'

Claire didn't know what to make of that remark and, putting down her fork, she looked at Ange closely, although she was still smiling. 'What d'you mean?'

'Oh heavens, I don't know,' and Ange chuckled. 'You know what I mean.'

'I don't.'

Ange sighed. 'I have known you for a number of years now, Claire, and apart from Matt and now this chap, there hasn't been anyone else, has there?'

'No, well, Alistair did ask me, but I said no.'

'Exactly.' She paused. 'Pity about that really.'

'What!'

'Alistair. You know, I really like him, I always have done. I mean he's incredibly good-looking and quite loaded from what I hear. Why don't you like him?'

'I don't dislike him,' Claire insisted. 'On the contrary, I think he's great as a friend. He really makes me laugh, but something . . . oh well, I don't know what it is . . . perhaps he's just too nice.'

'Rubbish! The trouble with you is that you don't know a good thing when you see it. Even when I made all those efforts to introduce you to people, you still wouldn't come. I used to seriously worry about you after Matt's death. Cooped up there all day long, no visitors, no family and now this! Totally out of the blue. I'm amazed!' She drank some of her coffee. 'Tell me, is this a case of good old-fashioned lust or are you going to get serious about this guy? What's his name, by the way?'

'James Lamont and at the moment I just don't know.'

'How about another cake,' suggested Ange suddenly. 'After all, as citizens of this parish, I feel it is our duty to regularly check the quality of goods that are on offer to make sure they are up to standard. What do you think?'

Claire smiled. She wasn't really hungry and certainly didn't share Ange's sweet tooth.

'Okay, I'll have a jam doughnut.'

After a couple of minutes Ange returned.

'I'm glad to hear your good news, Claire, it couldn't have happened to a nicer person and as for this James Lamont . . . well, should I start feeding you up or something? I mean, you know what they say about sex — it burns off loads of calories. There won't be anything left of you at this rate.'

Claire grinned. 'Hardly.' She then fell quiet. 'You know,' she said, 'I never knew it could be like this.'

'What?' Ange had sugar all over her top lip which she was licking off.

'Love, lust or whatever.'

'Oh dear, we have got it bad, haven't we?'

Claire took a bite from her doughnut and then ignored it.

'Definitely the first sign,' said Ange, helping herself to Claire's doughnut.

'What is?'

'Losing one's appetite. God, I wish it would happen to me.'

Her voice was louder and Claire could sense her depression. 'What's the matter?'

'Oh nothing really,' she said smiling ruefully. 'Except that Colin's virtually a workaholic, the twins are driving me to distraction and it looks as though Colin's mother might have to come and live with us.'

'Oh dear. Can't the old lady go into a home?'

'Have you any idea how much they cost?' She shook

her head. 'No, we could never afford it. Unlike you, we're quite broke. God! Can you imagine it? It's bad enough having the old bag living so near, but it would be simply awful if she was under my roof.' She angrily stabbed Claire's doughnut. 'If I had known what a hypochondriac neurotic she was, I never would have married Colin.'

'You don't mean that surely?' Claire was genuinely alarmed. She had rarely seen Ange so upset.

'Don't I? Do you know that since he took up his new appointment at the school, I rarely see him in the morning because he leaves so early and I don't see him at night because I'm so exhausted with the twins, I'm usually dead to the world by ten. And as for sex,' she added contemptuously, spitting out the words, 'forget it! I can't remember the last time we had any!'

'I'm sorry, Ange.'

'Why? You've got everything you want. I don't see why you should be sorry about anything!' and she took up her handbag. After a moment she found what she was looking for and lit a cigarette.

'I thought you'd given them up,' said Claire.

'This James Lamont,' Ange queried, ignoring her comment, 'when are you going to see him again?'

Claire pushed back her hair and began to fiddle with her coffee cup, turning it round and round in its saucer.

'He said that he might ring or come over some time.'

'When?'

'Yesterday.' She hadn't wanted to admit to it, but lying would have been useless. Ange's sixth sense would have spotted it immediately.

'And did he?' she asked.

'No.' Claire snapped shut her lips.

'Had his oats and gone then, has he?'

Now Claire was angry. What on earth was the matter with Ange for her to be so spiteful?'

'Look, Ange, he didn't turn up and no, he didn't ring, but that's no reason for him to not appear very soon. It just so happens that he has business problems in London and he told me that he might have to rush back. As a matter of fact, when I got home, he rang me but I just couldn't get to the phone in time.'

'He rang you?' Ange was amused. 'How do you know it was him?'

Claire was exasperated. 'I don't, but if it wasn't you, then who else could it have been?'

'But it could be anyone, Claire – Jack, anyone. How could you be sure it was him?'

'Because,' said Claire, trying not to lose her temper, 'he told me he loved me and he wouldn't just take off if he did, would he?'

Ange sighed. 'Dear Claire, you are very sweet, but unbelievably naïve. How could you swallow such crap?'

'Don't patronize me, Ange!' she warned, her eyes a brilliant green. 'He said he did and I believe him. Okay?'

Ange held up her hands in submission. 'Okay, okay. You don't think,' she added warily 'that his sudden appearance has anything to do with your amazing good fortune?'

Claire looked as if someone had kicked her in the stomach. 'What did you say?'

'I said, do you think perhaps this James Lamont is a fortune-hunter? After all, you're rich and maybe he isn't.'

Claire sat forward, her brows knitted, and pointed a finger at Ange. 'I just don't believe you could say such a thing. For a start, how would he know about me? The only people who know that are you and Alistair.' Her voice rose with indignation. 'How can you be so mean, Ange?'

'I'm not being mean,' she replied. 'Just practical. Here you are, head over heels with some stranger who suddenly appears very soon after you've inherited a great deal of money. Doesn't it even strike you as a little bit of a coincidence?'

'No,' replied Claire firmly. 'You're just a cynic, Ange, and, what's more, you're jealous.'

She hadn't meant to say it, but as her anger had got worse, it had just slipped out.

Now it was Ange's turn to feel enraged and like some old-fashioned ship's figurehead, pulled herself up straight and glared at Claire.

'If you seriously think for one minute that I'm jealous of you, then you are very mistaken. I'm not jealous, Claire, because unlike you, I am behaving with some restraint and common sense. I'm not jumping into bed with the first good-looking freeloader that comes my way. Good God, woman, heaven only knows what bacteria he's harbouring. You might be risking all sorts, not to mention a serious case of heartbreak. Still, it's your life and if you want to ruin it, you go ahead. Don't take any notice of anything I say. After all, I'm only your friend.'

'Huh! Some friend!' snorted Claire. 'I come here to share my good news with you and all I get is bitching and moaning.' She stood up. 'Thanks for the coffee, Ange. It hasn't been very nice at all. In fact, I can't remember a time when you were so bloody unpleasant. Goodbye,' and picking up her bags and coat, she walked out.

Ange's embarrassment didn't last long and hating waste, she finished off Claire's cake. Then feeling recklessly abandoned, ordered another slice of gateau. If she was going to make a pig of herself, then she might as well go the whole way. To hell with Claire and her bloody sex life. Just because everything was going well for her, there was no need to rub salt in the wound.

ELEVEN

She kissed him on the lips. 'Good morning, Alistair.'

He returned her smile. 'What time is it?'

'Ten o'clock. I've ordered tea.'

Five minutes later there was a faint knock at the door.

'Come in, Aditha.'

The maid kept her eyes downcast as she placed the tray on the bedside table.

Alistair smiled at her. 'Morning, Aditha.' She mumbled a reply.

'Aditha, tell Kevin to get the car ready, will you? We'll need it sometime later this morning.' Elyssa turned to Alistair and started to kiss him. 'Tell him,' she added, 'that he doesn't have to rush,' and she chuckled.

'Yes, madam.'

When she had gone Alistair said, 'You shouldn't have done that, Elyssa, you embarrassed the poor woman.'

'Did I? I'm sorry, darling. I'll be more careful in future.'

'And you can take your tongue out of your cheek as well, Elyssa. Why don't you let her go, and get somebody else? It's so obvious you don't like her.'

She passed him his cup of tea, a small triumphant smile on her lips. 'I'll think about it,' she said.

'Sometimes, Elyssa, you can be very cruel.'

'Who me, Alistair? How can you say such a thing?' She looked at him, the mischief returning to her face. 'I know, Ali, but you like it, don't you?'

She removed the cup from his hands, placed it on the table and then ducked her head under the duvet. Her voice was muffled. 'Alistair, you smell absolutely divine.'

He stretched back against the pillow as her delicious,

experienced lips explored him. Thinking himself completely drained after their afternoon session at the hotel, the lovemaking that followed after dinner and the sex at some early hour of the morning, he marvelled at her skill and the way he responded yet again.

It wasn't a fight any more. Now that he had pushed Claire to the back of his mind, it had become easier by the hour to let Elyssa take over. As long as he didn't think about Claire he could avoid the pain and languish in the pleasure; a pleasure that Elyssa gave so freely. Her enthusiasm encouraged him, stiffened his resolve and made him determined not to look back. It was his future that mattered now.

Elyssa was enjoying herself. It had been a long time, well at least a few weeks, since she had had such a handsome and wealthy man in her bed who wasn't already married. It made her want to give of her very best. Chances like this were few and far between as men like Alistair were inevitably snapped up as soon as they were spotted. What a relief that none of her friends knew about him. She could do without the competition.

'Are you enjoying that, baby?' she cooed.

There was a groan from the top end of the bed. She continued, using her teeth to nibble him.

She must be careful. She couldn't afford for things to go wrong. Rush him too much and he might get cold feet. If she were to succeed in her plans, she was going to have to watch her step. A change of attitude towards her staff would help. Alistair was overly sentimental about such people. If he saw her being snappy with Kevin or Aditha, it offended his liberal social conscience. She would be more careful in future.

Alistair stiffened. His whole body was shuddering. Elyssa crawled back up the bed, threw back the covers and lowered herself on to him.

'That's so good . . .' she sighed, her nails digging into his powerful chest. 'So . . . good.'

177

This was one of those occasions when Elyssa put on her best performance. It was in her interests to keep Alistair happy and for that she would do anything.

Elyssa wiped her mouth delicately with her napkin and replaced it on her lap. Alistair watched her; he thought she looked particularly beautiful today. She was wearing another of her suits; a short, well-cut skirt and matching bolero jacket in a fine dog's-tooth check tweed. Underneath she wore a black polo-necked sweater with a large and ornate gold and diamond brooch at her neck, and she had earrings to match. Her white skin was flawless with only the hint of colour in her fine cheeks and her lipstick was of a deep shade of plum red.

'Why are you looking at me like that?'

Her question caught him unawares. He held her hand.

'I'm sorry, I didn't realize I was being so obvious.'

'Not at all, Ali; I like it, it's very flattering.'

'Well, you do look very beautiful.'

'Thank you.'

She poured him some more coffee. 'Have you thought what we could do today?'

'I thought a visit to the National Gallery might be interesting. I haven't been there for ages. What about you?'

'Well, actually, I have some dreary fitting I have to go to. I saw this lovely dress at a show a few weeks ago and I thought it might be fun to buy it.'

'Might one ask how much?'

'You might, but I'm not sure you'd approve.'

'Go on then, shock me.'

She looked at him. He was teasing her.

'Five,' she said.

'Five? Hundred?'

Her laugh was brittle. 'No, Alistair, of course not. Thousand, silly. How on earth can I buy a haute couture dress for five hundred pounds? The idea's preposterous!'

He shook his head slowly, smiling. 'I don't know how you do it, Elyssa.'

She stood up and pecked him on the head. 'Well, you should know, Ali. Surely all solicitors know only too well the importance of money.' She lit a cigarette, apologetically. 'I'm sorry, but I just have to have one.'

'It doesn't matter.'

'How about if we meet in Manchester Square?'

'Where's that?'

'Behind Oxford Street. Given your interest in art, you might like to pay a visit to the Wallace Collection. I could meet you there if you like. About two?'

'Right, that suits me fine.'

'Can you make your own way there, darling? I really need Kevin to drive me.'

'Of course.'

'Stop looking so miserable, Kevin. It doesn't suit you.'

He opened the car door for Elyssa and she got in, gracefully crossing her long stockinged legs. She waved goodbye to Alistair who was standing on the front steps.

'How long is he staying?' Kevin looked at her through the rear-view mirror, his eyes blank.

'That is none of your business, Kevin.'

Her smile was tight-lipped. The impertinence! How dare he!

Alistair took the tube. The day was cold, clear and bright, and a brisk walk from the house to the station would do him the world of good and give him time to think.

He could kick himself. Furious with his weakness in the face of Elyssa's charms, he could no longer disguise the self-disgust that rose up from his stomach. So why did he stay? Because he couldn't help it. Elyssa fascinated him. At first he had tried to ignore her effect on him. It would pass, he told himself. Her hold on him had crept up unnoticed until it was too late to stop or do anything about it. He sighed as he put his tube ticket in his pocket. What a bloody mess! The woman he wanted was with someone else and the woman he had, he didn't want, well, not that much.

Sublimating, he decided, that's what he was doing. Redirecting his needs on to someone else and feeling thoroughly miserable as a result. He wondered how much longer it could go on.

Walking up the hill from the Embankment Tube Station he found himself in Trafalgar Square. The traffic was horrendous and the stinking air was beginning to make his eyes itch.

He climbed the steps up to the National Gallery door. He hoped that, as it was so cold and nearing lunchtime, he might be able to view the pictures in relative peace and quiet. He was wrong. It was packed. It was so different from the contemplative peace of Devon. He immediately headed off for the Turners. He had often come here and to the Tate Gallery when he was studying in Cambridge and spent many hours looking at his favourite art works. If anything would calm down the inner turmoil, *Ulysses Deriding Polyphemus* would be the one.

'This neckline doesn't suit me. I want it lowered.'

'That would be an . . . interesting idea, madame.'

The small woman, impossibly glamorous in her black Chanel, looked archly at Elyssa. Her mouth was tightly fixed in the deepest red lipstick. 'Perhaps, though, it might look a bit . . . ordinary?'

Elyssa looked at herself in the huge mirrors, the light from the chandeliers making the sequins sparkle.

'I want it lowered,' she repeated ominously.

'*Oui, madame.*'

The woman bustled round her, her quick fingers altering the bustline, a tape measure round her neck.

'And remove two of those buttons. They look ridiculous.'

'*Oui, madame.*'

Another woman walked into the room.

'Elyssa!'

'Claudia!'

They air-brushed each other's cheeks.

'And how are you, darling, after our little luncheon the other week? I was thinking that you looked a little depressed.'

'Oh really, Claudia? And what gave you that idea?'

Claudia, unable to resist the mirror any longer, turned to face it and pulled in her already flat stomach. 'Oh nothing,' she smiled, her eyes glinting with malice. 'You just looked a little . . . well,' she frowned, 'peaky, I think the word is.'

'Peaky?' repeated Elyssa, as she held out her arms for her dress to be altered. 'I look peaky?' Her voice was incredulous.

'Perhaps,' suggested Claudia, brushing some nonexistent fluff from the shoulder of her suit, 'you should go on holiday. Somewhere hot, maybe. I've always thought that redheads do terribly badly in our English winters. They look so pale and washed out.'

'Well, of course, Claudia, I bow to your superior knowledge. You are the expert on such things.'

'Rupert and I are going to Aspen, you know, in a few weeks. It will be wonderful,' she trilled, clapping her hands together like a little girl. 'He says it's a special holiday when we can be together; just the two of us. A second honeymoon.'

'Surely you're both a bit past that sort of thing?'

'Now, now, Elyssa. There's no need to be spiteful. Just because you can't get a husband . . .'

'Well, that's because some of us,' she replied tersely, 'are a bit more particular than others. Let's face it, Claudia, if you have any taste in men at all, it doesn't show. Rupert must be well past his best.'

'And how old are you?' retorted Claudia, flicking back a lock of her heavy, straight blonde hair.

The two women glared at each other's reflection as the tiny *vendeuse* continued to put pins in the dress.

'If you must know,' said Claudia, 'Rupert has just been for his annual checkup and Mr Leigh-Davidson, our consultant, says he is one of the best physical specimens for his age that he has ever seen.'

'Good God, you make him sound like a car going in for its MOT.'

'That's as may be, Elyssa, but at least I have a husband to be checked over. And,' she added, holding out her hand, 'you simply must see the ring he's just bought me.'

'No, thanks,' said Elyssa. 'Such things are of no interest to me.'

'Oh really?' laughed Claudia. 'You're so jealous, aren't you?'

Elyssa swung round, hands on hips and bristling with fury.

'Please, madame,' insisted the *vendeuse*. 'I'm trying to alter your dress!'

Elyssa stood her ground. 'Me!' she hissed. 'And why would that be?'

Claudia raised one perfectly arched eyebrow on her perfectly made-up face. Like Elyssa, she carried over the benefits of having been a top model. She looked as elegant now as she had in her twenties.

'You mean to tell me you're not, Elyssa? My goodness,' she said, holding her outstretched hand, sporting a massive collection of diamonds, against her chest, 'I don't believe it. Forgive me if I'm somewhat sceptical, my dear, but I have known you for many years and quite frankly I always thought you were just a teensy bit green eyed.'

182

'Oh yes?' Elyssa was furious now. Only Claudia could be this spiteful.

'Those two husbands of yours, Elyssa . . . Archie and whatever his name was.'

'William Hansen, the steel magnate. Surely you remember him? He was the one who rejected all your advances.'

'Oh yes, I recall him now. No taste, of course. You know,' she said stepping forward with a small smile on her lips, 'I heard some terrible rumours about him.'

Elyssa stood still, her eyes hard. She wouldn't put anything past Claudia. 'What?' she said at last.

'That he didn't have anything worth going to bed for,' whispered Claudia.

The small dark woman altering Elyssa's dress listened closely, but with her face a complete professional blank. Only the nimbleness of her fingers, which uncharacteristically dropped a pin, gave away her agitation.

'*Excusez-moi, madame.*'

'You bitch, Claudia!'

'Ah, so it's true then. Tut, tut, tut, you poor thing. How unhappy you must have been. Still, I suppose it gave you all the excuses you needed to return to your usual modus operandi.'

Elyssa was too angry to reply.

'Sleeping around,' said Claudia, with a satisfied smile. 'I hear through the grapevine you're getting desperate these days. You even, I've been told, pay for it. Is that true?'

Elyssa pulled herself up to her full height and stared at Claudia.

'How's Rupert's premature ejaculation problem?' she asked coldly. 'I always found that if you squeeze him just prior to orgasm, it generally delays things.'

Claudia's face blanched. It was rapidly followed by two bright pink spots in the middle of each cheek.

Elyssa smiled. 'Go away. I'm trying to get my dress altered,' and she laughed to herself as Claudia flounced from the room. Elyssa turned back to her reflection, her eyes as cold as the dead.

'Tell Veronique that I'll be back in two weeks and that I expect the dress to be ready then.'

'*Oui, madame.*'

The garment was removed and Elyssa's clothes were brought to her. As she got dressed, she smiled at herself. It was good to get the better of Claudia. She had become such a stuck-up creature since her marriage.

She left the building and went to find Kevin and the car. She had to raise the money to pay for that dress and only one man could help her.

'Manchester Square,' she said, getting into the back seat of the Jaguar.

She found Alistair wandering around upstairs. Standing at one end of the long room, she studied him. He was deep in thought as he walked slowly around, his hands clasped behind his back. She gave herself six months to get him to marry her. That would shut Claudia up.

'Alistair!'

He held out his arms as she walked towards him. He embraced her, kissing her on the cheek.

'Hello. Did you have a nice time with your dress?' His face was slightly ironic.

She pressed his lips. 'Now don't make fun of me, Ali.' Her eyes flickering at him coquettishly. 'I like clothes. I always have. Anyway, that dress will be worn enough times to justify its expense and it will last forever.'

He held her hand. 'Only teasing.'

They walked slowly down the room.

'How about you?' she asked. 'Did you enjoy the museum?'

'Yes, but I think I'm still a Philistine.'

'Why?'

'Well I stood in front of the Picassos and no matter what

the experts say, I'd still prefer to have an unfinished Turner on my wall than be lumbered with one of those monstrosities.'

Her high laugh echoed around the hall.

'"*The Swing*, J. H. Fragonard 1732–1806,"' he read. He stood back and admired it. 'What do you think?'

She shrugged. 'All right, I suppose. Bit insipid, I think, for my tastes.'

'I heard one of the curators telling an American couple that a certain well-known actress frequently comes here and spends many hours looking at this painting.'

'Really?' Elyssa looked closer. 'Well, perhaps it does have a certain quality to it; a lightness of touch maybe and the lighting gives the border a three-dimensional feeling.'

Alistair looked at her.

'Something wrong, darling?'

'No, no. Not at all. It's just that . . .'

'. . . I surprise you sometimes?'

He paused before answering. 'Yes.'

She squeezed his arm. 'I'm not at all sure, Alistair, that you have the right impression of me. Fickle, flippant and spoilt are adjectives that you can apply to some of my acquaintances, but they don't apply to me.'

He patted her hand which lay along his arm. 'Of course not.'

'Have you seen everything then?'

He nodded. 'Yes. Impressive, isn't it? The armour in particular. Heaven knows how they went into battle carrying that lot.'

'Well, let's go to lunch then. I'm starving. How about Harry's Bar in Mayfair. We can get a taxi.'

They collected their coats. He helped her on with her fur, gently settling it around her shoulders.

'I've really enjoyed my stay, Elyssa.'

Abruptly she turned to him. Something in his voice alerted her.

'You're not going yet, are you?'

They walked past the amiable smiling doorman into the cold fresh air.

Alistair pursed his lips and looked down at his feet as they strolled out of the drive.

'No,' he said guardedly. 'Not yet. But I will have to tomorrow.'

'Oh thank goodness for that,' she smiled, mightily relieved. 'For a minute there I thought you were going to say you had to leave now,' and her panic subsiding, she linked her arm in his. 'Let's go and find a taxi.'

Alistair smiled but his eyes didn't. For a minute, he wished he had said he was going now.

Kevin and Aditha sat opposite each other in the kitchen, their hands tightly clasped. Kevin never was one for words and tongue-tied with elation, it was all he could do to smile inanely at Aditha with a lop-sided sheepish grin. Aditha in her turn, smiled modestly back, her eyes fixed firmly on the table top. It wasn't often that a man told her how beautiful she was. Kevin's stumbling words had spread a warm glow through her insides.

'I mean it, Aditha.'

She nodded slightly. 'Yes,' and glanced up at him, her eyes sparkling.

Suddenly they stopped, their smiles vanishing. The front door had opened.

'Oh shit, she's back.' They let go of each other's hands. 'Not a word, Aditha. Not one word.'

TWELVE

Once, the isolation of the farm had been a comfort to Claire. Now she was beginning to hate it. After Matt's death, she had rearranged her life so that her days were filled with work. She reasoned that if she were busy she wouldn't have time to think about him. She was busy now but it didn't help. A whole week had gone past since her night with James and not once had he got in touch with her. No telephone calls, no letters, nothing.

At first she was puzzled. She had worked it all out so logically and had assumed that the minute he could, he would ring her. But he didn't. She then thought that perhaps there had been an accident after all and maybe he had been killed. After a day of unreasonable panic, she told herself not to be such a fool.

Coffee with Ange hadn't helped. Her words kept reminding Claire of a blunt truth she would rather not hear. Perhaps he had just wanted her in bed; perhaps Ange was right? But she couldn't believe that either. He loved her; he had said so and he wouldn't lie. Claire was convinced of it.

By the end of the week a deep cold rage had set in. She had been used and that was all there was to it. He had done exactly what he wanted and taken her for the stupid idiot that she was. She was furious with herself. How could she behave like that when normally she was so circumspect in her relations with men? He had wanted her for one thing only and the minute he had had her, he had disappeared, just as Ange said. Claire didn't know what was more embarrassing: her behaviour with James or falling out with Ange. She would have to eat humble pie.

The nights were the worst; lying awake, imagining he was there stroking and caressing her. It was nothing short of torment, the way it kept her awake. Unable to sleep, she would tirelessly walk about the house, trying to read, trying to watch TV, but always, always thinking of him.

With Matt her body had been dormant. Her meeting with James had changed everything. She was an entirely different woman, her whole senses alive with new sensations of taste, touch, sight and smell. A deep-seated need inside her newly awakened body would not leave her. Day and night, she ached to have him. He was the only answer to her need; the primitive instinct to have him again and again and again.

She had adjusted to her years of celibacy with little or no effort. She had never really enjoyed sex so it didn't matter if it were absent from her life. Now it did and she found it virtually impossible to maintain any semblance of normality when she was so unfulfilled. She sometimes touched herself, but it rarely calmed her. He was what she wanted; his hard, muscular body lying next to her and filling her up.

She was constantly on edge, irritated with herself and everything else. Even poor Rosie got shouted at and would slink under the table, mystified as to what was happening. Claire would always be repentant – Rosie was the last thing she wanted to hurt.

'Oh come here, sweetie. I didn't mean it,' and her dog would trot towards her, head down in appeasement, her tail wagging slowly. Once they had made up, it would all be forgotten – until the next time, that is.

Claire began to hate James: she wanted him, but didn't. He had betrayed her so cruelly but she still loved him. She was nothing without him.

She didn't know what she would do if she ever saw him again. It didn't bear thinking about.

* * *

She was in her greenhouse preparing the new season's bedding plants when she thought she heard a car pulling into the yard. She looked up expectantly but when the silence returned and Rosie wasn't barking, she returned to her work. She was probably just imagining it.

The greenhouse stood at the end of her long garden behind the house and as it was a grey February day, the rain falling windswept and furious against the glass, she didn't hear Alistair's footsteps. He knocked on the glass, making her start.

'Hi.'

She held her hand to her breast. 'Good heavens, Ali, you made me jump.'

He came in, Rosie following. She was, as usual, very pleased to see him.

'How are you, Claire?' He looked at her closely. She seemed pale to him, her normal fresh complexion white and drawn, her freckles standing out even more noticeably. He allowed his gaze to fall down her body. She had lost weight.

Her smile was brief. 'I'm fine.' She turned away from him and began sorting out some pots.

'Are you sure? You don't look too well to me.'

He moved closer to her. He couldn't help it. She was a magnet to him. Resistance was impossible.

'Yes, really, Alistair, you shouldn't fuss.'

'I'm sorry, I didn't mean . . .'

'No,' she sighed. 'I'm sorry. I shouldn't have snapped. Have you come for anything in particular?'

'I had to visit Jack Burrows. He was telling me about his new Charolais bull. Very proud of him, he is.' He paused. 'I just thought I'd pop in and see you that's all.'

'Oh.' She wiped her muddy hands against her jeans. 'That's nice.' She glanced at him. 'Did you see the bull as you drove past the gate?'

'Yes. He's a fine big animal, isn't he?'

'He certainly is. I shall be glad when Jack moves him. I

189

know he's a placid beast, but I'm still not sure about him being so close.'

'No, I can imagine that.' He watched her. She was nervous of him; her actions awkward and tense. She was trying to undo a bag of potting compost and getting nowhere. Just as he was about to offer some help, the plastic ripped, sending the dark mass spilling out across the table and onto the floor.

'Oh bugger it!' and she threw the bag to one side.

'Can I help?'

She held up a restraining hand. 'No, please, it's all right.'

'Are you sure you're okay, Claire?' He was worried about her. He had not seen her looking so bad and had never heard her swear before.

She turned to him, tight-lipped and ashen-faced. 'Fine, Ali. I'm just having an off day.'

He wanted to hold her so much, but his arms remained glued to his sides, his hands impotent in his overcoat pockets. What's wrong with me, he thought. All I have to do is reach out and touch her. But he couldn't. As much as he wanted to, something held him back. Something in her demeanour told him to hold fast. She was upset, very upset in fact, but she wasn't giving him any encouragement. Whatever he did, he had to be careful. He looked at his watch.

'Do you have time for a cup of tea, Claire?'

He noticed how her shoulders visibly relaxed and she looked up. She was relieved he had asked, as if his question had broken some kind of spell she was under.

'Yes, of course. How rude of me not to offer you something.' She walked up to him and stopped. When she spoke, he could see the slight tremor in her bottom lip. Her eyes were frighteningly bright. 'I'm not myself,' she whispered. 'I'm sorry. Please . . . bear with me,' and she gave a pallid smile.

He touched her arm and held it. 'It doesn't matter, Claire. Whatever it is that's bothering you, believe me, I

190

understand. Anyway,' he added with more cheer, 'I've got big enough shoulders for both of us.'

She lowered her eyes. Was it his imagination or did he detect a tear?

'I know, Ali, and I really appreciate it, but I don't think you can help me with this one.' She walked off.

He followed her across the wet grass, his mind racing. What on earth had happened? She didn't say anything until she made the tea and placed the mug in front of him. She sat opposite, both hands cupping her mug and looking out of the kitchen window into the garden. She was in no mood to hurry.

In the afternoon gloom, the room silent save for the kitchen clock, he studied her.

Something was very wrong. He didn't know what or whom it concerned, but he did know it had changed her. She looked lifeless, still and becalmed as if some terrible storm had been sweeping her along. She had never been the most extrovert person, but the difference between now and their last meeting at the farm suppliers was so extraordinary that he was very concerned for her. He put down his mug.

'Tell me, Claire, what is it? What's happened to upset you like this?' He kept his voice low. He didn't want to make matters worse.

She didn't answer but shook her head with a singular determination, her mouth shut against him.

He reached out across the scrubbed table and held her clenched fists. 'Please tell me, Claire. What is it? I'm your friend, you can trust me.'

At first her movements were so slight, he wasn't sure if he was reaching her at all, but then she turned round and faced him. The pain in her eyes almost made him gasp. He held her hand tighter. 'Oh my dear, what is it? What's going on?'

'Don't ask, Alistair, please I ... don't want to speak about it.'

'Why?'

She was adamant. 'It's . . . it's too embarrassing. I just don't want to talk about it that's all.'

'I won't be embarrassed, Claire. Nothing could embarrass me. I'm a solicitor, remember. I hear all sorts. People are always revealing their most torrid secrets to me.' He gave a small chuckle. 'I couldn't survive in my business unless I had a very thick skin and a very broad mind.'

She smiled weakly and flipped her plait over her shoulder. The misty rain had gathered in the tendrils of hair around her face so that they looked like dew-covered cobwebs.

'I know that you want to help and I really appreciate it, but this . . . well, this is different. I have to sort it out myself and there's nothing anyone can do about it.'

'Is it your money?'

'No, far from it.' She sighed heavily. 'I wish it was sometimes, and then at least I'd know who to turn to for help,' and she smiled warmly at him. 'No, it's not that.'

'Well, what then?'

She stood up and walked over to the cupboard, the eyes of both man and dog watching her intently. She got out a tin. 'Do you want a biscuit?'

He shook his head. 'No thanks.' He paused. 'You look as though you could do with some though. I've never seen you look so slim.'

She pulled her baggy jumper down. 'I'm fine, Ali,' she insisted, embarrassed that he had noticed.

'Really?'

She put the tin away without opening it and sat down again.

'So,' he said, 'apart from this thing that's upsetting you and which you won't tell me about, everything is okay, is it?'

'Yes.'

He took a sip of his tea. She could see he wanted to say

something, but was inhibited in some way. He kept fidgeting with his signet ring.

'Did Peter Collier come round that evening?' she asked brightly.

'No. In the end I went to London. I stayed with an old friend of mine. I don't know if I've mentioned her name before. She's called Elyssa Berkshire.'

'No, you haven't.'

'Well, we went out, had dinner, that sort of thing.'

'And you enjoyed it?'

'Yes,' he lied, 'very much.'

'Good. I'm glad you've found someone. What's she like?'

He smoothed his moustache. 'Tall, red-haired, slim, a few years older than me. I've known her for a number of years. She's divorced and she's good fun.'

Why am I lying, he thought. Oh Claire, she's nothing like you. She isn't soft or gentle; she's nowhere near as pretty as you and I really couldn't care less about her.

All these words and not one of them did he articulate. He despised himself.

'How about your dinner with your wonderful new neighbour?'

She shrugged. 'Okay.'

'Okay? Is that all?'

'Yes. Okay.' She looked at him and he could see immediately that she had no intention of saying anything else. The brick wall was still well and truly in place and there was no way round it. But still he tried.

'Are you going to see him again?'

She stood up and gathered together the empty mugs, which she placed in the sink. With her back to him she answered in a low voice, 'I don't know.'

That's it, he thought. All of this is because of him and his bloody good looks and cosmopolitan manners. Damn him!

'Is he around at the moment?'

193

Claire rinsed out the crockery with unnecessary force. 'I don't know. Maybe.'

She's being evasive, he thought. She doesn't want to face the fact that he might have dumped her.

'Maybe he's gone back to London,' she added. 'I don't know and I don't care. He's nothing to me.'

So, he had dumped her. No wonder she was in such a state.

'Well,' he said cheerily, 'no doubt we'll see him around soon.' It was the least offensive thing he could think to say under the circumstances.

She fixed him with a steady gaze. 'Look, Alistair, do we have to talk about him? I've got loads of other things to do, you know, apart from worry about him.'

'Of course.' He smiled. 'I'm sorry.' He felt better now, knowing that their dinner had not been the success that he feared it would be. Now that this Lamont chap had gone back to London, the way was clear again for him. He must not push it, though. Claire was clearly distressed by the whole episode and would only come round again if he took his time and moved with the utmost care. He didn't want to scare her off.

She wanted him to go. So far she had just about managed to hold back the tears. His probing about the dinner and about James was making it impossible. Only by digging her nails into her palms and by biting the inside of her mouth did she stop herself from breaking down. She couldn't bear it if he saw that. It would make him even more solicitous for her and he was bad enough at the best of times.

'I have to go and see to Jacky now.'

'Who?'

'The cow,' she said walking over to where her muddy boots stood next to the Rayburn on a piece of newspaper. 'She's having her calf soon,' she explained as Alistair followed her across the yard. Why wouldn't he go? 'Wouldn't come in if I were you,' she said. 'The stable tends to be a bit mucky,' and she pointed to his highly polished shoes.

'Oh that doesn't matter,' he replied, waving away her objections. 'I don't mind a bit of dirt. As a matter of fact, I used to work on a farm when I came home for the school holidays. My father thought it was only right that I learn how the real world ticks along and used to send me down to a nearby farm.'

Claire pushed open the stable door and walked in. If he wouldn't take a hint there was nothing she could do. Anyway, she didn't feel too bad now.

'I don't think I was ever much good at it, though.'

She ran her hand along the old cow's flank. 'Why?'

He stood in the doorway watching her. 'Well, I invariably got kicked or butted about. On one particular occasion I remember trying to get this recalcitrant beast into the milking parlour and whichever way I went, she managed to side-step me, eventually escaping back into the field.'

Claire chuckled.

'I don't think the farmer was too pleased.' Alistair was happy. She was smiling again. 'How much longer has she got?' he asked. The cow looked round at him, licking her nostrils with her long prehensile tongue.

'Not long now,' replied Claire.

'What will you do in an emergency?'

'Ring Mr Roberts, the vet, or Jack.'

'It's a pity I don't live closer,' he said. 'I helped out a number of times with the calving, and that part I enjoyed.'

'Alistair, I'm really surprised.' She looked up from mixing the cow's feed.'

'Why?'

'Well, because I just wouldn't have thought of it. I've always known you to be a "grey suit".' She went back to her mixing, then tipped the food into Jacky's trough. 'A man of unknown qualities, eh?'

He smiled modestly. 'Hardly.'

She finished up and he followed her into the yard. The rain had stopped and the all-encompassing blanket of cloud had melted away to reveal the strengthening spring sun. Puddles of water reflected the sparkling light, their colours dancing across the grey walls of the buildings.

She turned to him. 'Fancy a quick walk?'

'Why not?' He had a whole string of afternoon appointments, but nothing would have dragged him away from this.

'I'll just get my jacket,' she said, walking towards the house. Claire didn't know why she had changed her mind about Alistair. Something in his warm and caring attitude towards her had pushed its way through her defences. She was lonely – too lonely – and it was good to share his company again. Perhaps the lady in London had something to do with it, she thought, but he had changed. He was more relaxed for a start. He had never spoken to her about his childhood before. It was as if some door had been unlocked.

Alistair impatiently waited for her. This was the first time she had asked him to accompany her on a walk. It was significant. Perhaps there was an opportunity for things to change.

She came towards him, doing up her waxed jacket. 'I can't be too long away from the house.'

'Why?'

'Well, I'm expecting a phone call and I don't want to miss it.'

They walked along the lane, silently at first; Claire because she was enjoying the sun on her back and Alistair because he didn't know what to say. When he did speak, so did she. They laughed together.

'No, after you, Ali.'

'No, you first.'

'I was just going to say why here, why Devon? What made you decide to up sticks and move down here?'

'Mmm, pressure, I suppose. I was expected to follow in

196

Father's footsteps and help run his firm, but it didn't appeal to me. I spent most of my childhood and adolescence at boarding school deep in the heart of the countryside and just couldn't stomach the idea of working in London. So when I finished my training, this is where I came. What about you?'

She paused to admire a snowdrop in the otherwise bare bank.

'Well, you know about my mother and her problems. The other problem was my father. I never got on with him either. Most of the time he just ignored me and when things got so bad between Mother and me, I just left. It was the only thing I could do. I had no choice but to go and this is where I came, but when they split up, Mother came down too.'

'You have no brothers or sisters, do you?'

'No.'

'So it's just you then?'

'Yes.'

'You and Rosie.'

The dog, who was walking next to them, looked up at him and wagged her tail.

Claire stopped at a gate and looked out across the field which was full of ewes and their lambs.

'Do you suppose it will always stay like this?' he asked.

'What?'

'You and Rosie. Will it always be just the two of you?'

She looked at her hands. She had only recently taken off her wedding ring and her finger felt quite naked.

'I hope not,' she answered quietly. 'One day I would like to get married again, have some children and be like everyone else. It's just that it hasn't happened yet.' She stopped and looked away from him, screwing up her eyes against the sunlight.

He turned his back to the gate and leant against it. In doing so he had moved closer to her.

'It would have to be someone really special for me,' she

said quietly, feeling him watching her. 'Someone who I could spend the rest of my life with.'

'I suppose,' he said, giving a small deprecating laugh, 'I'm like that too. I know that when I fall in love it will be forever. Sounds clichéd, I know, but there just isn't any question about that and whoever that woman is she will be cherished and loved and wanted until the end of her days. I'm not a man who plays with people's emotions.'

Claire had turned even paler, her brow furrowed and her lips pressed tightly together. Unable to hold back the tears, they began to flow unchecked down her cheeks. She put her face in her hands and sobbed.

'Oh Alistair, what am I going to do?'

Instinctively, and without hesitation this time, he wrapped his arms around her shoulders and held her tight.

'Don't cry, my love. Shh, shh, don't cry.'

She wailed against his shoulder, her face full of pain as the tears fell. 'I'm so depressed. I just don't know what to do.'

He rocked her gently backwards and forwards, the feel of her body filling him with tenderness. She looked up at him, tear-stained and pathetic. It was then, before she could say anything, that he kissed her, the years of wanting bursting out of their restraining hold and washing through his body, warming his soul. And Claire, so lonely and vulnerable, gave way to him, responding in kind.

His lips were warm and soft against hers and the only noise he could hear was his heart thumping. If he had given in to his body's demands, he would have lain her down there and then on the wet grass and made love to her. But he didn't. She was so precious to him that he wouldn't do anything to hurt her. At long last she was his; the one and only true love of his life had finally come into being.

Claire was surprised at first. She hadn't expected him to kiss her and was even more surprised that she reacted the way she did. Despite the voice in her mind which kept telling her to stop, she was enjoying this. Then something began to happen; the animal was starting to wake up. At first she ignored it; go away, she told herself, go away! But it didn't. The need became stronger, insistent even. She pressed closer to Alistair, her whole body pushing against him, desire tearing at her insides.

Alistair responded. His breath came more quickly as he reached for the zip on her jacket. With the utmost care he pulled up her jumper and shirt and his cold hand met her warm flesh. She felt exquisite. All that time spent wondering about her, dreaming about her and here she was; in his arms and his at last.

Their kissing grew more frantic, she seemingly needing him every bit as much as he wanted her. Claire's legs began to feel weak. The effort of fighting herself was threatening to topple her. Stop it, the voice screamed. Stop it! But she couldn't. On and on the need went, stronger and stronger. If only it would stop . . .

'No!'

She pulled back breathless, her face flushed. Holding him at arm's-length she stared at him, her eyes filled with an emotion he had never seen in her before.

'Stop it, Ali, please stop it.' She shook her head, her lips full and red and half opened. 'I can't . . . no more . . . please don't make me.'

He gazed at her, her words unheard in the storm of his heart. 'What?'

'I said no, Ali. We can't do this. It's . . . it's wrong. We mustn't!'

He held her hands tightly. 'But why? What does it matter? There's only you and me. There's no one else.'

She removed his hands. This time she spoke with more calmness and control. 'You're wrong. There is someone else.'

The cold, hard stilettos of ice that inched their way around his heart left him without breath. 'What?' The word only just escaped his frozen lips.

'I said,' she replied, her voice steady, 'there is someone else. Someone I love and I can't betray him like this.'

She watched him as he turned away from her and faced the open fields. He had shrunk like a snail pulling itself into its shell.

At last, when he had control over himself, his hands gripping the gate so tightly that his knuckles had turned white, he said: 'It's him, isn't it?' His voice was distant.

'Who?'

He turned to her quickly and she could see his pain, his eyes staring at her. 'Don't play with me, Claire,' he warned. 'I'm not some stupid fool and I won't be treated like one.'

She looked away. She hadn't meant to upset him like this.

'It's that Lamont fellow, isn't it?'

Her silence was her assent.

'I thought so,' he added, standing up straight, readjusting his tie and putting his cold hands into his pockets. The silence between them continued. Claire didn't want to leave it like this. She wanted him to be her friend, not her enemy.

'I'm sorry, Ali.'

'Don't be.' He was tight-lipped. 'I've always known, I suppose, that you would never have me. It didn't matter what I did or said, it was never going to be, was it, Claire?'

She didn't answer. She felt ashamed that she was hurting him so much. This wasn't what she wanted at all.

'I'm sorry,' she repeated. It was all she could think of to say.

He reached out and touched her arm. 'Don't be,' he whispered. She looked at him with a gratitude that surpassed everything. He was forgiving her.

'Can we still be friends?' she croaked, on the point of tears yet again.

'Yes, yes, of course we can.'

'Thank God for that,' she smiled. 'It wouldn't be the same without you around.'

He smiled ruefully. 'Well, make the most of it, Claire, because I think maybe the time has come for me to move on.'

Now it was her turn to be surprised. 'Why?'

He looked at her and said, 'You know why, Claire.' He glanced at his watch. 'Time for me to go I think.'

The walk back to the yard was again in silence as they reflected on their own moods. Alistair had never felt so wretched in his life. She had been so close to him, within his reach and ready for him, and now this. The empty futile helplessness of it all depressed him beyond anything he had ever experienced.

Claire was embarrassed because she had let her desire get in the way of her good sense. She must make sure that it never happened again. Its power frightened her. She just hadn't realized how strong it was now that it had been released. So strong, in fact, that it would make her behave with total abandon with someone she didn't even love. As she walked she could feel the moist stickiness between her thighs. Oh God, another sleepless night, she thought.

They stopped by Alistair's car. Claire held out her hand. 'Goodbye, Ali.'

He looked at her hand and then up at her face. 'Must I?'

After a moment she said, 'No, of course not,' and then he kissed her; chastely on the cheek this time, his hands resting lightly on her shoulders.

'Goodbye, Claire, and thanks for the tea.'

He wanted to say much more; how he loved her, needed her, couldn't live without her, but all he was stuck with were polite banalities.

'I'll be around if you need me.'

'Thanks.'

That night was the worst Claire had known since James had left. No matter what she did nothing could calm her.

201

She scrubbed, hoovered, ironed, cooked, rode Bonny, walked Rosie again. But still she couldn't rest. As for sleep: that was unobtainable and she gave up even trying to think about it.

The physical excitement from her meeting with Alistair didn't die down at all. She was so hungry, desperately hungry.

It was James she wanted, only James, and nothing would be able to replace him. She would just have to wait.

After Alistair left the farm, he drove to the nearest pub and bought himself a bottle of whisky. He then drove to an isolated layby on the moor and proceeded, very rapidly, to get drunk. He wanted to be drunk; to be so drunk he would forget her and the pain she had caused him and the bloody awful mess it all was, and that bastard James Lamont. Just blot the whole thing out and pretend it didn't exist.

But it didn't happen that way. Her face filled his mind; her sparkling green eyes, her beautiful lips, her thick black hair.

He shook himself trying to break the spell, but it didn't work so he drank some more. She had been, was and always would be the only woman he ever loved and it was the awful certainty of that which hurt him more than anything. He carried on drinking until he finally passed out.

THIRTEEN

Alistair woke at about three in the morning feeling awful. He had a foul taste in his mouth, a thumping headache and a terrible nausea. While he had been asleep he had fallen over on his side so that he was laid across the two front seats of his car, the handbrake digging into his ribs, which now felt sore. He was also very cold.

He sat up, sending the empty whisky bottle clattering onto the floor. He grimaced in disgust: the car stank of alcohol and self-pity. Despite the biting cold wind it was a relief to open the window and breathe in the clean fresh air of Dartmoor.

As he drove back along the empty country lanes he tried not to think of what had happened. He was determined to close his mind to it; to shut it off, put it away, forget about it. It was the only way he could cope.

Bringing it out into the open and facing up to his pain and rejection would only serve to undermine his self-confidence and distract him from his work. Now that Claire had made it abundantly clear that she was not interested in him it was up to him to go out and enjoy life to its fullest. It was the least he could do. Exactly how, where and with whom he didn't know. Elyssa maybe? He rejected that idea at once. She was everything he didn't like.

He swung his Saab into George Hill. His house was near the top with superb south-facing views of the moor. This was the most desirable part of town, the big detached houses all commanding high prices when they occasionally came on to the market. Alistair had bought his soon after moving to Torhampton in the distant expectation that one day he would be getting married and raising a family. Now he was beginning to wonder if that would ever happen.

He put his car in the garage and walked across the crunching gravel to the imposing front door. All was quiet. The wind had died and the temperature dropped further, its cold tentacles finding their way into every cranny. He was freezing but not so much that he couldn't go in without first looking up at the pitch-black sky and wondering at its dusting of bright stars. He then turned away abruptly, his eyes beginning to smart. Such sentimentality was quite ridiculous, he told himself.

Angrily wiping his face dry, he stepped inside and pulled the door shut with a purpose.

After a hot shower he fixed himself a tray of soup and some French bread and cheese, and sat in his study in the soft light of a lamp in front of a roaring fire. He still felt rough, but not as bad as he had. He didn't try going to bed. He knew he would only lie there, awake and restless and unable to relax. Far better to stay up and do some work, at least then his mind would be occupied and he wouldn't have time to think.

He finished his meal and, cupping his hands around a mug of hot tea, he put his feet up on a low stool and laid his head back against the chair. Peace at last.

Claire; Claire: always she came back to him. Was he to be haunted for the rest of his days?

He finished his tea and stood up. On his antique writing desk lay numerous files from work that he really ought to look at. With a half felt sense of guilt, he sat down to work on them. If they didn't put him to sleep, nothing would.

Two hours later and he had had enough. He snapped shut the last file and pushed them all to one side. Wearily he rubbed his eyes. He ought to go to bed and try to get some sleep, but looking at his clock it hardly seemed worth while. It was getting on for six.

He opened the desk drawer to put his pen away and his

eyes fell on his photograph of Claire. When not at work he kept it in here, because his cleaning lady was apt to gossip and he didn't want anyone to know about it. He picked it up, delicately, as if it were made of the finest china. Holding it in both hands, his fingers caressing the silver frame, he studied it. No matter how often he looked at it, it never ceased to hold his attention. She was beautiful then in her wedding finery and was beautiful now, in her scruffy jeans. Although the photograph was now eight years old, time hadn't diminished it or Claire. If anything, she looked better now. Her loss and suffering had strengthened her, made her more resistant, but at the same time more vulnerable. He had seen all of that the previous afternoon. He sighed, kissed the photograph and carefully put it away. He still loved her.

Unlike Alistair, Elyssa was asleep, but only just. She too had spent most of the night restlessly awake, tossing and turning in her silken bed, increasingly desperate. Sleep only came when she gave in to her misery and swallowed two white sleeping pills with a large tumbler of whisky. She wasn't pleased with her behaviour, having sincerely promised herself that she wouldn't drink or take any more pills. But in the end, she knew she had no choice. As soon as the pills were down and drink finished, the slight tremor in her hands disappeared and she felt much better.

'See,' she said to herself. 'All I needed was a little drink. I can manage it. I'm not a drunk.'

She replaced the pill bottle in her bathroom cabinet and smiling happily to herself, padded across the carpet to her bed. She would sleep soon and she needed that so much. The last week had been awful: so depressing and such hard work. She had hardly got any rest at all.

After Alistair's departure and another threatening letter from the bank, she had thrown herself into a strict régime of aerobics, health foods, manicures and a hair cut. She felt exhausted but insufferably pleased with herself. Wait till Alistair sees me the next time she thought, he won't want to go home again: she would make sure of it. Except that Alistair didn't call. The telephone remained resolutely silent.

She went shopping, something she did with little interest or need, spending huge sums of money on a completely new wardrobe. Like some highly whipped ice cream, it satisfied her for a short time. Then her anxiety returned, nagging at her with an unspoken truth that maybe he wasn't coming back; perhaps she had lost her touch. Her panic increased.

She went to a small dinner party but didn't hear what the other guests said to her. She even overcame a lifetime's abhorrence and accepted an invitation to the opera. Her date for the evening was a handsome and wealthy German, blond and blue-eyed, and over on a short business trip. Under normal circumstances she would have enjoyed him, flirting with him and charming him into her bed with little or no effort. But not now. She wasn't interested.

She tolerated the first half, clapping politely at all the right places, but as soon as the interval came, she deliberately lost him in the bar and made her escape. She couldn't put up with it any longer.

Back at her house she stood by the phone, willing it to ring. If she truthfully faced the reality of her situation – her impending bankruptcy, her passing years and fading beauty – she would have panicked even more. What was really at stake was her pride. She found it inconceivable that any man could turn his back on her. She intended to prove to herself and all her so-called 'friends' that she could still have whoever she wanted and Alistair was who she wanted now. If Claudia could get Rupert and his millions, she would get Alistair and his.

But all the time, her irritation grew. Stalking the house like a caged tigress, she impatiently snarled at her staff, picking arguments with both of them. Nervous of her unpredictability and lack of self-control, Kevin and Aditha maintained a low profile. They did what was expected of them and no more. It all came to a head on Thursday.

She was angry. Her bank manager had rung her personally, requesting her presence as soon as it was convenient for her. She had pleaded illness and managed to fob him off. On top of that, the wine merchant apologized for not completing her order, but had given her all the outstanding bills she owed him, demanding immediate payment. He was unable to oblige her any more.

After spending most of the morning on the telephone, shouting at her accountant and stockbroker, she had a blazing headache. She was also sexually very frustrated. Since Alistair left she had done nothing in bed except sleep and only then fitfully. She didn't visit Kevin, nor had she had anyone else, preferring to turn down the one other opportunity, and she was beginning to notice it.

She started thinking about Kevin at lunchtime. She had spent the morning at Harvey Nichols trying on some new clothes and had enjoyed the sensation of dressing and undressing in the cubicle. The curtain was not quite drawn and the young dark-haired assistant was watching her closely. Elyssa was no lesbian, but she liked to be admired and the look on that woman's face was one of sheer admiration. Lust was pouring out of her and wafting over to Elyssa who did what she always did when someone wanted her; played up to it.

She ran her fingers slowly through her hair and then down over her bust, aware of how the nipples were standing erect through the flimsy silk of her shirt. The assistant's eyes widened, the dark brown of her irises following every move. When Elyssa pulled down the skirt she was trying on and stepped out of it, she began to trace the edge of her lace panties with her fingers until she reached her crotch. The assistant openly stared. Then suddenly another customer came in and the assistant reluctantly dragged herself away to see to her. Elyssa smiled. She had enjoyed that.

When she got back to the car, she looked at Kevin's neck thoughtfully. It had been a long time. An afternoon might be fun. She decided she wouldn't tell him about it. She would just turn up.

'Home, please, Kevin.'

He looked up, surprised, in the rear-view mirror. She hadn't said please for days.

She took her time getting ready. A long luxurious bath using some of her favourite bath oil was followed with an all-over application of body lotion. She combed her hair, made up her face and dressed herself in an ivory-coloured raw silk kimono. A spray of perfume behind her ears and on both wrists and she was ready. She stood in front of her full-length mirror and looked at herself. It pleased her very much.

It was not until she got down into the basement that she realized how quiet the house was. No Aditha, no Kevin, no music; nothing. Aditha was probably out somewhere with her Filipino friends, and Kevin asleep.

She walked briskly down the short corridor to his room, tingling with anticipation, and opened his door.

Those brief moments while her eyes adjusted themselves to the gloom would be remembered by Elyssa with startling clarity. They were the moments of her final self-delusion and beyond them she would no longer have the self-confidence of her appearance or imagined wealth.

Aditha and Kevin were both naked and in the act of making love, their legs and arms grotesquely entwined around each other, her brown skin contrasting sharply with his blondness.

The three of them froze. Caught in time like a photograph, but not smiling, their looks were ones of horrified embarrassment and instant rage.

'You bloody bitch!' screamed Elyssa. 'You fucking

She pulled away from him and helped herself to a tissue from a box on her bedside table.

'She made you do it, didn't she?'

He looked at her with puzzlement.

'Don't lie to me, Kevin. I heard her. I always do, she makes sure of it.' Her large brown eyes looked at him with gentle understanding accusation. 'I know what she like, Kevin, and you can't lie to me.' She clasped his hand, her small delicate brown one around his large white one.

He looked down at their entwined fingers, ashamed of himself and nodded. 'Yes.' When he looked back at her, her eyes had filled with tears again and her mouth wavered dangerously. 'But it doesn't mean anything. Honest,' he pleaded. 'She makes me do it.' He looked away across the room and added quietly, 'I don't want to do it. I want . . .' He was embarrassed and smiled awkwardly. 'I want you. You're the one I fancy. Christ, what bloke wouldn't?' He smiled, his eyes gentle. 'I've never felt like this about anyone before. Do you believe me?'

She kissed his massive hand. 'Yes,' and her breath was warm against his skin.

'I know,' he said, more hopeful now. 'You can go and stay at me mum's. She won't mind really. She's got a house in King's Lynn. Nothing special, just a council place, but she'll have you. You can stay there until I come and get you.'

She put a lock of her thick glossy hair around one ear. 'You very sweet, Kevin.'

He stood up and pulled her to him, lifting her bodily off the ground in a bear hug, grinning broadly.

'Don't worry. I'll take care of you. We'll get the old bitch back, won't we?' and they kissed.

Back in her bedroom, Elyssa, who had tried to cut down on her drinking recently, had such an overwhelming need for alcohol, that the pain was physical.

She looked at herself in her dressing-table mirror. Once she had got over the shock of those two . . . and here she shivered in revulsion . . . in bed together, it had been quite enjoyable. Kevin wasn't perhaps his usual enthusiastic self, but that didn't stop her from having fun. Elyssa liked that. It showed the boy appreciated who paid his wages.

She wasn't too sure about his taste for Aditha; she was so dark. Elyssa had never liked dark skin and unlike some of her friends who found such things attractive, she had always steered clear of them. Still, each to their own and she could hardly expect Kevin to have discriminating taste.

She picked up her tortoiseshell comb and ran it through her hair. The need for alcohol was passing now. She knew it would eventually. All she had to do was to find something else to think about and then it subsided. She smiled at her reflection. Aditha off her hands and Kevin back where he should be. The only thing that blighted her horizon was Alistair. If he didn't ring some time during the next twenty-four hours then she would contact him. She had been invited to a fancy dress party at the weekend and it would be fun to take Alistair along, especially as the party was given by Claudia and her decrepit old Rupert. Alistair's presence would certainly wipe the smile off her arch-rival's face.

Alistair was woken up by his cleaner prodding his arm.

'Mr Kingston . . . Mr Kingston . . .'

'Uh . . . yes?' He woke up with a jerk. 'Sorry? What's the time?'

'Eight forty-five, Mr Kingston.'

'Oh dear.' He got to his feet and immediately winced. Sleeping in his chair and lying with his head at an awkward angle for the last two and a half hours had made his neck sore. He rubbed it. Mrs Tucker smiled affectionately at him. She was a large jovial woman who radiated practical good sense and maternalism.

'Want me to make you some tea, Mr Kingston?'

Alistair was hurrying towards the door. 'Oh would you? And some toast, if you don't mind? I'm absolutely starving.'

'Of course.'

When he came back down from his shower, still doing up his tie, Mrs Tucker turned around from the sideboard in the kitchen and placed the plate of toast on the table.

'You sure you're all right, Mr Kingston? You don't look too good to me. Perhaps you should take the day off.'

Alistair picked up a piece of toast and began to eat it.

'No, really, I'm fine, Mrs T. I've just got an awful lot of work on at the moment and I was very tired last night . . .'

She poured the tea and placed a cup in front of him.

'Can I have next week off, please, Mr Kingston?'

'Oh, something nice?'

The dimples in her cheeks grew larger. 'Well, it's my son's wedding that weekend and I'd like some time off to get the final arrangements made.'

'Well, I don't see why not. Big affair, is it?'

'Oh yes, all the relatives are coming. My brother Jack is letting the young ones use one of his barns for the disco afterwards.'

'Is that Jack Burrows who owns the farm next to Tor Heights?'

'Yes that's right. Do you know him then?'

'Yes, I've just done some work for him. Do you see him often?'

'Often enough for him to keep me up to date with the gossip.' She smiled at him with an extra sparkle of delight as though she had a particularly juicy morsel to impart to him.

'And what gossip is this, Mrs T.?'

He rarely listened to anything she told him and only ever asked out of politeness, but as soon as she mentioned Claire's name his ears pricked up. He tried to keep his demeanour as indifferent as possible. He didn't want to give anything away.

'Well,' she began, sitting down next to him with her mug of tea. 'He told me that his lodger, that chap from London, entertained Claire Bromage for more than just dinner.' She sat back, pleased with herself, waiting for Alistair to ask her to go on. He didn't. 'I always thought that girl was just a bit too innocent-looking. Honestly, fancy spending the night with that man and he's only been here two minutes. Just goes to show, you never can tell what people are really like.'

'Really? And Jack saw all this did he?'

Alistair's heart was thumping and his appetite had vanished.

'Yes. He was up and about seeing to his cows when he saw that hussy leaving Briar Cottage in the morning.'

Alistair turned away from her and drank his tea, anything to distract him from wanting to smash Mrs Tucker's self-satisfied face into the table. How dare she speak of such things and with such gloating smugness? She and Jack and some of the rest of the locals infuriated him with their narrow minds and blinkered outlook on life. So what if Claire had spent the night with him? It didn't matter: it was none of their business. But he knew they wouldn't see it like that. All over town they would have discussed it and chewed it over, dissecting out every last bit of titillation until the next rumour hit the streets.

He finished his tea and wiped his mouth on his napkin. He stood up and smiled. 'I have to go to work now.' He kept his voice deliberately calm, to camouflage his real feelings.

Mrs Tucker looked deflated. It was a waste of time telling him anything. He never took any notice of it.

'All right then. I'll see you tomorrow.'

He went to his study and shut the door behind him. He turned on his stereo. When a particularly loud bit of Verdi's *Requiem* blasted through the speakers, he started to hammer the back of his chair with all his might.

Ignoring the pain, he pounded and pounded and

pounded, his rage, frustration and despair bursting up through him like a long-dormant volcano.

'How ... much ... more?' he asked himself. 'How much more?'

FOURTEEN

A car pulled up. Claire methodically took off her rubber gloves and laid them on the draining board. She undid her apron and hung it up. A few days ago she would have rushed out to see if it were James; but not now. She had long passed the time when her heart started beating faster every time she heard an engine. Her renewed cynicism had seen to that.

She could hear Rosie barking furiously, so it must be a stranger. She went to the back door and opened it.

A large saloon car sat in the middle of the yard. Expensive and sleek, it seemed entirely out of place in the rural surroundings. Its pristine paintwork was splattered with fresh mud which brought a satisfied smile to her lips. Serves him bloody well right, she thought. Damned cheek, coming up here! Who the hell did he think he was?

The unfortunate object of her mental scorn and derision was Philip Neale, property developer, acquirer of land and to her mind a totally unscrupulous creep who would stoop to any level to get what he wanted. And what he wanted was her field. She decided to string him along a bit. It would be fun.

The driver's window glided down smoothly and Neale poked out his bearded face.

'Can't you call that animal of yours off?'

'Why? She's only doing what she's supposed to do and that's guard me and my property from unwanted intruders.'

He gave a small ingratiating smile. 'Please, can't you do something?'

Rosie stood her ground about four feet from the car

door and barked furiously. She was wagging her tail and enjoying the game. He looked at her with concern.

'Why what's the matter, Mr Neale? Are you frightened?'

He pursed his lips and scowled angrily. 'I'm not frightened,' he insisted, 'but I don't see how we can have a civilized conversation if that . . . that,' and he pointed an indignant finger, 'if that animal isn't put in a barn or something.'

Claire didn't move. 'Who said anything about a civilized conversation?' Her words were tinged with sarcasm. 'I thought everything that had to be said, had been said, Mr Neale, through our solicitors. I had no idea there was anything else to discuss.'

'Well, I think there is.' He went to open the door and had one leg out when he hastily retreated. He was getting angry, his round face quite pink with irritation. 'Please, Mrs Bromage, can't you do something?'

'Oh all right, if I must.' She called Rosie. 'Come here, girl.' The dog looked round at her. 'Rosie, Mr Neale doesn't like being barked at because it frightens him, so be a good girl and come here.'

Rosie gave Neale a final blast and then trotted over to her mistress.

'Good girl. Now, in the house.'

With Rosie out of the way she said, 'Right then, Mr Neale, what is it you want?'

'Well,' he said, smiling once more with relief. He got out of the car and promptly placed a well-shod foot into a fresh pile of dung. 'Bloody hell!'

Claire smirked.

He looked up at her sharply and said, 'Sorry, dear, a gentleman should never swear in front of a lady.'

Some gentleman, she thought. He was such an irritating little man. Smaller than her but twice as broad, just about the only hair he had on his head was his thick luxuriant beard that covered the bottom half of his face and hid his immensely thick lips. His small hooded eyes twitched nervously from side to side as he spoke, pricing up his environment. He sweated profusely, whether from greed or fear she wasn't sure, but she noticed how he had a small tremor which seemed to increase the closer she got to him. Her bile rose at the sight of him. He stood for everything she despised.

'Well, I'm listening. What do you want?'

He smiled greasily. 'I just thought we could talk.'

'About what?'

'Please,' he said, 'you're not making this easy for me. Can't we go in and perhaps have a cup of tea?'

She shook her head. 'I only have friends in the house.'

His smile faded.

'Tell you what,' she added brightly. 'I have to move some hay bales. You can come in and help me if you like.' She moved off towards the barn not waiting for him. He followed her to the door, carefully picking his way through the detritus of the yard.

'Better take that overcoat off,' she advised. 'Moving bales can be a fairly dirty operation and we wouldn't want that expensive item to get messed up now, would we?'

'Oh okay.' He undid it revealing his flowery silk waistcoat. 'Where shall I hang it?' he asked looking around.

'Just put it there,' she said, pointing to an old gate propped up against one wall. He looked warily at it before brushing off some cobwebs and rust. He thought better of removing some dried chicken dung and managed to find a clean bit where he lay his coat. He brushed his hands together to clean off the dirt.

'Well then, what do you want me to do?'

Claire had climbed to the top of the stack where he couldn't see her. She appeared at the top heaving a bale. 'Here!' She dropped it off the edge.

It landed dangerously close to him and he stepped backwards a few paces. She watched him, amused.

'Right then, Mr Neale, what is it you've come all this way to discuss?'

He wiped his perspiring forehead and looked up at her. 'Please call me Philip, all my friends do.'

'Okay, Mr Neale, what is it?' She turned her back on him and disappeared again.

'I thought we might come to a friendly . . . um, arrangement, you know, one that would satisfy both our requirements.'

'I can't hear you!' she shouted.

'I said,' he repeated, 'we might come to an arrangement.'

She dropped another bale in his direction. 'Is that so? And what gave you that idea?'

He picked himself off the barn floor and brushed some hay off his trousers.

'I thought my solicitor told your solicitor what you could do with your arrangement, Mr Neale.'

'Ah yes, but that was before your neighbour, Mr Burrows, agreed to sell.'

She turned away. She didn't want him to see how she felt about that.

'You see,' he added, 'I now own nearly all the land that I need in order to build my exclusive estate.'

'Designer rabbit hutches, you mean.'

'My exclusive estate,' he reiterated, forcing a smile, 'and all I need is your co-operation to finalize the details. Now I know that the farmers round here are really suffering in this recession, especially the moorland ones who never do that well, even in the best of times. If you sold me Orchard Meadow, and for a very good price, I might add, then I'm sure that you could make a very tidy sum of money. Whatever objections you have to my scheme, Mrs Bromage, I'm sure I could lay them to rest provided you will listen to me.'

Another bale descended, this time only just missing him. Claire appeared, hands on hips and tight-lipped with anger.

'I don't give a damn what my neighbours do with their

219

land – that's their business – but I'm not going to sell, Neale.' She glared at him with utter disdain. 'You can offer me whatever you like, it won't make any difference. I'm not selling. Okay?'

He thought for a minute and then said: 'But people have to live somewhere. All I'm doing is providing them with homes. Surely you can see the logic of that?'

She stood at the top with another bale at her feet. Neale stepped back.

'No, I don't. You see, Mr Neale, you're not providing homes for the locals who are the real inhabitants of this place; you're providing houses for the incomers, people like you who come down here loaded with money and buy up everything they can get their grubby little mitts on, thereby pushing up the price of ordinary accommodation beyond the reach of the locals. And don't give me that rubbish about doing a service to the community because you're not. The only service you're doing is providing yourself with a bigger profit.'

'But isn't that what business is about?' he asked. 'You're a business woman, surely you recognize the sense of that. Your neighbours do, even if you don't. And anyway, you're no local either, so what gives you the right to criticize?'

'I may not be a real local,' she retorted, 'but only because I wasn't born here. I married a local and I work just as hard as any of them and like I said before, what my neighbours do is their business. I've made up my mind and I'm going to stick to it.'

'But what's all this,' he said, waving his short arms around, 'if not to make a profit?'

'But that's the difference, Neale,' she said, pointing an accusing finger at him, 'I make what little I do to exist; you make a fortune by exploiting others.'

He jutted out his chin with defiance. 'I resent that accusation very much, young lady.'

220

'Tough!' and she pushed the bale at him. He dodged to one side.

'I intend to build on that land, you know. I already have possible planning permission.'

Claire reappeared. She was simmering with a deep rage. 'You have what?'

'I said I have planning permission.' He smiled in triumph. 'I've consulted the town planning office and made contact with a number of councillors and they all seem to agree with me that Torhampton could only benefit from such a development.'

'Been greasing palms then, have you? Taking some of the old codgers out to lunch and flattering them with your oily charm so that you can get your way?'

'Now look here, Mrs Bromage, I didn't come here to be insulted by you. I came here to talk business.' His small eyes hardened and nearly disappeared into the folds of well-indulged skin around his brows.

'No, you came here uninvited and I'll say what I want to uninvited pests like you.'

She climbed athletically down the stack, jumping the last few feet and landing in front of him. 'You're wasting your time, Neale, and mine too. I have better things to do than stand here and listen to you prattling on.'

She turned and walked out of the door. He hesitated and then ran after her with short podgy steps.

'Okay, okay,' he said, breathing hard, 'perhaps I haven't exactly gone about things the right way and I apologize for that.'

Claire stopped and faced him. 'You've left your coat behind and you have horse shit all over your shoes.'

He looked down and swore. Claire was sure she heard him say something derogatory about country yokels as he turned away. In his absence she quickly ran to the back door and let Rosie out. She then ambled nonchalantly over towards his car. Rosie began to bark. When Neale

221

returned, struggling to put on his coat, flustered and bad-tempered, he eyed Rosie with caution, side-stepping away from her.

Claire stood smiling benignly with her hands in her pockets.

'Don't worry about her,' she said. 'She only bites if I tell her to.'

He reached his car with obvious relief as Rosie ran around him, playing with his feet. He climbed in and slammed the door in her face.

'You haven't heard the last from me, young lady,' he shouted through the window.

She walked over to him and leant down. 'Get lost, Neale, and don't ever come back.'

He angrily turned the ignition and reversed quickly across the yard, his rear bumper hitting a pile of steaming manure. She smiled as he skidded away, his tyres screeching.

'What a wally, eh, Rosie?' The dog wagged her tail and the pair of them went into the house.

That afternoon, when Claire was out hunting for eggs, she heard another car pull up. She was crouched down between two straw bales, trying to dislodge a malevolent, beady-eyed chicken from her clutch, when Rosie started barking again. She stood up and climbed out from between the musty bales.

'Oh who can it be this time?' She was angry. She had been annoyed ever since Neale's visit and no amount of hard work could relieve it. Already depressed and upset over James, the last thing she needed was any more unexpected visitors. If it was that bloody Neale back again, she would get really angry.

She climbed down the stack and stepped out of the barn into the weak spring sunshine. James was standing next to his red Porsche: suave and elegant, his arms were folded across his chest as he leant back against the door.

'Hello.'

Claire didn't reply, but stood quite still looking at him.

'Well,' he said, opening wide his arms, 'aren't you pleased to see me?'

She still said nothing, anger and surprise paralysing her. He waited.

'Go away, James,' she said coldly.

'Pardon?'

'I don't want you here. Go away.' Her voice was flat and without emotion. She turned away from him and headed towards the house.

'But, Claire . . .'

She rounded on him fiercely. 'Don't you "Claire" me!'

He came towards her, repentant and cajoling, his hands asking her. 'Please, Claire, listen to me. I can explain. I did try to phone, you know.' He put one hand lightly on her shoulder. She pushed it away with considerable force.

'Get lost, James. I'm not interested in your excuses. All I know is that you left me without any explanation.' Her voice was starting to tremble. 'Do you have any idea how much you hurt me?'

He removed his hand.

'Well, do you?' she shouted. 'I sat here night and day for the past week waiting to hear something, anything, ready to believe whatever you said . . . and what happens?' The tears welled up. 'Nothing. Absolutely bloody nothing!'

'Please, Claire, I'm sorry. Okay, I didn't mean it to happen. I just couldn't get through.' He tried to put his arms around her but she pushed him aside again.

'Go away, just go away! I can't believe anything you say any more.'

His hands hung limply by his side and he looked at her helplessly. 'Won't you at least hear what I have to say?'

'Why?'

'Because it's important, Claire.'

She impatiently brushed her wet eyes and stood up straight. She wasn't going to give him the satisfaction of

223

seeing her cry. When she had collected herself her voice was much colder.

'I don't like it when people take advantage of me, Mr Lamont, especially when it's done with such professional ease. God!' she exploded 'Was there ever a woman as stupid or . . . or as gullible as me that night?' She turned away from him in disgust at herself. 'You had me there in the palm of your hand, didn't you, like some little Miss Innocent from the sticks? You used that charm of yours to get me exactly where you wanted me and then . . . then when you return a week later after saying – do you remember that, James? – saying that you would come and see me again, you turn up as if nothing had happened!' She glared at him wide-eyed and furious, her face white with rage. 'I don't believe you could be so bloody selfish.'

'Claire . . . please.'

'Shut up, James!' she snapped. 'I haven't finished.'

'But if I could just explain – '

'Explain what? That you had someone else to see to? Some other lonely widow that needed seducing? What, James? What was it you were doing that needed so much time and attention that you couldn't be bothered to ring me? And don't give me that crap about not getting through. This is Devon, you know. Not the other side of the moon.'

'But I did ring, Claire,' he protested, 'honestly.'

She didn't wait for his reply but walked off. 'Come on, Rosie, let's leave this stupid man.' She looked back over her shoulder.

'Go back to where you belong, James, because I don't ever want to see you again,' and the pair of them left him standing in the yard. It was only when she had shut the door behind her that she gave way to her tears.

'You bastard . . . you bloody bastard!'

Her crying continued as her legs buckled and she slid down the door until she was sitting on the floor. She hugged her knees and buried her face in her arms. Rosie came to sit next to her and watched closely. Occasionally she whined.

James went back to his car, got in and stared thoughtfully through the window. He had badly miscalculated – very badly – and this was going to take a great deal of hard work before he got his plan back on line. No matter what she had said, he knew he would get round her again. Her little outburst was, of course, to be expected.

It was wrong of him to be so complacent when he arrived. He should have been more apologetic, brought flowers or something. Then when she had first come out of the barn, he could have softened her, maybe deflected some of her wrath. As it was, he was quite surprised by her reaction. She had a strong will and quite a pretty little temper on her too. He would do well to watch that in future.

He then smiled to himself. If she had reacted so strongly to him, that only meant one thing: he had got to her. And, if he had got to her then he could get round her. Simple really. Her indifference would have been far more difficult to cope with. Then he really would have problems.

He picked up his car phone. 'Directory enquiries, please.'

When he had finished his call he started the car and drove off. He was feeling quite jolly now and was in a much better mood.

From her bedroom window, with deep unhappiness, Claire watched him leave. It was no good lying to herself any more. She loved him and seeing him again so unexpectedly had brought back all those deep-seated feelings. Once again, she had caught his scent; again her body was drawn towards him, aching for his touch, and again she felt complete misery at his going. Why then, didn't she run after him and stop him? Because her pride prevented her. He had made her suffer; now it was his turn. If she had to spend the next few weeks, months or years getting

225

over him, then she would, because no man who treated her like that would get away with it. She had had enough humiliation, and she wasn't going to have any more.

Rosie was lying on the floor waiting for her. Claire knelt down and stroked her.

'You don't know how lucky you are, girl; these damned emotions of ours. They get in the way of everything.'

Rosie stood up and licked her face.

She was having tea when there was a knock on the door. She looked up tiredly from her baked potato.

'Who the hell can that be?'

Rosie barked.

'In your basket, you, and stay.' The dog reluctantly did as she was told.

Claire opened the door. It was James holding before his face a huge bouquet of flowers.

'For you, madam.'

She wanted to shut the door on him; slam it in his face, tell him to go away, shout and scream at him, but in an instant it all melted like the morning mist.

'Oh James!'

He opened his arms and the pair of them embraced. This time her tears were ones of relief. He kissed her, once more igniting her fire.

'I'm sorry, darling.'

'Me too. I shouldn't have shouted.'

'It doesn't matter.'

'I love you.'

'I love you too.'

'We're squashing the flowers.'

'Don't care . . . I love you.'

She took the bouquet from him and placed them on a dresser next to the door. And still they kissed, keen memories being brought back into focus as they held on to each other, tighter and tighter, as if releasing their embrace would be their end.

'It's cold . . . let's go in,' he whispered.

They stepped backwards over the threshold, still kissing. Unseen by either of them, Rosie sat up on her blanket and began to growl. They ignored her.

'Upstairs,' he whispered, his voice urgent.

'No, too cold. Sitting room. The fire's lit.'

Holding her hand he shut the door on Rosie and led her next door. They stood in front of the roaring fire, bathing in its orange warmth. He held both her hands and looked deep into her eyes.

'I have missed you so much,' he told her. 'I didn't think that it was possible to love someone like this.' He smiled briefly, a little sadly.

She stepped forward and kissed him like a child. 'It is possible. I know, because I feel it too.'

He held her face in his hands.

'Claire . . . Claire . . . Claire.'

Sprawled across the rug, hot and weary she lay in his arms.

'That was wonderful . . . really wonderful.'

He kissed her forehead. 'I thought so too.'

Silence.

'I love you, James.'

He squeezed her tight. 'Love you.'

A log cracked, throwing out a spark.

'We'd better get dressed,' she said.

'No. Let's lay here for a while and relax.'

'When did you ring me, James?'

'Just after you left,' he mumbled, 'after our wonderful night together.'

'So it was you then,' she muttered.

'You were in?'

She looked away into the fire, too embarrassed to face him. 'Yes,' she answered, her voice low.

'So why didn't you answer?'

'I was . . .' she shrugged. 'I was in the bathroom. I

thought it might be you, but by the time I got downstairs, you had rung off.'

He smiled and kissed her, a small peck on the end of her nose. 'Silly girl,' he teased. 'I wanted to say how much I had enjoyed myself and how, well,' he sighed, 'how much I loved you.'

'Why did you leave so suddenly?' She watched him as he pushed back his dark hair. His brow was furrowed and all the happiness had drained from his face.

'Problems,' he said.

'Problems?'

He nodded. 'I can't explain, Claire. It's a long and complicated story.' He seemed subdued and suddenly very tired.

'You're worried, James; what's going on?'

He kept his eyes shut and smiled. 'Nothing, darling, don't worry about it. There's nothing you can do.'

She started to pick at the rug. 'Is it something to do with your work?'

'Don't worry, Claire. I can handle it.'

'But I do worry,' she insisted. 'You tried to tell me this afternoon, didn't you, only I wouldn't listen.' She paused. 'Can't you tell me now?'

He opened his eyes and smiled, a soft gentle smile. 'No. It's neither the time nor the place.'

'Later then?'

'Maybe.'

She lay back down again, reassured. For a while they listened only to the fire, its heat warming their bare skin.

'There is something I want to say, Claire.'

'Yes?'

He hesitated.

'You're probably going to think me a bit presumptuous.'

'So?'

He hesitated further.

'What is it, James?'

'Well . . . given that we love each other, agreed?'

'Yes.'

'And given that . . . well, apart from this afternoon's little hiccup, that we get on very well.'

'Yes?' She sat up now, intrigued.

'Well,' he said, holding her hand, 'I was wondering . . . could we possibly make this a more permanent arrangement?'

Her stomach turned over. He couldn't really have said what she thought he had said. 'What did you say?'

'I said how would you like this to be a more permanent arrangement?'

'You're joking!' she stared at him, wide-eyed.

He shook his head. 'No, I'm not. I never joke about things as serious as this.' He watched her face as it slowly registered his words, her disbelief gradually giving way to pure joy.

'You mean . . . get married?' Her eyes shone.

He shrugged. 'Eventually. Why not?'

She threw her arms round his neck. 'Oh, James! I'm so happy! This is wonderful!'

He held her close and kissed her.

'Of course,' he added, 'you might not want me when you get to know me better.'

'Rubbish! Of course I will. I love you, don't I?'

When they made love again, Claire knew all her dreams had come true.

'What's it like, living in London?' She poured the hot water into the teapot.

James thought for a moment. 'Where I live isn't too bad. The streets are clean, the houses large and spacious and outside, in the square, is a private area of garden that is strictly kept for residents. There's a couple of tennis courts and a play area for the kiddies. I wouldn't mind my children growing up in such a place.'

He watched her closely as she sipped her tea. 'You would like it as well. It's near all the main shops – Oxford

Street and Knightsbridge. You'd find plenty of things to do during the day and then, in the evenings, we could visit the theatre, go and visit my friends.' He cupped her hand in his and said in a low voice, 'Or simply stay in and make love.'

She smiled briefly. Children? Houses? Since his proposal she had been running on autopilot; aware of everything she was doing, but numbed with a dizzy excitement. It was hard for her to maintain a semblance of normality and common sense. She stared vacantly at the table. He spoke for some minutes.

'Claire, are you listening to me?'

'Pardon?'

'I said what about the farm; what are you going to do about that?'

'Don't know. Sell it, I suppose.' She helped herself to another slice of cake. 'Still, it's not as if we'll need the extra money.'

He frowned. 'Why?'

'Well, as we're getting unofficially engaged now, I suppose I can tell you.' She paused, uncertain of what to say next. When it came, the words poured out hurriedly, tumbling over each other in her excitement. 'I'm loaded, rich. I've got pots of the stuff sitting in the bank. Some distant relative that I'd never met left it to me a few weeks ago.' Seeing his look of astonished surprise she added, 'I was wondering what I was going to do with it.'

He held both her hands and kissed them. 'Claire, that's wonderful! It really is.' He gave a relieved chuckle. 'What with all the problems I have at work, I can't tell you what a relief it is to have some good financial news for a change. And so unexpected.'

'What problems?'

He stopped, sat back and looked down, almost ashamed. 'Nothing. It doesn't matter, but it was why I didn't call you as often as I could have done.' He shrugged it off with a weak smile.

'And you're not going to tell me?'

He shook his head. 'No. Maybe later when it's all sorted out. I'm nearly there as it is, so don't concern yourself. Anyway, we don't want to talk about such boring and depressing things like work when we're together, especially on a day as important as this.'

'Why?'

He reached into his pocket and withdrew a small heart-shaped blue velvet box. 'Forgive me again for being so forward, but I brought this for you. I hope it fits.'

She opened it. Inside was a diamond and sapphire ring.

'Good heavens!'

'Go on then, put it on.'

She hesitated. 'No, you do it.' The ring fitted perfectly.

'It was my mother's.'

'Oh James! It's lovely!' She held it up in the light and it sparkled brilliantly. 'You shouldn't have! It's beautiful! I can't believe it.' She leant over and kissed him. 'Thank you, darling.'

Rosie sat on her blanket watching them, her eyes flickering from side to side as she followed their speech. She didn't relax.

'It's ironic really,' said Claire.

'What is?'

'Neale was here earlier trying to persuade me to sell.' She smiled, the corners of her mouth turned downwards. 'I more or less told him to get lost.'

'Who's Neale?'

'Philip Neale, property developer and all-round rip-off merchant.' She paused, frowning slightly. 'I'm not too sure where he comes from, somewhere up North I think, but I wish he'd go home. He's the most unpleasant creature I've ever met. He's only down here to make a killing and he doesn't care much who gets in his way. What really got up my nose was his assumption that I would sell to him, provided the price was right. Well, of course, I wouldn't!'

231

And then she laughed. 'But I might now. So much for principles, eh?'

'Yes,' he said slowly. He turned and looked thoughtfully out of the window. 'You know, someone who didn't know might say I was only down here to make money.'

She immediately flew to his defence. 'How? Why? But you're nothing like Neale.'

'Whoa, whoa! Hang on a minute, Claire. Let's look at the situation objectively, shall we?'

She relaxed once more.

'Here I am,' he began 'in a spot of bother, conveniently down here for a holiday, when I meet a beautiful woman who has recently become very wealthy.'

'Yes, but you didn't know that until today.'

'I know, but not everyone will see it like that.'

'But no one knows about my money, apart from my friend Ange, my solicitor and you. I've kept it very quiet.'

'Yes, yes,' he said soothingly. 'But you'll be amazed how these things get out and before long the whole damned neighbourhood will know about it and then they'll put two and two together and I'll be branded a fortune-hunter.'

Claire was alarmed. 'But you're not! Anyway, my friends would never betray me like that.'

'Wouldn't they? How did your friend — what did you say her name was?'

'Ange.'

' — Ange react?'

Claire thought back. Ange definitely hadn't been herself that day.

'Well,' she started, 'she was a bit upset, I suppose.' She was reluctant to admit it.

'And your solicitor?'

Claire shook her head adamantly. 'No. He definitely wouldn't. I've known him for years and there's no way on earth he would ever say anything.'

232

'Mmm, we'll see, shan't we? I'm sorry, Claire, but I know how people behave when there are large sums of money about and sometimes it's not very pleasant.' He smiled to reassure her. 'You're so trusting, aren't you?'

'Well, why not? Some of us have to be.'

He didn't answer.

'Anyway,' he said, 'back to the point. Do you think Neale will definitely want this place? I mean, look at it. It's a bit . . . well . . . rural, isn't it?'

Claire looked around the room, the faded light blue paint on the walls, the wooden shelves covered in kitchen equipment, the old Rayburn and the sash windows. To liven it up a bit she had put up the occasional postcard she had received from Ange and Alistair when they were away on holiday and posters about British wildlife. She liked the cosy familiarity of the room. 'What's wrong with it?'

'Well, we can't live here. If we want to be together, then you'll have to move to London.'

'Why? Plenty of people commute between Devon and London. Why can't you?'

'You don't understand, Claire. It's not just my work that ties me to London, but also my family. I promised my mother before she died that I would take care of my sisters and I can't let her down, can I?'

'What's wrong with your sisters?'

'Nothing – because I take care of everything; money, schooling for my nieces and nephews, the whole works. Without me handling things, they would be quite useless.'

She looked downcast.

'Claire, listen to me, darling, we don't have to rush anything. We have plenty of time to discuss things and make our decisions. I'm sure we could come to a compromise.'

She glanced up. 'I suppose so.'

He patted her hand. 'That's my girl.'

She got up and went to the sink to wash up her mug.

'How long are you going to be down this time?'

He put his arms around her waist, snuggling up against her back.

'I have to go tomorrow,' he whispered, kissing her neck. 'My accountant and I have a meeting on Monday, which I must attend.'

She said nothing, a heaviness descending on her, robbing her of all her joy. 'I don't want you to go,' she said. 'You're only here for two minutes before you have to disappear again. It's just not fair.'

He turned her round to face him and gave her a broad smile. 'My darling, Claire, life isn't fair at all sometimes, and do you know something?'

'What?'

'You look very pretty when you pout.' He pulled her bottom lip out even further. She brushed his hand away.

'Don't. You're making fun of me.'

'No, I'm not. Now come on, we've got the rest of the afternoon together and the evening and I'm sure we could think of something to do and after we've done that a few times we'll go out and celebrate; a proper champagne dinner with candlelight and all the trimmings. How about that?'

She threw her arms round his neck and cuddled him. 'Oh James, I do love you!'

He pulled away. 'Steady on! You're getting me all wet!' and they both laughed.

'Look,' she said, 'I've got to go and finish up outside. Why don't you have another cup of tea. I'll leave Rosie with you. That way you can get to know each other better.'

'Okay.'

He poured himself some more tea and then, when she had gone, pushed it to one side. The tea bags she used were cheap and very strong and he couldn't stand them. Then he noticed Rosie.

Sitting next to the Rayburn, she was staring at him.

Quite still and emanating real menace. He was intimidated by her. Her eyes never left him. He stared back.

'Don't like me, do you, hound?'

Rosie didn't respond, her gaze unflinching.

'You mongrel,' he said quietly. 'Ill-bred, ill-begotten mongrel, just like everything else round here. Well, just you wait, one of these days I'll make her see sense, I'll make her see what a flea-bitten useless good-for-nothing you are, and then we'll see who's the boss round here, won't we?'

Rosie stood up, her hackles rising. Despite his quiet voice, she sensed the antagonism of his words and she wasn't deceived by them. She stepped closer to him, each foot placed deliberately on the floor, her ears back, her teeth bared as she growled.

He didn't feel so confident now. She was a very large dog and left on his own to face her, he was unsure what to do. He wanted to escape, but the dog advanced, blocking off his exit. He began to panic. She was getting closer now and he could see, only too clearly, how much of a threat she was.

'Okay, girl,' he said, trying to placate her. 'It's all right. Yes, it is. It's all right. It was a joke, okay? I didn't mean it.' He spoke quickly, extending his hand towards her, but still she advanced.

Where was Claire? Why didn't she come back? He considered calling for her, but decided against it. She would only think him a coward and he didn't want that.

Damn the animal! It was unfit for human company and making a bloody fool out of him. The sooner he persuaded Claire to get rid of it the better.

Rosie still advanced. She was less than two feet away now, her whole body poised for launching at him. Any minute now . . . any minute now . . . and then he kicked her, lashing out blindly, his foot thumping against her shoulder. She yelped a high-pitched whine and slunk under the table.

'You bloody wretch! You bloody skunk!' he hissed, thumping the table, shuddering with an emotion that was half fear and half relief. 'Don't you ever do that to me again, do you hear? Never again!'

To make sure she understood he kicked her a second time. Rosie snapped at his leg, more in defence than anything else, and slunk off to her blanket, limping badly, her left front paw held up pathetically and her tail between her legs.

James went to the front door, his chest heaving. He needed to calm down; he needed a cigarette. He was still shaking as he lit up. If Claire had seen that little episode she would be on to him in no time. She adored that mongrel and wouldn't stand for anyone hurting her, not even him. He breathed deeply, his fear abating.

Wandering over to the barn, he found her looking over her cow. She smiled when he appeared.

'She's going to calve soon.' Claire moved round the animal, patting her. 'Fancy helping me?'

James backed away, holding up his hands in protest. 'Er, no thanks. Playing bovine midwife isn't exactly my idea of fun.'

'Come off it, James, those muscles of yours could easily help deliver a calf.'

He shook his head. 'No, I think not. I've never really got on with animals. I did try once. It was on my uncle's stud farm. One of the mares dropped her foal prematurely over Christmas when most of the staff were away. Most unpleasant it was too. I'm afraid to say I made a complete ass of myself and was gloriously sick all over the stable floor.' He shuddered at the memory. 'My uncle hit the roof and I was sent packing with a flea in my ear. Needless to say, I was never asked again, but then I wasn't that bothered. Like I said, I don't care too much for animals and most of them feel exactly the same way about me.'

'Well, Rosie likes you anyway. Perhaps,' she added, 'if

236

your uncle had been more sympathetic you might have got used to it.'

'No chance of that, I'm afraid. He belonged to the old school: children should be seen and not heard, et cetera, et cetera, and just to make sure we kept in line he had a very large and odiously efficient riding crop which he kept in his study for those odd lapses of concentration when we behaved like normal children.'

'Charming!'

'Yes. In fact, I'd say he was a real bastard.'

She walked over to him 'You didn't like him did you?'

'No.'

She leant towards him and kissed him. 'Well, you're with me now and all that can be laid to rest.'

He embraced her. 'Have you finished?'

'Yes, just about. I'll clear up the few other things later.'

Hand in hand they walked back to the house. It was later than they thought so they quickly shared a bath and got dressed to go out. It was only when Claire was downstairs putting on her lipstick that she realized Rosie was missing. She went back upstairs to her bedroom. James was standing in front of the mirror.

'Have you seen Rosie?'

He paused briefly from doing up his tie, looking at her reflection. 'No. The last time I saw her she was sitting on the blanket in the kitchen. I tried to make friends with her, but she wouldn't have it. I don't think she likes me.'

'Rubbish! Rosie likes everyone. Even the ones she's not keen on she still wags her tail at.' Claire sat down on the bed. 'I'll have to go and find her. I can't go out unless I know where she is. I'll just worry about her otherwise.'

He turned around to face her. 'Why? Surely if she's cold and wet she'll just go into the barn or one of the stables. She's quite capable of looking after herself, Claire. You really shouldn't fuss so.'

'I'm not,' she insisted 'It's just that I don't like her out

237

there on her own. There's other farmers round here who wouldn't think twice about shooting a loose dog, especially at this time of the year when all the lambs are about.' She stood up again. 'Oh James, what on earth am I going to do?' and without waiting for his reply, she left the room.

He followed her downstairs and was just in time to catch her going out in her wellingtons and waxed jacket. It had been raining for about two hours.

'Claire, what are you doing?' He held her gently by the arms.

'Please let go, James. I've got to find her.'

'But you can't. Look at you, all dressed up in your new clothes. You'll get soaked.'

She shrugged him off. 'It doesn't matter. I'll soon dry off again.'

He glanced at the hall clock. 'We've got to go soon. I've booked the table for half seven.'

'I'm sorry, I won't be long, I promise.'

He looked at her strong determined face. 'Okay,' he conceded. 'I'll help you find her. Have you got any spare wellies?'

She found him a pair of Matt's old ones and although they were a size too small, he put them on. She also found Matt's old waxed jacket, stiff and filthy dirty. James looked at it with distaste.

'Haven't you got anything else?'

'No.' She led the way out into the rain-lashed yard.

'You go that way,' she pointed, shouting over the wind. 'Look in the barn and then round the back. I'll go this way.'

He trotted quickly over to the building. The jacket was too small for him and rain was beginning to trickle down his neck. To hell with that dog, ruining things. She was really beginning to annoy him.

He pushed open the creaking door and felt blindly for the light switch, his hand pushing through dust and cobwebs. He ambled off across the hay-strewn floor, his feet rustling. He thought he could hear the small sounds of rodents, but he didn't see anything. From across the yard he could hear Claire calling her dog. He did the same only with far less enthusiasm. He didn't want her to get the wrong impression.

He sat down on a bale of straw and lit a cigarette. He reasoned that by the time he had finished it, Claire would either have found the animal or given up looking. Weather like tonight's was enough to put off even the most persistent.

Cigarette finished, he flicked the butt to one side. It landed in some dung. He stood up and left.

'Any sign of her?' she asked.

He shook his head. 'No.'

'Damn! Where can she be?' She stood dejectedly in the rain, her head down against the elements. He put his arm around her.

'Come on, Claire, let's go inside. We're getting drenched out here.'

She let him lead her back into the house without protest. As he took off her jacket he said, 'I know it's upsetting for you, darling, but we mustn't let this little setback ruin our evening.' He smoothed away some damp hairs from her forehead. 'Cheer up; Rosie is a very clever dog and far too keen on her food to go wandering. You wait, when we come back tonight, she'll be waiting for us.'

She sighed. 'I suppose so.'

'Good. Now come on, let's get going. We're late as it is and our champagne will be waiting.'

Despite herself, Claire was soon enjoying the meal. James was an exceptionally attentive companion that evening and they had a marvellous time. It wasn't at all difficult to push Rosie to the back of her mind and forget about her after a few drinks. Perhaps she did fuss too much.

*　*　*

239

Rosie was hidden in the barn between the bales, her shoulder throbbing. She had watched James when he came in and sat down. As trusting as she was, she didn't move when he called her. She knew better. In her pain and incomprehension she knew she was far safer where she was.

FIFTEEN

'Hello, Saskia.'

Terri stood on the doorstep, grinning. She was clutching what appeared to be a large canvas wrapped in brown paper and tied with string.

Saskia yawned and rubbed her eyes. 'What's the time?'

Terri stepped in and walked past her. 'Late.'

Saskia pulled the sash of her silk kimono and yawned again as she shambled off towards the kitchen.

'Christ, what bloody time did you go to bed?'

'Late.'

'I can see that. Well, is your lord and master at home?'

'Why?' said Saskia as she opened the fridge. She half glanced at the jumbled contents and then shut it again with a grimace. Terri stood up and pushed her to one side.

'Sit down, you. I'll make the coffee.'

Saskia slumped onto a chair, relieved that she didn't have to do anything. If her brain was functioning at all, she wasn't consciously aware of it. Her eyelids drooped.

'What time did you say it was?'

Terri looked at her watch. 'Half ten.'

'Oh God!' moaned Saskia. 'Why couldn't you have left it until later?'

'Because I wanted to see you, my darling.' She placed a mug of steaming black coffee in front of her friend. 'Now drink up and sober up.'

Saskia pulled a face, or as much as she could do, given the thumping of her skull. 'Thanks.'

They drank in silence for a few moments and then Saskia said, 'Who's the picture for?'

Terri got up and removed the paper wrapping. 'You,'

she replied proudly. 'It's to say sorry again for our little misunderstanding.' She stood up straight, one hand preventing the picture from falling over. Saskia stared, screwed up her eyes and leant forward, her head cocked on one side. At last she seemed to be waking up.

'That's the chap who was in the flat the day – '

' – You came round,' interrupted Terri. 'What do you think?'

Saskia smiled lasciviously. 'Very nice.'

'Apart from the obvious, Sas.'

'Like I said, very nice. Now where am I going to put it?'

Terri shrugged. 'I don't know. You've got loads of room here. I'm sure you can find somewhere.' She sat down again and offered Saskia a cigarette. They smoked contentedly, the overhead drone of the hoover permeating to them as the cleaning lady got on with her work.

'Why are you giving it to me, Terri? You don't have to, you know. You've already said sorry, that's enough. I mean, it's very nice and don't think I'm ungrateful because I'm not, but surely a picture like that you could have made some money on?'

Terri inhaled deeply and knocked some ash off her cigarette before answering. 'Yes, I could have done, but I wanted you to have it.' She hesitated, her eyes lowered. 'I made a fool of myself that day and I can't forgive myself for it. I'm really sorry, Sas.'

'Yes, I know that, Terri, but why give me the picture?'

Terri raised her eyes to the heavens in exasperation. 'For goodness' sake, Saskia, are you really so dumb?'

Saskia looked back at her, her eyes completely nonplussed. 'What are you talking about?'

Terri leant forward and touched Saskia's hand. 'Because, you numbskull, despite . . . everything and even if you're only my friend, I'm very fond of you.' She gave Saskia a wide smile, her eyes luminescent with a soft inner warmth.

Saskia's smile remained fixed. Unsure how to respond,

she took a rather-too-large mouthful of hot coffee and immediately choked. Terri jumped up, moved quickly round the table and proceeded to thump her on the back. When the coughing and spluttering had ceased and Saskia had wiped away the tears, she gave an unsteady smile, the corners of her mouth undecided as to which direction they should take.

'Feeling better now?'

Saskia nodded. Terri returned to her seat.

'That's why I asked if James were in,' she explained. 'I didn't want him to see this until it was up on the wall. Present him with a *fait accompli*, so to speak.' She smiled, more to herself than Saskia. 'I'd like to do that to the old bastard. Show him that there are other men out there, just as . . . how shall we say?' She looked at the picture, her face shining with anticipated delight. 'Accomplished as he is?'

Saskia didn't join in the laughter, which soon died away.

'Oh dear,' said Terri with heavy expectation. 'What's been going on this time?'

Saskia drank up sullenly. She didn't much care to be patronized.

'Nothing.' She averted her eyes, hoping perhaps that if she carried on staring into her now empty mug that Terri might stop probing. It didn't work.

'Don't lie to me, angel.' Terri reached out to touch her, only to be rebuffed.

'Don't.'

'Come on, Sas. Tell me all about it.'

'Don't want to.'

Terri lit a fresh cigarette from the stub of her old one. With measured tones she said, 'Think I might try to seduce you again, do you?' She watched Saskia from beneath the fringe of her thick black false eyelashes and constantly fiddled with her white loop earrings. 'Well come on, Sas, let's have it. Let's hear the "how much I hated it and it made me feel sick" routine.' She sneered at Saskia, even copying her high-pitched little girl's voice. 'Only it didn't, did it, Sas?' she added more softly. 'And you were rather enjoying yourself at first, weren't you?'

Saskia looked up, a veil of embarrassed defiance in her eyes. She shook her head. 'No. I wasn't.'

'What? You expect me to believe that? Come off it, Sas,' she laughed. 'I've had enough women to know when they want it. Even the straight ones like you.'

Saskia had no idea what to say.

Terri continued smoking, contemplating her next move. 'You can deny it all you want, Sas; it doesn't fool me.'

'I love James,' said Saskia at last.

'That's not what you said last time we met. Quite the opposite, in fact. Don't tell me,' she said suddenly. 'Don't tell me. I know what happened. He came back, didn't he, swearing undying love, promising he'd never do it again? Well?' she said, glaring across the table. 'That's it, isn't it? That's what the little shit did and you being you, dumb little doormat, swallowed it all!'

Saskia winced under the onslaught. 'No, I didn't,' she insisted. 'Anyway, you don't understand; he's in trouble. He had to go away.'

'Crap! You'd believe anything that man said.' Terri turned away in contempt. 'Honestly, Saskia, how can you be so stupid? Don't you realize what he's up to?' She waited for an answer. Saskia said nothing. 'He's screwing someone else!'

Saskia's face crumpled and she began to wail. 'Shut up . . . no, he's not . . . you don't know him like I do! He promised me he wasn't!'

'Oh Saskia, Saskia.' Terri walked over to the sideboard where there was a roll of kitchen paper, and ripped off a couple of pieces. 'Here,' she offered, 'dry your face and for heaven's sake stop bawling!'

The door opened and the cleaning lady poked round her wizened face. Seeing the emotional chaos she said in her thick Irish accent, 'I'll come back later to wash the floor.'

Terri smiled. 'If you don't mind.'

The door closed on the blue-nyloned figure. Saskia eventually took the kitchen paper and wiped her face. By the time she calmed down, Terri had made a fresh pot of coffee and refilled her mug. Saskia looked up shyly.

'Thanks. I'm sorry,' she mumbled.

'For what?'

'For being such a prat.'

Terri sat down and pulled in her chair. 'So you live with a bastard who's messing up your whole life. So what? So are thousands of other women. It's nothing new.'

'He can be very kind, you know.' Saskia was desperate to say something in James's defence.

'Oh I'm sure he can,' she paused for effect, 'when he wants something, that is, like money, sex, other women. I swear, Saskia, that he could charm the birds out of the trees if he wanted to. Only trouble is, you're one of them.'

Saskia glanced up, her bottom lip threatening to collapse once more. 'But I love him!' she cried. She leant forward on her elbows and hid her face in her hands. 'You don't understand, Terri. I . . . love . . . him. I can't help it!'

'Oh I see,' she replied jauntily. 'I'm a lesbian so of course I couldn't possibly understand what it's like to love someone. After all, I don't love anyone, I just try to seduce unwary little girls, don't I?'

Saskia put down her hands. Her face was an awful mixture of red and white that came after a good emotional blowout. It did no justice to her at all, only exaggerating her double chins. She absently started biting a nail.

'Look, I'm sorry about . . . about storming out and calling you those names. I shouldn't have done it.'

'But it's all over, eh?'

Saskia nodded.

'That's a real shame, you know.'

'Why?'

'Because the only person who really loves you isn't James.'

245

'I'm sorry. I can't help it. He says he loves me and I believe him. I have to,' she added with firmness.

'Then where is he?'

When Saskia answered she didn't look at her friend. 'Business. In Devon, if you must know.'

'Really? And is this business to do with another woman?'

'No. Money. Like I said, he's in trouble. Gambling debts.' Her voice was empty and flat.

Terri smiled disbelievingly and stood up. She had had enough. 'A merchant banker with gambling debts? Incredible! God, Sas, you do get yourself in a mess sometimes.'

She pulled on her short PVC mac, pulling the belt tight and walked towards the door. 'I've got to go. I'll see you sometime. Keep the painting.'

'No . . . no.' Saskia came over to her tentatively smiling. 'Please, Terri, not like this.'

The two women stood together, searching each other's face. Terri reached out and held Saskia's hand. She ran her thumbs over the smooth skin. 'If anything happens . . .' she began.

'I know. I've got your phone number.'

And then they kissed. Unlike her animal passion for James, Saskia felt real tenderness for the woman in her arms, although she couldn't admit it.

They heard a noise and immediately pulled apart. The cleaning lady, her face a mask of absolute horror, was watching them from the stairs. She had dropped one of her cans of spray polish. When Saskia and Terri turned around to face her, she hurriedly bent down, picked up the can and tottered her way back up the stairs.

'Bog-Irish Catholic,' said Saskia.

'Yes, and unlike we fallen ones, her soul will never burn in eternal damnation.'

They walked arm in arm to the door, close friends once more.

'Do you ever wonder,' queried Saskia, 'what will happen when you die?'

'You mean to my soul and all that?'

Saskia frowned. 'Well, it's not as though we've led completely blameless Catholic lives is it? The sisters at the convent would be horrified if they knew what we had done over the years.'

Terri let out a roar of disbelief. 'What! Do you mean to tell me you still believe all that crap they forced down our throats!' She laughed some more.

'Well, why not?'

'Look, angel,' said Terri patiently. 'Il Papa is male, celibate, an old age pensioner and childless. If that hypocrisy wasn't enough he also lives in incomparable splendour and is waited on hand foot and finger. He then has the gall to try and regulate our sex lives. Well, I say to hell with him. No man is going to tell me what to do, him or anyone else, and I'm not at all concerned about the after life either. Neither should you be if you have any sense. It's this world that matters, Sas, not that bullshit we got fed with at school, so don't even think about it.'

Saskia squeezed her hand. 'I wish I was like you sometimes,' she said quietly.

Terri pecked her on the cheek. 'You could be if you wanted to, you know. Think about it that's all,' and with a final glance, she left.

When Saskia returned to the kitchen, the nude painting was sitting accusingly on the floor, propped up against a cupboard. She looked at it thoughtfully. James definitely wouldn't like it. It was perfectly acceptable for him to look at his 'magazines' but the mere idea of this being in the house and he would go spare. She decided to hide it away.

Pity really, she thought, because on closer inspection the model certainly had a more attractive prospect than James did. She smiled to herself.

Alistair pressed the doorbell again. He was feeling conspicuous. Someone was standing behind the net curtain in the neighbouring house and watching him. He had seen the material twitch a couple of times. At last he heard some footsteps and his rising anxiety left him. Thank God. He was beginning to think no one was in. He expected Aditha, so Elyssa's unexpected presence almost knocked him off course from his prepared apology.

'Ah . . . Elyssa . . . um, in these days of sexual equality, is it acceptable for a man to change his mind?' She was watching him with an amused smile.

'Only if he agrees to accompany me to tonight's fancy dress party and is prepared to go as . . .' she looked him up and down '. . . Ares, the Greek God of War and lover of my Aphrodite.' She took the bouquet from him. 'Are these for me?' and cradling it in her arms, she inhaled the sweet aroma, her eyes closed in ecstasy. She then took his arm and pulled him into the hallway. 'Welcome back, darling. What a lovely surprise!'

She kissed him fully on the mouth. He responded, any thoughts of Devon now firmly shut away in the deepest recesses of his mind.

There was a slight cough behind them, which Elyssa ignored. Alistair found it difficult to focus his attention when Kevin was watching them. The chauffeur coughed again. This time Elyssa did respond. She whirled around about to snap his head off, but held herself back.

'Yes, Kevin?' she smiled sweetly.

He looked down, recoiling under her gaze. 'Everything's packed and the car's ready.'

'Fine. We'll be there in a minute. In the meantime, take Mr Kingston's luggage and put it in the car.'

'Yes, madam.'

'And,' she added, as he started to walk away, 'we will be going via the hire shop. After all,' she smiled, turning back to Alistair, 'we must get you something decent to wear.'

'Where is the party?'

They were on the A1 heading north out of London.

248

Alistair was relieved he didn't have to drive. Kevin was taking care of that, through nose-to-tail traffic.

Elyssa stretched out luxuriously on the leather seat. The Jaguar certainly had plenty of room for both of them.

'Stamford, Lincolnshire.'

'Will it take long?'

'Not at all, my darling. Quick drive up the A1 and we'll be there in next to no time.'

She held his arm and leant against his shoulder. 'I'm so glad you came back. I wasn't expecting it, you know. What made you change your mind?'

Alistair simply smiled. There was no way he was even going to begin telling her about Claire. It was out of the question. Far better for her to draw her own conclusions.

'Just couldn't resist my charms, eh?'

'Something like that,' and he kissed her hand.

When he looked away out of the window, his eyes were dead; dead with his own deceit, dead with his own misgivings. What was he doing here? He didn't know. It was as if the empty bleakness that clouded his life had made him throw all caution to the winds. Damn Claire! Damn her face, her body, her voice! If she wouldn't have him, then he would make himself stop caring about her. With enough drink and a woman who couldn't keep her hands off him, the pain would eventually go away. Or so he hoped.

Elyssa sighed and rested her perfumed head against his shoulder. Everything was going to plan. Alistair and his money were back, she was keeping off the drink, Aditha had gone and, most important of all and something that she looked forward to so much it made her insides curl with anticipation, was Claudia. Dear Claudia. She had invited Elyssa to her houseparty and now Elyssa could hardly wait to show Alistair off to Claudia and all her rich friends.

Rupert, her husband, may be rich and successful and mediocre in bed, as Elyssa knew only too well to her cost, but he was so old. Twenty-five years ago he was society's darling; debonair, suave, divorced. Women had chased him constantly, but now time had started to catch up on him. The money was still there but not youth, whereas Alistair was young, virile and handsome. Elyssa couldn't wait to see Claudia's reaction when she met Alistair. It was going to be a moment to relish.

'Happy, darling?' she asked affectionately, squeezing his arm.

'Mmm,' he nodded. 'Have you got any music we could listen to?'

'Of course, darling. Kevin will find something, won't you, Kevin? And in the meanwhile, let's have a drink.'

Alistair's gin was too big, but he didn't protest. If he was going to be in the right mood for tonight, he might as well start now.

'Chin-chin,' said Elyssa and the crystal glasses tinkled together.

The traffic lessened and the road flattened out. By now Alistair could feel that welcoming alcoholic numbness that preceded any drunkenness. When Elyssa took off her fur coat and got down on her knees between his legs, he was unprotesting. It felt very nice.

She deftly undid his trousers. She had already spent the previous ten minutes kissing and caressing him and he half expected from previous encounters that she wouldn't stop until they had reached a conclusion. The fact that Kevin was driving the car and well able to hear and see practically everything didn't seem to bother her at all. On this particular occasion, Alistair didn't mind either. He had had enough alcohol to quiet any protesting voice.

Elyssa had a mouth that was as soft and as gentle as any lover could wish for, but nothing happened. No matter what she did or how she did it, he remained quite unresponsive.

She looked up, holding him between thumb and fore-

250

finger and raised a questioning eyebrow.

He smiled apologetically and, taking her head in his hands, pulled her up towards him to kiss her.

'I'm sorry,' he whispered.

'Don't be. Doesn't matter. There'll be plenty of other times this weekend.'

'But it's never happened before.'

'Perhaps you're tired.'

He nodded. 'Yes, I think maybe I am.'

She moved to one side and sipped her drink. When she looked up and saw the knowing eyes of Kevin in the rear-view mirror, she glared at him.

They arrived at Rhodes House at about eight o'clock. Passing through the tall wrought-iron gates, with their lions rampant on either pillar, the car glided along the gently undulating road through the avenue of old beech trees. When they pulled up in front of the large, brightly lit house, a footman in black coat-tails was there to meet them. Other cars – Rolls-Royces, BMWs, Daimlers and Jaguars – were being driven off by chauffeurs round to the back of the large house to be parked. The door was opened and the man gave a slight bow.

'Good evening, sir; madam; and welcome to Rhodes House.'

Elyssa and Alistair got out whilst their luggage was removed from the boot.

'Very nice,' said Alistair, looking up at the numerous long windows on either side of the massive open door. From inside they could hear the general chatter of many guests.

'This way, please.'

They ascended the long sweeping steps. Inside the doorway the Hon. Rupert Myers, head of a vast international conglomerate that his father had built up since before the war, was greeting his guests. A tall, well-built man, his lush silver hair the only indication of his true age, he beamed good-naturedly at everyone, his blue eyes shining in his tanned face.

When he smiled at Elyssa the years rolled back and she saw him yet again as her lover, his trim body entwined with hers. No wonder she hated Claudia.

'Elyssa! Darling! How nice to see you.'

'Rupert!'

They kissed each other's cheeks.

'This is Alistair Kingston.'

The two men shook hands. Elyssa linked her arm through Alistair's.

'Hopefully my significant other,' she smiled.

'Really, Elyssa, and I thought that was going to be me tonight.'

'It would have been, Rupert, but you're already spoken for,' she teased.

'Kingston,' mused Rupert. 'You're not related by any chance to Rolly Kingston?'

'I am indeed. He's my father.'

'Well, in that case, welcome a second time. I've done a lot of business with him over the years. He's a splendid chap,' and he beamed again. 'Well, look, you two, someone will show you your room and I'll see you later. My wife's about somewhere, Elyssa. I'm sure you two have loads to catch up on.'

'Oh I'm sure we have, Rupert,' purred Elyssa.

'Nice chap,' commented Alistair as they followed a liveried butler up the staircase.

'Mmm, yes,' agreed Elyssa.

'Known him long, have you?'

'Oh no,' she replied, shaking her head and then more quietly added, 'Claudia knew him far better than I.'

Alistair glanced at her. What an odd thing to say.

It was the music which called them all downstairs. Booming, floor-vibrating music from a band set up at the back in one of the hired marquees out on the lawn.

252

As Alistair picked up his shield and arranged the belt to which his sword was attached, Elyssa walked in from the dressing room. Dressed in long shimmering white chiffon, which flowed about her like wafts of steam, her red hair pulled back and attached to a hairpiece, fully revealing her beautiful face, he stared. On all the occasions he had seen her, she had rarely looked as beautiful as this. Things were turning out far better than he had expected. Maybe he wouldn't have to get so drunk after all.

He stood up and came towards her. 'You look magnificent.'

She smiled with the instinctive confidence of one who has always been told that. 'Thank you, darling. You look quite superb yourself.' She floated past him towards the dressing-table where she picked up a small Lalique crystal bottle and dabbed some perfume on her neck and wrists.

'Shall we go?' she asked, holding out her hand.

As they walked downstairs the noise of the crowd rose and fell, interspersed with shrieks, guffaws, hoots and bellows. People hailed one another, slapped old friends on the back, tinkled in their cosmetic finery and flirted.

Taking Alistair's hand, Elyssa weaved her way across the large room, receiving compliments and 'hellos' from many acquaintances.

'Hello, Elyssa! How are you?'

'Fine, Bruno. How was LA?'

'Pedestrian.'

'Elyssa!'

'Charles!'

'Where were you last week? I didn't see you at my party.'

'Otherwise engaged, dear boy. Perhaps another time?'

'Perhaps.'

'Well Andrew and I don't go to the theatre any more. We find the intervals are such a waste of time.'

Alistair trod on somebody's toe. 'Oh, excuse me.'

'Not at all,' crooned the young woman, dressed in an

off-the-shoulder leopard skin, her wild unkempt hair flowing over her shoulders. 'I say, you're rather nice, aren't you? Doing anything later?'

'Do you mind?' interrupted Elyssa and firmly holding Alistair's hand, led him away.

The woman turned to her friend, who was dressed as Josephine Bonaparte, her already large bust further emphasized by her tight bodice. She was smiling aimlessly at two young men who couldn't take their eyes off her cleavage.

'Phillida, who is that wonderful-looking blond with that cheap Berkshire woman?'

They both turned round and looked as Alistair disappeared in the crowd.

'Don't know, but he's rather nice, isn't he?'

'Yes . . . very.'

'. . . So I was just dropping off when I heard this almighty crash.'

'What was it?'

'Well, the bloody mother, pissed as a fart, had driven the Porsche into the fountain. Cracked the statue and made one hell of a mess. The old man went spare.'

'I bet he did. I would too if my wife wrecked my car.'

'Oh, he couldn't care less about the car. Said he never should have got one that colour in the first place. No, he was more concerned about his fish. Yeah, it seems that goldfish and petrol don't exactly mix.'

'No, I don't suppose they do. Another drink, old man?'

'Elyssa!'

'Claudia!'

The women embraced but didn't touch. They viewed each other with deep dislike, their eyes hard.

'Alistair Kingston; Claudia Myers, Rupert's wife.'

'How do you do, Claudia?'

'Well, at last we meet. I heard that Elyssa had a new

254

man, but as I hadn't met you I was almost beginning to think that you were just a figment of Elyssa's vivid imagination. Obviously I was wrong.' Her small laugh was forced as she eyed Alistair up. She turned to Elyssa. 'And who are you this evening?'

'Can't you guess?'

'Should I? It's so hard to tell when there's so many of you all looking the same. I've seen at least four other women dressed as Romans.'

'Greek actually. Aphrodite.'

'Really? Goddess of Love, or in your case, Sex. One would never have guessed.'

'And you – what is this?' Elyssa's smile was fixed as she fingered one of the leather tassels that were hanging from Claudia's basque.

'Well, Rupert's the Marquis de Sade and I'm his accomplice. I even have a whip.'

She leant towards Alistair who was watching the proceedings with bemused detachment. 'What d'you think?' she said to him in a low husky voice. 'Shall I give you a little demonstration of my sado-masochism skills? Do you think Elyssa would mind?' and she grinned. The effect of at least half a dozen glasses of champagne shone in the light blue eyes as they vainly tried to focus on him. They kept gyrating from side to side.

Rupert, who was hovering nearby, took Alistair by the arm and drew him to one side to make further polite enquiries about Alistair's father, leaving the two women alone in each other's company.

'Have another glass of champagne,' offered Elyssa, taking one off a tray from a passing waitress, a tall ebony woman, dressed as a nymph. Across her pert bare breasts shone an iridescence of silver sparkles, matching the multitude of silver jewellery festooned about her neck, wrists and body. The only bit of clothing she wore was a tiny piece of translucent silk covering her pelvis. Haughty and disdainful, she carried the tray of full glasses around the room, completely ignoring everyone.

Claudia smiled and raised the glass in salute. 'I didn't think you were going to come, Elyssa.'

'Then why send me the invitation?'

'Because if I didn't, when would you ever get out? I mean, there you are, all alone, no children, no husband; it must be so dreary for you.' She paused, maliciously enjoying the discomfort she was creating. Elyssa stood proud.

'Poor you,' added Claudia. 'I had to do something. My heart bleeds for you.'

'Please,' smiled Elyssa, 'don't concern yourself on my behalf. Contrary to what you think about me, my life is nowhere near as dull as you paint it. Unlike you, of course, I don't have the luxury of having children, but then neither do I have the stretch marks and varicose veins to go with them. Tell me, did you ever get rid of them?' She smiled sweetly and then added, 'Neither, as you so rightly pointed out, do I have a husband. But then I prefer to take my time over making such an important decision and I'm not going to marry the first man who asks me.'

She leant forward to whisper in Claudia's ear. 'You need to wipe your nose.' And stood back triumphant, her eyes steely hard.

Claudia's face had begun to twitch; just a little one, a tic really, her left eyelid flickering shut of its own accord. She wanted to say something but nothing happened, her mouth remaining half open like a fish's. Then she took out her handkerchief and buried her face in it.

'Well,' said Elyssa, 'I mustn't keep you. I'm sure you would like to mingle with all your other guests. I'll see you later perhaps, and thank you for inviting us.'

She linked her arm with Alistair's, extracted him charmingly from Rupert, and led him away through the crowd into one of the large rooms that ran off the side of the main concourse. Food was being served in here. Plates and plates of the stuff, piled high and invitingly. Other guests were already helping themselves. More nymph-like wait-resses were on hand to assist.

They took some food and sat down by the roaring log fire.

'What did you say to her, Elyssa, to make her so upset?'

So Alistair had noticed. She carried on eating. He waited.

'Oh nothing really.' She smiled. 'You must understand something, Alistair: Claudia and I have known each other for a long, long time and we can't stand each other. It's almost a game for us. We don't mean anything really.'

She put down her plate and stared into the fire. 'We were both models, worked for the same agency and it all started because I went out with one of her boyfriends – well, he was her fiancé actually.' She paused and stared again into the fire. 'She never really forgave me and from that day to this we have been having this silly, ongoing . . . argument.'

She turned to him with genuine pain in her eyes. 'I know it's all a bit unseemly and if I promise that I won't do it again, will you forgive me? I'll even make up with her if you like. It's so idiotic of us to carry on like this at our age.'

At first he didn't answer her. It was difficult for him to understand such pettiness. For the moment he would let it pass. A few more drinks and he wouldn't notice anyway.

'Yes, of course.'

'Wonderful!' She leant forward and kissed him. She tasted of onions. 'Let's finish this,' she suggested, 'and go and party. There's loads of people here I want you to meet.'

He awoke slowly. He was lying on the bed, the sun streaming in through the window straight into his face. He screwed up his eyes because they hurt, and rolled over.

'Oh God,' he moaned. He felt awful. He ached all over. He was shivering because the window was open and he was practically naked. His costume, or what was left of it, hung around his groin. But worst of all, he had no recollection of anything. He sat up; too quickly. His skull pounded. Staggering to the bathroom, eyes almost closed with the pain of his headache, he stripped off.

He had been under the shower for about ten minutes before he began to feel remotely human. He sat down and allowed the water to spray against him. What had happened? He had no idea. And where was Elyssa? More to the point, did he care?

Dressed and feeling much better, he was sitting on the bed, putting on a clean pair of socks when she arrived. She looked radiant, her face delicately pink with morning freshness and her eyes clear. She came over and kissed him.

'Good morning, darling, and how are we?'

She sat down next to him. He stopped trying to put on his shoes: it was too much effort.

He smiled ruefully. 'Not too good.'

'Mmm, I can see the light shade of green about the gills. Well, I'm not surprised.' She gave a peal of laughter. 'You should have seen what you did last night.'

He pulled a face. 'Oh no!'

'Oh yes. I'm not sure that young girl knew what was happening to her.'

He held up his hands. 'Don't. I don't want to hear.'

She pecked him on the cheek. 'Only teasing, darling. You didn't do anything, so relax.'

He sighed with relief.

'Why, though, did you get so drunk? It's not like you at all. God, it's normally me who's, well, a bit tiddly.'

He shook his head. 'Don't know.'

She looked closely at him. 'Do you feel really terrible?'

He nodded.

'Oh dear, what a shame. I was hoping this morning that we might make up for yesterday. I believe that you and I have some unfinished business.'

He smiled awkwardly. 'Mmm ... yes ... well, let me

get some fresh air first and then maybe . . .'

'Maybe,' she finished for him, 'we can take up where we left off?'

He put his arm round her. 'Yes.'

They drove home after lunch. He still felt ill, with a pounding headache and sore throat. He slept most of the way, only waking when Kevin nudged his arm.

'We're back, sir.'

'Oh . . . right. Thanks, Kevin.'

'Miss Berkshire's gone in already.'

'Fine.'

He found her in the lounge.

'Well, what a wonderful scintillating conversationalist you were on the way back.'

He walked over to the fire. 'Please, Elyssa, I'm sorry. I'm just not used to such . . . activity, that's all.'

She went to the drinks cabinet and poured herself a large whisky. After a few minutes silence she said, 'Never mind, we'll stay in tonight. Have a takeaway or something. It won't matter.'

He looked up. 'Why, did you have something planned?'

'No, not really. There's a little get-together with some friends but we can skip that.'

Alistair yawned. He still felt tired.

'I suppose the best thing for us to do would be to go to bed.'

'It would?'

'Yes, you're exhausted. A good couple of hours' sleep would do you the world of good.'

She linked her arm in his. 'And when you're fully rested . . .'

It was devastating. Twice in as many days. Nothing had happened. And it didn't matter how often he apologized or the fact that she dismissed it as a minor inconvenience. It seriously disturbed him.

'The drink,' she said by way of excuse. 'That's all it is.'
She smiled to reassure him. 'You'll get over it.'

Alistair stared bleakly at the canopy above him.

What the hell was going on? But he refused to answer
the question.

SIXTEEN

'Wakey, wakey!'

Claire smiled, her eyes still closed.

'Wake up, darling. Breakfast is served.'

She turned over, fully conscious. 'James! You shouldn't have!'

'And why not? Surely the woman I love deserves only the best? Here, let me help you.' He plumped up her pillows as she sat up and then lay the tray over her legs. Toast, coffee and fresh orange juice sat before her with the carnation that had been given to her by the proprietor of the restaurant. She smiled; it was so good being with him. Matt would never have done anything like this.

'Aren't you going to join me?'

He stood up and undid his robe. 'No, unfortunately I've got to get back to prepare for tomorrow's meeting. Business, you know. I have to be there.' He buttoned up his shirt and then did his tie.

Standing in front of the mirror he said, 'You don't mind if I leave some washing here, do you, darling, only I really haven't got time to do it myself and I'll be back in a few days.'

'No, no, that's fine. Leave it downstairs in the scullery and I'll have it sorted out by the time you get back.'

'Thanks.'

She watched him dress. As male animals went, she considered him a prime specimen. Slim and muscular and still so handsome, despite their late night and rampant lovemaking, the memory of which melted her insides.

She felt protective and possessive of him. He was all hers. Nothing was going to come between them. Of that she had no doubt. She loved him totally. Every last molecule of her being was mesmerized by him and his overpowering maleness. It was their lovemaking that did it; the indescribable, wonderful sensations that enriched and enlivened her whole body. Never had she had so much energy and drive. All the time he was here she felt buoyant and happy. When he went, she slipped into the abyss of despair. Without him she was nothing. He had become the reason for her existence.

She put her tray to one side. She had to hold him, smell him, infuse her whole body with him one more time before he left.

'Do you have to go?' she asked quietly, putting her arms around his waist and brushing her face against his back.

'Yes, but I'll try to get back before the weekend.' He picked up his jacket. 'There now, how do I look?'

'Wonderful,' and then she sighed. 'I wish I were coming with you.'

He put on his jacket. 'No, you wouldn't like it. You'd be bored stiff. It's all business, business, business and very dull I can assure you.'

'But if I stay here I'll be jealous.'

'Why?'

'Because I'll be here and you'll be there and I won't be able to see you.'

She flattened out his collar and made unnecessary adjustments to his tie. 'I'll miss you. You'll be there with all those other women while I'm stuck down here with only my neighbour, Jack,' she pouted.

He smiled. 'Now listen to me, Claire. You have no reason to be even the remotest bit jealous. You're the only one I love and it's you I'll be coming back to, okay?'

She nodded. 'I know, but I can't help it, James. You'll be so far away from me.'

'And you'll be so far away from me,' he answered. 'I don't know what you'll be getting up to, so that makes two of us, doesn't it?'

'Me and Jack?' she laughed incredulously.

'Well, there's all the men in town as well. Any one of them might be after you, for all I know.'

An image of Alistair flitted briefly across her mind.

'No,' she said. 'There's no one.'

'Good. Going to see me off then?'

They stood by the back door. It was cold but at least the rain had stopped. On the horizon a pink sky showed where the sun was coming up in a clear spring morning. A bright star could be seen still shining in the purple heavens.

'Look,' she pointed. 'Venus, planet of love. The ancients called it that because it appeared at its brightest when men and women most made love; early morning or in the evening.' She smiled dreamily. 'I think it's beautiful; don't you?'

'Yes, it is rather. Can't say I usually notice things like that.' He looked at her sideways. 'Bit of a romantic, aren't you?'

'And why not?' she retorted. 'Romance oils our everyday existence.'

He held her close. 'Look,' he said glancing at his watch. 'I've got to go. I'll give you a ring as soon as I can, okay?'

They kissed. Then she watched his car as it sped off, its lights bouncing around the countryside until at last they too disappeared.

Later that morning, when Claire was about to look in on Jacky, Rosie appeared, her tail down, limping quite badly.

'Hello, sweetie, and where were you last night?'

The dog's tail wagged a couple of times then stopped. Her whole demeanour was cowed.

'What is it, my beauty? What have you done with that leg? Here, let me look at it.'

Rosie sat patiently and unprotesting while she was examined. She didn't flinch once, not even when Claire

263

touched her swollen shoulder, her fingers running carefully over the soft, bruised flesh.

'How on earth did you get that, eh? What happened to you?'

Claire was worried. Rosie never bothered any of the stock and stayed well clear of dangerous hooves and horns; Claire couldn't imagine how she had done it. She held the dog's head in her hands and looked into the pained brown eyes.

'If only you could talk, mmm? Still, I'm glad you're back and I'm sure it's only a bad bruise, otherwise you wouldn't be walking at all, so we won't need a visit to the dreaded vet, will we?' Rosie's tail swished. She was happier now. 'But I wish I knew what you'd been up to and where you've been all night. Honestly, you're such a pest. You had me really worried, you know.' She stroked the large glossy head. 'Come on then, ratbag,' she added affectionately, 'it's time for some grub.'

With a three-legged hop, Rosie followed Claire into the house for a well-deserved meal of meat and biscuits, topped with a raw egg. Heaven.

James pulled in at the Exeter service station and phoned Saskia. Everything was progressing so well he just had to share it with her. He wouldn't give her any specifics, but just enough to let her know that it was all going to plan. When she eventually answered the phone, her voice sounded dull.

'Yeah?'

'Hello, Sas.'

'Oh . . . James . . . Hello.'

'Still in bed, are we?'

'Yes. What time is it?'

'Seven thirty.'

'Seven thirty!' she exclaimed. 'What are you ringing me for at this ungodly time of the morning?'

'To say hi and to say I miss you. Sas, I was thinking.'

'What?'

'How would you like it if I gave you a superb massage when I get back?'

She said nothing.

'Followed by one of the best fucks you've ever had.'

Silence.

'Are you listening to me, Sas?'

Still nothing.

'I know what you're doing, you randy little minx, you're playing with yourself, aren't you?'

He glanced down at himself. He was getting interested too.

'Go on, Sas, tell me what it's like. Describe it to me.'

'Why? Can't you imagine it for yourself?'

'But it's not the same,' he insisted. 'I want you to give me the details.'

'Oh, James, I can't be bothered. Leave me alone, for God's sake. I want to sleep.'

'Do you know something, Sas?'

'What?'

'You're a real pain sometimes.'

'So are you.'

He sighed. So much for telephone sex. He enjoyed their pornographic conversations, but obviously she wasn't in the mood. He looked down at himself. Neither was he any more.

'Look, James, what do you want?'

'Nothing really. Just rang to say hello and that I'll see you later.'

'Fine. Well, hello to you and goodbye.'

She put the phone down. He stared at his receiver for a few moments in annoyance. Bloody cow! She was such an ungrateful bitch sometimes.

On Monday morning, Elyssa was busy. She was interviewing some girls that had been sent round from the agency to replace Aditha. There were four of them altogether;

none of them English and all intimidated by the experience. They sat in the kitchen quietly drinking their coffees, waiting to be called through to the drawing room.

Alistair was in the lounge reading his newspaper. Or rather he was trying to read. The only problem was that however hard he concentrated on the words, the newsprint seemed to remain static in front of his eyes, blurring into a grey, out of focus expanse. What he really wanted was to make a phone call. The telephone was distracting him, drawing his eyes across the page to the table. So far he was resisting the temptation. He read on. Then he stopped, threw down the paper in exasperation and reached for the phone. It was no good. He had to hear her voice.

Claire was having her mid-morning teabreak when the telephone rang. She rushed to pick it up.

'Hello?'

'Claire, how are you?'

'Alistair! How are you?'

'Fine, just fine, dear girl, never felt better.'

'Where are you? You sound a bit distant?'

'London. I'm in London at Elyssa's house.'

'Oh.' She paused. 'Do you think it's a good idea ringing me? I mean, she might take it the wrong way and get upset or something.'

He chuckled. 'Not at all. Of course she won't. I just wanted to see how you were after what happened the other day, although I can hear by your voice that you're much happier.'

'Oh Alistair, I am! You'll never believe what's happened.'

'What?' In an instant his stomach tightened, poised for the onslaught. He didn't know why he reacted as he did, but it happened automatically. Something in her voice, in her excitement, told him he wasn't going to like what he was about to hear.

'I'm going to get married!' she cried.

He felt sick. He reached over the table to a silver box, opened it and took out a cigarette. He had given up months ago. Now he lit up and inhaled deeply, supressing the inevitable cough. His eyes watered with the unfamiliar smoke. 'Oh, Alistair!' she continued. 'I'm so glad you rang. I had to tell someone. Aren't you going to ask me who it is?'

'I think I know,' he said flatly. He inhaled again, the hit from the nicotine clouding his brain. She's mistaken, he thought, she's not going to get married. It's a lie. She doesn't mean it. 'It's that James Lamont chap, isn't it?'

'Yes, that's right. He came down at the weekend and out of the blue proposed to me. Heavens!' she laughed. 'Just talking about it makes me go all goosepimply. I can't believe what's happening. It's all so sudden.'

'And you're . . . I mean, you really think . . .'

'Yes, of course I'm sure,' she interrupted. 'How could I not be? I love him, Ali. I don't think I've ever loved anyone like this before. It's . . . it's wonderful.'

'Well, I'm glad,' he said. His voice sounded very peculiar to him. Detached; as if it belonged to someone else; as though there was another Alistair Kingston who was sitting on the chair, making this phone call, listening to these awful words and saying all the right things. The real Alistair was somewhere else, far, far away, down on his knees in despair and screaming with rage and frustration at the gods or fate or whoever it was that ruled his life.

'You sound very happy,' he continued, 'and that's good. You deserve a bit of happiness after all this time.'

'Thank you, Ali. You know, you really are the best friend a woman could have. You always say the right thing at the right time and never get at all upset or angry. You're really sweet, Ali; you're like an older brother to me.'

'Am I?' Halfway between the two words his voice began to crack and it was only with desperate self-control that he managed to keep it all together. Perhaps it would be better if he changed the subject.

'What about your money, Claire? Have you made any decisions about that?'

'Ali!' she protested. 'I don't want to talk about that now. I want to talk about James and the wedding.' She hesitated. 'Don't you want to hear all about it?'

The cigarette was making him feel light-headed and nauseous, but he persisted in smoking it. He knew he was being perverse, but at the moment he couldn't care less.

'Yes, all right. Go ahead. Tell me all about it.' She couldn't hurt him any more than she already had so it wouldn't matter if he had to suffer for a few minutes longer.

'Well,' she began slowly, 'you know that day you came round and I was a bit off? I was like that because James hadn't contacted me. He said he would, of course, because he loves me, but he didn't and to be honest with you, I was getting really fed up with the whole arrangement. It looked as though he had just used me and dumped me. At least that's what Ange said, and I was beginning to believe her. Anyway, the next day he did turn up and although I was very angry with him, we made up . . .'

Alistair closed his eyes in torment. He couldn't didn't want to hear this.

'. . . and after that he suggested that we made it all a bit more permanent.'

'You mean he actually asked you to get married?'

'Well, not exactly. He said we would eventually, perhaps two years, that's if I didn't go off him before then . . .' she chuckled '. . . as if I would!'

'So what happens now?'

'Now I sell up and move to London.'

'What!' This was really unexpected.

'Well, what else can I do?'

'Couldn't he commute?'

'No; he has responsibilities, Ali, and he has to live in London.'

'But I thought . . . we all thought that Tor Heights meant everything to you.'

He stubbed out his cigarette, picked out another and lit it. He needed a drink as well, but the cabinet was on the other side of the room and he didn't know if the flex would stretch that far.

'It does, Ali, but things change; I've changed and now it's time to go.'

'But what about your animals? What about Rosie?' What about me screamed the voice in his head.

'I'll sell them all, except Rosie, of course. She's coming with me. I couldn't leave her.'

'But London?' It was no good, he must have that drink. He stood up and carrying the phone in his other hand, walked over to the drinks cabinet. His whisky was far too big for this time of day, but he didn't care.

'Yes, I know; it's not exactly open moorland and green fields, but James says he lives right next to a square and I'm sure Rosie would be happy wherever we go.'

'Really?'

'Oh Alistair, don't dampen things! You should be happy for me!'

'I am, I am, but don't you think, well, that it's all a bit sudden?'

She didn't answer immediately. 'Well, maybe,' she said thoughtfully, then quickly added, 'but I do know what I'm doing, Ali. It's not as though I'm some stupid little teenager, all dewy-eyed and romantic. I am old enough to make my own decisions, you know.'

'Yes, I know, but nonetheless, I am concerned for you. I just feel that perhaps you're rushing things a bit. For instance, what do you know of his background?'

'Oh Alistair! Now you sound like my father!'

'Well, someone has to look out for you,' he said, 'and as

your father has voluntarily abdicated any responsibility towards you, I feel I should step in to replace him.'

'Okay, okay.'

The force of his reply surprised her. 'He's taken Briar Cottage for the spring to get away from London and the reason he has to keep going back is because he has business problems. He hasn't said what exactly and I don't like to pry, but I think it's pretty serious.'

'So he's got money problems then?'

'Yes, I suppose so.'

'And that doesn't strike you as odd?'

'No, why should it?'

He took a mouthful of his whisky. It went down his gullet, warming his insides and calming his thumping heart. He would have to be very, very tactful here.

'Listen, Claire, you're probably going to get a bit upset when you hear what I've got to say, but please bear with me.'

'Okay.'

He took a deep breath. 'Have you considered the possibility, the vague possibility, that he might want you because of your money?' He waited. She had gone very quiet. He couldn't even hear her breathing.

'Are you saying what I think you're saying?'

'That he's after you for your money? Yes.'

'I don't believe it,' she muttered. She wasn't talking to him; more to herself.

'Claire – please, Claire, don't get angry. Just think about it. Just consider it even. Please. For your own good.'

She didn't answer. He finished his drink, thought about having another one and abandoned the idea. He had another cigarette instead.

'Claire . . . are you still there?'

Now it was her turn to be shocked. 'How could you, Ali?' Her voice was low, barely audible.

'Sorry?'

'You heard me,' she said louder. 'You . . . you . . .' she spluttered. 'Of all the rotten, bloody things to say, I don't believe it!'

'But, Claire – '

'Don't "Claire" me! First Ange and now you. You're as bad as each other!'

'Claire, listen to me – '

'No! Goodbye, Alistair.'

The phone went dead. He replaced it slowly, too full of his own pain to hear the click of another receiver.

Elyssa smiled to herself. So, she had a rival. Or rather, did have. And by the sounds of things, Alistair really liked her. Poor man! No wonder he had been feeling out of sorts for the last couple of days. Well, she would soon be able to deal with that now she had a clear field. She had suspected all along that he wasn't being entirely honest with her and had enough experience with the ways of men to know the various reasons for impotence, whatever his excuses.

She leant her face on her entwined fingers and considered the engraving on her silver tea service. There wouldn't be any problems now. There was only one thing she had to settle; and that was her marriage to him. She didn't love him but he was just what she needed. People like Claudia or the bank would never leave her alone until she had someone like Alistair. He was solid, reliable, and very, very rich.

She smiled again at the young Thai girl whom she was interviewing.

'And what did you say your name was again?'

Alistair sat still; thinking. There was time to change her mind, possibly even to stop her. All he had to do was work out how. He decided to ring a friend of his, an old chum from law school. He reached into his jacket pocket and took out his diary. He had his number somewhere.

271

The telephone rang twice before being picked up. A plummy female voice said, 'Du Pres residence, how may I help you?'

Alistair smiled to himself. Mortimore's nannies were always very 'nice' young ladies. She would be some finishing school bimbo with perfect manners and legs, who was only filling in time until some man whisked her off for marriage and children of her own. These girls were always more attractive than efficient, but then Mortimore always had been an aesthete and he wasn't going to change now. Alistair wondered how his wife stood for it.

'Mortimore Du Pres, please.'

'Whom shall I say is calling?'

'Alistair Kingston.'

'Thank you.'

A pause with the noise of children in the background and then: 'Ali! You sly old fox! Long time no hear, how are you?'

'Well enough. And yourself?'

'Fine, just fine, old boy.'

'And Pamela and the kids?'

'Delightful! Absolutely delightful. You must come round and see them sometime. It's been ages since you visited us.'

'I will.' Alistair smiled. He could picture Mortimore, debonair and relaxed, oozing confident charm, his large spectacles sitting on the end of his long beaked nose.

'So what is this: personal or professional?'

Alistair hesitated. 'Both,' he said at last, 'and not something I usually have dealings with.'

'Ah, is that so? Life in rural Devon a bit quiet then?'

'No, not really, it's just . . . well, I'm not sure I know where to start.'

'Spit it out, spit it out, you are after all talking to your oldest friend and one who's heard all manner of confessions over a few pints in the Nag's Head.'

'Yes, I know that, but this one . . . it's a bit, well, dodgy.'

'Really? Sounds interesting. Well, come on then, I'm waiting.'

Alistair reached for another cigarette. By now he had a headache and his mouth tasted foul, but he ignored it. He lit up and inhaled.

'It's like this, Mort: I would like someone investigated. Someone who comes from London and who I feel might be committing or is about to commit a grave act of embezzlement against a friend of mine.'

'Who is this friend?'

'Claire Bromage.'

'Bromage ... Bromage ... ah yes! I remember her. Wasn't she that delightful creature I met at some party you took me to when I came down to spend a weekend. Didn't she have on a glorious red dress, long black hair and, you know, fairly well developed . . .?'

'The same.'

'Oh charming creature, absolutely charming. Yes, pity about the neanderthal who was with her. Didn't say two words all evening as I seem to recall?'

'That was her husband who died shortly afterwards in a tractor accident, and believe me, Mortimore, he was no neanderthal.'

Mortimore was instantly contrite. 'Oops! Sorry about that, old man. Apologies offered.'

'Accepted. Now listen. The problem is she's met this Flash Harry who has asked her to marry him.'

'So? Perfectly normal behaviour for most people, Alistair, as you very well know. By the way, who are you squiring about at the moment?'

'Never mind about me,' said Alistair impatiently. 'The point is, she's only known this man for a very short time and she's just inherited a great deal of money.'

'Ah ha, I see!' said Mortimore slowly. 'And you suspect that this chap's motives aren't altogether honourable. That maybe ugly Mammon has come between him and his heart?'

'Precisely.'

'So you want me to arrange for one of my contacts to sniff around a bit, see what's going on, dig up some dirt or some such?'

'Not necessarily.' Alistair instinctively recoiled from such words. He was an honourable man himself and wasn't used to dealing with the more sordid side of life, especially when it involved someone like Claire. 'I just want your "contact" to find out about this man; where he comes from, what he does, what his financial background is. Anything really that I ought to know.'

'It's not like you to dirty your hands like this,' queried his friend. 'What's going on, Alistair? I mean, really going on? Is this Bromage woman someone special, someone you care about?'

'A friend, yes.'

'I see.'

His tone said it all, that he didn't believe Alistair. 'She's your "friend", nothing more, nothing less, and you don't want her to get hurt? Right?'

'Yes.'

'Really, Alistair, you must think I was born yesterday!'

'Look, Mort, I don't care what you think, I just don't want her hurt and if your chap can find out something that will stop it happening, then fine, okay?'

'All right, all right, I believe you.'

Alistair was angry and Mortimore surprised. He had known Alistair long enough to know when to back off, but even he was caught off guard by Alistair's over-quick reaction. 'Right then,' he resumed more quietly, 'give me the details.'

Alistair told him everything he knew. He tried to get the conversation over as quickly as possible because he knew Elyssa would be finishing soon.

'Okay,' said Mortimore, 'I'll get on to this as soon as poss and let you know the minute I hear anything.'

274

'Thanks, Mort. I owe you one for this.'

'Not at all. By the way, does Mrs Bromage know you're doing this?'

'Of course not.'

'So this is being done from a purely altruistic standpoint?'

'Yes.' Alistair was getting annoyed again and then he understood the reason behind the question.

'You're not implying that I might be in this for my own benefit, are you?'

'And why not? You said yourself that it's a great deal of money and that's a very tempting bite.'

'Good God, Mort! You're such a cynic.'

'I know, old boy, terrible, isn't it? Maybe I ought to come and work down in your neck of the woods where people are more honest with each other.'

'Don't be ridiculous, Mort; you'd hate it. It's far too quiet for someone like you. Anyway, with few exceptions, the women down here are more efficient and that would never do, would it?'

'Oh well, in that case I'd better stay where I am and become even more of a moral imbecile!'

Alistair grinned. Mortimore never did take himself too seriously.

'Look, Mort, I have to go now, but will you contact me as soon as you can?'

'Certainly, and it was good to hear from you again. Next time we speak, we'll arrange a get-together.'

'Yes. Fine. Bye, Mort.'

Just as Alistair had replaced the phone, Elyssa came through the door. She was dressed in black, the jersey dress figure-hugging. Her red hair was pulled back off her face and she had a large gold brooch on her breast. Alistair smiled benignly at her, his insides in turmoil.

'Alistair! You're smoking. I thought you'd given up?'

'You look lovely,' he said, ignoring her comment.

'Why, thank you. I'm glad you like it. It's by Louis Féraud and you know how much I enjoy dressing up for you.'

'Mmm, very nice,' and he managed a weak smile through his pain.

She came over to the sofa and sat down next to him. 'Are you feeling better now, darling?'

He said nothing.

She held his hand, looking deeply into his blue eyes and delicately ran her perfectly manicured finger along the inside of his thigh.

'I thought,' she said softly, 'that we might go out for lunch and then . . . later . . . perhaps?' She kissed him and smiled. 'Who knows?'

As Alistair told himself much later on the way back to Devon, Elyssa did have her good points. She was an intelligent conversationalist; she was outstandingly beautiful, for which she was much admired by both sexes, and her behaviour in bed was second to none, although even she hadn't overcome his little problem. He sighed. It had been stupid going to bed with her again, but like the lovesick fool that he was, he would try anything to rid himself of Claire. Served him right when everything refused to co-operate. Elyssa wasn't pleased at all and was still sulking when he left.

The answer to his problem was too obvious even to contemplate. He mustn't think about it; he would not think about it. It was finished; over; ended.

In time he would forget Claire. Sometime he would lay her ghost to rest. But until then, he had work to do. James Lamont; just who was he?

SEVENTEEN

It was very dark when Claire woke up. Most nights her sleep was deep and relaxed, but not this time. Something had disturbed her; something was wrong. She lay still, very quietly and listened. The only thing she could hear was Rosie's contented snores under the duvet. Claire nudged her.

'Be quiet you.' Rosie moved but soon started snoring again.

Then it happened: Jacky bellowing.

'Damn! Damn! Damn!' She hurriedly got up and fumbled in the dark for her clothes, stubbing her toe on the bed as she did so. She leant over and turned on the light: ten past three! Oh God! Why couldn't the silly animal wait until the morning?

She finished dressing and went downstairs, Rosie following her. Irritated, she clumped about, filling up the kettle to make some tea, eyes blinking in the bright light. If Jacky was going to calve at this unholy time of the morning, then Claire needed something hot to warm her before going out into the cold of the barn, especially as it was raining again.

Seated at the kitchen table, her hands cupping the mug of tea, she sipped slowly, letting the hot liquid spread its warmth inside her, Rosie lay on the floor by her feet. Since her reappearance she was even less inclined to let Claire out of her sight, staying as close as possible at all times. Claire looked down at her. She was worried; worried because some of the dog's bounce seemed to have gone. She just wasn't herself any more. She was nervous and clingy. Claire found it disturbing because she had no idea

277

how Rosie's injury had happened. The shoulder swelling and limp had gone and Claire reasoned that with time Rosie would soon be her old self again.

The cow bellowed, long and demanding. A cry like that would carry on the wind and be heard at least half a mile away. Claire had to move.

'Okay, okay, I'm coming.'

She drank the last of her tea and, while eating a biscuit, put on her jacket and woolly hat. Her wellies were cold to her feet. She opened the door.

'Come on, Rosie, let's go and see what the old bag wants this time.'

As soon as she switched on the barn light she could sense something was wrong. Used to a kind of blank, placid conformity in the faces of her cattle, she noticed at once how Jacky was now staring at the middle distance, frightened and wide-eyed as she braced herself for another contraction of her mighty uterus. As it came, she stretched down her neck and bellowed, her pink tongue pointing out over her large, square, stained teeth. Claire watched as one wet cloven hoof, new and shining, appeared from under the cow's tail then slipped back in again as the contraction subsided.

'Oh no!' It was a helpless cry of despair. 'That's all I need!'

The calf was lying awkwardly, unable to get out, a jumbled up mess of flexed limbs and possibly a twisted-back head. How long the cow had been fruitlessly heaving Claire didn't know, but even to her inexperienced eye, she could see it had been going on too long.

Jacky was vast, far bigger than during her last pregnancy, and looked very uncomfortable. The milk vein running along her belly was protruding out against the skin as it meandered to her massive udder which dripped colostrum from the engorged teats.

She was well into labour, but getting nowhere. Claire thought about doing an internal examination to see if she could find out what was going on, but rejected the idea at once. It looked perfectly straightforward when Jack or the vet did it, but she knew she wasn't up to it. She had to get help. She moved slowly along the cow, gently feeling her abdomen. The muscles underneath were taut with expectation.

'Oh you poor, poor thing!' she said, rubbing the cow's neck. 'It must be agony for you. Well, never mind, old girl, I'll get the vet and we'll soon sort it out. I just wish you'd chosen a better time for it, though.'

With a last pat on Jacky's neck, Claire turned to go back to the house, Rosie following. The phone rang for ages. 'Come on, come on.' She looked at her watch. Three twenty-five. Eventually a sleepy female voice answered.

'Torhampton 396, Mrs Roberts speaking,' and then yawned.

'Hello, Mrs Roberts, Claire Bromage here at Tor Heights.'

'Hello, Claire, how are you?' The voice was much warmer now she knew who she was talking to.

'Fine, except that I have a cow calving and she's having real problems. Can your husband pop out and see her?'

'I'm sorry, Claire, but he's over at Little Grebe Farm at the moment. One of Major Harrington's mares is having the same problem and I've really got no idea when he'll be back. You know what these things are like, my dear, it could take ages.'

Claire thought quickly. She had to do something. 'If your husband returns soon, could you ask him to come out?'

'Yes, of course. Just how bad is she?'

'I don't know. One hoof keeps appearing and disappearing and she's making one hell of a racket.'

'Right then, Claire, if Bill comes home soon, I'll pass on your message. In the meantime, is there anyone else who can help you?'

'I suppose I could ring Jack.'

'You do that then. Jack has vast experience of these

kinds of things. I'm sure he won't mind.' Claire could almost hear Mrs Roberts' smile.

'Thanks, Mrs Roberts. Bye.'

'Goodbye, dear.'

Jack answered the phone much more quickly. 'Yes?'

'Jack, it's me, Claire. I've got problems.'

'What problems?'

'My cow. She's in labour and has been for some time, only nothing's happening and the vet can't get here for ages.' She paused. 'Will you help me?'

She heard him sigh. 'Okay, see you soon,' and he put down the receiver.

She went into the kitchen and made a Thermos of tea. When that was ready, she found a half-bottle of whisky and put it in her jacket pocket. If it was going to be a long struggle, they would need something to keep them going.

Twenty minutes later Jack arrived, looking the same as he always did: blue overalls, mud-covered wellies and woolly hat. He came into the barn cursing.

'Bloody piss-awful weather, isn't it?'

She nodded in agreement.

'Well then, let's have a look at her.' He walked round the cow, feeling her belly. He lifted up her tail and inspected her.

'Got some soap and water?'

Claire watched as he washed his arm and inserted it into the cow, his wrinkled, weatherworn face frowning and puckered as he felt around.

'How long has she been like this?'

'Don't know. I only came over about an hour ago and nothing has happened since then except the one hoof that keeps coming out.'

He removed his arm and wiped it with straw. 'You've got twins in there and the head of one of them is blocking the other one's feet so that neither of them can get out. Have you got some rope?'

'Yes, in the scullery. I'll fetch it.'

The rope was hanging behind the door. She took it back to the barn and handed it to Jack.

'How are you going to do it?'

'I'll push one back and hook the rope over the other one's feet and pull it out.' He inclined his head towards the cow. 'She's knackered. If we don't help her she might give up altogether.'

He pushed his brown sinewy hand back into the cow, grimacing and straining as he tried to manipulate the calves out of each other's way and pull out the other hoof. Jacky didn't help much by having a ferocious contraction while this was happening.

'Ah damn bloody bitch!' he exploded, beads of sweat breaking out on his forehead as the exertion became too much.

When the two feet were finally out, he fixed the rope around them.

'Right, come here, Claire.' He positioned her next to him and gave her one of the ropes.

She wrapped it around her hand for a firm grip.

'When I say pull,' he instructed, 'pull. Okay?'

'Yes.'

'Only when she pushes, all right?'

The calf took an age to come out. Even with the two of them pulling with all their strength, it only slowly inched itself forwards.

'Christ! What bloody bull did you use on her?' asked Jack between contractions.

Claire glanced at him. 'Friesian. Mind you, if I'd known she was going to have twins, I would have gone for a smaller Hereford.'

Another contraction started and again they pulled, their faces contorted with the effort.

'Well,' he said breathlessly, 'if the other twin is as big as this one, it's no wonder the old girl is having so much trouble.'

The end came suddenly. The calf shot out towards them,

heavy and wet as it flopped out onto the straw.

'Good grief!' exclaimed Jack. 'Look at the size of that!'

'And she's got no tail!' said Claire, pointing.

'Well, I'll be buggered, so she hasn't!'

Instead there were a few hairy wisps, damp as a teased kiss-curl, sticking out above the animal's backside.

'I've only seen that once before,' said Jack as he lifted the calf up by its back legs and tried to shake it. Jack was tall, at least six feet four but the heifer stretched out longer than that, her forefeet dragging on the floor. Apart from the missing tail, she was a good-looking beast, black and white like her mother, with a white star on her forehead. She began to come to after her prolonged birth and blinked hazily in the strong light. Shaking her wet head she snorted and coughed as some of the birth fluid still filled her lungs.

Jack smiled to Claire, well satisfied. 'Let's get on then, see what other surprises she's got for us.' He reached back into the cow and felt around. 'Smaller,' he said 'much smaller. No movement either. Reckon we'd better get it out as soon as possible.'

After the struggle with the first calf, its twin arrived easily. They hardly needed to pull at all and when it was laid on the floor, they could see why. Much smaller as Jack had said, it was perfectly formed and quite dead.

'Oh dear,' said Claire disconsolately. 'What a shame!'

Jack agreed. They stood looking down at it, sad that their efforts hadn't saved it. Claire tapped its limp body with her boot.

'What d'you suppose happened to it?'

Jack scratched his bristly chin. 'Who knows? Perhaps it just wasn't strong enough to cope with the birth. Still,' he said, touching her arm affectionately, 'you've got one good calf and that's something.'

Claire looked at him sceptically.

'Okay, so it's got no tail,' he said. 'So what? She's still a good heifer.'

They both watched as the calf lay in the straw being licked dry by its mother. A car's headlights bounced across them and its engine stopped. Claire looked round

'That will be Mr Roberts.'

They went out to meet him. The old man got out of his car and tiredly rubbed his neck.

'Hello, Mr Roberts. Tough foaling, was it?'

He pulled a face, friendly and kind despite the long night. 'Yes. Very. Hello, Jack. Right then, Claire, lead on and show me this cow of yours. With a bit of luck, we'll get it over and done with and then maybe I can finally get back to my bed.'

She looked guiltily at Jack. 'Actually, it's all finished. Jack did it.'

'Oh really? Well, that's wonderful. And is the calf all right?'

'Twins,' answered Jack. 'One great big 'un without a tail and one dead little 'un.'

'No tail, eh? Well, I've never seen that before. Let's have a look at her.'

They trooped into the barn and watched smiling as the enormous youngster tried to take its first feed.

'They look very well,' said the vet, 'and the other one, where's that?'

Claire pointed to a feed bag. 'In there.'

He had a cursory look. 'Mmm, far too small. Didn't stand a chance really. Pity, though. It's got a wonderful tail.'

'Why did it die?' she asked as they went back to his car.

'Nature can be very cruel sometimes, dear. Only the biggest and strongest survive when it's a fight for the basics in life. That little calf obviously got far less food from the mother than the big one and it just wasn't strong enough. I'll be back in a couple of days to make sure the cow is cleaned out. So I'll see you then. All right?'

She watched him drive away into the grey dawn. Nameless shapes were beginning to take on their form as the sky brightened in the east. It was still raining, only much more gently now. Claire yawned and stretched. She was very tired.

'Want some more tea, Jack?'

He too looked pale and exhausted. 'Yes, why not?'

They sat at the kitchen table, too tired to talk, absently eating some biscuits and drinking their tea. Claire had placed the half-bottle of whisky between them and Jack topped up his cup with a generous measure.

'How's your bull then, Jack? I haven't seen him lately.'

'I've moved him.'

'Where?'

'Field next to Briar Cottage. It's got more grass and he needs to be in good condition for my ladies.' He helped himself to another biscuit. 'Course, that visitor won't mind, he seems to have other things to think about.' His eyes rose slowly from the table top until they were looking straight into Claire's.

She knew exactly what he was hinting at but remained impassive. She was determined not to talk about James. Any mention of their affair to Jack and the entire neighbourhood would know about it. Jack, though, was looking at Rosie now.

'Your dog's not herself. Anything wrong with her?'

Rosie looked up from her blanket and wagged her tail. She always knew when someone was talking about her.

'No, not really. She's a bit quieter than usual, but she's not ill.' Claire called her over. 'Come here, girl, come on.'

Rosie didn't move, but looked at them both from her blanket with her huge brown eyes.

Claire turned back to Jack. 'I think she's a bit stiff,' she explained. 'One of the beasts must have kicked her or something. She's had a slight swelling on her shoulder, but it seems to have gone now.'

'Surely she's got more sense than to go near their feet?' he queried, puzzled.

'Well, something must have kicked her,' replied Claire

yawning. She scratched her head and then lay her head on her arms.

Jack stood up. 'You're knackered and I've got to get back for milking. Thanks for the tea and I'll see you soon.'

Claire followed him out. 'Hardly worth going back to bed,' she said as they both watched the spring sun tinge the sky a vivid orange.

'No,' said Jack pulling on his boots. 'But that's farming for you.'

Claire was snoozing in her chair by the Rayburn when James arrived. He wasn't unexpected, as he had rung the previous day, but with the drama in the cowshed, Claire was too tired to give him much thought.

He stood behind her chair and put his hands over her eyes. 'Guess who?' he whispered.

'James!' She jumped to her feet and threw her arms around his neck. 'Oh it's good to see you, I've really missed you!'

They kissed.

'I've brought you something,' he said, going to his bag. He handed her a small packet.

'Here, take it.'

She slowly turned it over in her hands. 'What it it?'

'Unwrap it and see.'

She ripped off the paper. When it came to presents, she was a small child again. She opened up the red velvet jewellery box.

'Oh James! It's beautiful! Where did you get it? Is it real?'

She held up the pearl necklace so that it's muted opalescence shone in the light.

'They've been in the family for ages,' he explained. 'They were some great-aunt's. Here, let me put them on for you.' He took them from her. 'They'll look much better on you than they did on her.'

'No, you can't!' she protested. 'Look at me, I'm not

285

dressed properly.' She held out the sides of her trousers, smeared with mud and bits of hay. 'I'm a mess.'

He put down the pearls and held her gently. 'Rubbish; you look absolutely beautiful to me.'

For a moment they stood together, gently swaying to the beat of their hearts.

'Tell you what,' he said 'perhaps if you feel so dirty we ought to see if there's anything we can do about it.'

She looked up at him. As usual, he was immaculately dressed, every line of his tailor-made trousers and cashmere sweater fitting perfectly. His deep blue eyes twinkled and just a hint of a smile played about his lips.

'Meaning what?' she asked mischievously.

'Well,' he said, taking her hand and leading her towards the door, 'I have been led to believe on previous visits to this house that upstairs you have what is commonly known as a bath tub. Now, people who know of these things – stop giggling, Claire, I'm trying to be serious – people who know of these things have said, and of course we must take their word for it,' they were upstairs now and walking down the corridor, 'that these porcelain objects are for washing in, for the removal of dirt, for the cleansing of the body.' He put the plug in and turned on the taps. 'Maybe,' he said slowly, 'we ought to find out.'

Claire stood expectantly, unable to stop smirking. This was fun.

'Of course,' he said, undoing the buttons of her shirt, 'I'll have to join you, just to make absolutely sure that we haven't been misled by the experts.'

'Do you think so?'

'Oh, absolutely. After all, I wouldn't be doing my duty as your fiancé if I didn't make sure you were . . . totally . . . utterly and completely washed.' He pulled off her shirt with a flourish.

'Of course,' she replied in all seriousness. He turned her

286

around and undid her bra. She then faced him again.

'You know,' he said, slipping off the garment and running an index finger around her breasts, 'there are merely attractive women and women whom no adjectives can adequately describe, and you,' he watched his finger traverse her white breasts, 'are the latter.'

She looked at him, proud and confident, the real woman in her coming to the fore. She took off the rest of her clothes while he undressed as well.

'Do you suppose,' she said, wrapping her arms around him and kissing him, 'that maybe we should go and see if the bed is still flat. You know, make sure it's still horizontal?'

He began to caress her, his hands running over her body. 'Now whatever gave you that idea?' and picking her up in his arms, he carried her down to the bedroom, kissing her all the while.

It never ceased to surprise Claire how it was that she could be so tired one minute and yet aching with physical desire the next. It had to be because she loved him so much.

He stood her in front of the full-length mirror and began to undo her plait. She watched him closely, her moist lips slightly apart. They said nothing. His fingers deftly parted each strand of her thick black hair which he spread out across her shoulders like a fan.

'Beautiful,' he whispered.

Their eyes met, holding each other's gaze. There was no need for words.

He kissed her neck, gentle, warm, his lips brushing against her skin, sending shivers of delight through her as he played with her nipples. Down towards her shoulders he went and she shut her eyes.

'I love you, Claire,' he whispered. 'I . . . love . . . you.'

He turned her round and they embraced. He then picked her up and carried her over to the bed. Lying her down, he began to kiss her again. This time, it wasn't only her neck, but her lips, her face, her breasts, her stomach; he wanted all of her.

She too needed him. Her heart pounded and she became oblivious to everything: the sun streaming through the windows, the wind blowing gently around the eaves; the ewes calling to their lambs; she heard and felt nothing. Only James mattered.

His tongue licked one of her nipples as his hands explored her body, gently probing and teasing with each touch.

She pressed hard against him. Her body was on fire. Only he could do this to her and she wanted him so much.

Across her flanks and down her pelvis went his quick-silver kisses, each one a tantalizing frisson of nerve-tingling heat. He ran his fingers delicately along the smooth hot skin of her thighs, easing her apart, beckoning her towards him. He watched her closely, as the rose-pink blush of desire spread over her skin towards her neck. It wouldn't be long now.

Faster and faster he went; teasing her, enticing her, her frenzy increasing. When her climax came, he was ready for her. He covered her face with kisses as she strained beneath him, her fingers etching her ecstasy down his back with each contraction. He pushed harder. Mind blank, body in autopilot and violence about to grip his soul, he pinned Claire down and shuddered within her.

She held him tight, her legs wrapped around his buttocks as the storm passed; her hands smoothing the skin on his back.

Afterwards, as she lay in his arms, satiated and warm, she said: 'I love you, James, so very much. I don't think I could live without you.'

He pulled her down again. 'Shh, you mustn't say that. Of course you could.'

'Do you love me?'

He squeezed her. 'How could you doubt it?'

'I don't. I just want to hear you say it.'

He smiled. 'Sometimes, Claire, you are a child.'

'Sorry.'

'Don't be. It's very endearing.'

They lay quietly.

'I wonder why Rosie didn't bark when you arrived. Normally she makes one hell of a racket if someone comes to the farm.' She chuckled. 'Maybe she's used to you now.'

'Well, of course she is. I knew she'd make friends with me eventually.'

'You saw her then?'

'Yes. I said hello to her and then she went off into one of the barns.'

They were quiet again and then he said, 'Darling, I don't want to be rude or anything, but are you moulting?'

In his fingers were some black hairs. 'They look a bit short for you.'

She sat up, embarrassed and nervously cleared her throat.

'They're not yours, are they?'

'No.'

'They're the dog's, aren't they?'

'Yes,' she answered quietly.

'Really, Claire, how could you let that animal share your bed? It's positively unhygienic.'

She said nothing but sat hugging her knees.

'Well, what do you have to say about it?'

She got up. 'Nothing.' She stopped and looked at him. 'Before you, James, she was all I had and I don't think it matters one way or another whether she sleeps up here or not. She's my animal and it's my decision.'

He got out of bed. 'Okay, okay, let's not fight about it.' He tried to hold her, but she moved away, not yet ready to give in to him. 'Come on,' he teased, pushing in her pouting bottom lip. 'I'm only jealous. After all, I would prefer it if I got preference over Rosie when it came to the sleeping arrangements.'

She capitulated with a shrug and wry smile. 'I'm sorry,' she mumbled. 'Yes, of course you come first.' She looked up at him. 'Will you forgive me?'

He pushed some stray hair away from her face.

'Yes, but only if you make her sleep downstairs in future.'

'All right.'

'And you'll buy some new linen and covers? That one smells.'

'Yes, I will.'

'Good girl. Right then, shall we go and have that bath of ours?'

Claire had no food in the house, so James suggested he went down to Torhampton for her. As he had forgotten his chequebook and only had a small amount of cash, could she lend him some? She immediately obliged.

With him gone, she decided to tackle some of the washing that was waiting to be done. With so much happening since his last visit, she hadn't got round to it.

Her washing machine was in the scullery, a small narrow room that ran off the side of the kitchen. It was always cold in there, no matter what the weather. Matt used to say it was because of the stone floor that was now worn smooth and shiny by generations of unknown feet. Despite its coldness, it had a familiar welcome to it. It was almost as though it understood that Claire belonged to the house, just as it belonged to her. The room never bothered her.

Alongside the washing machine sat a chest freezer and next to that an old stone sink with a single cold tap. Around the walls were shelves and cupboards housing long-forgotten bottles of sheep medicines, garden insecticides and books on animal husbandry. It was the room where things went that had no other home.

Matt had kept his guns in there. He had two, which he kept for potting rabbits and clay pigeon shooting. They stood in a steel cabinet, a strong padlock on the door. Somewhere in one of the drawers was the key, but Claire had never looked for it. She hated guns and hadn't looked at them since Matt's death.

She put the linen basket down on the floor and started to sort out the washing. She always checked pockets, having washed a few bills and paper money over the years. In one of James's she found a folded piece of paper. On it, in crudely embellished writing, she read:

My darling Jamie
Am missing you more than I can say
Love you so much.
S.

Claire shivered. It was suddenly much colder. She angrily screwed up the note and threw it away, thought better of it and then picked it up again. This time she spread it out on top of the freezer and smoothed down each tiny wrinkle.

She read it again, concentrating on each word, willing it to speak to her. Who was 'S'? James wasn't Jamie – he was James. No, it was a mistake, it had to be. It didn't make sense. But she couldn't ignore it. She wanted to – she just wanted to forget that she had ever seen it – but it wouldn't let her. So she folded it up and put it away in her pocket. She would wait; that was best, wait and see. If he didn't say anything, then maybe she wouldn't either. There was bound to be a simple explanation behind it.

She slammed the washing machine door shut and switched it on. She then stood by the freezer and stared out of the window, her mind a blank, her emotions in a void.

While she watched, she became aware of Rosie standing in the doorway of the barn. The dog was waiting for something, her gaze fixed on the road. James arrived, but Rosie, instead of going out to meet him, stayed where she was. Claire thought it would be interesting to see how the two of them got on together when she wasn't there. She watched as James got out of his car with the shopping. He walked towards Rosie, apparently saying something. Whatever it was made Rosie run off with her tail between her legs. Claire was puzzled. She had never seen Rosie behave like that before. She went out to meet him.

'What's going on?' she asked, gesturing after the dog.

'You saw?' He was wary.

'Yes. I was watching from the scullery.'

He shrugged. 'I don't know. It appears that whatever I say or do, she's not going to like me.' He paused. 'Perhaps she's jealous.'

'Jealous!' Claire cried incredulously. 'How can she be jealous?'

'Easy. Here, hold this a moment,' and he passed her another bag of shopping. The pair of them walked towards the house.

'Your dog is besotted with you. She loves you very much. You are the centre of her world and then along comes this strange man who takes away her mistress and, well, it's obvious really, isn't it? Her nose has been pushed out of joint.'

He smiled, quite satisfied with his explanation and they went indoors. After they had put the food away, Claire made him some coffee. She placed the steaming mug in front of him and then put the note down next to it.

'What's this?' he asked, holding it up.

She sat down opposite him and looked blankly at him. 'Read it.'

He did and burst out laughing.

'Well, what is it?' she demanded, irritated by his reaction.

'Ah, that explains it.'

She was puzzled. 'Explains what?'

'Why you were so ready to accuse me of mistreating Rosie.'

'I said no such thing.' She didn't understand.

292

'Oh yes you did.'

She looked at him with annoyance, her brows puckered. What was he talking about and why had he turned it around like that? She stood her ground.

'I didn't accuse you of mistreating her.'

'As near as made no difference.'

'Well, what if I did?'

He arched his graceful fingers together and said in a manner that suggested he was talking to a four year old: 'Somehow or another, presumably when you were sorting out the washing, you found this note in one of my pockets. It means nothing, of course, but you don't see it that way and then, when you see Rosie and me together in the yard, you misinterpret her behaviour, just like you've misinterpreted the note, and start painting me blacker than black.'

She glanced at him and noticed how his eyes weren't smiling, even if his lips were.

'This note,' he continued, 'is a prank – a very silly one, I might add – by one of the secretaries at work. She is a young lady with a rather bizarre sense of humour who has done this sort of thing before and with whom I will be having serious words when I get back to London.'

'What's her name?'

'Sarah.'

'Sarah what?'

'Oh look, Claire, does it matter?' He frowned at her. 'I mean, it's only a joke. Surely you're not taking it seriously?'

She turned on him. 'Well, it may only be a joke to you, but it's damn serious as far as I'm concerned!' She was getting angry, her jealousy running out of control. She couldn't help it. 'When I first saw this, I felt absolutely . . . well, I don't know, sick, I suppose.'

'Of course you would, darling. Anyone would react in exactly the same manner. It's perfectly understandable and quite natural.'

She gave him a watery smile. 'Oh dear, I've made a bit of a fool of myself, haven't I? I'm sorry, James. I've been a complete wally over this.'

He kissed her hands. 'No you haven't.' Then he smiled. 'If anything, it just goes to prove how much you love me.'

She nodded. 'Yes, yes, I do so much. I couldn't stand it if anyone came between us.' Her eyes started to fill. Even the thought of losing him could stir her to tears.

'Now don't cry, Claire,' and he wiped her face. 'It doesn't matter if you were a bit hasty over the note and said things you didn't mean. We all make fools of ourselves sometimes.'

'Oh James! I don't deserve you.'

'Yes you do and you're the only woman for me.'

She came round to his side of the table and sat on his lap. They embraced tightly.

'Darling, I have some news for you. I think I've found a property for us.'

'You have?' She moved to the chair next to him, her face vibrant. 'Where?'

'As I think I said before, the flat I'm renting at the moment is a bit too small, so when I was in London yesterday, I rang a few property agents and got some addresses of a few likely sounding places. Well, I visited three or four and in the end settled on a place which is in a very nice part of town. It's called Portland Road and the house is one of a long terrace of four-storey Victorian buildings. I'm sure you'll like it. There's plenty of rooms: two main reception, two bathrooms, four bedrooms, a basement, an attic and, of course, a large garden. It's really very nice.'

Claire looked away. All this was unexpected. She didn't imagine things moving so fast and felt uncertain.

'Well, what do you think?'

'The garden's big, you say?'

'Yes, largish.'

'Good. Plenty of room for Rosie.'

His expression didn't change. 'Quite.'

She looked back at him. She was decided. 'So, what are we going to do then?'

He hesitated. 'Well, there's a problem, a small one really, but still a problem.'

'What?' Surprises again and just when she had calmed down.

'The agents say they need a decision fairly quickly and if we agree to it, it's all ours.'

'Great! I agree to it and so do you.'

'But that's not all of it.'

She was puzzled. 'What do you mean?'

'The money,' he began. 'That's what I mean.'

'So?'

'Well . . . I don't know how to say this . . . but – '

'What?' she urged.

'It's awkward.'

'What is?'

He sighed. 'I want you to understand that normally I would never ask you to do this, but under the circumstances, I have no choice.'

'What circumstances?'

He glanced to one side. 'Cash flow,' he mumbled.

'Meaning what?'

'Meaning,' he said after a deep breath, 'that I need help with raising the deposit.'

Claire sat back in her chair and looked at him. Alistair's warning suddenly took on significance.

'What d'you mean "need help"?' she asked.

He shrugged, his smile faltering. 'Well, Claire, it's like this. I made a great deal of money throughout the eighties boom years. A great deal,' he repeated. 'But then . . . well, I came a bit unstuck. It's only temporary you understand,' he added hurriedly. 'These things happen. After all, you can't win all the time. I'll get out of it.'

'You will?'

He held her hand. 'Now, now, there's no need for you

to sound so suspicious. Of course I will, and with you to help me I'll get out even quicker.'

'What if I can't?'

She thought she saw his eyes harden, but his voice was honey-soft when he answered her.

'My darling Claire,' he whispered, leaning forward and kissing her on the cheek, 'would you really not help me?'

'You do love me, don't you, James?' she asked, her eyes so anxious as she tried to believe him.

'Of course I do!' he laughed.

'Okay. How much do you want then?' She still wasn't completely happy about it but he did love her and that was the only thing that mattered.

'Are you quite sure?' he asked.

She brushed aside any doubts. 'Of course. If you say you've found a place for us and it's good enough for you, then it's good enough for me. I'll lend you whatever you need.'

'Thank you, Claire. I knew you'd understand.'

'Right then,' she said brightly, ignoring the cold lump of mistrust in her stomach, 'what do you need?'

'Mmm, a hundred thousand. If that's all right by you.'

She blanched. 'A hundred thousand!'

'Claire, houses in London cost a damn sight more than houses down here and you do want a nice place to live in, don't you? Anyway, you did say you had pots of money from that inheritance you received. A hundred thousand pounds should be nothing to you.'

'Well it is. Fifteen thousand is as far as I'll go, James.'

'Only fifteen?' He was incredulous. 'But that won't get us anything!'

'Yes it will. If, as you say, the estate agents want to tie things up quickly, then that and whatever you can raise will be enough of a deposit to be going on with.' She saw his look of disappointment. 'I'm sorry, James, but I think a hundred thousand pounds is a ridiculous amount of money to put down for a deposit. Fifteen thousand it is and fifteen thousand it'll stay.'

He glanced at her. He had underestimated her. Anyway, perhaps he had pushed a bit too far.

'Okay then,' he smiled. 'Fifteen grand will do fine.'

'Happy now?' she asked.

'Yes.'

She arranged it all the following morning after a night spent making love with James, when he was especially attentive and very passionate.

EIGHTEEN

'You bloody stupid bitch!'

'What?'

'You heard me! Leaving that note in my trouser pocket. It nearly ruined everything!'

'What d'you mean?'

'Don't play games with me, Saskia. You know bloody well what I mean. That little note saying how much you missed me. Christ! What the hell were you playing at?'

'I didn't think it would do any harm.'

'You didn't think! God, that's your problem, Sas, you never do!'

'Please, James, I didn't mean it.'

'Don't whine! I can't stand it when you whine, and for God's sake take that muck out of your mouth. It looks awful when you chew gum!'

She removed the offending piece and wrapped it in a tissue before putting it into the rubbish bin.

'Do you want some coffee?'

'Yes.'

He picked up his luggage and placed it on the table. 'Thanks to your stupidity, I've brought back all my dirty washing for you to do.'

She glanced up from her magazine. 'Maureen will see to it.'

With a slow reptilian smile, he came round the table and, taking her by the arms, pulled her to her feet. 'No, Sas, she won't. Just for once in your lazy, useless life you are going to get off your backside and do it yourself.' He glared at her. 'Understand?'

'Ow . . . James, you're hurting me, let go.'

'I'll do more than just hurt you if you answer me back again.' He shook her. 'Are you listening to me?'

'Yes,' she mumbled.

'Louder, Sas, I can't hear you.'

'Yes, all right.'

He threw her back into her chair with contempt.

For a while they drank their coffees in silence. She because she was frightened to say anything, and he because he was thinking of McArdle. He would have to go and see him again soon, probably tomorrow, and he wasn't looking forward to it. True, he had paid some of the money he owed him, and he had the rest, but that wasn't the point. McArdle was an evil bastard; unpredictable and violent. There were stories all over the place of how he had squashed his rivals and 'sorted out' those who didn't show proper respect. James didn't want to be one of his victims.

Saskia looked up at James. She saw how pale he was and noticed the unfamiliar worry lines around the corners of his mouth and eyes. She had never seen him look so tired, but it was hard to feel sympathy for him. She had made a promise to herself that she would stick by him whatever he got up to. She wouldn't ask any questions and she wouldn't pry behind his back, but it was getting more and more difficult.

'The bank rang yesterday.'

He glanced up, suddenly alert. He was on holiday and they knew it, so why did they want him? 'Oh yeah?' he drawled. 'Who was it? What did they want?'

She shrugged. 'I don't know. It was Guy, your boss, said he wanted to speak to you urgently. Something to do with a transaction of some sort. I didn't get all the details but he sounded a bit miffed when I said you weren't here. I think you'd better ring him, sweetie.'

'Oh do you? Well I don't. Any more calls from him and tell him I'm abroad or ill or something. I can't talk to him yet.'

'But why? If you don't, James, you might lose your job.'

'And if I do I might lose my job as well,' he retorted. 'Anyway,' he added with a smile, 'soon I won't have to work.'

Saskia frowned.

'Don't worry, Sas, you'll find out why soon. Very soon.'

'That woman in Devon?' she ventured.

'Never you mind. Just you concentrate on looking beautiful,' and he patted her hand.

She knew he loved her because he said he did, but that wasn't enough any more. She wanted firm evidence of it. She wanted to be married, to have kids and to live like everyone else did. She wanted to be cared for, looked after and cherished. Instead, all she got was his violence, his moods and his secretiveness and she didn't like it at all. She wanted him but he was pushing her away. His behaviour today was proof of it. All this business in Devon; she hated it. She wanted to believe that he was being faithful to her, but it was so difficult.

She was all prepared to welcome him home and if only he would be a bit nicer to her . . . But when he shouted at her, it was terrible. That note was only meant as a little joke. He really was a bastard sometimes.

'What happened in Devon then?'

'Nothing much.'

'Did you get any money?'

'Look, Sas, don't hassle me, okay? Stop asking questions. I'm not in the mood for it.'

'Oh stuff you, James!' she retorted angrily.

He glared at her. 'What did you say?'

Her defiance melted. 'Nothing.'

He leant towards her. 'Don't give me any lip or you'll be very sorry.'

She snorted. 'Oh yeah? And what if I do?'

He slapped her; a full-faced stinging slap, leaving his hand tingling. 'That's what will happen.'

She recoiled, her hand on her face. Then the tears came. 'You shit! You utter bloody shit!'

After she had stormed out, James settled back in his chair. He felt strangely better now.

Saskia had spent the night in the spare bedroom, the door locked, and refusing to speak to him.

The following day, James was about to leave for the club when the doorbell went. It was Terri. Today she was a Goth; her hair dyed blue-black, her face a deathly white with thick black eyeliner and black lipstick, her ears decorated with enormous silver earrings. She wore sprayed on black jeans with a baggy black jumper. On her feet were black Doc Martens. James looked her over with barely suppressed amusement.

'What do you think you look like?'

She smiled, ignoring him. 'Saskia in?'

He turned away from her. 'She's upstairs sulking. I don't think she loves me any more.'

'Well, you can hardly blame her, can you?' She watched him as he primped himself in front of the hall mirror.

He caught her eye. 'You don't like me, do you, Terri?'

'It's nothing personal,' she replied. 'I don't like any men.'

'And why's that then?'

'Mostly because they're crap in bed. I tried it a couple of times and I've never been more pissed off in my life. It was a complete and utter waste of time.'

'Ah, but then you've never met a real man, have you?'

She looked at him; levelly and unafraid. 'And you're one, are you? The last of the great white-hot lovers?'

He grinned. 'Could be. You'll never know, Terri, unless you give it a try.'

She laughed. 'Forget it, Tarzan. You know,' she added, 'you men have two main problem areas, from the neck up and the waist down, and I see absolutely no reason at all

301

why I should waste my time with either of them.'

He turned round and came towards her slowly, his eyes fixed on her face. 'How can some dyke like you know anything about men? You're unnatural, you're perverted, you're . . . evil. Women like you don't deserve anything.'

She backed away from him. Now she was afraid. Her hands met the wall. There was nowhere she could go. He put his arms up and pinned her in.

'Do you know what I'd like to do with you?' he hissed.

She wouldn't look at him. She was terrified. She could feel his spittle against her face.

'I'd like to fuck your brains out; I'd like to let you know what it really feels like to have a proper man; I'd like to – '

'James!'

They both turned. Saskia was standing on the stairs. Terri took the opportunity to duck under his arms and run towards Saskia.

He smiled, tired and resigned. 'Two little girls together, eh? Dear, oh dear, Sas, I think I'm going to have to do something about this.' And with that he left.

Terri turned to Saskia, her eyes frightened and filling with angry, impotent tears. 'Charming bloody bastard, isn't he?' and she broke down, covering her face with her hands.

Saskia instinctively put her arms around her friend and comforted her. This time Terri was right: James could be an absolute pig. 'There, there, Terri. He didn't mean it. Honestly.'

Terri's reply was muffled as she sobbed against Saskia's shoulder. 'Oh yeah? He meant it all right. God knows what he would have done if you hadn't arrived.'

'He wouldn't have done anything. He was only teasing.'

Terri stood back. Her eyes red-rimmed and her mascara running. 'Oh God, look at me!' she exclaimed, catching sight of herself in the hall mirror.

302

'Come upstairs, you can clean up in the bathroom,' and taking her hand, Saskia showed her friend the way.

Terri lay back in the deep, hot, scented water. It had been Saskia's idea for her to have a bath. It would help her relax, she said, so while Terri relaxed, Saskia fetched them both a drink.

'Here you are,' she announced, coming back into the bathroom. 'One glass of champagne, relaxing for the use of.'

'Thanks, angel. You are a poppet, even if I can't make you see what a bastard James is.'

Saskia sat on the edge of the bath. 'Please, Terri, don't.' She shrugged as she stared glumly into her glass, the tiny bubbles rising to the surface. 'I know he can be . . . well . . . a bit difficult, but really, if you knew him the way I do, you'd know he's not like it all the time.'

'Really?'

Saskia sighed. 'Look, let's not talk about him.' She smiled brightly. 'Let's just forget him. Have some fun.' And she refilled Terri's glass.

'In that case,' replied Terri, her eyes sparkling, 'why don't you take off your clothes and come in?'

Saskia looked long and hard at her friend. Could she? Would she? It seemed an age before she finally made up her mind.

'Okay,' she said quietly.

Terri's heart missed a beat. It was something she thought she would never hear.

Their lovemaking started slowly. Terri knew she had to be careful. Saskia had never done this before. One false move and the whole episode might disintegrate and she couldn't bear that.

They washed each other; gentle, considerate hands smoothing lather over pink-tinged skin. Very little was said. Mainly they spoke with their eyes: Saskia's questioning; Terri's surprised at how easily it had all happened. She was half-expecting Saskia to stop at any minute, but she didn't. Instead, Saskia grew impatient.

'Bed,' she said, her heavy breasts rising and falling with each hungry breath.

Terri nodded.

They didn't bother drying. Hand in hand they walked to the bed and lay down.

'Why?' asked Terri.

'Why not?' came the reply, and they kissed. Saskia let her mind go blank as Terri's hands explored her. She didn't know why but she did know she needed some kindness, some gentleness. After James's rough selfishness, it was so good to be in the arms of someone who truly cared about what she wanted. And Terri knew exactly what she wanted.

'Enjoying that?' Terri's voice was a distant whisper.

Saskia nodded, a wide smile on her face. With James it could be such an effort, especially when he was in a bad mood and needing his ego massaged. But not this time. Lying in Terri's arms and giving herself up entirely seemed the easiest thing in the world. When she came, it was one of the strongest she had experienced.

Terri worked her way up Saskia's body, kissing her, her lips like scorching needles. 'Was that good, my darling?'

Saskia lay exhausted, arms and legs outstretched, like a becalmed windmill after a storm. She couldn't speak.

'My turn now,' said Terri, and she took hold of Saskia's hand and guided her downwards. 'There,' she said quietly.

It was an odd experience for Saskia, watching another woman writhing to her touch. Odd and yet more satisfying. Men, she thought, were so predictable.

Terri's face contorted, her eyes screwed tightly shut, her lips pulled back almost in a snarl as her hands dug into the mattress, wrapping the sheet around her fingers. She grabbed Saskia around the neck and pulled her towards her as she orgasmed.

Sexually replete, they lay quietly, their limbs wrapped around each other. Head to head, breast to breast, thigh to thigh. Sleep followed.

After the sunshine of the street, the noise of the traffic and the crowded pavements, it took James a few minutes to get used to the dim interior of the club.

The place stank. Stale cigarettes, old beer and the cloying background scent of perfume and old body smells permeated the air. It disgusted him. At that time of the morning, he preferred fresh air.

A lone barmaid, peroxided and clinking with fake gold jewellery over her tightly encased bust, idly wiped some glasses, a cigarette dangling from her vividly painted lips.

James walked towards her, his footsteps echoing on the polished floor, acutely aware that he was now in enemy territory. He thought it strange that this place, normally so alive with punters from all over London, should now seem so dismal. Like a sleazy temple to man's baser instincts, it reeked of selfishness, money and greed; of flesh bought and sold and of souls destroyed. Momentarily he despised himself because he was one of those who came here to worship and he couldn't do without it.

'Where is he?' he asked the barmaid.

She said nothing at first, looking blankly at him with tired, heavily mascaraed eyes, dead long ago. From a distance he had thought she was in her twenties. He was wrong by about fifteen years. Then she inclined her head. 'Upstairs. Ron'll take you. Ronny!'

A tall, bald man, heavily built, with a cadaverous face, appeared out of the dark, his well-cut suit clashing with his scarred hands.

'Bloke 'ere to see the Boss.'

Ronny turned to him. His voice was very deep. 'Name?'

305

'Skerrett, James Skerrett. I came last week. He's expecting me.' Already James could sense his mouth drying and his stomach beginning to churn. He regretted now not having any breakfast.

He watched Ronny pick up a phone. The man continued to stare at him with his dull brown dead eyes. He was inscrutable.

'Boss says come up. Follow me.'

They went through a door at the back of the bar and up a short flight of stairs. At the top there was a narrow landing with several doors along the side. They all said 'Private'. The one at the end was McArdle's office.

He fidgeted with his tie knot. It felt too tight and he was finding it difficult to breathe. He hated this corridor. It had no windows and the red flock wallpaper and replica prints of old London made him feel claustrophobic.

He was pushed into a bare wooden chair and told to wait. Ronny then knocked on the door. James didn't hear any reply but Ronny went in, pulling the door shut behind him.

Someone began to talk loudly – it was McArdle, James realized – and then another voice would answer, not loud enough for James to make out what he was saying, but whatever it was, McArdle didn't like it.

McArdle spoke again, but it was still muffled. The door of the office was reinforced because of the safe that was kept in there, so the words were indistinct. However, that didn't matter. James knew what was happening. His whole body knew it and reacted accordingly. He began to shake. Some poor bastard was getting it in the neck and soon it would be his turn.

A scream. James jumped, eyes and ears alert, the adrenaline racing through his system and his heart pounding. McArdle shouted again. It wouldn't be him doing the dirty work. He never bloodied his hands. He always got one of his men to do it while he watched. James felt sick.

The second scream made the hairs all over him stand up

in fear. It was so long and drawn out; so piercing. His shaking was getting worse. At that moment the door opened and out came Ronny. He smiled crookedly but his eyes remained blank. James noticed there was blood on his knuckles. Ronny took out a large white handkerchief and wiped them clean.

James glanced fearfully from him to the door. Ronny saw him.

'Boss'll see you in a minute. He's just sorting something out.'

There was a final thump from the room and then silence. The door opened again and Ronny was summoned. When he reappeared, he was dragging a semi-conscious, blood-spattered, middle-aged man. The whole of the man's shirt front was coloured a bright scarlet from where blood had dripped down from his smashed face.

James was horrified and nearly gagged. He looked up. McArdle was standing in the doorway.

'Come in, Jamie my lad, come in.' He still retained traces of a Scottish accent. James rose unsteadily to his feet and smiled weakly. He followed McArdle into the office. It wasn't a big room. There was a good solid table with the ubiquitous desk-top computer, some filing cabinets, a couple of chairs for visitors to sit on and pictures of boxers and racehorses around the walls. On the floor, behind McArdle's chair, sat a very strong. heavy-looking safe.

'Petty cash,' smiled McArdle, noticing his look, 'and talking of which, I think you owe me something – the remainder of your loan.'

James swallowed hard and then shifted uncomfortably in his chair.

McArdle lounged back in his seat and luxuriously smoked an enormous cigar. He seemed in an unusually good mood today. He was almost smiling to himself, his pock-marked cheeks fleshy and red. He rolled the cigar appreciatively through his fingers.

'Best Cuban cigar, is this.' He sucked deeply and then

pursed his thick lips to blow out the aromatic smoke. All the time he was watching James through his heavy-lidded eyes: watching to see how James reacted and James knew it. Between his pride and his fear, he managed somehow to look straight at McArdle's chest and the thick gold chain that hung around his neck.

'Well, I'm waiting.'

James reached into his jacket pocket and pulled out an envelope. He pushed it across the table.

McArdle glanced inside, his experienced eye calculating the amount with precision. The door opened. James turned quickly and saw Ronny. The big man smiled and then stood with his arms across his chest against the wall.

'Haven't seen you around lately, Jamie my lad.'

James turned back. He nervously lit a cigarette. He had to do something with his hands. 'No, I've been busy.'

'Too busy to come here.' It wasn't a question. James knew he had to be careful. He couldn't afford to upset the man.

'I've been away,' he said hurriedly. 'Family problems.'

The truth was that even now James had paid off his debt, he wasn't coming back here again. These people unnerved him. He didn't like to admit it, especially to himself, but their brittleness and unpredictability, their veiled threats of intimidation were more than he could stomach. They brought home to him a truth about himself that he could no longer ignore: he was a coward.

McArdle leant forward. 'Come back and see us, James. You're a good customer. Bring your friends, enjoy yourself.' He smiled slowly. 'I want you to come back.'

McArdle beckoned Ronny forward. James tensed and watched out of the corner of his eye as Ronny came to stand next to him.

'Give James his present, Ronny.'

James instinctively flinched and McArdle laughed. The resulting embarrassment was obvious.

'We're not going to hurt you, Jamie my lad. We like

you. In fact,' he went on, enjoying James's discomfort enormously, 'we like you so much we're inviting you to join our little operation.'

James blinked uncomprehendingly. 'What?'

'Yes,' said McArdle. 'We're going to ask you to look after something for us. A little thing,' he assured him, 'and only for a few weeks.'

Ronny handed over the package, a small brown paper parcel.

McArdle pointed a stubby, heavily beringed finger. 'You're to look after that.'

James stared at it and then looked quickly at the two men. 'What is it?'

'Now don't ask questions, Jamie boy. I don't like being asked questions.' McArdle sucked on his cigar. 'Ronny, get me a drink.'

The huge man left the room.

'You see,' continued McArdle, 'we have a problem.'

James was sweating freely now, rivulets pouring down his back. He wiped his hand across his forehead. 'We do?'

'Well, to be precise, you have a problem.'

James swallowed hard. 'What?' he croaked.

McArdle looked at the envelope. 'You are short. In fact quite a bit short.'

'But how can I be? You said . . . I . . .'

McArdle held up his hands. 'Now now, Jamie, don't take on so. Just calm down, okay?'

James licked his lips, his brain racing. He couldn't owe more surely?

'The fact is,' said McArdle, 'I'm prepared to overlook the extra amount you owe us, if . . . and it's a big if . . . you look after that.'

The door opened and Ronny had returned. He placed a large crystal tumbler of Scotch on the table. James eyed it enviously. He was thirsty.

McArdle picked it up and swilled the amber liquid around in the glass. 'You know,' he said, 'I really like a good whisky. Only the best and this stuff is sixteen-year-old Bruichladdich from Islay off the West Coast of Scotland. It's a rare and wondrous stuff that can only be bought from the distillery.'

He stopped and sniffed the aroma. 'Ahh, magic. Once a year I go up there on holiday, back to my roots, so to speak, and spend three weeks fishing for salmon and sea trout. You get a better sort of tourist up there. None of your riffraff.'

James didn't see the point of this conversation, but he knew it was far safer to let McArdle talk. Under the circumstances he would be prepared to put up with anything so long as it stopped him getting hurt.

McArdle went on: 'Yes, every day, come rain, wind or sun, I'm outside contemplating the beauties of the countryside and breathing in the fresh air. It calms the soul, you know, and lifts away the cares and worries that a businessman like me has. And then,' he put down the glass and glared at James, 'and then I have to come back here and once again deal with the problems of running a business like mine, a business that is difficult enough without having minor irritations like you to deal with.'

James looked up quickly. The atmosphere in the room had changed. He began to feel even more apprehensive. What had he done to upset things? Christ! He hadn't said no to McArdle's request.

'You will look after that for us,' said McArdle, pointing to the package. 'Understand?'

James nodded.

'You won't ask any questions and you won't open it. Right?'

'Yes.' His voice was barely audible.

'And next time I ask you to do something . . .'

'Yes?'

'There will be no discussion.'

James looked down at the small parcel. He just wanted

to get the hell out of there. He would agree to anything at that moment, if only they would let him go.

'Show Jamie out, Ron.'

James sat up straight. Was that it? Was he really going? He started to smile, his lips moving about wildly of their own accord, his relief overwhelming him.

'Goodbye, Mr Skerrett.'

'Yes, yes, of course. Goodbye.' The hammering in James's ears was the sound of his own heartbeat and it was drowning out everything else.

He hurried out of the room clutching the package, not seeing the looks passing between the other two men. He was heading out the way he came when Ronny stopped him.

'This way,' he growled, and taking James's arm in his strong grip, he inclined his bald head towards another door. It was hard to disagree with him. Despite the smile and the well-cut suit, Ronny was all muscle. James walked on meekly. They went through a set of 'Staff Only' doors, down a short staircase and out into a linoed corridor. The pungent smell of cooking filled James's nostrils and once again reminded him that he hadn't had any breakfast.

A chef, dressed in his whites, was standing by the back door having a fag. When he heard them coming and saw Ronny, he quickly stubbed it out and scampered back into the kitchen.

James stopped to look in, but was urged on by the man. 'Okay, okay, I'm going,' he said.

Ronny pushed open the back door. They stepped into a small yard, smelly and dirty with a line of rubbish bins up against a bare brick wall. It wasn't a warm day and yet there were flies crawling over the waste food and half-eaten remains from last night's dinner. On the ground was a chicken carcass that rats had been eating. James was revolted. He turned and looked at Ronny.

'It's a bit . . .' and he trailed off.

Ronny was putting on reflective sunglasses and then pulled on some black leather gloves. A cold hard knot of fear gripped James's stomach.

'Mr McArdle told me to tell you that he doesn't like having to wait for his money.'

'But . . . I told him last week . . . I said . . .'

'Shut up!'

James stepped backwards, his knees beginning to buckle. He knew he was going to cry in a minute. 'Please . . . I couldn't help it.'

'Mr McArdle says you won't do it again and you will pay him the extra interest.'

'Yes, yes, I promise. Of course I will. I'll pay him.'

His eyes desperately searched the reflective screens for signs of humanity but he saw nothing except his own pathetic cringing figure holding out his ineffectual hands against Ronny's advance.

The punch, when it came, was so fast that he had no time to avoid it. In a way he was glad it was over. The waiting had been far worse. When he slipped into unconsciousness, it was with a relieved smile on his face.

He found himself propped up against a wet brick wall underneath a railway arch. For a moment or two he tried to get his bearings, grimacing with pain every time he moved. He was aware of the taste of blood in his mouth and when he ran his tongue slowly around, it caught on the jagged edge of his two broken front teeth. There was also a bad gash in his bottom lip. He touched it gingerly, exploring it with his fingers. 'Shit!'

He put his hands down on the ground to try and ease himself up, away from the puddle of stagnant water that he was sitting in. 'Oh God!' he groaned when he finally got to his feet. His trousers were soaking, one shoe was missing and the front of his shirt was splattered with blood.

As he slowly straightened himself up, his sight blurring,

he remembered the package. If he lost that . . . Frantically he felt inside his jacket, shaking with panic.

It had gone. So had his wallet.

Poleaxed with terror he looked around on the ground. He could see nothing. He got down on his hands and knees, turning over bits of soggy cardboard, pushing aside rusting tins and empty bottles and throwing them out of the way.

'Where is it? Where is it?' he mumbled. 'Oh God, where has it gone?'

His fingers tore through the filth and slime, which released the noxious smells of slowly decaying matter. Crawling through the half-light, straining to see where his precious parcel and wallet had gone, his despair mounted.

'Think, think, think,' he told himself. 'Use your brains, for God's sake!'

He pummelled his fists against his head, trying to force himself to concentrate. It only made his dizziness worse.

It was then he heard a moan. Animal or man he wasn't sure, but it was coming from behind a pile of cardboard boxes on the other side of the archway. He got to his feet and approached slowly, like a cat stalking a mouse. Nothing was of any importance now; he could only stare at the boxes.

Another moan. James stood still, each hair on his body quivering. In the silence that followed, the distant traffic roar a mere blur on the perimeter of his mind, he inched himself forward. He reached the boxes. With thumb and forefinger he carefully pulled away the cardboard, unsure of what he would find. Inside, finally revealed in all its squalidness, lay a figure.

He peered closer. It was hard to tell its age, colour or sex, although on closer examination the matted hair on the head ran around to join a filthy straggly beard. It smelt foul; layer upon layer of clothing of indeterminate age and colouring covered the man, welded together by sweat, vomit and the elements. James stepped back. He had never seen anything so revolting in his life. Dulled as his senses were by his injuries and the surroundings, he was still unprepared for this.

He stepped closer again. Provided he breathed through his mouth, he wouldn't have to smell the stench. He nudged it with his foot. The figure turned over, peacefully oblivious in his drunken stupor, carried away from the desperateness of his miserable existence. His mind, what was left of it, the one safe haven where nobody could get him. Clutched in one of his grimy blackened hands was a half-empty whisky bottle and in the other hand James's wallet.

James was paralysed with indecision. He wanted his wallet. He had to have it. There was a good few hundred in it, not to mention a whole battalion of useful names and contacts, but that meant touching the body and he didn't know if he could.

Taking a deep breath, he leant down as quietly as he could. Not only did the man have his wallet, but he also had the package tucked away inside his shabby coat. James could only hold his breath for so long, and stepped back. The dreadful smell of ordure that wafted up from the figure was making him feel queasy.

Recovering his composure, he moved forward again and was just easing the wallet out of the man's hand when he became aware that the figure was awake. From the blackened hairy face, two rheumy brown eyes gazed unsteadily at him.

'It's mine!' the man yelled, yanking it away from James, who had been caught unawares by the man's formidable strength and had been knocked back on the ground. The drunk sat up and looked at him, gripping tightly on the wallet.

'Piss off you, find your own. This is mine.'

Most of his front teeth were missing, with only a couple of browned stumps left. He spoke in a husky growl, the

314

beard around his mouth stained a dark nicotine yellow-brown.

James stood up. 'Give it to me!' he demanded, his hands on his hips. He was damned if he was going to let this scum get away with it. He was livid. That wallet and package were his and no one, least of all a piece of rotten old shit like this, was going to take it away from him.

The tramp clutched the whisky bottle and James's wallet even closer to him smiling toothlessly. He opened the wallet, took out the money and started to count it, placing each note carefully on the ground.

James watched him with a cold hard fury. The man was teasing him, using his money to show James what he had and what James had lost.

'That's my money, old man. You stole it from me and now you're going to give it back.'

'Fuck off!' snarled the tramp.

James hesitated. The man had already shown his unlikely strength and James knew that if it came to a straight fight, he would have more than a match on his hands. He needed an advantage. He looked around. The remains of a fire smouldered a few yards away, blackened pieces of wood still glowing dully at the ends. He went over to it and picked up the heaviest piece, testing it against his hand, making sure it was strong enough. He looked back over his shoulder. The tramp was engrossed in his counting, happily losing his way and starting all over again. James had been quite forgotten.

The wood made a very saisfactory implement. It stood up to James hitting the tramp across the back of his head, smashing it end first into his face and then, a *coup de grâce*, a direct blow to what was left of his unused and shrivelled testicles. As the body fell to the ground, blood running bright red from its nose and shattered mouth, James removed his wallet from the now willing fingers and gathered up the loose notes that had scattered about in the mud. He didn't hesitate at all when it came to retrieving the package, the tramp's filth not bothering him now.

It was a strange experience walking back to his car. Jaded city dwellers, long used to unusual sights, parted before him on the pavement, avoiding his gaze, shooing their children past as if he were untouchable. He smiled indulgently at them. He couldn't care less what they thought; he had his wallet, his money and his package back. That was all that mattered.

He was glad when he got home that Saskia wasn't there. Probably out on some time-wasting shopping spree with some of her equally dumb friends.

As soon as he stepped into the kitchen, he undressed. He gathered up all his soiled clothing and put it in a bin bag outside the door. The rubbish men could take it away. He then trooped wearily upstairs, taking the package and wallet with him. He had a locked safety box in which he kept all his important papers. He would put the package in there. That way it would be safe from Saskia's prying eyes. He could never trust her completely.

He got the box out of his wardrobe and, taking a small key from his wallet, opened it. For the briefest, and only the briefest moment, he thought about opening the package. Holding it in his palm, he looked at it. What was it? It felt quite heavy and it gave under his fingers. He was curious, but not curious enough to risk his neck, so he put it away. He then counted the money in his wallet. He wasn't sure, but he thought some of it was missing. The old tramp must have spent it on booze. Still, he was feeling magnanimous. What was a few quid when he had all of Claire's money to look forward to?

With aching head, grazed knees, broken teeth and a badly cut lip, not to mention all kinds of bruises that were beginning to appear where he must have been kicked, he went into the bathroom and turned on the shower. The filth of that tramp was so bad that he was beginning to wonder if he could ever wash the stench away.

An hour later, he was lying back in a hot, deep, perfumed bath, his eyes shut as he dozed. At last he felt clean. It was how Saskia found him.

'What on earth happened to you?' She immediately sat down on the edge of the porcelain bath and touched his face.

He pushed her hand away. 'Don't, it hurts.'

She looked at him with concern, her face pinched and white, despite the makeup. 'But what happened?'

He sat up. 'Pass the soap. Go fix me a sandwich and some coffee, and this time make it less strong. I get enough paint stripper down in Devon.'

She started to chew her bottom lip. 'I don't think I can, I think we've run out of bread.' He turned and looked at her. He was too damn tired for a fight. 'Then put on your coat and go and buy some, dearest, because if I get out of this bath and there's nothing for me to eat, I'm going to get very upset.' He sighed heavily. 'Understand?'

She didn't argue, but stood up and left. He heard her thumping down the stairs and slamming the front door after her. Stupid cow, he thought.

The sandwich was a doorstep with holes in it where the almost frozen butter had ripped it, but it filled him up and under the circumstances, that was all that mattered. The coffee wasn't too bad either. After he had eaten, he pushed his plate away and lit a cigarette. Saskia sat opposite him, watching.

'Well?'

He winced when he tried to pull on the cigarette. He would have to get his face seen to and maybe his teeth capped.

'I took some money to McArdle and one of his men got a bit rough.' The details he would leave out. She didn't

317

need to know anything else. Anyway, he would far rather forget the entire incident as quickly as possible. Talking about it would only serve to remind him of the terror and complete helplessness that he had felt.

Saskia's beautiful face creased with puzzlement. 'But why did he get rough when you had taken him the money? Wasn't that what he wanted?'

James shook his head. 'It wasn't enough. He's added on extra interest.'

'So what happens now?'

He drank some coffee cautiously. 'I have to look after something for him for a few weeks, that's all.'

'What?'

James looked at her sternly. She seemed excited, her eyes bright. This was a side of Saskia that intrigued him. Her fascination with violence and its overlay of sexual attraction was coming out more and more often.

'Mind your own business, Sas. It's got nothing to do with you.'

'That's not fair, James. It's got everything to do with me. After all, I'm the one who has to live with you, so can't you tell me just a little bit?' Now she was flirting with him, doing her little-girl-lost look, her baby-blue eyes wide and inviting. She took hold of his hand and began to caress it.

He watched, mesmerized, as she moved over his wrist and up along his arm. His cigarette burnt forgotten in the ashtray, blue smoke curling into the still air. She got up and walked behind him. Placing her hands on his tense shoulders, she began to rub.

'My poor baby.'

James closed his eyes and leant his head back until it was sandwiched between her luscious breasts.

'Come to bed, Jamie,' she said softly. 'Come to bed so that I can take care of you.'

His mind dulled. He was so tired. Saskia's voice seemed to be coming from a great distance; a call on the wind echoing down to him. Bed . . . yes, he wanted sleep, to forget everything, to lose himself in unconsciousness. Dimly aware of her hands moving over his chest, he relaxed more and more, letting a calm heaviness spread through his limbs. She began to kiss his neck. 'Please, Jamie, let's go to bed.' Her breath was hot against his skin, but he didn't hear her. It was only when she put her hand on his crotch that he reacted. He grabbed her.

'No. Don't. Leave me alone.' He stood up and walked to the window.

She came up behind him and put her hands around his waist. 'But why, Jamie? I've missed you.' She tried to kiss him. 'Please, Jamie, why not?'

'Don't call me that!' he exploded. 'Leave me alone! Can't you see I don't want you!' He roughly pushed her away. McArdle called him Jamie. That bastard! And no one else was going to; not now, especially not her.

'It's her, isn't it?' she cried. 'That bloody woman in Devon!'

James turned his back on her. 'Don't be stupid, Sas. Of course it isn't. I'm just tired, that's all. God Almighty! I get beaten up today and all you can think about is sex!'

She went quiet. 'I don't believe you,' she said at last. 'You're screwing her and don't tell me you're not because I know what you're like, Skerrett. Anyhow, what if I'd found someone else? You wouldn't like that, would you?'

He looked at her with wry amusement. 'Oh yeah? And who would that be? Come off it, Sas, no man in his right senses is going to want you.'

'You bloody pig!' she yelled, her high-pitched voice going right through him, making his headache even worse.

'Oh for God's sake shut up, Sas!'

'No I won't!' She took out a tissue and blew her nose. 'You know,' she said, a look of real malevolence on her face, 'if I find out what's really going on between you and that Bromage woman, I'm going to tell her everything and

319

blow your little plan to kingdom come.'

He came up behind her. The bitch! How dare she! Who the hell did she think she was?

He grabbed her hair. 'Saskia, just what are you going to say?' And he slapped her terrified face. 'Don't you ever threaten me, Saskia, because if you do I will not be held responsible for my actions. Okay?' He shook her hard.

'Owwww! You're hurting me!'

'Good, serves you bloody well right!' He threw her forward so that she cracked her head on the table. 'Just don't even think about it, Saskia, not once, or God help me!' He was shaking, partly because of his rage at her, but mostly anger at himself. He was such a craven coward and that morning McArdle had proved it.

He walked away, ignoring her sobs, almost crying himself. He hated it when she made him hurt her.

She found him in the lounge cradling a large whisky. She watched carefully from the door to see his reaction and then, when she could see it was safe, came in and sat down next to him on the sofa. He put his arm round her and kissed her blonde curls.

'Saskia, Saskia, you're a silly little girl. Do you really think I would want to go to bed with that oik? God, it's bad enough having to take her out and compliment her. I couldn't sleep with her as well!'

'I don't know, James,' she sighed. 'I just know I love you and that you're hurting me.'

'I'm sorry, baby, but it'll be over soon, believe me.'

'Honest?'

'Honest.'

It was at times like this he could almost believe he loved her.

NINETEEN

Saskia couldn't sleep. She lay on her back staring at the ceiling, restless and agitated. Something was wrong: James was wrong. He didn't want to make love to her. He was angry, even more so than normal and, as usual, it was she who was getting the worst of it.

It was pointless trying to talk to him about his problems. So far as that was concerned, he was a closed book. He wouldn't answer any of her questions and simply told her to mind her own business.

It's not fair, she thought. All this business with his inheritance and the woman in Devon and now McArdle's men beating him up. Why wouldn't he tell her what was happening? She had a right to know. She was his girlfriend after all.

She sat up and scowled in the darkness. Bloody pig, she thought. She looked down at his sleeping form. The desire to inflict more injury was tantalizingly close to being realized.

No, she thought, I mustn't. If I did that he'd kill me.

She sighed and then her eye caught something. On the dressing-table were his wallet and diary. Her heart raced. It was the perfect opportunity.

She slid out of bed, tiptoed over the carpet and picked them up. She glanced over her shoulder. James was flat on his back and snoring. The sleeping pill she had given him had more than done its work. She smiled to herself.

Downstairs she poured herself a large gin and tonic and lit a cigarette. She then sat down on the sofa, his wallet and diary on the coffee table in front of her.

Her hands felt sweaty. She rubbed them hard against

the sofa, but it didn't help much. With one last drag at her cigarette, she picked up his diary. What did he say that woman's name was? She remembered. Bromage: Claire Bromage. She opened the diary at the address section. Pages and pages of his distinctive heavy black script stared up at her. Some were just initials – girls, she thought – and some just surnames. At the end she found what she was looking for. Claire Bromage, Tor Heights, Torhampton, Devon and her telephone number. Taking a pad and pencil Saskia copied it down. She would hide it away in her bureau. He had searched that once, a long time ago, quite soon after he first moved in, and finding nothing there of any consequence, had left it well alone. He wouldn't think to look there again.

After his diary, his wallet. Some money, bits and pieces, but nothing much. There was even a photograph of her. Unexpected. It made her smile. Then she found the key. Sitting in her palm, its sharp coldness burnt into her flesh. Where did it come from?

She finished her drink and cleared up. The last thing she wanted was for him to come downstairs and start making a scene just because she left a dirty ashtray out.

Back upstairs, she replaced the wallet and diary on his bedside cabinet and slipped into bed, snuggling up to his warm back. She found it much easier to drop off this time.

'Where's he gone then?'
'Devon.'
Terri laughed. 'You're unbelievable, Sas.'
'Why?'
'The way you put up with him.'
They were shopping. Not for anything in particular, but just because they felt like it. Saskia's father had given her some extra money he had made on some shares he had sold for her, and Terri had sold one of her paintings. They were feeling extravagant.

322

'What about this one?' asked Terri, taking a dress off the rail and holding it to herself.

Saskia shook her head. 'No, wrong colour. You need something a bit lighter. That's too dark.'

Terri shrugged and put it back. 'He's an inveterate shagger, you know.'

'Who is?'

'James, silly. If it walks, it's female and under the age of sixty, he'd poke it.'

'Terri! How can you say such a thing?'

'Because he is, that's why! The only problem is you can't see it.'

'I can't see it because it's not true. Yes, that's a much better colour. Goes really well with your hair.'

'I'll try it on.'

Exhausted with shopping, they decided to rest in a café.

'How much were those trousers?'

'Four and a half grand.'

Terri gasped. 'What!'

'Well, ostrich leather is very expensive, you know, and all the best people are buying it now. Coffee or tea?'

'You're obscene! It's obscene! It looks awful!'

'Mmm, look at those cream cakes, aren't they lovely? A slice of that one, please.'

'How can you spend that much money on clothes?'

'Why not? It's all on credit card. Anyway, why should I care? If I don't pay it off at the end of the month, it won't matter. Daddy will pay it for me.'

'God! How the other half lives. It's absolutely sick! Here am I, struggling to survive, and all you can do is behave like there's no tomorrow.'

Saskia licked some cream off her lips. 'Well, a girl needs something to cheer her up.'

'Why? Are you depressed? You don't seem it to me. Your appetite isn't.'

Saskia reached into her handbag and placed a small key

on the table. She waited for her friend to say something.

Terri shrugged. 'Well what is it?'

'It's James's. I got it from his wallet the other night. I'm not sure what it belongs to, but I think if I search around I'll find it.'

Terri looked nonplussed. 'So what? I mean, what has it got to do with you?'

'You don't understand, Terri; I think James is lying.' She looked at Terri, her blue eyes level and determined.

'Wow! You mean you've only just discovered this?'

'Don't patronize me!' she snapped. 'I know I might have said differently before but . . . well, I needed time, that's all.'

Terri's face softened. She was glad. She had sat by for over two years now, watching Saskia struggle with her inner convictions as James used and abused her and at last she had woken up to him.

'What happened then?' she asked.

'It was the other night,' began Saskia. 'He was asleep, snoring, you know, so I knew it was for real, and I couldn't relax. I kept . . . I don't know, I kept thinking that he just wasn't with me any more, that something had changed him.' She paused. 'I don't know what it was,' she continued, 'but something inside me said enough was enough.' She picked the key up.

Terri took it from her hand and examined it. 'Does James have a strong box?' she asked.

'I don't know. He may have. I haven't looked.'

'Well, this,' she said, holding it up in front of Saskia, 'may belong to one. My father has one and the key is very similar to this.' She handed it back. 'What do you think's in there.'

'I don't know,' mused Saskia, studying the key. 'Something exciting, I hope.'

Terri looked at her closely. 'If it were money or something then we could go abroad. Get away from James and all this. Do you remember that time I said I was thinking of going to Australia?'

Saskia put down her coffee cup. 'Yes.'

'Well, why don't you come with me? For a holiday,' she added quickly, sensing Saskia's immediate caution. 'We could travel round, get some sun, have fun with the locals.' She smiled hopefully. 'I've heard Australian men are generally big, blond and randy. Just your type of chap, I would have thought. And if you don't like them . . . well, there's always just the two of us.'

Saskia stared into the distance, quite lost in thought. The idea of going away was beginning to appeal to her more and more, but not enough yet. She turned back to Terri.

'Give me time,' she pleaded and then more quietly: 'I think I still love him, you know, and I know he's every-thing you say he is, but . . . it's not as easy as you think. It takes a long time before you'll admit to yourself what a complete wally you've been and I don't think I'm quite there yet.' She gave Terri a small smile.

'I understand, but I need to know soon, okay?'

Four days later James's teeth had been fixed, his lip was healing nicely and he seemed to be his old self again, as bad tempered and as moody as always. Saskia had forgot-ten to buy some toothpaste.

'Oh God, trust you,' he snapped, zipping up his over-night bag. 'Now I'll have to buy some at a service station or something.'

She got out of bed and stood in front of the dressing-table mirror, pulling in her stomach. 'Do you think I ought to lose some weight, James?'

'For heaven's sake, woman, how the hell can you expect me to answer that when you can see I'm up to my eyeballs!'

Saskia pouted. 'Do you have to go back to that terrible

325

woman?' She pulled her stomach in further, thus sticking out her weighty bosoms.

'Yes, Sas, I've told you, I have to.'

He held her. 'Not much longer, darling, and then perhaps we can go away somewhere; a holiday somewhere hot. You'd like that.'

'Oh can we, James?' She hugged him and then pulled away looking at herself once more in the mirror. 'It's high time I got a proper tan.'

He moved behind her and cupped a breast in each hand. 'Frankly, my dear,' he growled in a dreadful American accent, 'I don't care what colour you are, provided you have all the necessary equipment.'

He watched her as she closed her eyes and leant back against him. Good. She was purring. That was exactly what he wanted. It had been a difficult few days for both of them. Her nonstop questions about McArdle, the money and his visits to Devon had put so much pressure on him. And now he was going away again.

'I won't be long this time, Sas, just a few days to get what I want and then I'll be home. If Guy rings up, tell him I'm ill. I'll speak to him when I get back.'

She half opened her eyes and nodded. 'Fine,' she said, not really listening. She moistened her lips. She then started to rub herself against him, her excitement mounting.

With little preamble he moved her round to the bed and pushed her down onto her knees so that she was lying face down across the duvet. He unzipped his flies. It was funny really; now he was going away for a few days and would be free from Saskia's intolerable pestering, he was as randy as hell.

Without resistance, he slid in from behind and began to thrust. There were times when it was more appropriate simply to take her and this was one of them. He didn't care if she didn't enjoy it.

Kneading her breasts, his heart pounding and sweat

beginning to prickle his back, he soon teetered on the edge of his oblivion. With monumental heaves, he pushed inside her dark velvety confines until he was quite drained. He lay against her back, breathing hard.

'That was wonderful, darling. You were great.'

She said nothing, but stared fixedly at the blurred pattern on the duvet cover. Nothing had happened for her.

He got up and rearranged himself, tucking his shirt in his trousers. 'I'll give you a ring when I get there, okay?'

'Fine.' She rolled over and sat up. She was still wanting.

He leant forward and kissed her. 'Bye, darling. See you soon and behave yourself while I'm away.'

He descended the stairs feeling much happier. Good old Sas! All he had to do was keep screwing her. That always put an end to her awkward questions.

She watched him leave from the bedroom window. 'Bastard!' she whispered. He hadn't made love to her, he had just screwed her. He was keeping the real stuff for that woman in Devon. She just knew it. God! How could she be such a fool? Then she smiled to herself. She still had his key.

She started to search. It wasn't long before she found what she was looking for. The metal strongbox was on the floor of his wardrobe. He hadn't even bothered to cover it up.

She inserted the key and heard the satisfactory click as the lock opened. Inside there were separate compartments and it was while she was searching through these that her hand touched the masking tape of the package that was sitting at the bottom underneath some files. She took it out, turned it over and felt it with her fingers. She was intrigued.

She tried to peel off one corner where the tape wasn't stuck on properly, but it only ripped the paper, so she stopped. She went to her dressing-table and in amongst all the mess, found a nail file. She pushed it through the

327

wrapping and withdrew it and her face lit up. White powder. She tasted it. It was cocaine. James must have bought it as a present for her and was keeping it as a surprise. What a wonderful thing for him to do! He must love her after all. How could she have possibly doubted him?

She poked the nail file in again, and with careful manipulation managed to make a big enough hole so that she could tip out enough for a good sniff. She didn't want to make it obvious that she had been helping herself, otherwise he might get cross. No; she would take some when she needed to and not say anything about it. Then when he gave it to her, she would pretend to be surprised.

She spent the afternoon in town, although she couldn't really remember much of it. She had a dim recollection of being ushered out of Harrods after screeching with laughter at some Egyptian pots and asking bemused customers what they thought of such tacky items. The floor manager approached her like a besuited exocet and took her by the arm.

'Excuse me, madam, but if you come with me I'll get you a taxi.'

'But I don't want one!' It was hard to focus on him.

He smiled grimly. 'I'm sorry, madam, but I really do think you ought to leave. Perhaps you aren't feeling well?'

'I'm perfectly well, thank you, and take your bloody hands off me!'

Without changing a muscle of his fixed smile, he walked her across the department and handed her over to the doorman.

'Find this lady a taxi, please. At once,' he ordered.

The doorman, young, spotty, clean-shaven and at least six feet eight held on to her. His voice was very deep. 'This way, madam.'

Saskia tried unsuccessfully to dig her heels in but it was futile and she only succeeded in sliding unceremoniously across the tiled floor. Once out on the pavement and still pulling against his hold, she stood sulking, her hair awry and her coat undone.

'You pig!' she shouted. 'Let me go!'

'I think, madam, perhaps if you would stand still . . .'

'Piss off!' she screamed, stamping on his foot.

He momentarily winced. 'Now now, madam, that's no way for a young lady to behave.'

'Oh yeah?' she sneered, 'and what would a peasant like you know about such things.'

A taxi drew up and with more force than he would customarily use, the doorman bundled her into the back seat. 'Take this slut home,' he told the driver.

'Slut! Slut! Who are you calling a slut!' she yelled as the taxi pulled away. 'Do you know who my father is? I'll sue you, you bastard! Just you wait, I'll sue the bloody lot of you!'

The driver watched and waited until she had crumpled into a heap of tears.

'Where d'you live, luv?'

That evening, satiated on smoked salmon, caviar and a second large slice of cream-laden gateau, she sat in front of the television watching a video of *Cinderella*. James would never stomach such things if he was around but, free from his control, she always indulged herself. As usual, it made her tearful so she had to have a large gin to calm her. That naturally led to another and another until eventually she had drunk her way through a third of a bottle. Easy to do, she thought to herself, when you are alone and nobody loves you. Even her own dear Jamie didn't any more. He said he did, but she knew he didn't really. She had another drink.

He only said he loved her so he could get round her, so she would stay with him, so she could bail him out whenever he got in trouble. Well, she wasn't going to have it any more. Absolutely not. Her parents had warned her about him, saying that he was a common little leech and she hadn't listened. Well, she would now. She wasn't going to be walked over or used just as it suited him. She was going to stand up to him and tell him she'd had enough. She had another drink.

'The shit, the dirty rotten bastard! He had used her for everything she had and now he was leaving her for that Bromage woman. She started to cry.

Now he was with her and kissing her and probably making love to her. Why? What could he possibly see in some horrible old woman who lived in a pigsty? What did she have that Saskia didn't have?

She stood up and tried to pull off her nightie. I'll show her, she thought, I'll show her what a real woman's body should look like. The room swayed and she cried, further blurring her vision. When she crashed over the small occasional table and landed heavily on the sofa it didn't come as much of a surprise. With her nightie pulled up round her throat like an Elizabethan ruff collar and the rest of her Junoesque body stretched along the sofa, she cried really hard, her white flesh wobbling with each breath and tears cascading down her face.

'Jamie . . . Jamie . . . I love you . . . you bastard . . . you fucking bastard!' she screamed, hammering her fists against the upholstery. 'I love you and you're leaving me! It's not fair!'

She rolled over, sending the full ashtray off the side arm of the sofa onto the floor, the grey ash and squashed butts flung out across the carpet. She reached for her glass but missed and it fell over, spilling the contents. She found this very funny and started to giggle. At first they were light little guffaws, but soon they were full-blown and explosive roars. Her face, red and blotchy, was screwed up in open-mouthed emotion as she rolled from side to side, holding her stomach, her fingers digging into the firm roll of fat. It stopped abruptly. She sat up and pulled down her nightie.

'I'll ring her,' she said.

She stumbled over to the telephone. After a few minutes of uncoordinated searching, she found the number. Clutching the telephone tightly to herself, like some prized possession, she dialled. At last the ringing stopped.

'Hello, Claire Bromage speaking.'

Saskia giggled quietly.

'Hello, who is this?'

Saskia held her hand over her mouth, suppressing her laughter.

The phone went dead.

Saskia grinned. 'Bloody cow!' she muttered. She ambled back to the sofa and gave herself another drink. Some time later, as she drifted off into a drunken tear-sodden sleep, she made up her mind to go and visit Claire whatever-her-name-was and give her a piece of her mind.

The first thing Saskia noticed when she woke up was the dreadful taste in her mouth; metallic and bitty. Her tongue tasted foul. She then realized why. Sometime during the night or early morning she had been sick. Luckily she had been lying on her side otherwise it would have choked her. As it was, it had run through her hair, down the front of the sofa and onto the floor.

'Oh no!' she moaned, closing her eyes again. This really was too awful. And her headache! It was blinding in its pain. She put a hand to her face and eased away the sticky strands of hair that had stuck to her cheek. When that had been done, and it seemed to take a very long time, she very slowly sat up, trying as best as she could not to make any sudden move.

She opened her eyes and surveyed the mess. Thank God James wasn't here. She closed her eyes again. The sight and smell of it all was making her feel worse. Perhaps if she asked Maureen nicely she would clean it up for her. If she slipped her an extra tenner, she would definitely do it.

She stood up, unsteadily at first, but then with more conviction. Shower first, everything else later.

Maureen, contrary to what Saskia expected, was uncooperative.

'No way, miss. I'm not clearing up that mess and that's final.' She folded her skinny arms across her sunken chest in defiance, her thin colourless lips pulled into a tight line. 'Forget it.'

'Oh please, Maureen, I'll give you some extra money.' Saskia waited hopefully.

Maureen gave her a shrewd sideways glance. 'How much?'

'Ten?'

Maureen turned away in contempt.

'Twenty?'

She looked back. 'Twenty-five,' she said with authority. She had worked for Saskia long enough to know she had the upper hand. The young woman was such a slut and in all her cleaning years she had never been in such a filthy house. And the things they got up to as well. Disgusting!

Saskia found her purse and handed over three ten-pound notes. 'I haven't got any change.'

Maureen pocketed it. 'Doesn't matter. Neither have I.'

After some brunch and a very large pot of coffee, Saskia sat at the kitchen table trying to concentrate on her next move. It wasn't easy. Maureen was hoovering in the corridor outside and singing some ghastly sea shanty in a high, off-key warbling soprano. Saskia eventually reached a decision. She would go to Devon and find out exactly what was going on.

She packed her bag and left at three. Five hours later she crossed over the county border, unsure of her directions, but determined to get there. Finding Torhampton wasn't difficult, but after that it became more complicated. She stopped several times to ask the way, only to stare blank-faced and uncomprehending at the replies. What were they talking about? She couldn't understand their accent at all. Finally she stopped a policeman. He, she did understand, and twenty minutes later found herself outside Briar Cottage. James's car wasn't there and the house was dark, but she could be patient; she would wait.

She sat in the car for two hours, playing some CDs and eating a pasty. By now she was getting angry. She was quite sure this was the address in his diary, so where the hell was he?

She got out of the car and looked around. This was getting ridiculous. She was damned if she was going to spend the night hunched up in the front seat. She had to have somewhere decent to sleep. On top of that, there was a pressing need for a bath. A whole day's travelling and her headache was returning. She felt dreadful.

She walked up to the front door and tried to open it. It wouldn't budge. She went round to the back of the house, her shoes getting wet and muddy on the rough path and tried the other door. It was also locked. She stepped back and looked up at the windows. Maybe one of them was open. It wasn't. She swore silently. There was only one thing for it. She would have to break in.

She elbowed in a back window, sending shards of glass tinkling onto the floor, and climbed through. Inside it was dark and cold but she soon found the light switch. Once she got the central heating on, it wouldn't be too bad.

It was with some dismay that she realized the only heating was an open coal fire and that she would have to make it up and light it.

'Shit!'

There was some kindling, but not enough, and it meant she had to stand outside in the wet garden wielding a heavy axe to cut herself some more. She broke two of her nails and was very annoyed.

She wasn't completely sure how to lay a fire. She had vague memories of the cleaner at her parents' house doing it, but that was years ago and it was a struggle to recall exactly what she did. With a heavy sigh she crunched up some newspaper, laid the kindling on top and then put on the coal. It soon flared up and she sat there hopefully watching the flames lick the back of the flue. Then they died down and vanished altogether.

She crunched up some more paper and this time opened up the grate. It went a bit better, but not much. She then realized she needed a draught and spread her Aquascutum mac across the front. The flames roared and she smiled. Success: that was until she realized she had burnt a huge hole in the garment.

'Shit! Shit! Shit!' she yelled as she stamped out the flames, leaving a black smouldering mess.

When searching the kitchen for food, she found half a stale loaf, some remains of butter in its wrapper and a tin of soup. She couldn't get the tin opener to work so using a skewer, she punched two holes in the top and emptied it out that way.

Eating her pathetic little meal in the sitting room while she watched a flickering picture on the black and white television, it slowly dawned on her that James wasn't coming back that night. He was with Claire. She knew it. He couldn't lie to her this time. Still she had her little treat. She had helped herself to a supply of cocaine before she left, and that would cheer her up. She also had a bottle of gin in the car, just in case of emergencies – and it was definitely an emergency now.

James wasn't asleep but pretended to be. Lying quite still and staring at the thin flowered curtains, he couldn't relax. Why the hell, he thought, hadn't she changed them? She had the money, for God's sake.

He rolled over slowly and looked at her. Relaxed and unworried, her calm face registered only her inner peace. For a moment he envied her.

It had been a difficult day. She had been overjoyed to see him – even if her mongrel wasn't – but it took a fair amount of lying to allay her worries about his injuries. When at last he had persuaded her that he had only been mugged, and yes, he had reported it to the police, she finally relaxed. She then wanted to seduce him. Tired, anxious and not really enthusiastic, he resorted to his usual way of satisfying her: he switched into autopilot. This talent allowed him the luxury of doing his job well without disappointing anyone, and nothing distracted him. His services had been bought over the years by women who were well past their prime but still he satisfied them. He was well-known for it and Claire was no different. He had to maintain his pretence. One slip of his façade and she might begin to suspect something.

He lay quietly listening to the night sounds. Sometimes it was a cow, sometimes a sheep, but mostly it was eerily quiet. The only noise that regularly broke the silence was the chime from Claire's grandfather clock down in the sitting room. He began to resent it very much.

McArdle: he wanted more money and he wasn't prepared to wait this time. And then there was that package. It had to be drugs. There was nothing else it could be. He had better make sure Saskia didn't find it. And there was the bank too. Guy must have discovered something. James thought he had covered his tracks well. That Berkshire woman's account, among others, had served him well over the months, supplying most of his gambling money. He meant to pay it back all of it, and sometimes he did, but he knew at the time he might have gone a bit far with her. Still, he reasoned, she asked for it. Threatening to call the police in when she caught him signing one of her cheques. What the hell did she expect? She wasn't really to his taste, far too skinny. It was a relief to get back to Saskia.

Saskia: he wondered where she was now. Probably drunk or stoned, or maybe both. He would have to take her away somewhere when all this was over: somewhere hot, where the police didn't ask too many questions and he would not be extradited to face charges for fraud and deception. He sighed. No wonder he couldn't sleep.

He irritably rolled over and pulled the covers up around his shoulders. At least Claire had got rid of that smelly old duvet.

When he did awake she had got up and the sun was pouring in through the open window. To James that said it all: a thin poor miserable existence, at the mercy of the elements. He hated it, all of it, and wanted to get away from it as soon as he could. He was damned if he was going to help bring in the cattle like she had suggested the previous evening. He had other, more important things to do.

He got dressed and went downstairs. Claire had left a note on the kitchen table telling him she was over at Jack's and would be back at lunchtime. She also wrote that she loved him. He screwed it up and dropped it in the Rayburn. Such sentimentality he could do without.

Picking up his car keys, he decided to leave. Even being back at Briar Cottage was better than staying here. At least there he didn't have to put up with the dreadful smell of the farm.

When he reached the cottage, he nearly didn't stop. Saskia's car was there, parked in front of the door. He cursed quietly. That was the last thing he needed.

He found her fast asleep stretched out along the carpet in front of the dying fire with her burnt mac over her shoulders. He yanked her up.

'What the hell are you doing here, Sas?' He sat her unceremoniously on the chair, his foot clinking against an empty gin bottle.

'Christ, you stink!'

'Leave me alone!' she muttered feebly, her eyes barely open, the combination of drugs and drink making it difficult to rouse her. She saw his blurred figure and heard his strident voice, but it didn't register. She smiled aimlessly. 'Hello, James.'

'God, you're hopeless, Saskia.' He put his arms around her and roughly manhandled her towards the bathroom.

Without any protest, he stripped her, sat her in the large stained bath and turned on the cold shower at full blast. Up until that moment she had been giggling and smiling, but when the water hit her . . .

'Turn if off, you bastard! Turn it off!' She flayed her arms helplessly as she tried to protect herself from the cold. She started to speak again but he directed the water straight at her face. She coughed and spluttered.

'You sod! Leave me alone. Stop it!'

'Sober now, are we?' he asked with malicious glee.

'Yes . . . yes . . . please, James, stop it!' She was crying now. 'Leave me alone!' she wailed.

He put down the shower and adjusted the water so it ran hot. 'Get washed and I'll see you in a minute.'

She looked at him bleary-eyed and sulky.

He made some coffee and lit a cigarette. Saskia appeared, wrapped in his bathrobe, her hair wrapped up in a towel.

'Well, what do you have to say for yourself?'

He wasn't angry, more resigned. He should have known better really. This was exactly the kind of thing she would do; unexpected and stupid. She could have jeopardized everything.

'Well? I want an answer, Sas.'

She sat down avoiding his gaze and sipped her coffee. 'Can I have a cigarette?'

'No.'

'Oh please, James, I've run out.'

He impatiently pushed his pack across the table. She took one.

'What's going on then and how did you get this address?'

She looked down at her nails. There was no way out now.

'I looked in your diary.' She glanced up quickly. There, she had said it. If he went berserk it was only to be expected.

'What! You did what?' he exploded, standing up and

337

leaning over to her. 'You looked in my diary?'

'Please, James,' she whimpered. 'I had to. You don't tell me anything. I had to. Please don't hit me.' Her face crumpled in apprehension.

'I ought to bloody well thump the living daylights out of you for what you've done!' he roared, smashing her coffee cup to one side so that it shattered against a cupboard and left a stream of brown splashes down the wallpaper. She winced.

'You never tell me anything, James. I had to know,' she started to sob. 'I love you, Jamie, you bastard; don't you understand that?'

He sat down again, breathing rapidly, his mouth pinched with fury. 'And what were you going to do now you're here?' He stared at her, cold and hard. 'Thinking of seeing her were you? Perhaps tell her something, was that it?'

She violently shook her head. 'No, no,' she insisted. 'You've got it all wrong, James. I came here because I love you, that's all.'

'Well, listen to me, Sas, and listen hard. Your coming here could easily ruin everything and if you love me as much as you say you do, then pack your things and get the hell out of here. If Claire gets to hear anything about this, then we've had it.'

'Why?'

'Oh for God's sake, Saskia, don't be so dumb. Can't you understand anything?'

Her bottom lip trembled.

'And don't start wailing again!' he snapped. 'You look bloody terrible as it is.'

'But I love you,' she protested, 'and you're sleeping with her, I know you are.'

'Of course I'm not!' he shouted. 'How can you be so idiotic?'

'Then where were you last night?' she blubbed. 'Why didn't you come back?'

'Because,' he said through gritted teeth, 'I was in town playing backgammon and it went on a bit longer than I anticipated, that's all.'

'You're lying,' she stated flatly, her face a picture of abject misery.

He sighed heavily and came round to massage her shoulders. 'Listen, Sas,' he said quietly. 'I don't have to prove anything to you; surely you know that by now? There's only one person I love and that's you.' He bent down and kissed her neck.

'Only you, Sas, believe me.'

The tension in her shoulders started to go and gradually he could feel her relax.

'Try to understand, my darling, I have to do this. I have no choice. If I'm to get hold of the money, *my* money,' he emphasized, 'then I've got to do this. Honestly, do you really think I enjoy it?'

She sighed. 'I don't know. You haven't been yourself lately. You haven't wanted me as much as you usually do.' She turned round to face him. 'I don't know what to think any more.'

He lifted her chin and smiled at her. 'Saskia, how can you accuse me of that? I have a great deal of travelling to do. I'm up and down the bloody motorway like a Jack-in-the-box. No wonder I'm tired. Tell you what,' he stood her up and undid the bathrobe, 'why don't you and I go upstairs and I'll show you exactly how much I want you?'

She needed no further encouragement.

She stood in the small hallway. 'Do I have to go home, Jamie?'

'You shouldn't have broken that window, you know. And yes, you do.'

'Well, how else was I going to get in? I couldn't spend the night in the car.'

'No, I suppose not. I'll see the farmer who owns this

place and make him some kind of recompense.' He ushered her towards the door. 'Now, have you got everything?'

She looked down at her bag. 'No . . . I've left my face cream in the bathroom.'

'Stay there, I'll get it.'

The phone started ringing just as James found the pot. He raced out to see Saskia pick it up. He snatched it from her just in time and pushed her against the wall.

'Hello? Oh Claire.'

'James! What are you doing over there? I've been looking everywhere for you.'

He glared at Saskia who sat in an undignified heap on the floor, glowering at him.

He tried to sound cheerful. 'I just thought I'd pop back and make some calls while you were out.'

'Will you be back for lunch?'

'Yes, of course I will. I'll be back as soon as I can.'

'Okay, I'll see you then. Bye.'

He replaced the receiver slowly and deliberately.

'Don't you ever pull a stunt like that again,' he said, pointing a finger at Saskia, 'because if you do, God help me, woman, I won't be responsible for my actions.'

She stood up and backed away. 'It was her, wasn't it? That's why you didn't want me to speak to her.'

'Shut up!' he roared.

She picked up her bag. 'You lied to me. All along you've been lying. Well, I'm going to get my own back on you, just you wait and see,' and before he could stop her, she ran out, jumped into her car and screeched off.

He went to the doorway and watched her fast-retreating car. He began to laugh, a chuckle at first, but then much louder.

'Silly cow!' he shouted. She didn't have the bottle for anything.

TWENTY

'So who is this Lamont chap then?'

Alistair was worried. He stopped himself picking at a jagged fingernail and then decisively ripped it off.

'Not Lamont, old chap,' said Mortimore, 'but James Lamont Skerrett, twenty-eight years old, living with the daughter of a wealthy construction firm owner, a vacuous bimbette called Saskia. He works for Michelberg & Sons, a merchant bank. But that's not all he does. He also has a bad gambling habit and a taste for escorting rich older women, including, until fairly recently, Elyssa Berkshire. You remember her, don't you? She was that model we met at Cambridge.'

Alistair felt sick. This couldn't be right. Surely not. How could Elyssa even contemplate such a thing? He closed his eyes with disgust as he fought down the nausea.

'Are you sure?' he croaked, his voice no more than a whisper. This was far worse than he had expected, and to think that he had slept with Elyssa. It appalled him.

'Oh yes, no doubt about it. My chap is very thorough and can be relied upon entirely. You do remember Elyssa, don't you? Imagine her paying for the services of a young buck? Incredible, isn't it?'

'Absolutely, but I'm not sure I can remember her, actually.'

'Oh you must do, Ali. She was that gorgeous redhead. Mind you, she's probably not so gorgeous now.'

'Oh . . . was she?' Thank God Mortimore couldn't see him. He hated lying.

He leant back in his chair and rubbed his forehead. Poor

Claire, he thought, what was she getting into? More to the point, what had he got into?

'Well, I'm sorry to be the bearer of bad news, old chap,' said Mortimore cheerfully.

'Look,' said Alistair, regaining his composure, 'is there anything else you can tell me about him? I've got to have as much info as possible if I'm going to prevent an almighty cockup.'

'Rather you than me, old boy.'

'Meaning what?'

'Meaning that if you have any ideas about preventing this marriage, you'd better be prepared for an awful lot of flak. After all, how would you like it if a so-called friend told you that your beloved was an out-and-out crook who was only after your money?'

'Not very much, I suppose, but are you sure that's what he is? You know, the gambling and . . . the gigolo stuff?'

'Of course I am. My informant,' explained Mortimore, 'tells me that this chap Skerrett is mixed up with a very unsavoury character called McArdle. Now McArdle is one of the underworld's less pleasant representatives and well known for his racketeering; you know, nightclubs, prostitution, drugs, all that kind of thing. We don't know what the connection is between the two of them, but I can tell you this, it won't be any kind of legitimate deal. I would guess,' he added, 'that it's to do with money, which could well explain why he's sniffing around your friend.'

Alistair didn't reply. Just the thought of the creep seducing Claire was making his gorge rise.

'What are you going to do then, dear boy?'

'Don't know, Mort. I really don't know.'

'By the way, who was it you said this girl had inherited the money from?'

'I didn't.' Alistair was puzzled. 'But his name was Carter-Browne.'

'The Carter-Browne of racehorse owning fame; the one that ran his own investment agency?'

'Yes, I believe so.'

'Ah well then, it all falls into place. Carter-Browne was Skerrett's uncle . . . he brought him up as a child – '

'And if for some reason he cut Skerrett out of his will,' interrupted Alistair, 'it would explain why he's down here chasing after Claire – to get what he sees as his rightful inheritance.'

'Exactly! Heavens, what a charming individual! Carter-Browne probably disinherited him for a good reason. His will caused a huge rumpus because he left most of his private fortune to a dogs' home!'

'Yes, I knew that. Skerrett must feel highly aggrieved.'

'Precisely. So, what now?'

'Don't know,' repeated Alistair. 'I've got enough ammunition to sink that Skerrett chap for all time, but the trouble will be convincing Claire.'

'Mmm, I don't envy you, old boy.'

Alistair thanked him and put down his phone with relief. He sat quite still staring out of the window. It was bad enough finding out about Skerrett and his unpleasant private life, but discovering that Elyssa was caught up in it as well . . . it was a spider's web of filth that he wished he had never touched. Then he got angry with himself. He should have known better. There was no excuse for it. Elyssa had always been exactly the same: a woman who liked men and a good time and there was no doubting Skerrett's good looks. What really galled him was his own gullibility. She had used him in the same way as she used all the others. He smiled ruefully to himself. What a time to learn such a lesson.

His mind then turned to Claire and how he should break the news to her. It was not going to be easy. She could be very stubborn sometimes and wilful. If he wasn't careful she might take it all the wrong way. The only reassurance he had was that when it came to matters of the heart, she was a fairly practical woman; her choice of husband proved that. Matt was nothing like James. A solid, reliable individual whom Alistair had found a bit dour but totally genuine. How then, could she be so fooled by Skerrett? What did he have that so mesmerized her? He pressed his intercom.

'Can I have some coffee, please, Julie.'

'Yes, Alistair.'

Fortified with a good strong brew, he rang Claire's number. No answer. He let it ring continuously for about three minutes. Nothing. He replaced the receiver thoughtfully. Maybe it was a good thing she wasn't there. He wasn't sure how to broach the subject and a bit more time would allow him to think things through. As Mortimore had said, to come between lovers was not a sensible thing to do and in Claire's present situation, where she was probably quite volatile, he had no idea how she was going to react.

Claire was at the farm when Alistair rang, but deliberately chose not to answer the phone. There had been several calls over the last few days, randomly timed and without reason, and they were all the same: the phone would ring, she would pick it up and then there would be silence. No heavy breathing, no whispered obscenities, nothing; just an eerie silence.

The first puzzled her, the second and third annoyed her, and all subsequent ones had frightened her. She began to dread the phone's ringing, never knowing whether it was friend or foe. She wished she could tell James about it, but he had gone back to London to 'sort things out', as he had put it. She longed to ring him; to hear his voice and to whisper his name. She felt sure that if he knew about it, she would feel better able to cope. But she couldn't. He was very evasive about her contacting him in London.

'It's not that I don't want you to, my darling,' he had whispered, while kissing her neck, 'it's just that I'm so busy at the moment. It's easier if I ring you when I know I'm not going to be disturbed.'

She believed him but then it was easy to believe anything he said because she loved him. No man had loved her the way he did. Nothing was too much for him. If she wanted something, he would get it. He did most of the cooking, took her out for meals, gave her presents: he was wonderful. He made love in a way that she didn't think was possible, bringing her out of the darkness and into the light. When he was there everything else became unimportant; she concentrated entirely on him. When he was gone the life drained out of her and it was difficult to find any reason to go on. She would die for him.

Then there were the letters. The first one was such an amateurish and pathetic effort that after reading it, she had chucked it in the Rayburn and watched it dissolve in the flames.

The second was different. It knew too many details and intimately described things that had happened between her and James which only they could know about. Whoever had written them obviously knew James sexually. They weren't written but typed so she had nothing to compare them with and neither were they postmarked in London. From what she could see, it was somewhere in Surrey.

She told herself to remain calm. All would be explained when James came down at the weekend. He would know what to do. But it wasn't so easy.

At night, lying alone in her bed, she would continuously think about the telephone calls and letters, running them over and over again through her mind, unable to let go of the graphic details and salacious jeering. Then she would blush and, filled with embarrassment, hide her head under the blankets. In the dark, her jealousy grew.

James didn't ring. He said he might if he had time, but she knew he didn't mean that. He loved her: of course he would ring. And so she waited by the telephone, the hedges untrimmed and the eggs not gathered. All she had for company was Rosie.

It was nice to be alone with her dog again. When James was around, she knew she rather neglected her, as Rosie wouldn't come anywhere near the house. Claire had tried getting her to come in, bribing her with a handful of dog biscuits, but that didn't work either. If James was there, Rosie slept in the barn and there was nothing Claire could do about it. Man and dog seemed determined to ignore each other. James wasn't concerned. He said that that was where Rosie belonged. She was an animal, for God's sake, nothing more, nothing less, and Claire was being very silly about it. Surely the only relationship which mattered now was the one between the pair of them, and how could Claire not see that? Then he would make love to her and she would temporarily put Rosie out of her mind until the next morning when she would go out to the barn and there would be Rosie looking at her with her big brown eyes, silently chastising her.

Claire hated herself then, torn apart by guilt and love because both James and Rosie meant so much to her. So she waited until James left and as soon as he was gone, Rosie would move back into the house, but not upstairs. Ever since that day when James had told her off about the dog hairs on the bed, she had made sure Rosie slept on the blanket in the kitchen.

At first Rosie had hated it and pitifully whined whenever Claire went to bed and left her, but now she seemed to have accepted it. In the morning, Claire would come downstairs and Rosie would stay put, not even getting up to welcome her. Claire felt hurt.

It wasn't only Rosie who shunned her. The letters and phone calls had disquieted her so much that she decided to call Ange. It wasn't a successful conversation.

'Ange, hi, it's me, Claire.'

'Hello.' Ange was subdued. Normally she would gush over with friendliness.

'How are you?'

'Fine.'

'And the kids?' It was hard going but Claire persisted.

'They're fine too and so is Colin. Now is there anyone else I've missed off the list?' It was a rebuff and Claire knew it. She breathed deeply.

'Look, Ange, I'm sorry, okay? I shouldn't have spoken to you the way I did and I'm sorry if I offended you.'

Silence and then in a flat unemotional tone Ange said, 'Think nothing of it. After all, I'm only a good friend of yours and if friends can't have the odd argument now and again, well, what's the point?'

'I mean it, Ange. I'm very sorry,' insisted Claire.

Ange sighed. 'Okay, okay, I'm sorry too, so let's put the whole bloody episode behind us, shall we?' Her voice changed. Now it was the old Ange who was talking. 'So, how are you?'

'Actually, I'm getting married again.'

'What!' Ange screeched down the phone. 'Not to him, surely? I mean I can't believe it.'

Claire was hurt but swallowed it. 'Yes, actually, it is him and despite what you said about him getting his oats and disappearing, the truth was, as I expected, that he had a great deal of work to do and had to go back to London for a few days. Of course, when he got back, he explained it all to me.'

'Well, what a turn-up for the books and I take back everything I said.'

Claire refrained from adding, 'I told you so.' She had no intention of crowing over her friend. She could not quite dispel her suspicions, however. The phone calls and anonymous letters were constantly nagging at her. But even as she spoke to Ange, she realized they could never come from her friend.

'So,' continued Ange, 'when did all this happen?'

'Very quickly,' laughed Claire, finally pushing all doubts behind her. 'Naturally I accepted his proposal, but we won't be getting married for a long time, perhaps two years, it just all depends.'

'On what?'

'Well, I've got to get rid of Tor Heights for a start. All of James's family and business contacts are in London. We couldn't stay here. It's just not practical.'

'But what about you? I mean, what about your animals, your land and all the rest of it? I thought Tor Heights meant everything to you, especially since Matt died.' She paused. 'I can't believe, Claire, that you are prepared to give up all that you love on the strength of a marriage proposal from someone you have only known for two minutes.'

Claire looked heavenward and bit her tongue. Everything Ange was saying was true and she knew it, but she didn't understand: she loved James and that was all that mattered.

'You don't understand, Ange; we love each other and it's much simpler for me to move up there than it is for him to commute.'

'Why? Plenty of people commute from the West Country every day. Why should it be different for him?'

Why indeed? Claire didn't have an answer for that and all she could say was, 'but I love him.'

'Yes, Claire, and I love Colin, but I'm not prepared to give up my friends and way of life just on his say-so. Ask yourself this: who is going to be stuck at home all day twiddling her thumbs with nothing to do while your lord and master is making megabucks on the Stock Exchange or whatever he does?'

'Well, me, of course.'

'And how long d'you think that will last before you go out of your mind with boredom?'

'I'll get a job, silly.'

'So who looks after Rosie?'

'There was no answer to that either. If Claire was working, Rosie would be left on her own all day. It was a cruelty Claire couldn't accept – her beautiful dog left alone in a strange house with no one to walk her or keep her company.

'I'll work part time,' she answered at last.

'Really?'

Claire could feel her anger starting to rise. It seemed to her that no matter what she said, Ange always found obstacles to her happiness. She decided to end the conversation. 'Well, I have to go now, Ange. I've got loads of things to do. Why don't we have coffee somewhere soon? I'd love to see you again.'

'Yes, why don't we?' Ange too seemed reluctant to carry on. It was as if the pair of them knew there was nothing more to say. 'I'll give you a ring then, Claire. Bye.'

Claire went back out to the kitchen and made herself some tea. Everything Ange had said was right and she knew it. In her heart of hearts, she realized she couldn't leave the farm, or take Rosie off to London. She was beginning to feel utterly hopeless, a heavy indecision dampening her love.

'Oh to hell with it!'

She needed a walk.

The crocuses and daffodils were in full bloom, their white and blue petals and yellow trumpets waving in the gentle breeze. The whole landscape felt refreshed after its long winter sleep and a carpet of new greenness covered the fields and hedges. Birdsong filled the air and the intermittent sun felt warm on her back. Rosie appeared, wagging her tail.

'Hello, my precious, where have you been?' She patted the dog's back. 'Come on then, let's go for a walk.'

They set off across the moor, woman and dog together, enjoying the clean fresh air and spring sunshine. When they reached the top of one of the rugged grey granite tors she stopped to admire the view. Beneath her, in the wide open vista of patchwork fields and distant white farmhouses, she could see across miles and miles of the rolling

Devon landscape. Further away, along the horizon, land and sky blended together in a faint blue haze.

Her love for James had its price and this was it; leaving behind all of this. However nice the house they were going to buy, nothing could replace the view she had before her. This land had its grip on her and she knew that when the day of leaving came, she would be heart-broken.

Tears filled her eyes and ran down her cheeks. She sat down on the cold rocks and put her arm around her dog.

'Oh Rosie,' she whispered, 'what am I going to do?'

The town was quiet when Claire got in. It was late in the afternoon and most of the shoppers had been and gone. She knew what she had to get and clutching her small list, ambled around the town centre buying her goods. Then she saw Alistair and was about to set off in the opposite direction when he hailed her.

'Claire! Claire!' He jogged up behind her, smiling and trim, looking much better than she had seen him in a long time.

'Hello, Alistair. I didn't see you there.'

'Well, it's a good thing I saw you then,' he laughed. 'Are you busy? There's something I need to talk to you about. I've been trying to ring you but you must have been out in the fields or something.'

She glanced down at her scrap of paper and then put it in her pocket.

'No, not really.'

'Fancy a cup of coffee?'

She nodded. 'Okay.'

He gently took hold of her arm and steered her across the road towards a delicatessen.

'They make the most delicious pastries here,' he informed her when they found a table. 'You sit down and I'll go and get some.'

She watched him with renewed curiosity as he stood at

the counter. There was something different about him; something in his manner had changed. He was very pleased to see her, of course, that hadn't altered, but there was a hint of anxiety about him. She couldn't be more definite than that, but she knew he wasn't his normal self. He looked much better; of that she did approve. A good stone had disappeared from around his waist and his clothes had improved enormously. A double-breasted suit made him look taller and slimmer and its dark charcoal grey showed off the blond of his hair and the light blue of his eyes. He was certainly more handsome and she liked it.

He came back with a laden tray and put it down on the red and white gingham tablecloth.

'What d'you think of this place then?'

'Very nice,' she replied. 'I haven't been here before. Has it been open long?'

'Oh a couple of months. It's mainly vegetarian, lots of wholefoods and, of course, it's no smoking, of which I heartily approve.'

'Alistair!' she exclaimed 'So health conscious! What's brought this on?'

He grinned sheepishly. 'Well, I just thought it was time I made more of an effort. Do you like it then?'

She smiled at him. He was looking very attractive. 'Yes.' She paused and then said quietly. 'You look very handsome, you know.'

He blushed. 'Why thank you, Claire. To be honest, I never thought I'd hear you say that.'

'To be honest, neither did I.'

He looked at her, his eyes warm and gentle. 'You always look beautiful to me.'

She lowered her gaze. Now she felt uncomfortable.

'Well, anyway,' he said quickly, realizing his mistake, 'where were we?'

* * *

'Where are we?'

'Nearly there. Not much further. About a couple of miles, I'd say.'

'Good. I'm getting really fed up with this journey. If I'd known it was going to take this long I would have flown down.' Elyssa sighed. 'Put some more music on, Kevin, something that will put me in a better mood.'

Kevin turned on the radio.

'Not that, for heaven's sake!' she complained. 'I can't abide that rubbish. Find something a bit more soothing.'

He glanced in the rear-view mirror and, seeing her sulking face, made no comment and did as he was told. They drove on.

'Have you booked yourself somewhere to stay?' she asked, sipping a large Scotch.

'Yes. It's called the White Hart. Two nights' B & B, just like you said.'

'I expect to see the receipts,' she said.

They reached Torhampton.

'Alistair's office is somewhere in the centre of town. You can drop me off nearby and I'll find my own way after that. I'll give you a call when I need you.'

'Yes, ma'am.'

Bloody bitch, he thought. I hope he stands you up. It will be the least you deserve.

Kevin had been expecting the weekend off and had made arrangements to visit Aditha at his mother's house in King's Lynn. It would be an opportunity to look round for a job up there too. He was very annoyed to be informed late on Thursday afternoon that he was to drive down to Devon tomorrow. When he telephoned Aditha, she started to cry.

'Oh Kevin, I so wanted to see you.'

'Me too, love. Listen, I'll get up to see you as soon as I can, okay? You and Mum getting on all right?'

'Yes, she very nice, very kind. I miss you.'

'Yeah, I miss you too. Look, I've got to go, the old bag's coming back. Ring you soon. Bye.'

He only just got out of the kitchen in time. Down in his room he could hear her high heels clacking across the tiles but she didn't come down. She never did now. Since that day when she had fired Aditha, she had kept well away from him. He sometimes wondered why, but mostly he was relieved.

Elyssa finished her drink and then thought about having another. She decided against it. She didn't want Alistair to think she was a drunk. She wasn't of course, but he might think so. She leant forward.

'Got any of those extra strong mints, Kevin, you know, the ones I gave you for your halitosis?'

He silently passed her the tube of sweets. He really hated her. She watched the back of his head. The spots around his neck were as bad as ever. It didn't matter how much special cleanser she bought him, they just didn't go away.

She smiled to herself. Poor Kevin. No compliant little Aditha to screw and no mistress either. It must be difficult for the poor chap. Maybe he was screwing the new maid. Elyssa thought not. She had deliberately chosen the ugliest of the four candidates to work for her, and even Kevin, however frustrated he got, couldn't possibly find the woman remotely attractive. She was a real eyesore. Completely efficient, of course, but dead ugly.

It was all part of Elyssa's new plan. She had decided that if she was going to get Alistair, then she really had to make a bit more of an effort. It was no good simply inviting him up to London and having sex with him. She had to show more of an interest in his way of life; in the countryside, in animals, and in rural life in general. Being faithful would help as well. The last thing she needed was any inopportune little infections. That would take too much explaining and so far as she could see, Alistair was a very straightforward chap.

He was also very rich. Elyssa had spent her time profitably since she had last seen him and with the help of an old friend of hers, had discovered exactly how rich Alistair's family was. They were loaded and all of it old inherited wealth.

Elyssa knew everything about wealth, especially the subtle differences. There was the stuff that she had, young and worthless, and there was what Alistair had: old and valuable and she intended to get her hands on it.

Kevin stopped the car and opened the door for Elyssa. Some of the locals stopped and stared. Elyssa disdainfully ignored them as she pulled her full-length fox fur tighter around her waist trying to keep out the blustery wind.

'God, what a dreary little place.' She turned to Kevin. 'My bag, please, and then vanish and remember . . .

'Yes?'

'I want to know exactly how much money you spend.'

'Yes, ma'am.'

With the professional carriage of one used to having people watching her, she strode off across the square. Despite her haughty appearance, she secretly enjoyed the envious glances and when some workmen started whistling, it made her day.

She found Alistair's office without difficulty and went in. There was no one behind the reception desk so she let herself into his office. She was reading some of his correspondence, which he had helpfully left out on his desk, when the door opened. It was Julie.

'Excuse me, but what on earth are you doing?' She hurried over and snatched away the papers, clearly irritated. 'I don't know who you are, but you can get out. This is a private office and you shouldn't be in here.'

Elyssa smiled. 'Now, now, you shouldn't frown you know, you'll get wrinkles, or should I say in your case, you'll add to the wrinkles.'

Julie flushed red, her round face aghast at this stranger's cheek. 'What! How dare you!'

'Simple really. I'm just stating the obvious. Now listen, my name is Elyssa Berkshire and I'm a very close friend of Alistair's and I've come to see him. So where is he?'

'I . . . don't . . . know,' spluttered Julie, unused to such effrontery. 'He's out in town somewhere.'

Elyssa turned away and ran her finger over the side of Alistair's desk. She looked at the ensuing dirt.

'Oh how tedious! Is he meeting a client or something?'

'No. Now look, I really think you ought to leave. Wait out in reception, he'll be back soon.'

'Is there somewhere he goes for coffee or for a drink?'

Julie shook her head. She desperately wanted to get rid of this rude woman. 'There's a new place called The Bakery off the square. He was talking about it the other day.' She looked at Elyssa. 'Now will you please go.'

Elyssa smiled as she walked past her. 'You know,' she said, 'whoever does your cleaning in here aren't very good, are they?' and she held up her smudged finger.

Julie bit her tongue. 'Please leave at once, Miss Berkshire.'

'Are you all right, Claire?' asked Alistair softly. 'I must say you don't seem your usual bouncy self. If anything, you look decidedly pale and drawn.'

'I'm fine, Alistair, really I am.'

'And James, how is he?' Her smile is too bright he thought.

'Great! He's back in London at the moment, but he'll be down soon.'

'Good.' He pushed his empty plate to one side. It was far more difficult than he expected to tell her his news. He prevaricated.

'Have you contacted Peter Collier yet?' Neutral ground, this, he thought.

'No. There seems little point in it now. When I move to London I'll see someone up there. James will help me, of course. He's very good at that sort of thing.'

Alistair's stomach churned. 'Do you think that's altogether wise?'

She glanced at him, instantly alert for any attack on her beloved. 'What do you mean?' Her voice was cold.

'I mean,' he said hurriedly, trying to talk himself out of an awkward situation, 'that James's opinion – and I'm sure it would be a very good one – will be a subjective one. People like him usually work at the high-stakes end of the market. You know, big risks, big wins, but also big losses.' The tension was lessening and she had stopped looking quite so fierce. He continued: 'Peter, on the other hand, deals almost exclusively with small-town rural investors like yourself who generally require a safe return on their money. Nothing extravagant, of course, but it's all safe blue-chip stuff with a guaranteed income.'

He waited. His words were making sense to her. She was staring at some point in the distance. There were faint blue circles under her eyes and he knew she hadn't been sleeping properly.

'Of course,' he said, 'I realize that James is probably an expert in his field and no doubt,' he chuckled, 'he'd tell me what I could do with my advice, but Peter is also an expert and I think he's worth listening to.'

He reached out and tentatively took her hand. She didn't withdraw it. It was the first time he had touched her since that day at the farm and he felt his insides melting. God, how he loved her.

'Take my advice, Claire, even if it's the last thing I ever say to you, and please go and see Peter; please, for your own sake.'

Whatever reverie she had been in, she snapped out of it and looked at him. Her eyes were bloodshot and moist and she was having the greatest difficulty in controlling her trembling bottom lip. She withdrew her hand from his and took a less than successful mouthful of coffee, some of which spilt down her jumper.

'Oh bother!' She picked up a paper napkin and dabbed it furiously before throwing it back on the table. In that moment of anger, she had regained her composure. Her eyes were clear again and her mouth relaxed.

'Yes, all right, Alistair,' she said tiredly. 'I'll go if it keeps you off my back. I'll go and see Peter Collier.' She smiled crookedly, her full lips not completely synchronized.

Alistair beamed. A small triumph, and what's more it would keep that Skerrett chap away from her money. Feeling encouraged, he then decided to take the plunge.

'I know someone who knows James in London.' His voice was quiet. He didn't want to startle her.

She leant forward, much more interested. He glanced up at her; her eyes were very green today. 'Who?'

He fiddled with his cup and saucer before putting some sugar in his coffee.

'That's the second time you've done that,' she remarked.

He sipped it. It was far too sweet. 'Oh well,' he smiled. 'Never mind, it all goes down the same way.'

'Who is this person then?'

'A friend of mine, a solicitor called Mortimore Du Pres.' He could feel his heart beginning to thump faster and the skin on his back was prickling with beads of sweat. He started to wish he could have a cigarette.

'And what does this friend of yours know?'

He avoided her gaze. He knew she was ready to pounce, to defend James to the hilt, but it was too late now. He pressed his lips together and smiled, trying to placate her.

'Not much, really. He just says James is well known in some circles, that's all.'

'But of course he is,' she insisted. 'His uncle ran a very large and successful business.'

'Yes, well, you see, that's the problem really.'

'Why?' She ignored her untouched pastry and the congealing coffee. She was bristling with intensity.

'His uncle was called Carter-Browne.' He looked up at her. 'The same Carter-Browne who left you the money.'

'So we're related. So what? It must be very distant.'

'Claire,' he began slowly, 'I don't think you fully understand the ramifications of what I'm saying.'

'Well, what are you saying?'

He knew he was on thin ice, but having got this far, he saw no point in holding back. 'The circles James moves in are not perhaps the ones you imagine.'

'And?' Her voice was very cold as she stared at him. Alistair took a deep breath. He had to tell her.

'He's a banker not a broker and he's also a gambler, a big gambler. That's how he makes most of his money – or should I say, loses it. He's up to his eyeballs in debt to some underworld character who's putting the squeeze on him. Apparently he's in a great deal of trouble. It would seem that James was depending on some money from his uncle, but for some reason, was cut out of the will. You got the money instead and that's why James is down here.' He stopped.

Claire was shaking her head. 'I don't believe you, Alistair,' she said, looking at him with defiance. 'I can't believe you would do this to me.'

'Do what?' He was puzzled.

She leant forward again, her face pinched and white. 'You've been digging around behind my back, haven't you?' She paused. 'Well, haven't you?'

He held up his hands in defence.

'Now look, Claire, I was only thinking of your best interests.'

'Crap!' She exploded and then realizing that some of the other customers were watching her, lowered her voice again. 'Without my permission you have been doing some investigating so that you could come up with enough muck to throw at James, hoping that I would break if off.'

'Now look here, Claire – '

'No! You look!' she said, pointing a finger at him. 'I

358

haven't asked you for anything except to be my solicitor, for which I might add you get paid enough bloody money, and I don't need you to act as my moral welfare officer.' She was livid, boiling with rage at his presumptuousness. 'How dare you pry into my private life! What he does in London or what he has done in London is between us, not you, and I don't ever want to hear you say anything against him again!' She stood up, chest heaving.

He took hold of her arm and tried to pull her back down again. 'Please, Claire, just listen to me. There are things you ought to know.'

'Get off me!' And she wrenched her arm away from him, her mouth tight with suppressed anger. 'You're just like Ange. Do you realize that? Everything I've done or said about James she has criticized and now you're doing the same.' She bit her lips, draining them of blood, forcing herself not to cry. 'Well, I have some news for you, Alistair. I love him, he loves me and no matter what he's done or said in London, we are going to get married.' And throwing her napkin onto the table with as much finality as she could muster, she picked up her shopping and left.

He watched her go, as did most of the other customers. It was then that he noticed Elyssa's smiling face. She came over to him, most of the customers staring at her. How could she wear a fur coat in a wholefood restaurant?

'Well, well, well,' she said. 'What a fine little performance that was.'

'What the hell are you doing here?' he demanded.

'I came to see you.'

'Sit down then,' he said irritably, 'and for heaven's sake, take off that coat.'

'Huh! If you say so.' She turned around and clicked her fingers in the direction of the counter. 'Coffee, please.'

'Well, Alistair, are you going to explain what all that was about?' She smiled encouragingly.

'No,' he said at last. 'It's none of your business. She's

just an old friend who refuses to listen to me and I guess there's nothing more I can do.'

Elyssa's coffee arrived. She ignored the way it was thumped down on the table.

'Pretty little thing,' she commented.

'Yes she is.'

'Oh come off it, Ali, don't give me that. She's delectable and your eyes were falling out of your head. Is she the one you've been mooning after all these years?'

He quickly glanced up. 'No.'

Elyssa smiled. 'I thought so. Well anyway,' she said, shaking back her bobbed red hair. 'I'm down here to take your mind off such things; to distract you; to bring some joy into your life. So what do you think of that?'

He sat back in the pine chair and glared at her. After what Mort had told him he wouldn't touch her with a ten-foot barge pole.

'Where are you staying tonight?' he asked frostily.

Her smile was very wide. She seemed impervious to his bad mood. 'I hadn't thought about that. Do you have any suggestions?'

'Yes, I have a spare room.'

Her face fell. 'Only a spare room?'

'Yes. Only a spare room. Take it or leave it.'

Claire was crying. After leaving the café, she had rushed back to the car park, forgetting about the rest of her shopping, and climbed into the front seat of her van where she could have a good howl. And there she sat, paper tissue in one hand, dabbing and wiping her face as a fresh load of tears rolled down her cheeks. She couldn't believe it; just couldn't believe it. Both of her so-called friends ganging up on her like this. Both so anti-James and they hadn't even met him. How could they be so prejudiced?

Anyway, she reasoned, as her tears started to abate. What if he was a distant relative? They weren't first cousins so the question of consanguinity was irrelevant and if he was in trouble, it didn't matter. She could always help him out.

She reasoned that the only real problem was their jealousy. Ange because she was tied down with two children and a husband who was hardly ever at home, and Alistair because he had always fancied her and now James had come along and ruined it. Well tough, she thought, it's just too bad. She was going to do what she wanted and nothing was going to stand in her way.

She blew her nose, started up her van and drove off. James was coming down soon and she would make it a visit he would never forget.

TWENTY-ONE

'I'm sorry, Claire, but I'm up to my eyeballs at the moment.'

'But you promised.'

'Yes, yes, I know, my darling, but I can't, I just can't.'

She sat down heavily on the chair next to the telephone table and fought back the disappointment. James sensed the tension in her silence.

'Look, darling,' he said, his voice soft and consoling, 'it isn't that I don't want to, honestly, it's just that I'm so busy. I've been having non stop business meetings. It's no joke, you know, trying to keep one's head above water. I've got to be here to sort things out. I mean,' he said, giving a small cough, 'you don't want to marry a bankrupt, do you?'

'Oh James, that doesn't matter, does it?' she insisted. 'I've got all the money we'll ever need. It would be all right.'

'Yes I know, Claire, and it's very sweet of you, but no thank you. It's very important for me to do this by myself.'

'Can't I help? If there are money problems, surely I can do something?'

'How?'

'Well, with a loan or something.'

'Well, that's very generous of you, Claire, but I'm talking big bucks here, not a few thousand.'

'But surely if it's that desperate – '

'Okay, if you insist,' he interrupted, 'we'll talk about it when I next come down.'

'And when will that be?'

'On Tuesday, I think.'

'What! That long?' she wailed.

'I'm afraid so, dearest. Of course if I can come down sooner, I'll let you know.'

'But Neale is coming over tomorrow to look at the farm and I wanted you to be here.'

'Claire,' he cooed, 'you're more than capable of seeing to that man by yourself, you know. You don't need me to help you. Just let Rosie see to him. She can frighten anyone if she tries.'

'But he's horrible. He gives me the creeps. Can't you come down sooner?' Her disappointment was crushing.

'Look, Claire, I've got to go. Something has just come up and I really haven't got time to speak to you at the moment.'

'Please, James – '

'Sorry, darling. I really have got to go. Speak to you later.'

'Oh all right.'

'That's my girl. Love you. Bye.'

'Bye.'

Claire was beginning to resent her telephone. The bloody thing had taken on far too much importance in her life. She impulsively knocked it off the table so that it clattered on to the floor, giving a little ring.

'Stupid thing!' she yelled.

She had so wanted to tell James about the silent phone calls and anonymous letters that were plaguing her like some insistent and irritating insect. Night and day it went on. Sometimes the phone would ring on the hour every hour and always there was silence. Then, at breakfast time, there would be more letters, sitting on the doormat, staring up at her like flat white missiles, each one getting closer and closer to breaking her defences.

She didn't read them now. They usually went straight into the Rayburn with only the most cursory glance. It annoyed her so much that something ordinarily so inoffensive should be so intimidating.

She picked up the phone. It was silly to take out her anger on it. If she broke it, she would have no way at all of speaking to James. It rang almost immediately. She tentatively picked it up.

'Hello?'

'Ah, Mrs Bromage, Neale here.'

She relaxed. Even Neale's voice was better than nothing. 'What do you want, Mr Neale?' She may be relieved it wasn't one of those calls, but she still saw no reason why she should be polite to him. He felt differently.

'Now now, Mrs Bromage, that's no way to address a prospective buyer of your farm.'

She ignored him. 'What do you want, Mr Neale?' She heard him breathe deeply, obviously annoyed.

'I can't get there tomorrow. My wife has decided that she has to do some urgent shopping that really can't wait and that we can't come down now until Tuesday. Is that all right with you?'

'Yes, I suppose so, given that shopping comes way down the list of my priorities, you can almost guarantee that I'll be here.'

She couldn't resist having a dig at him, although she had to admit that he sounded almost as fed up as she did. Perhaps it wasn't all his fault. He didn't rise to the bait.

'Well, fine then. We'll be there at about eleven o'clock, providing the traffic isn't too bad on the motorway.'

'Where are you coming from?'

'Birmingham. It should take about five hours.'

There was a brief silence and then he said, 'Look, Mrs Bromage, I know we haven't exactly seen eye to eye over this matter and that you have no particular fondness for me or what I stand for, but I would hope that you would put all those considerations to one side, especially as we are now going to be doing business together.'

'I guess so,' she answered flatly. She didn't care what he thought. However, she was too well mannered to continue in this vein and had to concede that if she wanted to sell her farm it would be to her advantage to be nice to him.

'Okay, Mr Neale, when you and your family come down I'll make sure I'm on my best behaviour and I promise not to make any sly digs at either your politics or morals.'

'Well, that's very generous of you, Mrs Bromage.' The ironic tone was not missed on her. 'So we'll see you Tuesday. Goodbye.'

She didn't answer him, but replaced the receiver.

'Stupid little man,' she said as she walked back to the kitchen. She was in a foul mood now and saw no reason to be nice to anyone. She pulled on her wellingtons and stomped out into the yard.

James was having problems, especially with Saskia. He had returned from Devon the day after he had sent her home and found her unconscious on the sofa.

'Christ Almighty!' He rushed over to her and shook her. 'Saskia! Saskia!'

Nothing. He leant down and smelt her breath. He winced. She stank of alcohol. He picked her up again, but she only flopped to one side, her head lolling against him.

'You stupid bloody bitch! What the hell have you done now?'

As he moved her over to one side he saw the empty pill bottle. He picked it up. Saskia took lots of pills.

'Ativan,' he read. Anti-depressants. 'You silly cow!' he shouted. 'You've taken a bloody overdose, haven't you?'

Her sweetly smiling face lay against his arm, a dribble of spittle coming out of the corner of her mouth.

'Come on, stand up!'

He was panicking now. She mustn't die; she couldn't die; if she went, he'd have nothing. He struggled with her heaviness. She was going through one of her periodic fat cycles when her weight ballooned. He staggered across the room.

'Come . . . on . . . Saskia. Wake up, damn you . . . wake up!'

Her feet trailed behind her and her face looked very pale. More spittle began to appear. Now he was really worried. He lay her down on the floor, remembering dimly from school first-aid classes that she had to be on her front in case she choked. He raced to the telephone and rang the emergency services.

The ambulance arrived within minutes. When the men walked into the room, their faces were professionally blank and neither said anything to signify their feelings as they quickly set to work.

James showed them the empty pill bottle and the half-empty gin bottle that stood on the table. With a quick glance and a businesslike briskness, they carried her into the ambulance and sirened off through the city traffic. James sat next to her, holding her chubby hand. He was very shocked; far more so than he liked to admit.

The next two hours were horrendous. Disgusted by all things medical, James was nauseated by the very smell of the accident and emergency department. He tried vainly to answer the young doctor's questions about Saskia, but was soon relieved of the chore when they realized how upset he was. He was then left outside in a disinfectant-smelling linoed corridor while they got on and did the necessary. A young nurse brought him a cup of sweet tea.

'Here you are, Mr Skerrett, drink this. It'll make you feel better.'

'Oh . . . thank you.'

He took the cup, his hand shaking, and ignored her pretty smile.

Saskia required a full stomach washout, followed by twenty-four hours' observation to make sure there were no aftereffects. It turned out that she had only taken a few pills and that it was heavy drinking that had knocked her out. Eventually James was allowed to see her and was ushered in by a tiny Asian nurse.

'Don't stay long, Mr Skerrett.' She had a beautiful lilting accent. 'Your girlfriend is still very ill and she must not be distressed in any way. Remember,' she added, her dark almond eyes studying him closely, 'she is a very unhappy woman and her actions were a desperate cry for help.' She squeezed his forearm for encouragement. 'Try not to be angry, Mr Skerrett; she needs your support now more than ever.' She gave him a beautiful sparkling smile which only made him feel more guilty.

The nurse pulled back the curtain and let him in. He stopped in his tracks.

Saskia, whiter than he had ever seen her, with large blue rings under her closed eyes, lay stretched out on the bed, her beautiful face crowned by her thick blonde waves. She had a drip in one arm. He pointed wordlessly at it.

The nurse shook her head. 'Don't worry, Mr Skerrett, it's only a precaution to replace some of the fluids she has lost.'

The nurse left them alone and he sat down on the chair next to the bed and gingerly held Saskia's hand. How on earth had they got into this mess? It was ridiculous. All he was trying to do was secure a future for both of them and she had to go and nearly screw it up by doing this. Silly woman.

He wearily lay his head on the bed. Sometimes it seemed it was all just too much. Why couldn't she see that he loved her? Why did she have to go and frighten him like this? She was just so damned selfish sometimes. He felt a light touch on his hand.

'Hello, James.' Her voice was weak and hoarse; her eyes barely open.

He looked up and smiled at her. He was too relieved to be angry.

Her smile got bigger. 'Been a bit silly, haven't I?'

He nodded. 'Yes. Just a bit.' It was very late into the evening now and he had been at the hospital since lunchtime. He felt dirty and wretched. He pushed his hand through his unkempt hair.

'You frightened me, Sas.' He stopped. It was difficult to

go on. 'When I came back and found you like . . . like . . .' he waved his hand about, 'I didn't know what to do. Why, Sas? Why did you do it? You know I love you.'

She turned her head away, the tears rolling silently down her cheeks. 'No, you don't,' she whispered. 'Not any more. It's not me you want. It's that woman in Devon.'

'But it's not, Saskia,' he insisted, 'it's you. I've told you that before. Believe me, if you saw her you wouldn't think the way you do. She's nowhere near as pretty as you.'

She turned back to face him, her mouth pulled tightly shut as her tears overflowed, dripping onto the pillow. 'Don't lie to me.'

'But I'm not, honestly, Sas.'

'You are, you bastard, because when I left you I stopped off at Tor Heights and asked her the way back to Torhampton.'

Her face changed. Instead of the blank pathetic misery of before, anger, raw and powerful suffused her whole being and her eyes glared at him.

'What!' He couldn't believe it. 'You did what?'

'I said,' she repeated through clenched teeth, 'that I saw her. I spoke to her. You lied to me.'

He slowly stood up and walked to the end of the bed.

'I haven't, Sas – ' he began.

'Yes you have!' she cried.

The little nurse returned, throwing the curtains to one side as she rushed in. She glanced briefly at James with barely concealed disgust and then said to Saskia, 'Are you all right, dear?'

Saskia nodded and wiped her face. 'Yes.'

'Well, if there's anything you need, please don't hesitate to ask, will you?' She picked up the buzzer and lay it on the bed. 'You only have to press this.' As the nurse turned to go she whispered to James, 'Please keep the noise down, Mr Skerrett, we do have other patients in here, you know.' She snatched back the curtain and left.

He sat down again and tried to hold Saskia's hand but she wouldn't have it.

'She's beautiful that Bromage woman, isn't she?'

He said nothing but gazed steadily at his feet.

'Long legs, slim too, and lovely thick hair.' She paused. 'I always wanted legs like that, legs that went on and on. It's not fair,' and then she started to cry again. 'You shit, James! You bloody bloody shit!'

'Please,' he cajoled, 'don't, Saskia, it didn't mean anything, honestly. I had to do it.'

She looked up through her tears. 'Why?'

'Because,' he said exasperated with her, 'if I didn't I wouldn't be able to get the money off her.' He paused, watching her. He had nearly convinced her. 'Listen, Sas, the only way it's going to work is if she believes me. Anything less than a totally convincing performance and I've had it.'

'But why?' she sobbed. 'You didn't have to sleep with her.'

He feverishly kissed her hands. 'But, Sas, I want what's mine, what's rightfully mine by law, and if it hadn't been for that stupid uncle of mine, I'd have it now. Can't you understand?'

He had to placate her, get round her. If she left him, he would have nothing and that he could never face.

She stopped crying. 'You lied to me,' she said. 'Right from the beginning you spun me a load of bullshit.' She looked at him, her mouth quite determined. 'I'm not going to stand for it, James, not any more. I've had it with you.'

'But, Saskia, please listen, please.' She stared ahead of her, refusing to relent.

'Saskia,' he began. 'There's a great deal of money at stake and it requires me – ' he spoke slowly, searching for the right words – 'it requires me to behave in a way that I might not otherwise normally do.'

'Crap!' she exploded.'You don't need money as a reason.

Anything will do for you. I just can't trust you. You're a liar. You always were and you always will be.'

'No I'm not. I have to get Claire to believe me, because otherwise she's not going to co-operate.'

Saskia faced him again. This time she had some colour in her cheeks. 'Huh! Lying to her as well as me! Christ! I've got a good mind to ring her up and tell her everything. That would scupper your plans, wouldn't it, James?'

'No, Saskia, please don't do that.'

'And why not?' She tried to sit up but was too weak. Lying down again she said, 'Give me one good reason why I shouldn't. After all, you're playing with her just as you have done with me. You're stringing us both along and lying through your back teeth, so why shouldn't I tell her?' She pouted petulantly and folded her arms over her ample bosom. She had James nailed and they both knew it.

He took her hand and put it to his lips. He kissed it gently. 'Please, Sas,' he mumbled. 'Please, for both our sakes, don't do this to us.' He kissed her some more, watching her closely. 'Remember all the good times we've had: the parties the nightclubs, the holidays – '

'Which I paid for,' she snapped.

' – the dinners,' he continued, ignoring her. 'And think of all the good times to come. We could go abroad, somewhere hot, of course, and lie out in the tropical sun, the sea lapping against our feet while someone brings us some nice long cold drinks. I could rub oil into your back, your breasts, your legs,' he whispered, turning over her arm and kissing her white skin. 'There is no one like you, Sas. No one has your style, your beauty, or your body. It just isn't the same with other women. None of them know how to make love like you do.' He stopped.

She was watching him, a slight smile on her lips. 'You really are full of bull, James.'

'Please, baby, it's true.'

He tried to put his hand inside the voluminous armhole

of her nightie, but she slapped him away.

'Leave me alone, James. Keep your bloody mits to yourself. Or better still,' she added, 'go play with yourself.'

'But I need you, baby!'

'Get lost!'

He stood up. Now was obviously not the time to try to appeal to her better nature. He held up his hands in surrender.

'Okay, okay, I can see you're not really in the mood for this. Perhaps when I come back tomorrow you'll feel a bit better.'

'Don't bank on it, James! Now piss off and leave me alone.'

'Now come on, Sas, that's no way to speak in a hospital.'

'Fuck off, James!' she hissed. 'And stop telling me what to do!'

With a rueful smile he turned round and reluctantly left the cubicle. The oriental staff nurse was watching him. She was highly amused about something. He acknowledged her with a nervous smile and a nod of the head.

'I think she's getting better,' he said.

The nurse's smile grew larger, showing a row of large, very white teeth. 'I'd say so, wouldn't you?'

James didn't reply.

'Perhaps if you come back tomorrow, Mr Skerrett, you'll find her in a more accommodating frame of mind.'

Faced with such unfamiliar hostility from the opposite sex, he allowed himself to be ushered out.

On the way home he realized just how close he was to losing everything.

He slept badly that night, tossing and turning well into the small hours before eventually falling into a black and dreamless sleep.

There was so much to think about: the money, McArdle, the package, the bank, Saskia. As if faced with a huge avalanche of snow thundering down the hillside, he felt woefully out of control. He was running and running as fast as he could but it kept getting closer and closer. And then, even though his legs were moving, he wasn't running at all. As if in some kind of slow motion, he turned around, looked up and saw the massive wall of snow rear up above him, huge hands and claws appearing out of the whiteness on either side of a terrifying face. One look at that face and he screamed. It was his uncle.

He sat up suddenly, sweat drenching his brow, his heart pounding.

'It's okay,' he told himself. 'It's only a dream.' He shuddered.

The package!

He got out of bed and took his wallet out of his jacket pocket. The key had gone.

He systematically went through every bit of it but it wasn't there. He sat down on the bed and forced himself to think. Maybe he had left it at Claire's in his other trousers; maybe he had lost it. No, he was sure, convinced even, that he had put the key in his wallet. In that case, where was it? Perhaps it had fallen out or maybe Saskia had taken it. The heaviness of a dead certainty gripped his stomach. The bloody bitch! She had taken it! He knew he couldn't trust her. Well, there was a simple way to find out. He had brought her handbag back from the hospital with him. She kept all her precious bits and pieces in there.

The bag was downstairs. He opened it and tipped the contents out onto the kitchen table. A jumble of makeup, letters, bills, addresses, telephone book, sweets and money spread everywhere. It took him twenty minutes to search through it all and there was no key. He must have lost it.

With a large whisky and a cigarette, he went back to bed. He felt better now; more confident. He would get everything sorted out. There wouldn't be any problem. There just couldn't be.

* * *

He fetched Saskia the following lunchtime. During the morning he had decided he would tell her everything. Given that she knew so much, it would be easier to let her in on things than to try and deceive her further.

'So that's it then, is it?' She watched him closely. They were sitting in his Porsche in the hospital car park.

'Yes.' He flicked his ash out of the open window. 'McArdle wants more cash, the full amount this time, and I also have to look after a "little package" for him.'

'What little package?'

He glanced at her, suspicious again.

'It's no good looking at me like that, Jamie. Either you tell me or it's all off.'

He sighed. 'Drugs, of course. I'm presuming that one of his henchmen is going to come round and fetch it sometime so I wouldn't go poking around if I were you. If any of that goes missing, we really will be in trouble.' He ran his fingers thoughtfully round his lips. They had healed up now but he still remembered the pain; vividly. 'They don't mess about, McArdle's men. When they mean business, they really mean business.'

They smoked quietly. When he had finished his cigarette, he flicked the butt out of the window.

'So, I'm taking you down to your parents in Surrey.' He started the engine.

'I'm not going, James,' she announced defiantly crossing her arms.

He swung round on her. 'Yes you are!' he yelled, the veins in his neck protruding under the skin. 'You're going because I say so, because I don't want you around when McArdle's men come to the house.'

His eyes blazed at her and she retreated. She always did in the face of his anger.

'Do you have any idea what they are capable of?'

She said nothing.

'Well, do you?' He turned away from her in sheer helplessness. 'No, how could you?' He gave an ironic snort. 'The pampered only daughter of wealthy parents who sent her to a covent: you know nothing, nothing at all. Well, listen to me, my girl; if they come after me and they find you first, they will cut you up into tiny little pieces, understand?' He stroked her hair, his eyes almost painful with the love he thought he had for her. 'I don't want that to happen.' He paused. 'You're all I have and I want to keep it that way.'

Her bottom lip trembled. 'Oh, James!' And she threw her arms round his neck.

The journey was uneventful and he left her in the quiet countryside, sure in the knowledge that she wouldn't get up to any trouble. Her mother didn't ask him in.

Back in London and completely drained by the events of the last twenty-four hours, he decided he needed a break from everything. So he rung Claire and told her he wasn't coming down until Tuesday. He knew she would be disappointed, but it couldn't be helped. He was too damn tired. He got the distinct impression that she was desperate to tell him something but he didn't want to know. It was probably some boring detail about the farm or one of the animals and she was quite capable of sorting out anything like that herself, so he hurried her off the line.

When at last all was quiet, he took out his address book and looked for a number.

A woman answered. 'Hello?'

'Fran? It's James. James Skerrett.'

'Oh yeah, and what do you want?'

'Well, I thought we might get together again, you know, bit of fun, that sort of thing.'

'Why?'

'Oh come on, Francine, you know why. You like it as much as I do.'

There was a silence. James could picture her in his mind's eye; blonde, leggy and with the most enormous pair of breasts. She worked as a croupier at the club and tonight was her evening off.

'I'm tired,' she said.

'No you're not, Fran. If you come round here I'm sure I could wake you up again, arouse your interest, so to speak.'

'God, you're an arrogant bastard!'

He smiled. 'Mmm, I know.'

In the silence that followed he could detect her indecision. 'I'll make it worth your while, Fran.'

'Why should I? I've heard McArdle's after you. You're bad news, James, and I don't want to get mixed up with anything like that.'

'I'm not scared of him,' and he laughed dismissively. 'What do you think I am?'

She sighed heavily. 'All right. See you in about an hour and, Jamie . . .'

'What?'

'I expect to be met with champagne. Understand? Vintage champagne.'

He smiled when he put down the receiver.

'Did you send those letters, Mum?'

'Yes, yes. I followed your instructions exactly.' Her mother glanced over the top of her tabloid. 'You're not in any trouble, are you, Saskia?'

'No. Should I be?' Saskia smiled, her eyes very large and blue.

'You know your Dad and me wouldn't like it if you were.' She straightened out the newspaper. 'It's bad enough that you should live with that horrible boyfriend of yours.'

'Oh for heaven's sake, Mum, don't start that again!'

'Well, it's not right. I can hardly hold my head up for shame when I go to church.'

'Then stop going, for goodness' sake. You don't believe in any of it. Just leave me alone!'

The two women regarded each other from long-established lines of defence and then the older woman, who was a deeply tanned, bottle blonde, with lots of gold jewellery and very long bright red nails, capitulated.

'Oh all right, babes. I won't say anything else, only don't mention his name in front of your Dad. He'll go mental if you do.'

The doorbell rang. Then a maid came in, quickly followed by Terri.

'Hi, Saskia!'

'Terri!'

The two women embraced.

'Hello, Terri,' said Saskia's mother. 'That will be all, Conchita.' The maid withdrew.

'What are you doing here?'

'I've come to see you. I rang James and he grudgingly told me where you were and what happened.'

'Well, come next door and we'll talk.'

Saskia sat her down on the huge white leather sofa.

'Why didn't you tell me you were upset? Why didn't you ring me or something?'

Saskia shrugged. 'I don't know,' and then she smiled. 'I'm glad you're here.'

'So am I. I've missed you.'

Saskia's mother came in. She smoothed down her bright pink tracksuit. 'Well, you must excuse me, girls. I'm off for my golf lesson with my new instructor and he doesn't like to be kept waiting.' She twinkled at them both.

'He's only thirty,' Saskia said to Terri out of the side of her mouth, 'and very dishy by all accounts.'

'Now now, Saskia, that's no way to talk. I'm a respectable married woman, you know.'

After she had gone, leaving behind a slipstream of strong perfume, Terri leant forward and kissed Saskia on the cheek.

'You idiot,' she said softly. 'What if you had succeeded? What would I have done?'

'I don't know. I was just so miserable,' and the tears began to flow.

Terri handed her a clean hanky. 'You've got to leave him. This can't go on. If it does, then one day it might go too far, and then what?'

'But he said he loves me.'

'I know, angel. He would say anything to keep you. That's how he operates and that's how he's got you so upset.'

'He's not always like it,' Saskia sobbed.

'I know.' She hugged her friend. 'Come on, let's go for a walk.'

They stepped out through the large French windows onto the stone-flagged patio. Tubs of crocuses and daffodils were waving their open blooms in the gentle breeze. The girls took the steps down from there onto the sweeping manicured lawns that gently ran downhill to a large ornamental lake.

'It's beautiful here,' observed Terri.

'Mmm, it is nice. Bit quiet, though. I much prefer London. There's so much more going on.'

'Of course, but London isn't the only place. There's Sydney, Brisbane or even Perth, and if that doesn't grab you we could always stop off at Bali or Singapore.'

Saskia looked towards the lake. 'We have some rare ducks down there. Michael, our gardener, did tell me what they were called, but I've forgotten.'

'You're not listening to me, are you?' Terri linked her arm through Saskia's.

'Come on, let's go and see the ducks,' said Saskia.

'No, let's not. Let's talk and get this thing sorted out.'

Saskia pulled away. 'But I don't want to!' and she ran off across the grass.

Terri caught up with her by a large willow tree, the tips of green leaves starting to appear on its trailing branches. 'Listen to me, Saskia. He doesn't love you.'

They walked along the lakeside, their feet sinking in the wet earth.

'He does!'

'He *doesn't*!' Terri insisted. 'When I rang your house last night, guess who answered the telephone?'

'Who?'

'A woman!'

Saskia's face registered shock and then crumpled. 'That's it, that's it, I've had enough!' she cried. 'That bloody, bloody man! After everything he's said, I just can't believe it!'

Terri held her closely. 'Shh, shh, shh. It's all right, Sas. I'm sorry. Maybe I shouldn't have told you that,' and she patted her friend's back as the sobbing intensified.

They stood together under the gently swaying branches of the willow tree, the sunlight sparkling off the lake's surface and rippling across their faces.

'Come on, Sas. Don't cry. He's not worth it, you know.'

'I . . . I can't help it,' and again she sobbed.

Terri's shoulder was getting soaked through but she said nothing. She liked holding Saskia. It felt warm and comfortable. After a while, Saskia pulled back and, taking a crumpled tissue from her pocket, wiped her face, but the tears didn't subside.

'How could I have been so silly?' And she smiled weakly as fresh tears fell. 'After everything he said and everything he did you'd think by now I would have learnt my lesson.' She squinted out across the water. When Terri took her hand and squeezed it, she reciprocated. 'I'm such an idiot, Terri.'

'No, you're not,' came the warm reply. 'We all make mistakes and James has been yours.'

'But why?' Saskia looked at her, her eyes yet again full of tears. 'Why me, and why did it take me so long to realize?'

'Because, my angel,' said Terri, leaning over and brushing away the tears, 'you just didn't want to hear. I told you, or tried to tell you, on numerous occasions and you knew about his other women. I mean, where d'you think he goes most evenings?'

'To the club?'

'Yeah and why?'

'To gamble.'

'And screw, Saskia: he screws and he gets paid for it.'

Saskia's bloodshot eyes were round with disbelief.

'He's a gigolo.'

'I . . . I don't believe you.'

Terri nodded, her mouth a down-turned tight line. 'I'm sorry, angel, but it's true. One of my friends used to work in that place while she was "resting" from the theatre. She told me. Apparently he's well known for it. It seems he prefers rich, older women.'

Saskia's mouth hung open and she gazed unblinkingly at the ground. 'I don't believe it.' She swung round on Terri. 'You mean to tell me that all the time he's been living with me he's been working as a male whore and you didn't tell me?' Her voice had risen to a high pitch which made the ducks flutter away across the lake.

'Yes. Look, angel, I'm sorry. I really am, but . . . I tried, really I did.'

'You're sorry?' hissed Saskia under her breath. 'You wait until I get my hands on that bastard, then he'll know the meaning of the word sorry. When I've finished with him, I'll make him wish he'd never met me.'

'How?'

Saskia turned her head slowly. She looked anything but defeated now.

'I don't know, but I'll find a way somehow.' She paused and then said, 'He has a large supply of good quality cocaine already bagged and waiting to be sold sitting at home in London.' Her eyes widened. 'Why don't you and I sell it for him? I'm sure we could find a willing buyer.'

'You know, angel,' Terri said, smiling in return, 'I never thought I'd see the day when you fought back.'

'You know, Terri, neither did I. What say we go and have a little celebratory drink?'

TWENTY-TWO

'Who's Claire?'

Elyssa handed him a cup of coffee and then sat down on the bed next to him. Alistair took a sip. It was very hot and too strong. He put it on the side cabinet and leant back against the pillows. He wasn't fully awake yet. He closed his eyes.

'None of your business, Elyssa.'

She got off the bed and walked over to the window. She hadn't liked sleeping in the guest room but Alistair had been adamant. She pulled back the heavy velvet curtains and the sun streamed in, showing up the plethora of minute particles of dust that hung suspended in the still, warm air.

Alistair turned his head and looked at her. She was dressed in a gossamer silk negligée, and he could quite clearly see the outline of her slim nakedness through the material. It disgusted him.

'Was she that woman in the café yesterday?'

'Leave it alone, Elyssa.'

She turned and glared at him. 'What's the matter, Ali? I'm only being friendly.'

'Intrusive, more like.' He drank more of his coffee. 'Anyway, why do you ask?'

'Because you talk in your sleep. Quite loudly, in fact. Loud enough for me to hear everything.'

'I do? When?'

'Back in London. In the days when we shared the same bed,' she sneered.

She returned to the bed, his eyes fixed on her. She gave

a small triumphant smile and then leant forward and kissed him on the cheek.

'No need to be so alarmed, Alistair. You didn't give away any state secrets. Although,' she added, 'I'm not sure there's anything to give away any more.'

'What do you mean?'

'Oh come on, Ali, I'm not some silly little teenager, you know, and I can see quite clearly what's going on under my nose.'

'There is nothing to see, Elyssa, and it's got nothing to do with you.'

She looked at him. 'Yes, you're right, there isn't any more. She doesn't love you, Alistair. She never has and she never will.'

'Listen, Elyssa. I don't wish to discuss this with you, so just leave it alone.'

But she was not so easily put off. 'Oh but you do, Alistair,' she said purposefully. 'You and I can help each other a great deal in this situation.'

'How?' he asked with more irritation than he intended to show.

She gave a knowing smile. 'Well, I have need of you and I think that you have need of me.'

'I'm not sure that I follow you, Elyssa.'

'Then let me make it a bit more obvious.' She pursed her nonexistent lips. 'I want someone to marry and have children by. Now,' she said, holding up her hand, 'I know you might think that is quite ridiculous, but it's true.' She looked straight at him. There was no guile in her face now. 'I'm forty-odd years old and even someone like me who's filthy rich and can afford the best medical treatment, reaches a time in her life when the biological clock starts running down. If I am to have children, then it's got to be soon.'

He frowned. 'But what has this got to do with me, Elyssa?'

She sighed and looked heavenwards. 'Can't you see,

Ali? It's you I want. I want you to be the father of my children.'

Alistair simply regarded her with amazed disbelief. Eventually he said, 'Are you serious?'

'Why not? You're reasonably young, you're healthy, you come from a good family and are independently wealthy. A five-thousand-acre estate in Norfolk is not to be sneezed at.'

'Have you been making enquiries about me?'

'No more than you were making about this Claire's boyfriend, so I wouldn't start criticizing me if I were you.'

Alistair flung back the bedclothes in disgust. 'I'm going for my bath,' he announced.

'No, Ali, please not yet, listen to what I have to say.'

He held her wrists. 'I've heard enough, Elyssa, from you and others, and I have no need to hear anything more. Your plan is preposterous!'

'Well, I don't think so,' she replied angrily. 'Just sit down and hear me out. Anyway, what do you mean by "others"? Has someone been talking about me?'

He ignored this but said, 'All right, I will listen, but I warn you, I think your whole idea is completely out of the question.' He sat down, crossed his legs and stared at her. 'Well, let's have it then.'

She turned away from him. Someone had been stirring things up. Maybe that was why he was so angry. Perhaps she ought to change tack.

'Look, Alistair, I'm sorry, I haven't put this at all well.'

'Damned right you haven't.'

'Okay, I'll start again.' After a minute or two of pacing, while she was clearly gathering together her thoughts, she began, faltering at first, but then with more fluency.

'You love this woman . . . I know you do. It's obvious the way – ' She looked away from him; his anger was too much for her to handle.

'I know you do,' she continued more softly, 'and I envy her because you are a very special person, Alistair, and I wish it were me, that's all.' She violently twisted a large gold ring on her finger.

'But ... she doesn't feel the same way. She loves another ... and although you've done your best to stop it, it's not going to work, is it? She's going to marry him and there's nothing you can do about it.'

The silence in the room was almost palpable. Alistair couldn't look at Elyssa. He could feel her eyes penetrating his lowered head as he gazed at the carpet, the subtly patterned Axminster blurring in his vision. Had he been so obvious all these years? More to the point were the utmost clarity and truthfulness of Elyssa's words. Hearing them from someone else stabbed his heart with a hard cold knife. He had always known the truth of the situation, but when she said it, it shattered him.

'I know,' she continued, 'that you will never love me.' She cleared her throat. 'But that doesn't mean we can't have a working relationship that suits both of us. People from our background have invariably to reach some kind of compromise in their lives. No one marries for love, Alistair; that's an old wives' tale. It's commerce that makes the world go round and we must protect our livelihoods.'

'Please, Elyssa – '

'No, Ali, I haven't finished yet. You're wealthy and so am I. I could have any man I wanted if I chose to, but most of them are only after me for my bank balance. Most of them, except you that is. You are my equal and so in that respect we could both maintain our lifestyles with the minimum of readjustment.'

Alistair lowered his head again. It was much easier to let her simply babble on.

'You could stay here in this beautiful house or you could come to London and live with me. I know your father wanted you to work in the family business so it would be very easy for you to do that if you lived there. The other thing is,' she paused, 'I don't know what you're going to think of this, Ali, and please don't laugh, but I'm lonely.

You're lonely too; stuck here in this great big house with no one to love you or take care of you. It's not right, Alistair. There are other alternatives and one of them is me.'

She stopped. She had to check if he was listening. 'We get along fine, we have good sex and we share many interests. It just seems to me the best possible compromise. I get a husband and hopefully some children, and you get someone to keep you warm at night. So what do you think?'

Alistair looked up slowly. Had she finally stopped?

'Well, what do you think?'

He stood up, shell-shocked, his legs feeling quite weak. 'I'm going for my bath.'

He lay in the long white tub, staring at his knees. He was so dumbfounded by all that he had heard that he couldn't comprehend any of it. It was utterly and totally idiotic. How could he marry anyone that he didn't love? And he certainly didn't love Elyssa. The news from Mortimore had cauterized any feelings he might have had for her. He wasn't even sure if he liked her any more. He loved Claire, only Claire didn't love him. And then he started to cry. He hadn't done that since he was a child and his favourite pony had to be put down after breaking its leg. The unfamiliar hot tears ran through the sweat and steam on his face, getting caught up in the red-blond hairs of his moustache.

Elyssa, having dressed, was downstairs in the kitchen making herself some fresh coffee. She wasn't too perturbed by Alistair's abrupt exit from the bedroom. He was shocked but it wouldn't last long. She had practised long and hard over what she was going to say and having got it out of her system, she felt quite relieved. His reaction hadn't been nearly as bad as she had anticipated and now that he was mulling it over, he was bound to see the good sense of it before long. He was a practical chap and she felt confident that he would come round eventually.

Half an hour later, he appeared. Smiling, debonair, clean-shaven and his hair still damp from his bath, he looked relaxed and comfortable in his cords and jumper.

'Any toast for me?'

'Oh sorry, I didn't think . . .'

'That's all right, Elyssa. I'm fully aware of your dislike of anything culinary.'

He made himself something to eat and then sat down.

'When are you going back then?'

She looked up, startled. 'Well, um, actually, I thought I could stay a couple of days.' She smiled. 'I was hoping we could go out together somewhere today.' She cocked her head on one side, her finely etched eyebrows arched in expectation.

'I'm sorry, Elyssa, but I really do have to get down and do some work today.'

'But it's Saturday!' she protested.

'Yes, I know, and as a solicitor my work is never done, especially when it's a one-man practice. So I'll run you down to the station if you like.'

Her smile faded. 'You don't have to. My chauffeur brought me down,' she said coldly. 'I'll just give him a ring.'

'Good. You do that. The telephone is in the hallway.'

She regarded him sullenly. 'I take it then you didn't think much of my suggestion.'

'That we should marry?' He shook his head and chuckled ironically. 'No, I don't. Even if Claire doesn't marry me, or even love me, I couldn't marry you.'

Elyssa bit the inside of her cheek. She mustn't cry; she wasn't going to give him the satisfaction of seeing how much he had hurt her. 'I'm not talking about love, Alistair. I'm talking about making practical decisions, based on common sense situations.'

'Well, that may suit you, but it doesn't suit me and I'm sorry, but I simply can't go along with it.'

She said nothing but carefully wiped her mouth on a

386

napkin. That way she could hide her trembling lips. She blinked rapidly. 'I'll make that phone call now.'

Alistair had seen her tears but he saw no reason to say anything about them. He was emotionally worn out himself, without having to cope with her as well, particularly when she had brought it on herself.

Elyssa stood by the telephone, hand on the receiver, but not dialling. She had the telephone book open on the right page, but she couldn't focus on the numbers, her eyes were full of tears. It was ten minutes before she could make the call and by then her makeup was ruined.

Kevin arrived shortly afterwards. Wordlessly he picked up Elyssa's one small case and placed it in the boot. He then walked off to a discreet distance so that she and Alistair could say their goodbyes. Elyssa held out her hand. 'Well, Alistair, it's been an eventful twenty-four hours. A pity the conversation wasn't exactly to your taste.' She pulled her fur coat tighter around herself in the brisk wind, her red hair lifted up around her ears. 'I'm sorry I couldn't be any better company for you, but I guess it just wasn't meant to be.'

'No, Elyssa, I don't think it was.' He took her hand and shook it briefly. He didn't want to touch her at all.

'Can't we still be friends, Ali?'

He glanced down at the gravel beneath his feet. 'I'm not sure about that.'

He heard her sniff and looked up to see her wiping away a tear. She smiled brightly, too brightly. 'I'm off to Montserrat next month. Sunshine and warm seas: should do me no end of good. I do find this English weather so dreary after a while. The winter is just too long.' She looked at him. 'Would you like to come?'

He laughed, his head thrown back as he gave a deep throaty roar. 'You never give up, do you, Elyssa?'

She sparkled once more, the lights in her eyes brightening up her whole face.

'I think not,' he said, 'I've got other things to do.'

'But won't you even think about it, Ali? Please. It would mean so much to me.'

'It's time you went, Elyssa. Kevin's waiting.'

She glanced around and squinted in the bright sunlight. When she next spoke her voice was flat. 'I'll wait for your call, Ali.'

He didn't reply but watched her leave, a perfectly manicured, bejewelled hand waving out of the back window. From now on, he was going to stay well away from her.

Elyssa poured herself a large Scotch from the in-car bar. With a sigh, she lay back against the warm leather upholstery and smiled to herself. She'd get Alistair. She didn't care what he said. Somehow or another she'd work him round her little finger. He'd already sort of agreed to come on holiday with her. He hadn't said no, so that was half the battle won already.

Claire sat in the barn watching some chickens as they scratched for food in the mud and straw.

Depressed and tired, she couldn't summon up the energy for anything. She picked out a piece of straw from a bale and started to pull it to pieces. Everything had been going so well and now it was all falling apart. She had rowed with Ange and Alistair; she was about to sell her farm, which she didn't want to leave, and James was too busy to come down and see her. She lay back on the bales and absently chewed on the stalk.

It was a beautiful day again, which only increased her feelings of despondency. Small white fluffy clouds skidded across the bright blue sky, blown along by a warm southerly breeze. Blossoms were breaking out along the hedgerows, their scent filling the air, and in the distance she could hear her now well-grown lambs bleating. She would be selling them soon and really ought to be contacting the market, but she didn't. It wouldn't be her responsibility for much longer, so it could wait.

She sat up again. It was time to go for a walk. Anything was better than simply moping about like this.

'Come on, Rosie,' she called. 'Walkies!'

They ambled down the lane until they came to a gate. Jacky and her calf were in the field enjoying the new grass. Big to start with, the calf had flourished after its difficult birth. It was bigger and taller and absolutely full of life, bucking and running around with sheer exuberance. At first its taillessness seemed odd, but Claire didn't notice it any more. It was a fine big heifer and a pure breed too. It would make someone a good milker.

For Jacky the future was far more uncertain. She was easily ten years old and well past the prime of life. When the time came to sell up, she would have to go straight to the knacker's yard. No one would want a cow as old as she. The vet said she mustn't have any more pregnancies. She had only just survived this one. Claire sighed. She liked the old beast; she was a nice friendly animal and Claire would miss her.

Bonny was in the field too. When she saw Claire, she came over to greet her, her brown coat covered with patches of dried mud from where she had been rolling. She stood next to the gate snorting at Claire and nudging her arm until Claire relented and gave her a sugar lump, a supply of which she kept in her pocket. As Bonny took the titbit with her velvet lips brushing against Claire's open palm, Claire patted her neck.

'And what are we going to do with you then?'

The horse tossed her head and shook her mane, temporarily dislodging the flies that buzzed around her. She was a fine strong animal and quite big enough to carry far more than Claire's light weight. Viceless and well mannered, she would make someone a very good horse. There was an equestrian centre not far away that did day trips for holiday makers during the summer. They were always on the lookout for good animals that didn't mind the fumblings of once-a-year jockeys. Claire would give them a ring. She gave the horse a last pat and then walked on down the lane until she came to a stile which led on to the moor. She climbed over while Rosie pushed through a well-worn hole in the scrappy hedge. They then continued along the stony track. Small groups of moorland cattle and ponies stood around grazing on the sparse vegetation. Looking unkempt, their long winter coats were beginning to moult, revealing patches of glossy new growth underneath. Bits of discarded hair lay everywhere.

Rosie ran about sniffing the smells, occasionally stopping over something particularly interesting. Claire watched her. It was then that she realized how unfair it would be to take her to London. She was a farm dog, country born and bred, and used to the freedom of the fields and moorland. To shut her up in a house and only take her out for a couple of walks each day would be purgatory for her. She needed to run; she needed to work; it was what she was bred for and there was no way Claire could deny her that.

The dog ran about, her long hair flying in the wind, her mouth open and her pink tongue hanging out. She was so happy. Claire turned away. It would be difficult to leave her, but there was nothing else she could do. Jack would have her. He always admired her and she would make him a fine companion and worker. Claire could trust Jack to take care of her.

The other reason for not taking her was James. As much as Claire didn't want to face it, she had to. James and Rosie didn't get on. They never had and Claire saw no reason for it to change. Far better then to make a clean break and keep the pair of them apart. She could always come back and visit her dog. James couldn't object to that.

There was only one problem in her well-thought-out-plan: it would devastate her. Saying goodbye to her pet, who had been constantly by her side for two and a half years and had helped her get through the most depressing time of her life, was going to break her to pieces. Even thinking about it was upsetting her.

She stopped and called Rosie to her. The dog came happily, her tail wagging, her mouth open in a broad grin.

Claire knelt down and holding Rosie's face in her hands said: 'You have no idea how much I'm going to miss you, do you?'

Rosie cocked her head on one side. She knew when Claire was saying something of importance. Her bright eyes stared back and she gave a small whine. Claire started to cry, her warm tears blown across her cheeks by the wind.

'Oh Rosie, Rosie, what am I going to do without you?'

The dog pulled away and started to prance. She had found a stick which she picked up and dropped at Claire's feet. She wanted to play.

'I see,' said Claire standing up. 'No time for tears, eh?'

She picked up the stick and threw it down the hill. Rosie ran after it, reaching the stick almost before it had landed. She came back with it and there followed five minutes' tug-of-war before Claire got it back.

They played their game for another twenty minutes, after which they were both hot and thirsty. Rosie lapped at one of the cold moorland streams.

'Come on you, time to go home.'

Held together by love, freely given and reciprocated, they went back.

That evening when all the chores were done, Claire was sitting in her kitchen polishing Bonny's tack. It occurred to her as she buffed the seat of the saddle that something was unfinished. The one jarring note in her ordered existence was her row with Alistair. A few days' reflection had mellowed her feelings and she decided that despite what he had said about James, none of which she ever wanted to hear again because it was just malicious gossip, he was still her friend and she really ought to apologize to him. Having made up her mind she acted at once. She put away her polish and saddle soap and went out into the hall.

'Hello?' his voice resonated deep and rich.

She hesitated. 'I'm sorry, Alistair.'

'Oh Claire, how lovely to hear you.'

'I shouldn't have shouted and I'm sorry.'

'How are you?'

'Alistair, aren't you listening to me?' This was typical of him. No matter what their disagreements, he always behaved as if nothing had happened, which only compounded her guilt. 'I said I'm sorry.'

'Yes, yes, and that's the third time you've apologized and I accept it and what's more, I'm sorry too. You were quite right, of course, I had no business doing what I did and you had every reason to be a bit miffed, so I would say it was six of one and half a dozen of the other, wouldn't you?'

Trust him. He was so nice. 'Oh Alistair, you really are such a good friend to me.'

'Well, someone needs to be, you know. I saw Angela Wilkinson the other day and she hinted that you had had a similar disagreement with her.'

Claire was ashamed. 'Yes, I'm afraid we did, but I did say sorry afterwards,' she added quickly.

'Yes, she told me.'

'Did . . . did she say anything else?' She knew they both disapproved – that they had made perfectly obvious – and she couldn't face it if they were sharing their concerns. If only they would understand. It would make all the difference.

'No, Claire, we didn't talk about you and your chap if that's what you're asking, so you have no need to feel worried.'

She exhaled slowly. She hadn't realized she was so tense. 'Oh . . . good.'

'So,' he asked brightly, 'what are you up to now?'

'Well, at this precise moment, I'm cleaning my horse's tack. It's absolutely filthy.'

'No, I don't mean that, silly. I meant you and James.

How are things going with your plans?'

'Haven't you heard then?'

'Heard what?'

'Oh I thought you solicitors shared information and all that.' It was a dig at him and his contact in London and she instantly regretted it.

Alistair ignored it. 'Should I have heard?'

'Stapletons contacted me direct to say that Mr Neale wants to buy the whole farm. Apparently that day he came up here and I was really rude to him hasn't stopped him viewing the whole place as his second home or something. He's coming here on Tuesday and with a bit of luck we'll make a deal.'

'But you said . . . I mean, I thought that . . .' He trailed off.

'That was before I met James, Alistair. Since then everything has changed. Anyway, you said yourself you might be moving away. So new pastures for both of us.'

'Yes . . . exactly.'

'James has found a place for us in London,' she continued gaily, 'so the sooner I off-load Tor Heights the better, don't you think?'

'But I thought Tor Heights meant everything to you.' Claire didn't hear the pain in his voice.

'Well it does, Alistair, but James means more than that. I mean, what does a dilapidated old farm like this mean to anyone? It's only bricks and mortar and if we're to get married, then I'm going to have to move up to London.'

'But you said you weren't getting married for at least two years.'

'Well, things have moved a bit quicker than I anticipated, that's all.'

He didn't reply at once. At last he said quietly, 'Claire, are you quite sure you're doing the right thing? I mean, is there anything I can say that might make you change your mind?'

She was determined not to get upset so she answered

slowly and clearly. 'No, Alistair, there isn't. I know you and Ange only want the best for me and believe me, I appreciate that, but I know I'm doing the right thing. I love James and James loves me and the sooner I move up there and be with him, the happier I shall be, right?'

'Of course, Claire.' That word; why did she have to say that word? How could she possibly love someone whom she hardly knew?

Claire thought Alistair sounded convinced but she was glad he wasn't standing in front of her. She knew from experience that he had a way of looking at her that made her doubt the very words she was saying and she didn't want to doubt anything. Everything had to go exactly as she said it would; it had to.

'But, Alistair, I do have something to ask you. Will you do my conveyancing for me?'

'Oh Claire, how could you think I wouldn't?'

'I thought you might be a bit upset and wouldn't want to.'

'Silly,' he chastened with affection. 'Of course I'll do it, so long as you listen to my advice.'

'Yes I will.'

'Right then, I'll look forward to hearing from you, okay?'

She put the phone down with satisfaction. Talking to Alistair had cheered her up. She called Rosie from her blanket.

'Come on, sweetie, last trip round the garden.'

She stood on the back lawn, her slippers getting wet with the dew while Rosie sniffed about.

It was a cold night with few clouds and little wind. High above her the stars hung from the black velvet sky, shining down on the sleeping land. In the distance, she could hear the harsh call of a vixen and she knew all around her that nocturnal eyes were watching her from the darkness. On a night such as this Dartmoor was a hauntingly beautiful place and she felt privileged to see it.

* * *

Kevin didn't know what he was looking for, but there had to be something of interest in her bureau. She kept all manner of documentation in here so he was sure to find something. He silently slid open another drawer. The first one had been useless. Mainly old letters, personal and official. He only gave them the briefest inspection before returning them. Careful to replace everything as he had found it, he felt sure she wouldn't notice.

It had been easy once he had made up his mind. With Aditha's help they had concocted a plan in his mother's front room in King's Lynn.

'It's a bit risky,' he said. 'What if she catches me? She's bound to find out and then I'll get trouble from the police.'

'But you can do it, Kevin,' urged Aditha, looking at him with her huge brown eyes. 'I know you can. We know you can,' and she took his hand and placed it on her belly.

He smiled. 'How far gone are you now?'

'The doctor say twelve weeks.'

Kevin grinned, pink with pleasure. A dad; he was going to be a dad. His mum was really pleased when he told her. None of his mates had a girlfriend like Aditha. All they had were local girls. They weren't half jealous when he first took her down to the pub.

'We have to do it, Kevin, for baby. For your son.'

'How d'you know it's a boy?'

Her smile was enigmatic. 'Trust me, I know.'

She knew everything: where to find the papers, how to get them, how to make sure he wouldn't get caught. He couldn't do anything without her. He truly loved her.

So here he was, flashlight in hand, sifting through Elyssa's bureau. Aditha had told him that she had seen the papers one day when she was cleaning. She knew it was something of importance because when Elyssa came in and saw what she was reading, she was so angry that she had smacked her across the face. From then on Aditha had stayed well away from the bureau and she knew that Elyssa kept it locked.

It hadn't taken long for Aditha to find the key. She had ample opportunity to search Elyssa's bedroom on the pretext of giving it a good clean and it was on one of these days, when she had inadvertently opened the bedside table, that she found it. Within the space of an hour, she had removed it, got it copied and replaced the original. Elyssa never knew anything about it.

Kevin now had the duplicate key. After he had searched the drawers and found nothing, he unlocked the roll-top and pushed it back. It made a protesting squeak which echoed around the room. He gritted his teeth and hoped she was still blacked out. When they had got back from Devon, she decided to have one of her increasingly liquid suppers. She was so drunk by the time she had finished that he had had to carry her to bed.

He leafed through the mass of papers, the torch on the desk: bank statements – he was amazed at the figures – credit card statements – could she really spend that much? – and legal documents concerning her divorce. Then he stopped. There it was: that was what he was looking for.

In his surprise he drew up a chair and sat down. Change of Name Deed said the title. With eager anticipation, he opened it. Aditha was right, my God was she right! They would make a packet out of this.

There were several photocopies of the original document. He took one, folded it up and put it in his back pocket before replacing everything where he had found it. As he was doing so, he came across her birth certificate. He laughed out loud at that one, but quickly stifled the sound. He must not wake her.

He locked up the bureau and left the room, shutting the door quietly behind him. Pleased with his deception, he decided to go and check on her to make sure the old cow was really asleep. It would be nice to gloat.

Up in her bedroom, he stood next to her bed looking down at her peaceful face. Forty years old indeed! Who the hell did she think she was kidding?

Elyssa stirred, rolling over to one side and grunting. Kevin grimaced. She stank, as did the room. Stale alcohol and strong perfume didn't make a pleasant combination. He turned to go when – 'Alistair?'

He froze.

'Alistair, don't leave me, please don't leave me.'

Christ! What was he to do? He turned round. With relief he could see that she was still asleep. He stepped out.

'Alistair!'

He glanced back. Her eyes were open. He had everything to lose so he ran for it. As he bounded down the stairs, he could hear her cries.

'Alistair! Alistair! Don't leave me, Alistair!'

TWENTY-THREE

James arrived at Briar Cottage on Tuesday morning only to find Saskia's car was already there. She was sitting in the small sitting room listening to some music.

'What the hell are you doing here?' he asked brusquely.

She turned her lovely gold head to him and smiled. 'You always were so polite, James. Don't I even get a hello?'

'No.' He let his bag fall to the floor with a thump. He was tired after his journey and it was an unwelcome shock to find her here.

'Why aren't you at your parents'?'

'I was bored so I thought I'd come and keep you company. I knew I'd find you here. You never could resist the smell of money, could you, James? Especially when you need it so badly. Guy even rang me in Surrey to ask where you were. Why don't you ring him?'

He glowered at her. 'Who let you in?'

'That nice Mr Burrows, you know, your landlord. He came by earlier this morning, saw me sitting in the car and offered to let me in. I don't know how you follow his accent, I couldn't understand a damned word he was saying. He lit the fire for me and chopped up some more wood so I wouldn't run out of fuel. So, here I am.'

'Yes, so I can see,' he said dully. He went into the kitchen and returned a few minutes later with a coffee. He sat down next to her. 'This visit isn't just to see me, is it?'

'Oh James,' she said innocently, her eyes very wide and blue, 'how could you say such a thing?'

'Because I know you. You're down here because you don't trust me with Claire.'

'Whatever gave you that idea?'

'Cut the crap, Saskia, it doesn't work with me.'

'So, what if I am here?'

He gave her a flash of a smile, his eyes remaining quite sullen. 'I'm flattered, darling, but it won't work. You'll cramp my style and if Claire gets suspicious then she's not going to play ball.'

She leant forward to kiss his cheek. 'Jamie,' she breathed, 'I won't get in your way, honestly I won't. I'll be very careful.'

He pulled away from her. 'Listen, Sas, I've got her to think I'm on the verge of bankruptcy.'

'But you are, darling, and what's more McArdle and the bank are after you as well.'

'Shut up, Saskia. I don't need you to remind me of the mess I'm in.' He sipped his coffee, not really tasting it. 'Anyway,' he continued, 'so far I've refused all her offers of help, making her think that it's not the sort of thing a gentleman would do, but when I next see her, I'm going to accept. I'll take whatever she offers me, maybe even push the figure up a bit.' His eyes were bright with the tantalizing vision of all the riches which were just out of his grasp. 'I've got her right where I want her, Sas; she's ripe for the picking and I can't afford to have anything go wrong. I bumped into one of the women who works at the club. She said that McArdle is rapidly losing his patience with me. I've got to move fast. Understand? I've got to.'

'Bumped, eh? Is that what you call it now? And what about me? I'm just supposed to put up with all of this, am I?'

She was pouting like a spoilt little child, her red lips full. He could hardly believe it. Never mind all his plans, the only thing that mattered to her was herself. It was incredible.

'What about you? Listen, darling, I've told you what

we're going to do. We'll take the money and run. Our passports are all up to date and once we're out of the country McArdle can't get me.'

'You mean – '

'That's right,' he finished for her, 'I'm not going to pay him anything. That bastard can go screw himself before he gets any more out of me. Christ! I've paid him enough already.'

'But what if he comes after you? What about the bank? They're looking for you.'

'Fuck the bank and McArdle,' he said dismissively. 'Don't worry, we'll be okay. I don't foresee any problems, do you?'

Saskia smiled. 'If you say so, James.'

Getting rid of Saskia was a damn sight more difficult than James had envisaged. She wanted to stay around to see what happened she said; to see how he would get the money from Claire. He would have none of it. Any interference from her was bound to end in disaster. He had to persuade her to leave and the one way he knew to do that would be to have sex with her. It temporarily shut her up and right now, he needed that. He was about to make the first move when, curiously, she did.

'Why don't we go to bed, Jamie, have a small siesta? You know, recover from our journeys?' Her eyes were shining provocatively as she sidled up to him and ran her fingernails down the side of his face.

'Come on,' she whispered, 'it's been too long. I need you.' After Terri's revelations in the garden in Surrey, Saskia had done some thinking. It was a novel experience for her, but with Terri's help, she had sat down and worked out what she was going to do. In that one afternoon, over plentiful supplies of coffee, biscuits and tissues, she had cried, laughed and plotted her way to her revenge on James.

She had been a fool; she knew that now. She could see

only too clearly and painfully exactly how he had used and abused her over their time together. As the full realization of what he had done to her dawned, she began to feel a strange and unfamiliar optimism fill her insides.

'I'm going to make him pay, Terri,' she said quietly, her red-rimmed eyes staring at the table top. 'He's not going to get away with it; not this time. This time he's gone too far. Christ! How could I have been so stupid?' and her tears renewed with extra intensity.

'Don't, angel, don't blame yourself,' soothed her friend. 'So you messed up? So what? That's what life is all about.'

Saskia looked at her. 'I know,' she sniffed, wiping her nose, 'but I bet most people don't screw up like I do.' And she blubbed some more.

'Here, have another biscuit,' and so it went on, Saskia crying, Terri soothing, plans being made.

Now Saskia was at the cottage putting on the performance of a lifetime.

'Come on, baby, let's go upstairs. I want you.'

She kissed him on the mouth, full and passionately. She knew what his response would be. It was all so damned easy. He responded just as she knew he would, his hands grabbing at her. After a while she pulled away.

'Not here, James. Upstairs.'

In the bedroom, they tore off each other's clothes. Familiarity had bred impatience, with no time for subtleties. James didn't need to seduce her like he had Claire. With Saskia flat on her back and her legs apart, he simply got on with the job.

He took a generous mouthful of nipple while he fondled her other large breast. There was a fine balance he had to maintain between rushing her out of the cottage and satisfying her sexual needs. Too much haste and she would not co-operate.

'Like that, baby?'

She held onto his head, pressing him against her. 'Mmm, very nice.'

It's not the same, she thought. Two weeks ago, she would have melted when he touched her. Not now. The knowledge that he had been paid to have sex with women had turned love to hate and desire to distaste. Her flesh crawled to his touch.

'Hurry, darling, hurry,' she urged, pulling him up to her. It would be easy to rush him; to get him out and off her.

She closed her eyes. It's not him, she thought, it's not him. If she tried really hard she could make believe it was Terri.

James was puzzled. This wasn't like Saskia, but he didn't worry too long. If she wanted it, he would oblige.

It was a relief to Saskia when he finally entered her. Either he was rough or she wasn't ready, she wasn't sure, but he hurt her and she gave a little gasp.

He looked at her, a small frown on his face. 'Okay, baby?'

She nodded and he continued grunting in her ear.

Not long, she thought, not long now. There were cobwebs in one of the ceiling corners where a large spider was sitting waiting for its next unfortunate meal. Saskia smiled over James's shoulder as he bumped against her. There was little difference between them. It would have its fly and she would have her James.

James didn't answer the question in his mind. He just knew something was up. Quite what, he didn't know, but something; some little thing about her didn't make sense.

After making love, she had rushed to get dressed and was downstairs waiting for him calmly smoking when he entered.

'So everything's okay then?' he asked as he sat down and helped himself to a cigarette.

She smiled brightly. 'Of course, why shouldn't it be?'

'And you know what to do then?'

'Yes.'

He glanced at her and frowned. 'Are you sure, Sas?'

She tutted. 'Yes, of course I do, James.'

'Right then. You'd better get ready to leave.'

By 11.30 Claire was getting annoyed. Eleven o'clock had been the agreed time and she didn't like it when people stood her up. She could understand the odd five minutes, but half an hour? That was just plain rudeness, especially for someone who was busy like she was. There were so many other things she could be getting on with. She stood in her yard looking down the lane and could see nothing.

'To hell with you, Neale,' and with that she headed off back to her garden. She was sufficiently angry now to give her potato patch a really good dig. She had just picked up the spade when she heard a car engine and Rosie started to bark.

'About bloody time too!' She put down the spade and went off to meet the Neales. It wasn't something she looked forward to.

She found them sitting in their car looking apprehensively at Rosie who, knowing she had them at bay, was making the most of seeming big and ferocious. Claire smiled; it was so nice having a dog with a discerning taste.

'All right, Rosie, stop being a bully and come here.'

The dog gave one last half-hearted woof and trotted over to her mistress. Neale and his family got out and Claire could see immediately that they had not come dressed for a morning tramping over the fields. Mr Neale was encased in his everyday office garb of sober grey suit, psychedelic waistcoat and matching tie, while his wife looked as though she had just stepped out of the fashion pages of an up-market women's magazine, her peach dress and matching silk scarf flapping in the breeze. Her carefully coiffured hair didn't move at all.

The two sulky teenagers, both pustulating and greasy, wore makeup, sprayed on black jeans and had shaved parts of their heads so that their remaining multi-coloured dreadlocks hung over their faces.

Claire wiped her dirty hand on her jeans and offered it. 'How do you do?'

Mr Neale shook it, Mrs Neale's hand passed over Claire's like the breath of a ghost and the two teenagers ignored her completely.

'Say hello, you two,' ordered their father.

They grunted.

'I'm sorry we're late,' he added, looking sideways at his wife who hadn't stopped wrinkling her nose, 'but I'm afraid to say we were unavoidably delayed.'

'That's all right,' said Claire. 'I've only been waiting for the last half an hour, and you know we farmers, always plenty of time to waste.'

'Quite.' He smiled obsequiously. 'So where shall we start?'

Claire indicated the house. 'In here, I thought.'

'Of course,' he nodded. 'Come along, you two.'

The teenagers were lagging behind. One look at Claire's yard and they had made up their minds. They slouched after their parents.

'The scullery,' pointed out Claire, 'approximately eight by six. It's cold enough in here for the freezer, and you can see it's where I keep my washing machine.'

'Is that a gun cupboard?' asked the boy, his face lighting up at last.

'Yes.'

'Are they real guns? Do you use them?'

'Yes they are, and no I don't. I don't like guns, and prefer to have nothing to do with them.'

'That's enough, Jason,' interrupted his father. 'Let Mrs Bromage continue.'

Mrs Neale made no comment at all, only giving it the briefest glance. Then she raised an eyebrow and said, 'Small, isn't it?'

'Yes dear, but we can soon change that,' encouraged her husband taking her hand. 'Just look on the positive side,

Betty.' His smile was ingratiating and Claire found it difficult not to laugh.

She led them through into the kitchen. Rosie was lying next to the Rayburn. She instantly sat up and started to growl. The Neale family regarded her with suspicion.

'Big, isn't she?' said Mr Neale.

Claire noticed he was beginning to perspire, a faint wet sheen had appeared on his bald head. His wife, a good five inches taller than he with her high-heeled court shoes, gave the room a perfunctory look.

'Really, Philip, just how am I going to entertain in this . . . this . . .'

'Room?' offered Claire.

'Well, if you can call it that,' she replied disdainfully.

Neale gave a forced laugh. 'Really, dear, there's no need to be so frank.'

The two women looked at each other with barely concealed hostility. The idea of selling to them was rapidly receding from Claire. She found them repugnant and it was difficult to even be remotely civil to them.

They trooped after her into the sitting room. When Claire had first moved in, the place was almost uninhabitable with damp rot, dry rot, an antiquated plumbing system and the most appalling décor. She and Matt had done all the necessary repairs, spending weeks plastering, rewiring and digging up floorboards. When that was finished they had stripped down all the walls and painted them magnolia throughout the house. Claire thought the colour suited the rooms well and had left it alone since then. Given the age of the house and her eclectic taste in furniture, which she had gathered together over the years, she thought it all looked homely.

Mrs Neale, however, disagreed and said sotto voce, but still loud enough for Claire to hear: 'It's ghastly, Philip, positively ghastly. Just look at it. I couldn't possibly live with that.'

He waved her quiet and turned to Claire. 'Well, it's not too bad. Needs redecorating, of course, but apart from that it's okay.' He wanted to be nice. Claire could see that, but she still disliked him. The rest of his family left her speechless.

'It's a bit small,' he added, seeing her look, 'but I could get some people up here to knock down a few walls.' He tapped the skirting board with his foot, listening. 'Yes, it wouldn't take long. We'd soon have this place shipshape.'

Claire inwardly groaned. She didn't want to think of her lovely house being ripped apart by Neale and his workmen. They would turn it into a Lego box, just like the ones he intended to build in the valley. She looked at the teenagers. They were bored to death, their faces masks of long-suffering duty.

'Perhaps you two would like to go outside?' she asked.

Neale looked with disgust at them both. The idea that two such genetic cockups had come from his loins was deeply insulting to him.

'Okay Jason, Lorraine, off you go and play outside.'

They looked at him, their lips curled with sneering embarrassment. 'Play? Play?' they exclaimed in unison, their voices derisory. 'God, Dad, you're so gross!' and with that they slouched out, the chains on their jeans jangling.

'Excuse those two,' he said apologetically, 'it's their age.'

Claire said nothing, but led the adults through to the dining room, pointing out before Mrs Neale did that yes, it was small, and no, it hadn't been decorated recently, but no doubt Mrs Neale would have plenty of ideas about that. It had a panoramic view of the moor and if they stood here they could see both Haytor and the Three Wise Men. Mrs Neale wasn't impressed.

Claire loved this room, especially on summer evenings when swifts and swallows would screech around the eaves and the sinking sun was shining yellow and gold against the granite tors. When the tourists had all gone and only the moorland animals remained, it was a time for people like her, the privileged few, to sit and really admire the moor's isolated splendour. She considered it one of nature's most glorious sights.

She turned away from the window. She felt a stab of poignant sadness because she wouldn't be able to enjoy it much longer. The feeling changed to quiet anger when she saw the two idiots who wanted to buy it. Such a sight was wasted on them.

'Yes,' said Mrs Neale, 'and are there any decent shops around here?'

Mr Neale stayed longer. 'I think it's quite beautiful.'

Claire looked at him with renewed interest. Perhaps she had misjudged him.

'Gets cold up here,' she said, 'very cold. But of course I have the Rayburn going all year round and that gives me all the hot water I need.'

'You mean you don't have central heating?' Mrs Neale was incredulous.

'Central heating?' queried Claire. 'What's that?' and she turned away to stifle her giggle. She felt sure Mrs Neale was suffering from severe rural shock. As she walked out of the room, she could hear Mr Neale trying to placate his wife who was rapidly heading for a blue fit of hysteria.

'I can't possibly live here, Philip. I don't care what you say, it's out of the question. The place is just too awful.'

'But it won't always be like this. We can have done whatever you like. You can choose the colour schemes, a new kitchen, an extension, anything. Whatever you want, Bunny, you can have.'

Bunny! Mrs Neale was anything but small and furry. Cuddling her would be like embracing a cross between a viper and a sack of bones. Claire had never seen anyone who was so thin and still standing. Angles stuck out everywhere and one puff of a Dartmoor gale and she would blow over. Bunny indeed!

She led them upstairs. There were three bedrooms she told them: the main one which she slept in, a second double which she used as a storeroom, but was now cleared out, and the smallest one which she had intended to use as a nursery.

'Oh, so you don't have any children then?' asked Mr Neale.

Claire walked on.

She opened the door of all three rooms, stood back and watched as the Neales walked about. Judging from the look on 'Bunny's' face, her mind was made up. Of course, there were still the fields and farm buildings to look at, and if Mrs Neale needed any further convincing, then a tramp about in mud and animal dung should finally clinch it.

'Bathroom's at the end,' she said when the Neales had left the final bedroom. Mr Neale opened the door but his wife refused to go in. It was all too much for her delicate sensibilities.

They went downstairs. Claire made some tea and they sat around the kitchen table. Mrs Neale didn't touch her cup.

'Tea all right?' asked Claire.

'I'm just not thirsty, that's all,' she replied, trying to smile, but achieving only a sneer.

Claire liked her tea strong. Mrs Neale seemed not to share her taste.

'Well,' said her husband, 'I think this place has potential. It definitely has possibilities and when we get back home, I'll chew things over with an architect friend of mine and see if we can't come up with a plan. I could be making you an offer fairly soon.' His piggy eyes shone with brittle optimism as he spelt out his ideas. Claire's heart sank. So this was it. She knew she had to sell up, but still her heart wasn't in it.

His wife said nothing, she sat quite rigid and upright, pointedly ignoring them and trying, if it were at all possible, not to touch anything. She held her arms tightly at her sides, her knees were glued together and her mouth a thin bloodless line. Claire found it difficult to imagine what two such disparate characters had in common.

'More tea, Mr Neale?'

He put his hand over his cup. 'No, no, that was quite enough for me.'

'Well,' she said, standing up, 'perhaps you would like to see the outbuildings?'

'Yes, yes, of course,' he said. He helped up his wife, who seemed quite overcome at the mere idea of the suggestion, and out they went.

The yard was generally quite clean at this time of year. All the ewes and lambs were out in the fields and Jacky came in only once a day to be milked. A few chickens were scratching about, but there was little mess. There was a fine healthy aroma in the air emanating from a big steaming dungheap, but Claire didn't notice that. Mr Neale wrinkled his nose a couple of times and commented on the 'strong country smell' while Mrs Neale held a white lace hanky to her nose. When they got to the barn, she stopped completely.

'Really, Philip,' she began, fanning her hand across her nose, 'you can't possibly expect me to go in there surely!'

'Well, stay out here then.'

'I think I'll go and sit in the car. At least it smells nice in there.'

When she had gone, Neale turned to Claire and whispered, 'Has a delicate stomach, you know.'

'Really?'

They went in and surveyed the interior.

'Well, Mr Neale, what do you think of this?'

The barn with its whitewashed walls and beamed cob-webbed ceiling, was practically empty. There was just a small stack of last year's straw at the back.

'Very nice,' he said. 'Very nice. I know exactly what I'll do with this.'

'Yes?'

'I'll turn this bit into a garage and the bit at the back into a games room, you know, pool table, computer games, that sort of stuff.'

'Bit big for a garage, isn't it?'

'Oh no, not at all,' he beamed. 'I collect motorbikes as well as having the BMW.' His face had gone quite pink and for the first time that day, he looked genuinely happy, sheer contentment on his face. 'Yes,' he continued, 'big fat motorbikes. I have a Harley Davidson Electroglide, a BMW 1000cc and a Honda Goldwing Full-Dress. I love to go for a run.'

Claire found it difficult to believe how a man of his short stature could ride one of those huge machines. She had ridden a bike occasionally. Matt had bought a second-hand 250cc Suzuki, which they sometimes used to round up the cattle with, providing the weather had been dry and there was little mud. It was hard enough managing that little thing and Claire was a good few inches taller than Neale. Maybe, she thought, they made special attachments for the shorter man.

They left the barn and walked over to the stables, passing Mrs Neale who was sitting in the front seat of the car, listening to classical music on the stereo. She didn't acknowledge her husband's small wave.

'What will you do with these?' asked Claire.

'Swimming pool,' replied Neale with certainty.

She was amazed. 'How will you do that?'

'We'll keep the place virtually intact so that it still blends in with the countryside, but we'll gut it. Then we'll put in the pool with panoramic windows down one side. Easily done,' he added, seeing her disbelief.

Claire looked round the place. To her it would always be the stables, a place where she had kept the young bullocks and where Jacky and Bonny lived during the winter. All this talk of making it into a swimming pool seemed sheer fanciful nonsense. A wave of bittersweet regret swept over her. To lose so much . . .

'About how many acres do you have altogether then?'

'Fifty. Most of it up here, but a few acres down past my neighbour, Jack Burrows.'

'Orchard Meadow?'

'Yes. Five acres in all, plus I have common grazing rights on the moor, but I don't suppose you'll be taking advantage of that.'

He chuckled. 'Hardly. My two spend all their time hanging out with their very unsavoury friends. The idea of either of them on a horse is quite ridiculous.'

She smiled agreeably. 'You know, Mr Neale, I can't understand why you've decided to buy this place. I mean, I wasn't exactly polite to you last time you were here. In fact, I was hoping I might have put you off ever bothering me again.'

'Oh, I've been at the receiving end of far worse than that. No,' he said twinkling, 'I've always had an eye for potential. It's why I'm so successful, I suppose. Where other people might see a run-down old shack, I see it rebuilt, redecorated and resold, making me a nice little profit.' He glanced around the building. 'I wasn't born wealthy, you know. I had to work for it and in the early days when me and Betty were dirt-poor, I worked all the hours God sent, I can tell you.' He scratched his beard. 'I know that you don't like me much, and it's no good pretending otherwise, but I am what you see: a self-made millionaire – well,' he shrugged, 'on paper anyway, and I don't give a damn what anyone thinks about it.' He stuck out his little chin, bristling with defiance. Claire thought he reminded her of a bulldog and that maybe he wasn't so bad after all. There was something mildly attractive about his honesty and she warmed towards him. He had no illusions about himself and she liked that.

'Come and see my land, Mr Neale. I think you might like it.'

'Right.'

They didn't even bother to try to entice his wife out of the car. She sat there, stubbornly refusing to move, her stick arms crossed over her nonexistent bosom.

Claire waited until they were well out of earshot. 'You

411

know, Mr Neale, I hate to state the obvious, but it seems to me that your wife doesn't like this place.'

'Oh don't worry about Betty,' he said quite unconcerned. 'She's a very ... well, strong-minded person sometimes, but I always get round her in the end. You see, every time we move I say it will be the last time and then one day I'll see somewhere else and, well, before you know it, I've got that itch to go again.' He gave her a small reassuring smile. 'Once I give her a free hand to do as she wants inside the house, she usually comes round and I don't suppose she'll be any different this time.'

Claire showed him her flower garden and explained how beautiful it looked in the summer when the roses all bloomed, their scent wafting over towards the house. His interest lapsed even more when she took him to the vegetable patch. She gave up altogether when it came to explaining about soil quality because she could see he wasn't listening.

'Your fields,' he said, good-natured and patient. 'Where are they?'

She looked at his shoes. 'You're not really dressed for them, Mr Neale.'

He followed her downward gaze. 'Oh dear, I didn't think to bring any boots with me.'

'Well, we don't really have to walk through any mud. We can just walk down the lane. You can see most of the land from there.'

They went back through the yard. Mrs Neale was still ignoring them.

As they came up to the first field where Bonny, Jacky and the calf were, they heard a loud yell, followed by a screech of high-pitched laughter. A brief look at each other and they ran to see what was happening, Claire stretching out her long legs while Neale's short stubby ones followed close behind.

What Claire saw made her burst out laughing too. Neale came panting up behind her and did the same.

'Heavens! Look at him! Whatever is your wife going to say?'

The two teenagers came over to them, the girl giggling, the boy red-faced and angry.

'It was her fault,' he said, pointing at his sister. 'She said that if I could ride that old nag over there she'd let me borrow her Iron Maiden tape. Look at me!' he wailed. His jeans were covered in mud and his T-shirt had a rip in it.

'What happened?' asked Claire when she finally stopped laughing.

'That bloody horse, that's what,' he said, pulling off some grass that had stuck to him.

'Now now, Jason,' said his father, 'there's no need for that kind of language in front of Mrs Bromage.'

Claire waved away his objection 'And?'

'Well,' said his sister, eager to tell of her brother's misfortune, 'he climbed onto the horse but it wouldn't go so I managed to get its head up and with Jason kicking it and me hitting its bum, we finally got it going. Well, it went faster and faster and then it stopped.' She squealed with laughter. 'And Jason fell over its shoulders into the hedge!' The girl started to climb over the gate. 'Just wait till your friends hear about this. Talk about street cred.'

She just managed to avoid her brother's blow and ran off down the lane towards the yard, the boy following in hot pursuit, swearing all kinds of dire revenge if she so much as opened her mouth and uttered one syllable.

Neale turned to Claire. 'Kids, eh? Who'd have 'em?'

Claire shrugged. 'Mmm, yes, who indeed?'

Maybe me sometime, she thought.

She showed him as much of the land as she could from the road. He seemed pleased with what he saw and Claire could tell from what he said that he probably had ambitions to become one of the local squirarchy.

They walked back to the farm. Claire was all prepared to say goodbye to them when Neale said he wanted to go down to Orchard Meadow and have another look at the land he was buying. Claire pointed out that as it was quite a way from the farm, that they would have to take her van.

Neale had a word with his wife. Nothing doing. She refused point-blank to forsake the clean comfortable surroundings of her car to sit in what she imagined to be Claire's filthy van. On this particular occasion, Claire had to agree with her. The van was a mess. The Neales had another whispered but heated conversation, which eventually resulted in Claire getting into the front seat of the Neales' car while his wife sat in the back between their two delightful offspring. The daughter wasn't laughing now. The son had apparently caught up with her and before Mrs Neale could intervene, had wreaked his revenge by heartily thumping her. The pair now moaned continually about how dreary and awful the place was, and what about their friends and what would they do at the weekends?

Mrs Neale, her patience worn to a frazzle by the undue demands of the day, finally snapped, and in a very commanding and surprisingly loud voice yelled: 'Shut up now!'

Silence descended. Claire smiled to herself.

Saskia stood by her car. Everything was packed up and she was ready to go. James came out and smiled at her. It had all been so easy.

'All set then?'

'Yes.'

'Good.' He rubbed his hands together. 'Right then, I'll see you in a few days' time when I've got things sorted out here. Wait for me at the house and get the passports ready. Book a couple of tickets to . . . well, I don't know, somewhere hot anyway, and I'll see you as soon as I can.'

He went round and tested her boot. It was firmly locked. He took her in his arms, kissed her.

At that moment, the Neales' car drove past the end of

the drive. Neither of them noticed it. A couple of minutes later, when it came back again and stopped there, Saskia opened her eyes and immediately saw who was watching them.

'James,' she whispered in his ear, 'we have had a good time, haven't we?'

'Yes, what makes you say that? We always have a good time.'

He had his back to the car in the lane and couldn't see anything.

'Well, can we have another good time? Right here, I mean, out in the open, an alfresco one?'

He cuddled her. 'No, Sas. It's too cold for one thing, and for another I've got to get ready for Claire.'

'Huh! I see, she gets the best of you while I get the brush-off.' She was smiling.

'Not at all, darling. You know how much I love you.'

'Well show me then. Show me how much I mean to you.'

'What? Right here?'

'Well, why not?' she asked petulantly.

Then they kissed again, deeply this time, an unmistakably passionate kiss, and while they did so, she had her hand on his crotch and he had his hand on one of her breasts.

The road down to Orchard Meadow ran past Briar Cottage. James was due back soon and Claire glanced up the drive as she always did when passing, willing him to hurry up. She wasn't expecting to see him, but she did.

He was standing by his car kissing a blonde woman. Not just pecking her on the cheek, but really kissing her, a deep unmistakable kiss.

She felt sick: someone had just pounded her in the stomach. Neale was rabbiting on about something, but she wasn't listening. He asked her a question.

'Pardon?' Her voice seemed to be coming from somewhere else. It was very, very peculiar to be so detached from everything.

'Are you all right?' It was Neale again.

'Sorry?'

'I said are you all right? You've gone very pale.'

She gazed out of the window, the greenery flashing by unseen.

'I've got to go home, Mr Neale.' Her voice was quiet, dead almost. It had no emotion because as yet, she was unaware of feeling anything. She just knew she had to get home.

'Yes, yes, of course.' He glanced back briefly at his wife, the pair of them exchanging mutual looks of incomprehension. He did a three-point turn in a gateway and headed back to the farm.

As they were coming back to Briar Cottage Claire forced herself not to look. It had been a mistake she told herself; James wasn't kissing that woman. All of it had been imagined; it was her imagination playing tricks on her.

Just as they reached the end of the drive they had to stop. Jack was coming the other way on his tractor and the only place the two vehicles could pass was the driveway.

Claire froze and hid her face behind her hand. She didn't want to see anything, but she did. No more than one hundred yards away, James and the woman were still kissing. As Claire peered through her fingers, she could see it all. The gut-wrenching certainty of his infidelity. The stabbing in her stomach became intense.

Everyone else saw it too and just to rub salt into an already raw wound, the teenagers began to make wet sucking noises to accompany the erotic scene that was being played out in front of them.

'Don't be so disgusting, you two!' snapped their mother. The teenagers giggled. 'Oh for heaven's sake, Philip, can't you drive on! Those two up there,' she announced, ruffled and indignant, 'it's obscene.'

Jack passed and Mr Neale pulled away leaving the lovers behind him.

* * *

416

'Time to go I think,' said Saskia.

'But I thought – ' he began.

'No, I don't think so, James. You're right. It is too cold.'

She got into the car, did a three-point turn and stopped next to him. She rolled down the window.

'It was great to see you. Absolutely fantastic, and I'll never forget it.'

He knelt down and smiled at her. 'What do you mean, Sas? I'll be seeing you in a few days.'

'I am the best, aren't I, Jamie?' and she checked her makeup in the rear-view mirror.

'Oh yes. No one does it like you do.'

'Good,' she said, looking back at him and revving up the powerful engine, 'because you won't be seeing me again,' and before he could respond, she had roared off down the drive, sending bits of gravel flying into the air. He stood up slowly and stared after her. What did she mean?

She skidded to a halt and poked her head out of the window. 'Oh by the way,' she shouted, 'here's your strongbox key. I've sold the coke. My dealer gave me a good price. He said it was excellent quality. Bye!' and she raced off, waving out of the window.

It was some time before the full import of her words hit him. He stood there, impotently watching the last faint whiffs of her car's blue exhaust fumes vanish in the breeze, completely unable to comprehend anything.

The best? A good price?

He walked over and picked up his small key. The intense fury that was beginning to bubble up inside him made him grip the key so hard that it dug painfully into his palm. He stood upright and looked heavenwards. 'You bitch!' he shouted. 'You fucking bloody bitch! I'll kill you for this! I'll kill you!'

But no one answered him.

Claire felt numbed. Somewhere in the recesses of her mind she was aware of a deep roaring sound as the walls around her suspicions, which she had so carefully built up to keep them at bay, began to crumble. She didn't feel like crying: not yet, and she didn't feel angry. She just felt very, very cold.

By the time they got back to the farm she was collected enough to pass pleasantries with Neale and to assure him that she was fine, really she was. It was probably just some bug she had picked up. That made Mrs Neale's day. On top of everything else, they had probably exposed themselves to some horrid virus. Neale shrugged his shoulders and got into the car next to his furious wife.

'I'll be in touch Mrs Bromage, but . . .'

He didn't have to say anything else, his wife's face said it all. The thing was, it didn't matter any more. Claire wouldn't be selling her farm; to him or anyone else.

After they had gone she went into the house where she was violently sick. Afterwards, feeling utterly wretched, she made herself some tea and sat down at the kitchen table. She had to think.

TWENTY-FOUR

'It's all right, Tao, I'll get it.'

'Yes, madam.'

Elyssa pulled back her front door. 'Claudia! What a surprise,' she drawled. 'I would have thought after your party that you and I had no more to say to each other.'

The other woman smiled as she turned around, the breeze catching her long blonde hair trailing out over the collar of the black fur coat.

'What rot, Elyssa. Of course I wanted to see you again. My social life wouldn't be the same without you to bitch with. Can I come in?'

'Of course. Tao will take your coat.'

The maid stood by silently, dark and squat compared with Claudia's lofty fairness.

'This way. Drink?'

Claudia's laugh was like the sound of a small crystal glass shattering. 'Hardly.'

'Well, you won't mind if I do.'

'Not at all. Don't break the habit of a lifetime simply because I'm here.'

She gracefully sat down on the large Chesterfield.

'So,' said Elyssa, sitting down opposite her with a large whisky and water, 'to what do I owe this dubious pleasure?'

'Oh Elyssa, don't be so cruel. I've come here because I wanted to see you. After all,' she smiled, 'I am one of your few friends.'

Elyssa ignored her stab. 'Really? Is that what you call yourself? I always thought first-class bitch was more your thing.'

Claudia regarded her with contempt. 'I will have that drink if you don't mind.'

'Help yourself, you know where it is.'

Claudia returned holding a tumbler full of Martini. She touched the enormous diamond ring on her finger. She liked to see how other women reacted and sure enough, Elyssa always did. Even if it was only the tiniest of envious glances, Claudia still noticed it.

'I tried to catch your attention the other day in town but it appears that you were otherwise engaged.'

'I was?'

'Yes, you were talking to some fearfully spotty character in a uniform.' She paused. 'I say, he's not your chauffeur, is he?'

'Yes.' Elyssa kept her face straight. She was not going to allow Claudia the satisfaction of seeing her angry.

'Well,' said Claudia, 'as they say, nice body, shame about the face.'

'He does his job,' answered Elyssa coldly.

'Oh I'm sure he does, my dear, in and out of bed if I know you. But how can you stand those spots? They're perfectly frightful.'

'He's only my chauffeur, Claudia, nothing else.'

Claudia sipped her drink. 'Oh well then,' she said archly, 'I must have misunderstood the gossip.'

'Not hard to do when you have such a limited cranial capacity.'

'Mmm, Elyssa, such big words, are you sure you know what they mean?'

They regarded each other with pure venom.

'Look, Claudia, I'm busy. Say what you have to say, then leave. I have better things to do than sit here chatting with you.'

'Like what? I'm enjoying this.'

'Like going for a deep colonic irrigation.'

'Oh well, dear, whatever turns you on.'

Elyssa bit her tongue. Damn the stupid bitch!

'As I was saying,' said Claudia, crossing her elegant legs, 'I saw you the other day coming out of a travel agent's. Are you thinking of going abroad?'

'And what if I am?'

'Now now, there's no need to snap. I simply enquire because Rupert and I are off to Singapore next week. He's taking me on a trip to the Pacific as a special wedding anniversary present.' And she gave Elyssa a perfect closed smile with her full, red-painted lips. It was the one thing that Elyssa envied about her. The only way she could have lips like that was with injections of collagen every six weeks. 'So where are you going and is it with anyone special?'

'As a matter of fact it is,' said Elyssa with a rising sense of triumph. 'You know that chap I brought to your house party?'

'The blond? What was his name again, I don't remember catching it.'

'You were drunk and his name is Alistair Kingston.'

'Ah yes, I remember now. Very nice-looking, as I seem to recall.'

'Well, we're going to fly to New York, do some shopping, I expect, and then fly down to Montserrat.'

Claudia raised a perfectly arched eyebrow. 'My dear, how interesting! And does this mean that you and this chap are . . .?' She waggled her manicured hand from side to side.

Elyssa smiled, a genuine one. It didn't matter that Alistair had refused her offer. Claudia wasn't to know that. Anyway, there was plenty of time for her to change his mind. She wouldn't give up that easily. No man, and certainly not Alistair, could resist her for long. She would get her way yet.

'Yes, I'd say so. I think very possibly that sometime in the not too distant future, that Alistair and I will be getting married.'

'Really? And are you sure about this? After all, six years

421

by yourself has given you the perfect opportunity to sample a wide variety of men. Are you really prepared to give up such freedom?'

Elyssa took a sip of her drink. There was far too much water in it and not nearly enough whisky. It tasted ghastly, but she persisted. She needed all its help at the moment, however transitory.

'You know as well as I do, Claudia, that marriage is simply a state of being that is most conveniently recognized by the Church and State and if I am to have children . . .' Claudia laughed but Elyssa carried on '. . . if I am to have children, then I need to give them a recognized name and background. Alistair happens to fit the bill perfectly.'

'Yes, he comes from one of those good old-fashioned families, doesn't he? The ones where wealth has been passed down from generation to generation? It will be quite a triumph for you if you do marry him, won't it?'

'Why?'

'Because,' said Claudia with a satisfied smirk, 'you're so ordinary.'

Elyssa flinched. She stood up and smoothed down her clothes. 'I think you have said enough, Claudia, and that it's time for you to go.'

Claudia only smiled. 'Sit down, Elyssa. I haven't finished yet.'

'I will not and if you don't move that skinny behind of yours off my sofa, I'll get Kevin to throw you out,' and she glared at the other woman.

'I think not, Elyssa. I have important news for you and I really think you ought to hear me out.'

She stood up and the two women faced each other. They were roughly the same height and build, and each carried her confidence like a well-made garment.

'Do sit down, Elyssa, you're far too sensitive about your background. Anyone would think you had something to hide.'

Elyssa smiled tightly.

'Another drink perhaps?' offered Claudia holding up her empty glass.

Drinks replenished, they sat and faced each other again.

'So,' said Elyssa 'what is it you have to tell me?'

'I'm pregnant.'

Elyssa took a large mouthful of her drink and tried not to choke. She deliberately wiped the corners of her mouth. 'Don't you think,' she chuckled, 'that perhaps you and Rupert are a bit . . . past it for playing mummies and daddies? I mean, by the time this new addition to the tribe is ten years old, Rupert will be well into his dotage and you'll be . . . what?

'Well . . . on your third facelift at least.'

Claudia frostily ignored her. 'By my calculations I'm easily three years younger than you, if not more.' She shrugged her vast padded shoulders. 'As I see it,' she continued in the face of Elyssa's sullenness, 'I'm forty-two and fertile and you're forty-five, forty-six, and barren, so there's really no more to be said is there?'

'Forty-three, if you don't mind.'

'Really? Is that what you say nowadays? Well, whatever, I just thought you'd like to hear my good news.'

Elyssa glanced at her grinning face. 'I'm not sure that I am actually. I thought all your child-bearing days were well and truly over. I mean you have the two girls by that fool Henry. Don't you think this rabbit-like behaviour is a bit undignified?'

'Not at all. I have an extremely good consultant gynaecologist who will be taking care of me throughout my pregnancy and I've been constantly reassured that I'm in perfect health and that there are no problems.'

'Oh well,' said Elyssa, raising her glass in slow salute, 'the very best of luck.'

'Thank you, my dear, that's very generous of you. Rupert, of course, is delighted. Contrary to what you said

423

at the couturier's — and that was very unpleasant of you, you know — he is in full functioning order. I now have the visible proof of it.'

Elyssa leant forward and opened a silver box. 'Cigarette?'

'Elyssa! How could you? You should know by now how dangerous cigarettes are for the unborn. Of course I won't have one. They make me feel sick.'

'Oh dear, how awful,' she said and lit up, inhaling deeply and blowing the smoke in Claudia's face.

'So, when is this new member of your family due?'

Claudia fanned the smoke away, wrinkling her nose in disgust. 'November, so that will give me plenty of time to sort out the basement and get a new nanny installed. The colour scheme down there is absolutely foul and one feels quite sorry for the nanny and baby if they had to put up with it. Previous owners, you know,' she confided. 'No taste whatsoever,' and she looked around the room before giving Elyssa a pitying smile.

Elyssa stood up and walked over to the drinks cabinet. 'I take it you don't want another one?'

'No, dear, thank you. I must take care of the offspring, you know. Rupert's hoping for a son this time, after his three daughters by his previous wife. Someone to take over the family business. I want one too. I couldn't bear it if I had another daughter. My two are already helping themselves to my makeup and trying on my clothes. They're far too pretty for their own good. Perhaps I should get tested at that new gender clinic. Get rid of it if it's the wrong sex and then have another go.'

Elyssa sat down and lit another cigarette. Her third whisky should begin to have the desired effect on her soon. It would deaden her brain, uplift her spirits and keep out the pain, and that was what she wanted. Claudia's continuous crowing over her fertility was sharply irritating. She mustn't get too drunk, though. She didn't want Claudia to go away with the wrong impression.

424

'So, will you be having a white wedding?' asked Claudia.

'Sorry? Oh yes. Alistair. Well, what do you think?'

'Mmm,' mused Claudia. 'It would be a trifle far-fetched, wouldn't it, and one can't expect all our friends to suspend their belief for the day. That really would be asking too much.'

She looked at Elyssa with her head tilted questioningly on one side, so that her heavy blonde hair hung down straight to her bustline. Elyssa had to admit it; pregnancy had given Claudia more vibrant colouring. Everything about her had brightened and made her look years younger.

On the other hand, it could be just because she was having such a good time at Elyssa's expense. She always was such a cat.

'I hear that before your wedding you flew to Tokyo to have one of their hymen repair operations. Was it a success?'

Claudia's smile was tight-lipped. 'You must be thinking about someone else, my dear. I needed no such thing.'

'In that case, I must have misunderstood the gossip.'

Touché, she thought.

Claudia stood up. 'I must go now,' she said. 'I think I've taken up more than enough of your time.'

'Oh Claudia, surely not? I'm enjoying this.'

'Yes, I can see.' She paused. 'Tell me, Elyssa, do you believe in reincarnation?'

Elyssa shrugged. What was Claudia getting at now? 'Hardly. I don't really think about things like that.'

'No, I don't suppose you do. You never were the intellectual.'

Elyssa sighed. 'So what of it?'

'Well, what do you suppose you were in your previous existence?'

Elyssa chuckled disbelievingly. 'Heavens, I don't know. I could have been anything.'

'I was at a friend's house the other day and she showed

me a picture of this dreadful thing called a hagfish. Apparently this creature, which looks a bit like an eel, swims around the ocean until it happens upon a likely looking victim whereupon it bites into the unfortunate fish and hangs on for grim death, sucking the life out of the poor creature.' She smiled briefly at Elyssa. 'Reminds me of you somewhat, the way you line up these wealthy men and then bleed them dry.' Her smile faded. 'I don't think,' she added slowly 'that you'll be half so successful with the next one. It won't take that new man of yours any time at all to work out what you're up to. There'll be plenty of people to tell him of your . . . colourful past.'

Elyssa eyed Claudia coldly. 'And you,' she said icily, 'remind me of a female praying mantis. Do you know that they eat their mates while having intercourse with them?'

Claudia was puzzled. 'And what has that got to do with Rupert?'

'Nothing, but it has everything to do with you.' She stepped closer to Claudia and saw her momentarily waver, her eyes quickly scanning Elyssa's face. 'If I am what you say I am, Claudia, it's because like recognizes like. Don't forget,' she added, poking a long nail into Claudia's shoulder, 'that we've both come up the hard way. Neither of us was born to this.'

Claudia's smile spread slowly over her face. 'Except,' she said, turning towards the door, 'that you're going to come unstuck and I'm not.'

Elyssa followed her into the hallway. 'What makes you say that?' She was angry now and the drink wasn't working. Claudia took her coat from the maid and turned to face Elyssa.

'Tell me, you do bank with Michelberg & Sons, don't you?'

'Yes.'

'I thought so. Well, keep an eye on the news tonight. You might have a bit of a shock.'

'Why? What's going on?'

Claudia pulled her coat tightly round her middle. She seemed very pleased with herself. 'Rupert says that he's heard a strong rumour concerning widespread fraud and curruption at the bank. Apparently it involves one of your ex-boyfriends. A chap called Skerrett.'

Elyssa blanched. 'Skerrett? James Skerrett?'

'Ah, so you do remember that sordid little episode? Wasn't he one of those young studs that you paid for?' Elyssa didn't answer so Claudia went on, revelling in the effect her words were having. 'Yes, Rupert says that the Serious Fraud Office and the Bank of England are having talks at the moment to see what can be done. It seems that this Skerrett chap and a couple of other managers have been cooking the books, or should it be computers now-adays? Anyway, the bank's in serious trouble and is out to get him. It seems that several members of the staff have already fled the country. Still,' and she smiled encourag-ingly, 'a little matter like this shouldn't affect you too much, should it? An ex-boyfriend in jail for fraud will give the gossip columnists a whale of a time but you'll have your wonderful Alistair to take care of you, won't you? I'm sure he'll be delighted to fend off the press as they dig up all the dirt.'

Elyssa had gone numb.

'Goodbye, Claudia. Tao will show you out.'

'Oh by the way, Elyssa, Rupert says that if the bank collapses, compensation will probably be paid out — eventually — so that's something to look forward to isn't it?' and she left in a swirl of coat like a triumphant Roman general.

First things first: a drink; a very big strong drink and once she had drunk that, she would have another one and then perhaps another. In fact, she would have the whole bloody bottle. She didn't care. It couldn't be true what Claudia had said; it couldn't be.

She tried to ring the bank but she couldn't get through.

Even going through the operator was a waste of time. It was hopeless. No one she spoke to, from her accountant to her broker, could give her a definite answer. Everyone had heard the rumour but no one knew for sure. The only thing they could tell her was to calm down and wait and see. There was nothing else she could do. The bank was closed for business by this time. If it was true then there might be a way of rescuing her funds; if it wasn't, then it didn't matter. So Elyssa went to bed, taking a bottle with her. There was no way she was going to sleep without a little drink.

'Kevin! Kevin!'

He could hear her yelling but he took no notice. He glanced down at his suitcases. Everything was packed and the only thing left to do was to tell the old bitch what she could do with her job. He smiled to himself. It should be an interesting morning.

He picked up his cases and took them out into the corridor. Tao was standing in her doorway and watching him with a brown-eyed blank expression. She was nothing like Aditha. She was ugly. He smiled at her and she nodded cheerfully, showing her crooked white teeth.

'Kevin! Will you come up here now! I want to speak to you!'

He shrugged at Tao and she tutted. She had only been here a short time, but she already knew the malicious vagaries of their mistress.

'You go, Kevin. She doesn't like waiting.'

'Yeah I know, silly old cow. Still, I'll be gone later. Wish you all the best, Tao. You'll need it.'

'I fine. She no bother,' and she burst into a peal of girlish giggles holding her hands in front of her plump face. 'She drunk. She always drunk.'

Kevin smiled too. Despite her looks, she was a good-hearted soul.

'Oh well, I'd better go now. Bye.'

When he got to the top of the stairs, Elyssa, red-eyed and angry, was waiting for him.

'Where the bloody hell have you been? Didn't you hear me calling! Christ, I've been yelling for ages!'

She glared at him while she poured herself a large glass of fresh orange juice, slamming the fridge shut so that the milk bottles rattled in the door.

'I was busy,' he said.

'Oh yeah? Doing what? Or maybe,' she said, fixing him with a salacious leer, 'I shouldn't ask. I can't imagine you're so desperate you want to poke Tao.' She turned away with a chuckle and put her empty glass in the sink. 'Well, come along, we have to go. I want you to drive me over to my bank.'

Kevin stood still. 'No.'

Elyssa stopped. 'Pardon?' She looked at him with open-mouthed amazement and then started to smile. 'Did I hear what I think I heard?'

'Yes,' he mumbled. 'I'm not taking you. In fact I won't be taking you anywhere ever again.'

She walked towards him. She wasn't smiling now. 'You ungrateful, ill-mannered, ill-bred little shit!' she hissed. 'Don't you tell me when or where you're going to drive me. I want you to take me out now and I mean now! So get your uniform on and move it!'

He looked at her. 'No,' he repeated quietly. 'I'm going. I've had enough of you and all this. I'm bloody well leaving.'

She sat down and rubbed her temples. She had a terrible headache coming on.

'And just where are you going to, Kevin? Eh? Back to the dole office in King's Lynn or whatever the name of the godforsaken hole is you came from?' She glared at him. He avoided her gaze. 'And what do you think you're going to do? Well, I'll tell you,' she went on, 'nothing. You're going to do nothing because you haven't got the brains or the balls to do anything!' She was breathing heavily now and could really do with a drink. She got up and went to a cupboard. Just as she thought, there was an unopened bottle of whisky. She undid the cap and thankfully poured herself a large one.

'You, Kevin,' she said, after she had a deep drink, 'are a thick little bumpkin. Before you came to me you hadn't done anything except sign on every fortnight. I, Kevin, I,' she shouted, 'have given you a home, a job, a reasonable wage and generous time off and this is how you repay me?'

He went to say something.

'And don't interrupt me, you stupid bastard, I haven't finished yet.'

She had another drink. The anger was subsiding now.

'Look, Kevin, I know we haven't always seen eye to eye about things and that maybe I was a little bit hasty about getting rid of Aditha,' and she noticed his quick pained expression, 'but it was for your own good.' She sighed. 'You don't want to be tied down with one of these foreigners, Kevin. The only thing they're after is a white man's name and passport so they can become British citizens, so if you've got any ideas about marrying her, forget it.'

He reached into his pocket. 'I have something of yours here,' he said, holding up a document.

Elyssa craned forward. She couldn't quite make out what it was. She frowned. 'So what is it?'

'A copy of a Change of Name Deed. It says here,' he read out, ' "I the undersigned Sharon Lesley White of 48 Butts Park, Romford in the County of Essex do hereby absolutely renounce and abandon the use of my former names – " '

'Stop!' she cried.

'Sharon Lesley White, eh?' he laughed. 'I couldn't believe this when I first read it.'

Elyssa had turned her face away. 'Where did you get that?'

430

'And I had even more fun tracking down the rest of your family.'

'My bureau. You bastard! You've been prying in my bureau!'

'Yeah, that's right. Not only that, but your sister told me all about you. Nice woman, isn't she? Nothing like you.'

He walked over to her and took the whisky bottle. When he had poured himself a drink he sat down at the opposite end of the table.

'I took her out one lunchtime, a pub near where she lives and after a few drinks, she was very obliging.' He sipped his drink. Elyssa said nothing.

'She told me,' he continued, 'how you were always the really good-looking one in the family and how you were determined to get on in the world. You didn't do too well at school, but still managed to get into college where you trained as a hairdresser. At the weekends you would come up to town and it was then that you were spotted by a modelling agency. After that you more or less dumped everyone; friends, family, even the boy you were engaged to. You never had time for anyone once you made it and especially when wealthy men started taking you out. Of course, being called Sharon didn't fit your image so you dumped that as well. Only trouble is,' he said, waving the paper around, 'you didn't hide it too well, did you, and when Aditha found it, she told me.'

Elyssa looked up at him. 'So you're in this together, are you? God,' she laughed, 'I might have known. You would never have the intelligence to do anything like this by yourself.'

'I don't give a damn what you think any more, lady. The thing is, though, do I tell that Claudia woman about this or will you pay me to keep quiet?'

'I see, going to blackmail me, are you?'

'Well, why not?'

'Because, you moron,' she snarled, 'you'll never get

away with it. Do you honestly think I'll pay up to a couple of idiots like you?'

'Yeah, because that Claudia doesn't know anything about this. Nobody does. I've checked. I've spoken with her, carefully like, so she didn't know what I was on about and I can tell you this, she was very interested.'

'You wouldn't dare.'

'Oh yeah, want a bet, lady?' He was cocky now, confident even. He had her right where he wanted her.

Elyssa went quiet. She was weighing things up. She got off the stool and came round to him. He quickly folded up the document and put it in his back pocket. He sat down again. She wasn't going to get it off him. She stood next to him and then moved closer. He watched her warily. He didn't trust her as far as he could spit.

'Kevin,' her voice was low and soft. There was none of her previous bravado. 'Kevin, do we have to fight like this?' She ran a long painted nail across the back of his hand and then up along his sleeve. She was smiling coquettishly at him, her bloodshot eyes twinkling. 'I mean, there were times when you and I got on really well. There were times,' she murmured, brushing a breast carelessly against his arm, 'when we would get together and have a really good time.' She kissed his ear. 'We could do that again, Kevin. We could go to bed right now and have the best fuck you've ever had.' She looked at him closely, smiling. 'Come on, Kevin, let's be friends. Let's go to bed and forget all about this little incident and then maybe afterwards I'll review your salary: get you some more clothes, give you the bigger room downstairs.' She kissed his lips. Her breath stank of booze. Kevin pulled back.

'Listen to me, Kevin.' She was getting desperate. 'I'm going abroad soon with a friend of mine. We're flying to New York and then down to Montserrat. You could come too if you like. We'll need a driver. I'll pay for it, all of it. I'll get you a really good room in the best hotel.' She smiled again. 'Please, Kevin, think about it. You can have whatever you want, only please give me back my document.'

They looked at each other in silence; she hopeful and he . . . he held her arms which were now around his neck.

'Your breath stinks,' he told her as he removed her arms and pushed her back. 'In fact your whole body does.' He laughed with contempt, a hoarse callous laugh. 'You make me sick, lady, you always have. Do you honestly think I want to go to bed with a bag of old bones like you? Christ!' he roared, thumping his clenched fist down on the table, 'I hated it, all of it, the way you touched yourself, the way you made me do all those things. You're perverted. You're an old whore and I hate you!'

She staggered back, flinching under each verbal onslaught. She couldn't believe him. What was he saying? It wasn't true. None of it was. He was only saying it because he was poor and she wasn't.

'Shut up!' she screamed. 'Shut up! I don't want to hear any more. Shut up!' With hands over her ears, she spat out the words, hot angry tears racing down her cheeks. 'You fucking peasant! Don't you tell me what I am! I know what I am. I'm someone who crawled out of the gutter and made it to the top, whereas all you'll ever be is a heap of shit!' and she threw the whisky bottle at him. He ducked without any trouble.

A few minutes passed when the only noise was her sobbing.

'I want ten thousand pounds,' he said firmly. 'I know you've got it. You keep it in the safe behind that painting over the fireplace.'

She wiped her face and sipped her drink. 'Seven thousand,' she replied. This was business and she was quite capable of dealing with it. She would pay him off, get back her document, then throw him out. She was sure the police would like to hear about it.

'Nine thousand.'

'Seven.'

433

He paused. 'Eight,' he said, 'my final offer.'

'Seven thousand, five hundred. My final offer. Take it or leave it.'

He nodded his head. 'Done!'

In the lounge she made him turn away while she undid the safe. Into his grubby paws she handed the crisp clean notes, which he then stuffed into his various jeans and jacket pockets.

She held out her hand. 'My document, I think.'

He shook his head. 'No way, lady. You don't think I'm that stupid, do you? You'd be ringing the police as soon as I'm out of here. Forget it. I'll keep it. It will be nice and safe with me and Aditha, and it will make damned sure you keep off our backs!' He smiled and then stood up straight. 'Goodbye, Sharon. It's been an experience knowing you and a very profitable one.' And he smiled as he waved a wodge of notes at her.

She watched him leave from her bedroom window. When his jaunty figure had left the clean-swept square, she sat at her dressing-table and looked at her reflection.

She leant forward and ran her fingers over the mirror's tired drawn face. He was right, she looked every bit as old as he had said.

'Never mind,' she told her reflection. 'A holiday will do us the world of good. There's still Alistair and no matter what that bastard said downstairs, we know we will survive, don't we?' The reflection stayed mute. 'But we'll have another drink first, won't we?'

TWENTY-FIVE

Claire was out when James came round that afternoon. She had no intention of seeing him yet and took off across the moor with Rosie for a long walk. First she had to think and then she would confront him.

Numbed with disbelief, embarrassment and humiliation, as well as any number of other emotions that swept over her in alternate waves of hot and cold sweat, she found herself aimlessly wandering. When she was too washed out to cry any more and tiredness had overtaken her, she sat down on a warm rocky outcrop and rested her head on her knees. Rosie sat next to her, panting, her long pink tongue hanging out of her mouth. She had been unusually subdued, unwilling to run off and explore the exciting smells. If Claire hadn't been so wrapped up in her own misery, she might have noticed how Rosie, sensing her mistress's unhappiness, was trying to offer comfort and support.

Claire looked up and surveyed her surroundings. About a hundred yards away were the ancient tumble-down remains of a Neolithic village, the stones poking up through the heather and gorse. On previous occasions when she had come here, she had been with other people but still aware of its eerie emptiness. A long-forgotten aura of death and sadness still clung to it after all these centuries. In the gloom and murk of a midwinter's afternoon, she could well imagine shadowy figures flitting about, vague and intangible, slight of form but almost real.

Old people who knew this part of the moor would gather together their eager audience around a pub fire and frighten them all with tales of unexplained events. Claire, like the rest of the listeners, enjoyed being tantalized and unnerved in the security of the fire's warmth and would laugh it off with modern secular logic that they all professed to. However, she never came here alone. Until now that is.

The sun was shining warm against her face. High above her she could hear the loud piercing song of a lark as it hovered in the breeze. All around her was the steady drone of insects exploring the flowers. It gave her peace; an emotional balm to the turmoil which threatened to rend her apart. Over and over again, she kept asking herself how she had been such a fool. Why she had believed in him when her friends had so quickly seen him for what he was. Goodness, even Rosie disliked him. How could she have been such an idiot? And then she closed her eyes with embarrassment, so ashamed that she couldn't even look at herself as she remembered the days and nights, especially the nights, when they had lain together in her bed and he had stroked and caressed her, telling her he loved her and showing her the paths of sexual fulfilment that ran along her body.

She shuddered and forced open her eyes, her nerves so raw with pain that she could no longer think about it. He had cut her to the quick: pulled apart the layers of protection she had so carefully cultivated and buried his poison. Now, like the cancer it was, it was reaching out to all parts of her mind and body and slowly destroying her.

She put her hands over her eyes and let the anguish and betrayal spill forth.

On the other side of the hill, down in a valley, a teacher was taking his class of ten-year-olds along a stream, looking for small creatures that could be gathered up in nets, collected in jam jars and examined back at school.

When he first heard the screaming, or rather what he thought was screaming, he stood up and listened, the hairs on his neck and arms bristling.

'What is it, sir?' asked a small freckled boy, his trousers wet, despite his wellingtons. The teacher listened again. He felt sure he had heard something, but the wind was blowing in all directions and whoever or whatever made the sound, it was hard to pinpoint it.

'I don't know, Simon.' He smiled to reassure the boy whose face was puckered with worry. 'Perhaps it was just an animal.'

He and the young boy then went back to their work, now oblivious to the pathetic wrenching cries.

Claire stopped. Enough was enough she told herself sternly, wiping her face and sniffing. 'Okay, I've been stupid and everyone was right and I was wrong.' She faltered.

However hard she tried, she couldn't stem the tide of tears. 'For Pete's sake!' she yelled out loud. 'Stop it! Stop it!' She hit herself with her clenched fists, pounding her legs, stomach and arms until it all subsided.

She looked up. Rosie was watching her, her head on one side, frightened and bewildered at Claire's strange behaviour. She stood, tail down and quite motionless until all quietened.

Realizing her dog's incomprehension, Claire held out her arms. 'Oh Rosie, come here, sweetie, come here.'

The dog rushed over, joyful again and relieved. The two of them rolled back into the heather, smiling and whining, the dog licking Claire's face.

'All right, all right, that's enough, silly. Now stop it.'

Rosie stood back and then bounded off. She wanted to play games. Claire looked round until she found a suitable piece of wood. She threw it and watched Rosie chase after it.

At least I still have you, she thought, and to think I almost got rid of you. Incredible!

She looked at her watch. It was four o'clock. It would take her at least an hour to get home, another to do her

437

chores and by then she might feel ready to face James. She didn't yet know what she was going to say to him, but she knew she would have to be careful. If everything Alistair had said about him was true, and she now had no reason to disbelieve him, then James was going to be a pretty formidable enemy. His all-round deceit and the way he had so blatantly used her for his own ends made her fear for his reaction when she told him it was all off. She didn't want to face him, but something told her that she had to finish things properly. She didn't like loose ends and more to the point, she wanted to see how he felt when he realized he wasn't getting any more of her money.

She got up, brushed herself down and set off back to the farm. Tired, emotionally drained and resigned to her fate she felt happier now and more at peace with herself than she had done for ages. Her sickness, her obsession was receding.

'Come on, Rosie, it's time to go home,' and the dog ran after her.

James rang Claire about an hour after Saskia left. It had taken him that long to recover from her revelations and he could still hear her triumphant laughter as she screeched off down the drive.

He couldn't eat or relax, although he did drink and smoke. He did lots of both, pacing the small sitting room while he tried to work out what he was going to do.

At first he just panicked. When McArdle and his associates found out what had happened to the drugs, his life would be in danger. He knew from his long association with the club and the stories and rumours that he had heard, that McArdle was a very formidable enemy. God, he had seen it with his own eyes the day he had gone there with the money. When McArdle found out about Saskia's little sting he would be down on James like the proverbial ton of bricks – or rather one, perhaps two, of his henchmen would. James knew he had to do something and do it quick.

He poured himself another drink and lit a cigarette.

Claire; she was the answer. She was the only hope he had. If he could persuade her to give him enough money, then he might, if he were lucky, get McArdle off his back.

He paced up and down. How to get the money? That was easy; he had already laid the foundations of his plan over the telephone. Now was the time to pull her in, accept the money and run. He smiled to himself. She was such a poor dumb cow. It was like taking sweets from a baby. A good meal, a couple of bottles of wine, take her to bed – that part he least looked forward to. Other men might appreciate her slimness, but he liked his women big. However, he was a professional. He had been called on to perform in far more onerous situations than this one and he saw no reason why he couldn't do it this time. Then, with a little bit of luck, she would hand over a nice fat cheque to help towards his 'business' and he would disappear. It should all be tied up by tomorrow.

Then there was the bank. Guy must be on to him. They must have discovered his fraudulent withdrawals. If he went back to London he would probably be arrested.

He gulped his drink. God! What a bloody mess!

Come on, he told himself sternly, think clearly, think! Get the money, pay off McArdle and disappear. There, it wasn't that difficult when he thought it through.

He finished his drink and stubbed out his cigarette, allowing himself the luxury of a warm satisfied feeling that spread through him. He loved it when a plan came to fruition.

A wash; he had to have a wash and get rid of the smell of Saskia. It was things like that which made all the difference to a successful seduction.

Once ready, he raced down to Torhampton and bought the food for the evening meal. With the two bottles of wine standing in a cardboard box on the floor of the car, gently clinking as he drove to Tor Heights, he felt much better. He was so cheerful that he actually found himself whistling. Stuff Saskia and her butch friend. He would get by without them and after this, who knows? With his looks anything was possible.

He drove into the farmyard. It was silent. Claire's van was there, as was her tractor, so she had to be somewhere around. He got out and, taking the box of groceries, went to the door. It was open, as always. It amazed him how trusting she was.

The thing that struck him most was the absence of Rosie. Normally by now she would be barking dementedly at him, although since that little scene in the kitchen, she always kept her distance.

He put the food on the table. He wasn't angry, just puzzled. He assumed that she was somewhere out and about with her beasts and would be back soon, so he sat down and waited. After a while he decided to make himself a coffee. He noticed that she was still buying a cheap brand and that amused him. All that money and she had no idea how to spend it.

Two cups later and she still hadn't appeared. By now his good humour had evaporated and he was getting annoyed with her. But he remained where he was. He used deep breaths to dissipate his mounting anger. He must control himself otherwise she would suspect something and he couldn't have that. There was far too much at risk.

Half an hour later and he angrily slammed down his coffee cup. Where the bloody hell was she? He decided to leave. He had had enough of this waiting. Damn her! She had ruined everything.

Claire watched him go. She had been in the barn for some time quietly waiting. The minute she had seen his car in her yard, she and Rosie had crept into the barn as stealthily as they could. She knew he would leave eventually because he was impatient and she wasn't. So she sat and waited. She had no intention of seeing him yet. Rosie instinctively knew she had to be quiet and only gave the smallest growl from the top of the haystack as they watched him come out of the house, slam the door and walk towards his car.

'Shh, Rosie, shh!'

The dog fell silent. It was difficult to growl when Claire had her hand around her mouth.

The car raced off but Claire gave it a good five minutes before she climbed down. She walked to the end of the yard and double-checked the lane before going back inside. She didn't want any nasty surprises.

She found his box of food on the table. She was starving. She emptied it.

'Well, how nice of the man. What shall we do then, Rosie, eat it or chuck it?' She sat down, undecided. 'Oh to hell with it!' and common sense prevailed.

The meal was very welcome. She hadn't realized just how hungry she was until she saw the food and then when she started to cook it, it was almost overpowering. She sniffed the aroma of garlic that came out of the Rayburn from the prepared chicken Kiev.

'Mmm, lovely. I don't suppose you'll want any of it, dog?'

Rosie wagged her tail. Food was food so far as she was concerned.

When all was ready, Claire sat down to eat. She helped herself liberally to the wine and stuffed herself on the meal. Rosie had her own dinner but still sat underneath the table waiting for titbits.

'You're a pig, Rosie.'

Her tail thumped on the floor, and the scraps vanished without trace.

After her meal she cleared away and sat thinking. She really needed to talk to someone first to assure herself that she was doing the right thing. Alistair was the one who had all the relevant facts about James, so she decided to ring him. It was 5.30 P.M. but she knew he never left his office before six o'clock. As she waited for his secretary to pick up the receiver, she briefly ran over in her mind what she should tell him. It wouldn't be much; she was too ashamed.

'Hello, Mr Kingston's office. Can I help you?'

'Oh hello,' said Claire tentatively, still undecided about her actions, 'can I speak to Mr Kingston, please? It's Claire Bromage.'

'I'm sorry, Mrs Bromage, but I'm afraid he's not here. He's been in court in Exeter all day.'

'When will he be back?'

'I'm afraid I don't know. It's rather a complicated case and he could well be spending the evening there. He did say he had some business to discuss with another solicitor. I expect he'll be back about ten or eleven. It shouldn't be too late, though, because he's got to be here first thing tomorrow morning. Is there any message I can take? If it's at all urgent, I could pop a note through his door on the way home.'

'No, no, thank you. That's fine, but thank you for offering. I'm sure I'll see him soon.'

'All right then, Mrs Bromage. I'll just leave a note on his desk to say that you rang.'

'Thanks very much. Bye.'

Claire replaced the receiver. She was disappointed, but at the same time relieved. She knew Alistair would never gloat or anything as bad mannered as that . . . but she was still pleased she didn't have to face him yet.

With everything done there seemed no reason to delay the inevitable. She put on her waxed jacket, pulled on her boots and went out to get Bonny. By riding over the moor to Briar Cottage she could avoid the unexpected. She didn't know if that blonde woman was still there and she would be able to check unseen from the hill behind the cottage.

Bonny was frisky. After her little scene with the Neale

children, she hadn't calmed down. Using a handful of pony nuts as a bribe, Claire eventually caught her. She was covered in mud and had to have a good brush before she could be saddled.

Half an hour later and hot and glowing from her exertions, Claire mounted. Bonny needed no encouragement. She wanted the exercise.

The evening was drawing in and a grey twilight was descending all around. Dark clouds were beginning to obscure the horizon, blotting out the sun so that its orange rays lit up their edges as if they were on fire. The wind was rising too and Claire could feel the first faint dusting of rain. She pulled up the collar of her jacket and buttoned it against her throat. She was prepared for anything that the elements might throw at her.

It didn't take long to reach the cottage. Bonny, unexercised for some weeks, pulled hard at her reins, tossing her head impatiently as Claire tried to control her. As the wind blew harder, the horse became more skittish.

They stood on the hill some two hundred yards from the cottage where Claire could get a good view. Only James's car was there. The blonde had left. The lights came on in the kitchen and she caught a glimpse of him as he filled up the kettle and made himself some tea. It was then that she realized she didn't feel anything for him. As she watched his tall, muscular physique, his dark hair and regular features, all she could think of was how much he had betrayed her; how he had played on her defenceless-ness and wormed his way into her heart with his seductive charm. She didn't hate him, not yet: she was just icily indifferent.

She trotted down to the road and then up the drive to the cottage. She tied Bonny to a tree and with a deep breath to settle her nervous stomach, she walked to the door. He answered almost immediately.

'Claire! My darling! How lovely to see you.'

She allowed him only the briefest of embraces. She

found the smell and touch of him repulsive.

'Hello, James,' she answered quietly, pulling herself out of his arms.

He tried to kiss her but she turned away.

'Don't.'

He wouldn't let her go. 'What's wrong, Claire? Are you all right?'

She stepped past him. 'Can I come in?'

He followed her to the sitting room and went over to the drinks. 'Want one?'

'No.' She didn't look at him. She couldn't. He poured himself a large drink and sat next to her on the sofa. He tried to put his arm around her, but she pushed him away.

'Please don't.'

Abruptly she stood up and moved to one of the other chairs. He sat watching her, quite motionless, his face inscrutable.

'What is it, Claire?'

For the first time she turned to face him. 'You tell me,' she said in a cold voice.

He held out his hands as if in supplication. 'But I don't know what you're talking about. You're acting as if I've committed some dreadful crime or something.'

'Haven't you then?'

He looked down at his glass and took a swig. 'Someone's been talking to you, haven't they?'

Saskia, he thought, the little bitch. She had done exactly what she had threatened to do. He smiled wryly to himself. If he ever had the good fortune to meet that woman again, she wouldn't know what had hit her. He would see to it personally and thoroughly enjoy himself in the process.

'No.'

It was the truth and she said it as such; cool and without emotion. 'It's not what anyone has said, although plenty has been said to me by my friends. No, it's more to do with what I saw.' She paused, waiting to see what would happen. He didn't react. 'What I saw this morning when

444

you and that blonde woman were out there kissing, and I don't mean in a friendly detached fashion. I mean really kissing.'

He looked up slowly, the realization hitting him. Her face was rigid.

'I was in the car, James, at the bottom of the driveway, waiting for Jack to pass on his tractor and I saw everything.' She crossed her arms with emphatic resolution and sat back in the chair.

He tiredly rubbed his eyes. 'It's not what you think, Claire.'

She stood up, her anger rising. 'Isn't it? Because from where I sat in the front seat, getting a grandstand view of it all, it bloody well looked like it to me!'

'Claire, Claire, don't shout,' he said. 'Now listen, darling.'

'Don't "darling" me!' she snapped. 'Because that's one thing I'm definitely not any more.'

'Okay, but just listen to me, will you?' he reasoned. 'That woman you saw was just an old friend of mine, that's all, and she was here on a brief visit. I was saying goodbye to her when you saw us.'

'Oh I see, you kiss all your "old friends" like that, do you?' She stared hard at him, her green eyes like pieces of glass, shiny and brittle. 'Just what do you think I am, James, a complete moron?'

He didn't reply, but laughed nervously, a small twitch appearing in one eye.

'Well, you listen to me, James. Up until this morning, I had swallowed just about every damned lie you'd given me.' He tried to interrupt but she wouldn't have it, carrying on over his feeble protests. 'You came down here from the big city with one specific purpose in mind and that was to fleece me; to get your grubby little hands on as much of my money as possible.'

That was it, she had finally said it, the nagging nameless purpose of his being here had crystallized in her mind the minute she had opened her mouth. He was a fortune-hunter and he had hunted her.

The atmosphere had gone very cold but she carried on. He had hurt her so much that she no longer cared what he felt. To hell with him. It was now his turn to suffer.

'And, oh how I fell for it; all that charm, all those good looks, all that lovemaking. You really took me to the cleaners, didn't you, James? You had me right where you wanted me as if I was some stupid little sixteen-year-old!'

She stopped. Her tears were forcing their way up again. She checked herself. She didn't want him to see her crying.

'I fell for it,' she said more quietly, 'because I wanted to, because I was lonely and because I loved you.' Her voice broke and she gave way to the emotion.

With a tissue covering her eyes, she didn't see him get up and come towards her, but she did feel his hands on her shoulders and the firm sensuous touch as he started to massage her.

'Claire, Claire, Claire, listen to me, darling,' he whispered, leaning down and kissing her neck. She closed her eyes. It felt so good. It would be so easy to forget all of this and fall into his arms.

'No!' She flew away from him. 'Leave me alone! Leave me alone!' she shouted. 'You're not going to get round me, you're not! Everything's off, d'you hear, everything! I want nothing more to do with you. Now let me go!'

He walked towards her, his eyes cold, and took hold of her arms, his fingers digging into her flesh.

'Claire, you're being very silly.' As smooth as silk, his voice rumbled up from deep inside him, a playful smile about his lips. She stepped back from him, trying to loosen his painful hold. He was frightening her now.

'Stand still, Claire, I'm not going to hurt you.'

'No!'

He slapped her.

The stinging shock of it and the pain that spread across

her face instantly stopped her struggling, took away her breath and left her wide-eyed with horror.

He shook her. 'Now . . . listen . . . to . . . me!'

She stood quite still. When he thought she was calm enough, he sat her down on the sofa.

'Now I know it seems as though I'm a complete bastard and that everything you've heard about me from your so-called "friends" paints me blacker than black, but it's not like that, Claire, really it isn't. Even that scene out there this morning has a perfectly reasonable explanation if only you'd listen to me.'

She wasn't hearing him. She could taste blood in her mouth. She gingerly reached up and touched her lip. No one had ever done that before.

He went on: 'I might have seemed a bit callous or scheming to you, but that's not how it is at all.' He took another sip of his drink. 'Remember, Claire, whatever your friends have said about me, it's only because they're jealous. Perfectly understandable, of course. After all, you are a very wealthy woman and, as your friends, they don't like it when an outsider appears on the scene and tries to take their potential pot of gold away. Believe me, Claire, money and friends do not go together. They only want you to stay in the vain hope you might hand out some of it to them.' He looked at her to check her reaction. She was staring at the carpet.

'When I met you and saw how beautiful you were, I couldn't help falling in love with you.'

She still kept silent.

'Oh come on, Claire,' he added irritably. 'Do you really think I could have made love to you the way I did if I didn't love you?'

She finally looked up and smiled a slow ironic smile. 'Of course you would, James. After all, that's what you're paid to do in London, isn't it? Except, of course, I'm not a rich old lady, but a young one, which must make it easier for you. Perhaps I should just settle up now for services

447

rendered. Tell me, James, how much do you charge for your cock and do I have to pay VAT?'

His mouth had almost disappeared, his lips thin and colourless.

'James, I don't believe anything you say any more. All that rubbish about my friends is just that: rubbish. They have done nothing but help me since I've met you and I would trust them with my very life. You, by comparison, are a complete shit. There is nothing about you at all that is remotely commendable and all I can say is thank God I found out in time. Of course,' she added, 'I did have some unexpected help. Whoever wrote me this letter obviously knows you far better than I do,' and she placed the anonymous missive on the arm of the chair.

He picked it up and with shaking hands read it. It was from Saskia; he knew that immediately. He looked at the postmark – Surrey. The letter contained graphic descriptions of what he was like in bed, how he earned his living and how much he was in debt. At the end it warned Claire to leave him because he was using her to get to her money.

The bitch! The absolute bloody bitch! She said she would do it, but he never believed she would.

'And just to make sure I was taking notice of everything she said – I assume it was a woman, heavens!' she laughed, 'it really would be awful if it was a man! Anyway, she used to ring me up, sometimes three or four times a day. She never said anything, but just listened. I tried to tell you about it once, but you were "too busy" as you put it. No doubt some wealthy old dowager was waiting for her afternoon snack. God, James, you really are the most contemptible human being I've ever met.'

She moved to one side of him. 'I'm going now. I've had enough of this. I don't ever want to see you again. Goodbye, James.'

She took a step forward only to be stopped by his grabbing her arm.

448

'Oh no you're not!' he hissed. 'I haven't finished with you yet.' He pushed her down on the sofa, leering malevolently. 'Do you know what I like most about being a man?'

She stared wildly back at him, her heart pounding. She had to get out of there.

'No, Claire? Don't you know? It's having the strength to take what I want whenever I feel like it.' He gave a sickly grin. 'And right now I want you. I want to teach you a lesson; a lesson in manners so that in future you will learn to do as you're told by your betters. Now, stop struggling!'

He knelt down, his face no more than six inches from hers.

'You're not going anywhere, Claire, until I've finished with you. Understand?' and still smiling, he started to undo her jacket, pulling down the zip. 'Poor little Claire, all that money and no idea how to spend it. I could have helped you, you know.'

He yanked her up and pulled off the jacket, throwing it to one side. He put his hand on her trouser zip. She angrily smacked it away.

'Leave me alone!'

'Temper, temper, temper, little lady. Don't sharpen your claws on me, Claire, because I'll get really angry.' He grabbed her plait and pulled it. 'Okay?'

'Please,' she whimpered. 'Please don't.'

'Don't what, Claire? Don't you like this? I thought the only thing you really wanted was a good fuck. Christ! You couldn't keep your hands off me before! It was like being mauled by a farm cat, all hair and appetite. Well, now I'm going to give you what you always wanted.' He laughed hollowly. 'My dear little Claire, such an innocent.'

He pulled down his zip, one arm pinning her to the sofa, his full weight leaning on her breasts.

'You're hurting me!' she yelled. 'Get off me, get off!'

He slapped her again. 'Go on, Claire, keep yelling, no one's going to hear you.'

He pushed his hand into her unzipped jeans. He was cold against her warmth.

She began to struggle again, kicking and lashing out, her arms and legs thumping against him and the sofa.

'Leave me! Leave me alone! No! No!'

He pushed deeper, forcing her apart, his nails digging into her flesh.

'Like that, Claire? It's what you always wanted, isn't it, eh? You oversexed cow!'

Her penknife had fallen out of her back pocket. As he bent down to bite one of her exposed breasts, she felt underneath for it. He was undoing his trousers. With utter panic she saw what he was going to do to her. She took the knife and flicked it open.

Her legs were rigid, her fear was blinding and she could hardly breathe as he pressed down on top of her.

'You bastard!' she screamed. 'You bastard!' The tears were racing down her face.

He ignored her, pulling down his trousers, his livid eyes fixed on her.

As he leant over, about to climb on top of her, she lashed out one last time. The knife was blunt. She only used it for cutting baler twine, but it was still sharp enough to cut flesh.

'Ahhhhhh!'

He threw himself onto the floor, clutching the small of his back where she had stabbed him. Claire froze in horror. Seeing him curled up on the floor in agony paralysed her. What had she done?

Writhing on the floor, blood spilling out across the carpet, he screamed. 'You . . . bitch! You fucking bitch!'

She got up, slowly at first, but then with more urgency. She had to get out of there.

As she ran out of the door his cries still filling her ears, she hurriedly pulled up her trousers, stumbling and falling over her feet. Out in the drive, she climbed onto Bonny and fled, galloping down the driveway out into the lane and then off across the darkening moor. The wind howled, and his screams faded.

She didn't stop galloping until she was a good distance from the cottage and its lights had vanished into the gloom. He wouldn't follow her now. He couldn't do anything after what she had done. She hadn't meant to stick the knife in him like that, and she felt nauseated when she remembered the way it had sliced into him with such ease. She closed her eyes and shuddered. She must have really hurt him. And the way he screamed . . . it was awful.

She trotted on, the wind buffeting her. She felt wretched; cold and shivery. She was in pain as well. She knew that pain. It was a familiar aching cramp that came every month. It wasn't too bad at the moment, but it would get worse. When she got home she would take some aspirin. That would make it better.

She pulled Bonny to a stop. Just for a minute she had to get off and rest.

'Whoa, girl. Good girl. Stand still.' The horse stopped and carefully taking her feet out of the stirrups, she slid down onto the wet ground in a heap.

'Oh God,' she cried. 'What have I done?' She started to cry, great heaving, racking sobs of self-pity mixed with fear and relief. James had tried to rape her. There were no two ways about it. He had pinned her down and tried to rape her.

She felt giddy, the nausea rising again. She gagged, but nothing came. Despite the cold, wet and blustery rain, she was hot. She turned her sweaty face to the wind, closed her eyes and breathed deeply. After a while she felt better. When she got home, she would have a bath and wash the stinking traces of that man off her. How dare he do that to her! Who did he think he was?

'You bastard, James!' she howled into the wind. 'You bloody, bloody bastard!' And then with her head bowed and the tears falling onto her already wet trousers, she cried again. He had found a way to her heart that no other man knew about. Somewhere deep in the pit of her soul, he had moved her in a way that she had come to think was entirely impossible. And now he had betrayed her.

It was only when the wind blew too cold and she was completely sodden that she got unsteadily to her feet, gathered up Bonny's reins and with difficulty, remounted.

It was time to go home, to her dog and to safety.

TWENTY-SIX

Elyssa tried repeatedly to ring the bank, but she couldn't get through. She tried her accountant and was told he was busy, so then she tried her lawyer and was told he was at court today.

'Oh fuck it!' she yelled at the innocent receptionist. 'Isn't anyone in?'

'Well if madam would care to leave a message,' said the haughty voice, 'I'm sure Mr Benson will get back to you as soon as he can.'

'Look, you stupid cow, I want to speak to him now! Where is he?'

'I'm sorry, madam, I can't possibly divulge the telephone number. It's a very important case he's working on.'

'Stuff you, you silly bitch! Don't you patronize me!'

'Really, madam,' said the offended voice, 'might I suggest you ring later when perhaps you have calmed down?'

Elyssa slammed down her phone. She would ring Alistair; he would know what to do. She did, only to be told he was also out at court. Realizing, somewhat belatedly, that she had already offended too many people that day, she held her tongue.

'And when will he be back?'

Julie's rounded Devonian burr sounded very rural in comparison with the last receptionist she had spoken to.

'Oh later, about ten, I suppose. I don't really know. Can I take a message?'

Elyssa left her name and number and asked him to ring her back as soon as possible. She then went and poured herself a very large drink. She opened the silver box on the coffee table but the cigarettes had all gone.

'Oh shit!'

Her handbag – she would have some more in there. But there weren't any. She threw the bag down and called for her maid.

'Tao! Tao!'

No answer; she remembered then she had given her the afternoon off. That meant she had to go out and get her own cigarettes. How irritating.

She put on her coat and took her car keys and purse. There was a newsagent's around the corner. She hurried off.

There was no space to park outside the shop but that didn't stop her. She double parked, leaving her warning lights flashing, and ran into the shop, her fur coat flapping about her knees.

'Twenty of those.'

Her eye caught the headline on the *Evening Standard*. She picked up a copy.

'Oh my God!'

'Pardon, missus?'

'Nothing.' She handed him a twenty-pound note.

'Don't you have anything smaller?' he asked plaintively.

'No, I don't,' she snapped, not looking up. She read on, oblivious to him. The top story was about the bank and its unexpected and spectacular collapse. The front picture showed large numbers of concerned investors standing outside the main branch demanding information. The news item concluded that they stood to lose all their savings.

'Your change, missus.'

She didn't hear him.

'Miss, your change.'

She took it without comment and walked out slowly as if dazed. A traffic warden had just written out a ticket and stuck it on her windscreen.

'What's that?'

'Shouldn't park here, miss.'

'But I was only popping in for some ciggys.'

'Sorry, miss, rules is rules.'

'Oh fuck you!'

The long-suffering traffic warden ignored her.

When she got home and had poured herself another drink she rang Alistair again, only to receive the same message from Julie. She put down the phone, trying to control her rising panic. Everything that she had was in the bank.

Alistair got back to his office at seven o'clock. He could have stayed overnight in Exeter. The offer had definitely been made by the prosecuting lawyer, an attractive woman in her late thirties whom he had known for some time. But he refused.

'Well in that case, Alistair, having been so politely let down, I'll let you off this time.' She smiled warmly at him. 'Another drink?'

Alistair liked her very much. She was an intelligent, highly respected lawyer and good fun but that was as far as it went.

'Look, Margaret – '

She stopped him with a warm hand on his arm. 'No need to explain, Ali, I understand. So, what do you think the verdict will be?'

And so they chatted on, the bar gradually filling up with city workers having a quick drink before hitting the traffic, the atmosphere getting thicker and thicker with cigarette smoke.

He glanced at his watch. She saw him.

'Well, Alistair, I think it's time I went.' She got up and slipped on her coat. 'I have the most wonderful selection of two-minute microwave meals at home and I can't wait to eat one.'

'Yes,' he said, appreciating her irony with a smile of his

own. 'Being single does have its drawbacks and one of them is in the culinary department. Come on, I'll walk you to your car.'

The drive home to Torhampton was easy considering the amount of traffic there was on the A38. He glided along in his Saab, some Mozart playing on the radio, feeling at peace with himself. Since his last meeting with Elyssa and her bizarre suggestion, he had given himself a couple of days off, allowing a full recovery from the emotional upset she had caused him. The revelations from Mortimore about her private life had disturbed him far more than he liked to admit. The telephone call from Claire had helped him get over Elyssa too. It was really nice speaking to her again, even if it was only to apologize for her outburst and to reaffirm her intention to marry that Lamont chap.

He sighed. It was all wrong; he just knew it was. There was no way she was meant to marry that man. How could she not see that he was only after her for her money? Still, it was none of his business any more. She had made that very plain.

Once he got to Torhampton, he drove directly to his office. Normally he wouldn't have bothered but lately he was spending more time at work, especially in the evenings. Being busy meant he didn't have to face an empty house and at the moment he couldn't do that. All those rooms and only his voice to fill them. He would have to sell up soon and move on.

He parked the car and got out. It was very windy, the cold rain blowing all around him, seeking out those crevices of his clothing that weren't done up properly. He pulled up the collar of his mac and fastened the top button. Then, bowing down into the gale, he walked across the dimly lit and echoing car park until he came to the main square.

He let himself into the office, stamping his wet feet on the doormat and taking off his soaking mac. On his desk was a message. Claire had rung. There was her name among the bits of paper that his secretary had left for him. He immediately dropped the others and picked up the phone. The rest could wait. He wanted to speak to her now.

Her phone rang. She wasn't answering. He let it ring longer. Still no answer.

'Come on, come on,' he murmured urgently. Nothing. He put it down and wondered where she could be. It wasn't like her to be out on a night like this when the weather was so bad.

He smoothed down the ends of his moustache and stared at her name on the paper, contemplating his next move. All the message said was that she had rung and wanted to speak to him — no hint of what it was about. He was desperate to know.

He picked up the phone and tried a second time. Still no answer. He put it down and looked at his watch: 7.16 P.M. Where was she? He looked up at the window. The wind was blowing itself into a real storm, the rain coming down in torrents against the glass. He was worried about her, she shouldn't be out on a night like this.

He stood up. There was nothing much in his other messages: a couple of bills to sign, some queries about the conveyancing on some houses and a note saying Elyssa had called and would he call her back tonight if possible. He screwed that one up and chucked it in the bin. He certainly didn't want to speak to her.

When he got outside and locked the door, he looked skywards, grimacing in the rain. It had started to hail. Lightning and thunder could be seen and heard across the moor. It was a foul night. He nearly decided to go straight to Tor Heights and see if Claire was all right, but changed his mind. If he did turn up unexpectedly she might get a bit off with him again. In her present frame of mind, he was unsure how to treat her. So he left it and hurried back to his car.

Once at home, he made himself a hot meal, opened a

457

half-bottle of wine and sat with the food on a tray in front of a roaring fire while he watched the end of the news. He switched on just in time to hear the announcer report on the collapse and subsequent closure of the Michelberg & Sons Merchant Bank which was now being investigated by the Serious Fraud Office. Some members of staff were even helping police with their enquiries.

He sat down in his chair and watched intently. Michelberg? Michelberg? Where had he heard that name before? Oh yes, it was Elyssa's bank.

He ate his grilled chop without looking at his plate, so interested was he in hearing all of the details.

Afterwards, as he was sitting legs outstretched towards the heat and enjoying his wine, he thought of the possible consequences for Elyssa. He knew she was wealthy, or at least she said she was. She had made two advantageous marriages and she had done well out of them. He knew also she had a large portfolio of stocks and shares which, if the worst came to the worst, could always be sold to raise some capital. And there was her house. A substantial Georgian detached residence in the most desirable part of town. It had a large garden and ample staff accommodation. Someone would want it and pay a lot for it.

He sipped his wine. There was no need to worry about her, he thought to himself. If there was one thing Elyssa knew all about, it was money.

Alistair picked up his phone. Quite out of character, he had dozed off in front of the fire. He hoped it was Claire ringing him.

'Alistair, it's Elyssa.'

'Oh hello, Elyssa.' He sat down at his desk and wearily rubbed his eyes.

'Didn't you get my message?'

'Yes I did.'

'Then why didn't you ring me, Alistair?' she whined.

'This is important. I needed to speak to you ages ago!'

'Well, I'm sorry, Elyssa, but I've been very busy in court all day and I was too tired to do anything when I got back. However, now that you've found me, what's the problem?'

'Have you seen the news?' Her voice was jagged although the words were still distinct. That meant she was only half drunk. 'It's terrible, Alistair, awful. I might have lost everything. I don't know what to do. Oh please help me. I don't know who else to ask.' He could hear her crying now but it aroused little sympathy in him.

'Okay, okay, Elyssa. Calm down and speak more slowly. What's terrible and what have you lost?'

'My money, Alistair! All of it. The bank's collapsed.'

'Ah yes, I saw the news when I came in. I thought it was your bank. I'm afraid I didn't get much of the story.'

'Well, it's shut. They closed it down today. It says so here in the *Evening Standard*.' He could hear her rustling a newspaper. ' "The Bank of England were forced to go in and close it",' she read, ' "due to serious irregularities that were brought to light by the auditor." Oh Alistair,' she wailed, 'what am I going to do?'

'I'm afraid I don't know, Elyssa. As you're aware, I don't specialize in finance. Surely the best person to talk to would be your financial adviser?'

'I tried to earlier but he wasn't available.'

'Well, you'll have to try again tomorrow. He is the one to speak to, Elyssa. He'll be able to give you the best advice.' He paused and then, less businesslike and in a more conciliatory voice said, 'I'm sorry, Elyssa, really I am, but I'm afraid I can't advise you in this particular circumstance. You really will have to see an expert.'

'I know,' she answered, more subdued now.

'What about your stocks and shares? Don't you have some you can sell? I mean, if you need the capital?'

'What you're really saying, Alistair, is if the bank can't pay up, how else can I raise some money?'

'Well,' he answered, 'I didn't really want to paint the worst scenario.'

She sighed heavily. 'The answer is yes, but not nearly enough. I've been selling my assets over the last few years, ever since my divorce, in fact. I was given a few thousand shares as part of my settlement, but they're nearly all gone now.'

'Why?'

'Because, Ali,' she said with vehemence, 'how do you suppose I live like I do? It costs money, all of this, lots of it and I had to raise it somehow.'

'I realize that, Elyssa, but I had no idea things had become that desperate.'

She gave a brittle laugh. 'They haven't, Ali. It's just that I like the good life and for that you have to pay. God, how do you suppose I can afford haute couture dresses?'

'Well,' he said, 'I always did think you were a bit extravagant.'

She didn't reply.

'What about the house?' he asked. 'That must be worth something at least.'

There was silence down the other end of the line.

'Elyssa? Are you still there?'

'Just lighting a ciggy, Ali.'

'The house, Elyssa, surely you could sell it?'

'Yes and no,' she said slowly.

'Meaning what?'

'Meaning it's mortgaged to the hilt, I owe the building society thousands and even if I did sell it, in this recession, I would hardly make enough to cover my costs.'

'Elyssa!'

'Yes, yes, yes, no need to sound so shocked, Ali, but I needed the cash. I told you that. I can't manage in some tiny little flat, you know I can't.'

'But . . . but this is ridiculous! You mean to tell me that contrary to all appearances, you have nothing?'

'In a word, Ali, yes. And now that the bank has gone

bust, the only money I have left is the couple of thousand left in my safe.'

She closed her eyes and tried to wipe out the memory of Kevin and his greed. She had given him practically everything.

'Well, I am surprised,' he said at last. 'So what are you going to do now?'

She sounded very tired when she answered. 'Sell what I can and leave, I suppose. I'm going on holiday first though.'

'Do you think that's wise, Elyssa? After all, you're in no fit state, financially speaking, to spend any money.'

'Rubbish, Ali! God, you always were a boring old fart, weren't you? No, I've paid for it, so I'm going. Fuck the bank and everyone else. I'm going out as I came in — indefatigable!'

Now she was really drunk. Alistair knew for sure the minute she started getting hysterical.

'Don't let me stop you then, Elyssa.'

There was a pause. 'Won't you come with me, Ali? Please. I've got an extra ticket. We could fly out together.'

He needed no time to think over his reply. 'No, Elyssa, it's absolutely out of the question. I know we had some pleasant moments, but really . . .'

'Okay,' she said brightly. 'No need to rub the salt in. I can take a hint. I know when I'm not wanted.' He remained silent. 'It's all right, Ali, I understand. You'd just rather spend time with that bumpkin of yours. Honestly, Alistair, don't you understand anything? She doesn't love you.'

'Elyssa,' he said sharply, 'put down the phone and go to bed. You've said enough.'

'Why should I? You're not my husband. I can do as I like. I don't need some miserable old sod like you to tell me what to do.'

'Right, that's enough, Elyssa. I'm putting the telephone down now. Goodbye.'

It was some time before he stopped feeling angry. He sat at his desk staring into the distance. Despite her cruel words, he hoped she wouldn't come too unstuck. But then he always was the gentleman.

Elyssa stared at the receiver with sheer rage. How dare he speak to her like that? After all the good times they had shared together. It just wasn't on.

'You bastard!' and she flung the irritating machine across the room, knocking a Lalique crystal vase off a table and smashing it.

She slumped onto the Chesterfield, bereft of venom or ideas. There was nowhere else to go and no one else to turn to.

She glanced up at the drinks cabinet. At least she still had that and a good stiff drink always helped her in times of stress. She got up and wobbled over to the bottles.

'A drink,' she told herself, 'just a little, little one to help me relax. It won't do any harm.'

The ice cubes fell into the tumbler with a satisfying clink and when the amber whisky flowed over them she felt very calm. Oblivion wasn't far away.

'Right then, have you got everything?'

Terri looked up at Saskia, her pixie face animated with excitement. Saskia turned round and glanced back into the dark and quiet house. She wasn't happy at all.

'Yes,' she sighed, 'I suppose so.'

'Susie, the cat?'

'With the neighbours. Daddy is coming up to town next week to put the house on the market and he'll take Susie back to Surrey.'

'Switched everything off.'

'Yeah.'

'Oh come on, Sas, show a bit more enthusiasm, for heaven's sake!'

Saskia frowned. 'I don't know, Terri, if we're doing the

right thing, that's all,' she complained.

'And what do you suppose will happen if we don't go?'

Saskia looked at her, her bottom lip pouting like a child's.

'Well, I'll tell you. Lord and master will come back from Devon pretty damned quick and will be after you like some demented bounty-hunter!' She put her arms around her friend. 'Come on, Sas, cheer up. It's not the end of the world. He's a bastard, you know he is, and the best thing to do is forget about him, so stop snivelling and blow your nose. Here, use my hanky. It's clean.'

A car blew its horn outside.

'Come on, that's the taxi.'

'All right,' and with one last lingering look, Saskia turned her back on the house, her two years with James now a memory.

They didn't speak much on the way to the airport or while they waited to board. When they did, Saskia was very quiet, simply staring out of the window.

'I've never been Club Class before,' said Terri as she tested the seats. 'Nice and wide, much better than those cramped things next door.'

'Well, I wasn't going to spend the entire trip unable to stretch my legs, I can tell you.'

'Wow! This is so exciting, I can't wait to get there.'

'What about your flat and paintings?' asked Saskia.

'Oh I've dumped the lot off at the parents. Mother doesn't approve, of course, but who cares? She's so square, you can see the corners on her head.'

'Doesn't she like nudes?'

'No, not much.'

The plane lifted off.

'Where are we going first?' Terri's excited face turned to Saskia.

'Brisbane. I have some relatives there. They live near the beach. It should be fun,' and she gave Terri a wide open smile.

Terri took her hand and kissed it. 'I can't wait.'

'No,' said Saskia, 'neither can I.' And then she looked out of the window at the tops of the white clouds floating past underneath the plane. Her eyes started to fill until a single tear rolled down her cheek.

James – her James. She would always love him.

'There you are then, that's the lot,' and Kevin sat back proudly as his mother and Aditha stared amazed at the money.

'My goodness!' said his mum. 'How much did you say was there?' and she picked up a fresh clean note.

'Seven thousand, five hundred and all in brand new notes.'

She looked at him quizzically. 'And you won it on a bet?'

'Yes. Why, don't you believe me?'

'Huh,' she sighed, 'you take after your father where money is concerned and I don't trust you as far as I can see you.'

'Mum, how can you say such a thing about your only son?' he teased, his face crinkling into a smile.

'Oh well,' she said, standing up and clearing away the teacups, 'can't complain, I suppose,' and she waddled out of the room, leaving Kevin and Aditha grinning at each other. She immediately came over and cuddled him.

'I so proud of you.'

He kissed her cheek. 'Yeah, great, wasn't it? Worked a treat that plan of yours.'

'So, what we do with it?'

'Dunno.'

She smiled at him. 'I know.'

'What?'

'We open restaurant.'

'What! With only seven and a half grand? You must be nuts! That's not enough to get started.'

She reached into her handbag which was sitting on the

floor and took out a passbook. 'But I got this,' and she showed it to him.

He looked at the figure. 'Bloody hell! Where d'you get this from?'

Now she shrugged. 'Oh, here, there, I work in many houses and there always ways to make money.'

A sly smile spread over his face. 'You crafty bugger.' He grabbed her. 'Come here, you, I want a kiss.'

That done, he tapped her expanding belly. 'How's the young 'un then?'

She smiled, showing her row of dazzling teeth. 'He fine, he very fine.'

TWENTY-SEVEN

It was some time before James could get off the floor. He lay in agony. An undignified heap of painfully snuffed out sexual desire with trousers halfway down his thighs. A rage of mammoth proportions was beginning to ferment inside him.

'You bitch . . .' he whispered, his sweaty face screwed up into the carpet. 'You . . . bloody . . . bitch!'

He carefully reached behind him, his hand accidentally brushing against the knife, which was still stuck in his back. The sudden pain was excruciating.

'Shit!'

He looked over his shoulder. He could clearly see the handle of it sticking out of his flesh, gently vibrating with each of his shuddering breaths.

'Bloody hell!'

He got on to his hands and knees, each movement causing him to wince and cry out. Once that was safely negotiated, he put his hands on the sofa and eased himself onto his feet. At first, the room seemed to be swaying, but it soon settled down when he took some deep breaths.

'Must . . . get . . .' but he had to stop. Talking, however little, caused stilettos of pain to race across his back.

He carefully made his way out of the room and into the kitchen. There was little bleeding from the wound, but he still had to pull out the knife. Once he had made his way to the sink, shivering and sweating, he ran the cold water tap and splashed some on his face. He instantly felt much better. He looked to one side. There was a clean tea towel hanging next to the cooker. He wrapped it around his hand, gripped hold of the knife and pulled.

'Ahhhhh!'

He collapsed on the floor, his face pressed up against the cupboards and his legs sprawled out across the cold lino. He was crying.

'Just . . . you . . . wait, Bromage. I'll get you for this!'

He felt his back. There was a small trickle of warm blood oozing down over his buttocks. He wiped it away with the tea towel.

It was so unfair. All his inheritance; all his money, and it was now gone. She had it, stuck away in her bloody little bank where it was doing nothing when he needed it so much. Why hadn't his uncle given him his share? It was enough to make anyone cry. Well, he wasn't going to just sit here and accept it. No, he was going to teach that little peasant a lesson; something she would never forget and then, when he had got his back seen to, he would be off. Somewhere; anywhere; as long as it was abroad and out of McArdle's and the bank's way.

He stood up and splashed his face again. Now that he had made up his mind over what he was going to do, he felt better. The injury to his back certainly wasn't going to hinder him. He had business to do and there was no time to waste. He looked at his watch: 7.30. Claire should be at home.

It took him ten minutes to get to her farm. The yard light was on so she had to be around somewhere. He parked his car and got out, standing quite still in the howling wind and listened. There was nothing except the moaning of the trees and the rain lashing against his face.

He walked across the wet concrete towards the kitchen door. As he went to open it, Rosie started barking.

'Bloody animal!' he yelled. 'Why don't you shut up? You will when you see who's out here!'

He touched the door again and her barking renewed

467

with even more ferocity. He could clearly see her through the glass panel of the door, her massive white teeth bared as she growled at him.

'Going to play nasty then, are we? Well, I can play a damn sight nastier than you.'

He stepped back. It was no good. He would never get in that way unless he could get rid of that flea-bitten animal.

He shouted up at the dark house: 'Come on out, Claire. I know you're in there!' but the house stayed quiet. The only voice that could be heard was his own, echoing round the empty buildings.

'So you're out then? Well, if it's just me and that hound of yours, I suppose I'll just have to teach it a lesson.'

He turned back to the yard and walked over to one of the stables, the dog's staccato barking still following him. She was a large dog, powerfully built and very strong. It would take exactly the right sort of implement to do the job he had in mind.

As he searched the stable's dim interior he soon found what he was looking for. It was the broken-off handle of a garden fork or spade. Heavy and blunt with a jagged wooden dagger at one end. He tested it against his leg. Good; it would do.

He walked back to the kitchen, gripping his weapon tightly.

'Come on then, let's see what you're made of!' he yelled.

He rattled the door, sending Rosie into a fit of barking. When he judged the time to be right, he pushed it open just far enough for her to get her head out. Her eyes blazed at him as she tried to free herself. Her lips were completely retracted, exposing her white teeth. He had real difficulty holding the door just tight enough against her neck. Her strength was formidable. He knew he had to act fast, otherwise she would work herself free and surely attack him.

Adjusting his hold on the handle, he brought it smashing down onto her head. A blow like that would have felled a man, but apart from a small yelp, she carried on, determined to defend her territory.

He hit her again, this time in the mouth. She began to bleed quite profusely. He could see he had dislodged several of her teeth, her torn gums red raw. Again he hit her, and again and again and again, the wooden club smashing against her skull, sprays of her warm blood splashing up against his clothes, mixed with bits of bone and flesh.

Finally he stopped. There was no need to go on. Her limp body lay in the doorway, bloodied and pulped, her face unrecognizable. But she still breathed.

James stood over her, panting and hot. He wiped his face, smears of blood left across the back of his hand. When he had recovered, he bent down and cautiously touched her. There was no reaction. He pushed open the door and dragged her out by the scruff of the neck into the yard, her body leaving a trail of blood in the mud and rain.

He stood up and looked down at her. In a strange way he admired the dumb creature. She had put up a damn good fight and for that he congratulated her. She wasn't dead, but he could soon rectify that. Turning the wooden handle round so that the sharp end was facing her, he plunged it into her chest using his full weight.

She twitched and was still.

He threw the handle to one side while he decided what to do next. He wanted Claire to find her in such a way that she would never forget it. She had really hurt him. Her refusal to hand over his money was something he could never forgive. Well, now it was his turn.

He decided to hang the dog up in the stable. He went into the house and searched the scullery. Claire kept all kinds of rubbish in there and he soon found a suitable

469

piece of rope. He also saw the gun cabinet.

'Huh,' he said. 'If I'd known about those I could have shot the mongrel ages ago.'

He slipped the rope through her collar and dragged her across the yard; her body gathering up pieces of dirt and straw as it went.

In one of the looseboxes there was a wooden stairway which led up to the next floor. It was in here that Claire kept the animal feeds. James pulled the body up the stairs, switching on the light halfway up, the heavy weight thumping against each plank of wood. It was harder work than he expected but then she was a very big dog.

He stood panting at the top. His hands and clothes were filthy and he would have to have a good wash when he got home.

There was a heavy wooden beam traversing the roof space, twelve feet long and a good foot wide. He threw the rope over it and hauled the body upwards. It took all his strength. There was a convenient hook in the wall and he tied the rope around it, knotting it tightly so that it didn't come undone.

When he had finished, he smiled with satisfaction at a job well done. Rosie's body hung heavy and lifeless, the eyes opaque and blood dripping on the floor from her many injuries.

'For you, dear girl,' he said, rubbing his hands together, 'a little present, with love from your Uncle James.'

He descended the wooden staircase and turned off the light. Now he would ransack the house. After all, it would be a shame to waste such an opportunity. If Claire was stupid enough not to lock up when she went out, then she only had herself to blame if she got burgled.

There was nothing, of course, except her purse, which contained a few pounds and her jewellery box, which had a couple of rings in it; one dress ring and an old wedding ring. There was also the ring and the pearls he had given

470

her. He rejected them with a shrug. Bloody waste of time, he thought as he drove away.

By the time Claire got home, the storm was raging at full spate, the wind howling and moaning over the land as it looked for some hidden place that it hadn't discovered yet.

It was blowing right through her. She was in such a hurry to leave Briar Cottage and get away from James that she had left her waxed jacket behind. She was completely soaked and frozen to the marrow. Her hands were numb. She couldn't feel her feet and the ache in her belly was getting worse. She sat hunched up in the saddle feebly trying to keep out the cold, but it didn't work. She was utterly miserable.

Exhausted and aching all over when she got home, she stopped and wearily dismounted, grimacing as her feet hit the ground, sending small shockwaves up her groaning legs. She led Bonny into the stable and started to unsaddle her. Steam rose from the horse's wet back as the saddle was removed. She tossed her head and impatiently stamped her feet. She wanted her feed.

'Okay, okay, in a minute. Let me dry you off first.' Claire picked up some hay and began to rub down the horse's flanks and withers.

A drop of water fell on her head as she bent over. She wiped it off and carried on drying Bonny. Then another drop hit her and ran down her face. She impatiently wiped that off too when suddenly she saw there was blood on her hand; bright red blood and it wasn't hers.

Her heart began to race. She looked around. There was blood everywhere; on her, on Bonny, on the floor. She slowly looked up. There was a dark maroon patch on the ceiling and drops of blood were falling from its centre. She stared at it transfixed with horror.

'Oh my God, please . . . please don't let it be her, please, God no.'

She put down the hay and still not taking her eyes off the ceiling, walked slowly to the staircase, oblivious of everything except a pounding in her ears.

She ascended the steps with fear, swallowing hard and fighting to keep down the nausea.

Halfway up was the light switch. She turned it on. At the top of the stairs, her eyes lowered, she paused. She hardly dare look up because there in front of her, on the dusty floor, was a large pool of blood. She looked up.

Splintered; everything: her life, her world, her face. It all came crashing down around her ears in a shower of broken glass.

She stared at the obscenity that gently swayed before her, the face unrecognizable in the smashed and broken flesh, patches of bloodied fur barely noticeable among the swollen excresence that was once Rosie's muzzle. The blood running down the body was dripping rhythmically with a dull thud onto the floor.

Claire lurched forward onto her hands and knees and violently threw up, her whole body rejecting the unholy sight. When the vomiting had stopped, she wiped the mess from her mouth and gazed upwards again, steeling herself. Propelled by the sheer horror, she unsteadily got to her feet. With one hand outstretched, she started to circum-navigate her dog, the tips of her fingers barely touching the wet fur.

'What ... did ... he ... do ... to ... you?' she whispered. 'Oh my God, what has he done to you?'

She knew it was James. He was the only person in her life who was capable of such unprovoked cruelty, and it was all her fault. She had got mixed up with him; she had let herself be fooled by his warm smile and easy charm; she had allowed herself to be willingly led further and further into his devious abyss because she was a weak, stupid, idiotic woman. Her need for love and affection had far outstripped her common sense and made her blind to his faults. This was her punishment; this was the price her

472

dog had had to pay because she hadn't been there to fight him herself.

Rosie, her valiant friend and loyal companion, who had only ever shown her unconditional love and affection, had fought him on her behalf and lost.

The body swayed and Claire saw the gaping, angry hole in Rosie's side.

'No! . . . No! . . . Nooooooo!'

With hands over her mouth, she recoiled from the corpse, repelled by its awfulness, and sank to her knees. And then she started to cry.

From puppyhood onwards Rosie had been all Claire had. There was no one else, only her, and she gave unquestioningly. However moody or bad-tempered Claire felt, her dog stood by her. She had infiltrated herself into Claire's world so well that she no longer considered herself a separate entity. It was always Claire and Rosie; inseparable; thinking, doing and living together and now she was dead.

She must cut her down. She stood up and with renewed vigour struggled to undo the knot that James had tied too tightly. When it gave way, it happened so suddenly that the rope rushed through her fingers, burning them, and the body thumped to the floor.

She moved over to it, hesitant and blinded with tears, choking and gasping through her sobs, saliva running unchecked out of the corner of her mouth. She pulled the rope through Rosie's collar and sat down on the floor cradling the dog's head in her lap. Uncaring of the mess, she ran her hand lovingly over the torn and battered flesh.

'Rosie . . . Rosie . . . I'm sorry, so very, very sorry. What have I done to you?' She rocked backwards and forwards, comforting her dead animal. 'My poor, poor girl.'

She kissed the dog's matted head and then lay her warm face against her own, her tears running over Rosie's fur.

* * *

It was some time before she realized she must move. Rosie deserved a better resting place than this old barn. Claire got to her feet. She was weak and light-headed but ignored it. There was work to do.

With a great heave, she picked up the dog's inert body and came stiffly down the stairs, straining under the weight. She walked out to the yard and it was there, under the force of the relentless wind and rain that she stumbled and fell over. The fall tore a hole in her jeans and grazed her knee so that pinpricks of her blood joined the dying ooze of her dog's.

No longer physically capable of carrying on or able to restrain the huge grief that threatened to overwhelm her, she gave herself completely to her howling cries of pain. Sodden and wretched and well beyond the parameters of normal grief, her inhuman wails filled the air, only to be drowned out by the thundering rain and tireless wind.

'No! . . . No! . . . No! . . . Noooooo!'

It was later.

Claire was sitting in her kitchen, her hands clutching a thoroughly sodden hanky that she had been using to stem her tears, but they still came. Silently now, rolling down her cheeks and dripping off the bottom of her chin.

When the worst was over, she had got to her feet and carried Rosie into the house where she had laid her out on the kitchen table. She stood and looked at the body. She decided to light a candle. The overhead light was too harsh. That done, she filled a bowl with cold water and taking a cloth, had gently washed Rosie clean, running the damp cloth over her face and ears as she pieced together the fragmented remains of her muzzle.

Sometimes Claire stopped and turned away. Sometimes the images of violence that flashed before her of what Rosie must have endured were so clear that she had to blink her eyes and force herself to concentrate on what she was doing. And all the while she whispered, 'I'm so sorry, I'm so sorry.'

Soon the bowl of water was bright red with blood. She emptied it and started again. She was determined that her dog would be clean before she buried her and that she would have washed away any last remains of the horrible, horrible man. She couldn't bear to think of his hands touching Rosie's fur. She wanted all traces of him gone.

When she was done and the third bowl of water was emptied, she stood the candle on the table next to Rosie's muzzle and offered up a small prayer. She hadn't done that since Matt's death, but it seemed appropriate. She wasn't sure if she was speaking to anyone in particular, but it gave her some comfort to think that maybe she was heard.

Then she sat very, very still, her hands in her lap and her mind blank. She still cried, but they were quiet tears, a gentle ripple of grief after the storm. Soon they too stopped. She was just too damned tired to go on any longer.

Later, she went out into the scullery to find an old feed bag. She wanted to cover Rosie up, give her some dignity before she buried her. She kept a pile of bags under the sink. She turned on the scullery light and knelt down to look for them. As she did so, her eyes fell on the gun cabinet. For a while she didn't move, only stared at it. She had fired a gun once before, a long time ago. She detested them, but she could still use one if she wanted to.

She turned away. Such thoughts were ridiculous. She could never take her revenge like that even if James had killed Rosie. She couldn't do it and that was that.

Back in the kitchen Rosie's pulverized skull, still warm in places, had stuck to the table top. As Claire lifted up the head, a piece of smooth, white bone stayed behind. She screamed.

'Damn you, James! Damn you! Damn you! Just look what you've done! Look at it!'

It was the final straw. The feed bag forgotten, she raced back into the scullery. Somewhere there was a key for the gun cabinet. She pulled out a drawer and rummaged about but couldn't find it. She pulled open the second drawer but that was empty, and it clattered, ignored, onto the floor.

In the third drawer she found it, a small brass key that fitted the lock. She kicked the empty drawers to one side and knelt down.

She took the guns out with reverence. They felt cold and heavy, almost too heavy, for they were meant for a man to use.

She briefly checked them. Matt had been keen on clay pigeon shooting and had spent long hours cleaning his guns. Even though they hadn't been used in over two years, they still worked smoothly, the barrels clean and the firing action not too tight.

She weighed each one in her hands and decided on the lighter one. She must have a gun she could manage.

Now that she had made her decision, she felt no fear. To her it was perfectly straightforward: he had killed Rosie and now she would kill him. Simple really. She helped herself to some orange cartridges from a box on the shelf and went back into the kitchen. Rosie's body, lying there in all its pathos, made her decision all the more determined. No one would kill her dog and walk away from it; no one.

She put on Matt's old waxed jacket and, once more bracing herself against the storm, left the house.

She took her van this time. The wind was so strong that it even buffeted the vehicle, trying its best to push her off the lane. Bits of newly grown leaves occasionally caught in her windscreen wipers as they were whipped off the trees by the strong eddies and all the time it rained: a torrential downpour of water.

She arrived at Briar Cottage to see the lights on and James's car backed up against the front door, its boot open.

He was packing to leave. Claire smiled to herself. That's what he thought.

She drove along the rutted drive and parked her van at an angle to his car, effectively blocking him in. There was no way he could leave now.

She had enough self-perception to realize that she had no fear of him any more. He may have frightened her that afternoon, but that had passed. Rosie's death had changed everything. She viewed him now with no more interest than a pile of dung which she was going to tread on. Whatever he might have meant to her no longer applied. He was a worthless creature and he didn't deserve to live.

The door opened. He saw her van and immediately stopped what he was doing. He was confident; she could see that. One hand rested nonchalantly against the door frame while the other one sat on his hip.

Claire glanced at him. She then methodically and without any rush loaded up the gun. Wordlessly and without expression she got out of the van. With the gun held behind her, she walked towards him.

As she got closer, she could see he was smiling, a crooked leering sort of smirk that ran diagonally across his face. He was jaunty and arrogant and had no time to waste with her.

He watched her advance with bored indifference until she came within the light of the doorway. Then he noticed how pale she looked; how her red-rimmed eyes were sunken and dead against her white cheeks. Strands of her wet hair, long escaped from the confines of her plait were blowing around her face as they danced on the wind. She looked terrible. He was sure he could get rid of her with little difficulty.

'What d'you want?' he demanded. 'It's late and I'm cold and I'm in no bloody mood to talk to you. Surely I made that obvious enough this afternoon?'

Claire said nothing, but squeezed the comforting wooden butt of the gun.

'Find my little present, did you?' he leered, his lips pulled back in a sickly grin. He gave a hollow laugh. 'Oh my poor little Claire, what an innocent you were and so easy to please as well. Really, my dear, imagine you thinking you could get the better of me. You hurt me, of course, very much with that knife of yours. And you've stolen my money. There was no way you were going to get away with that. No way. God!' He spat. 'There was no bloody competition, girl. You had it coming, you know. You deserved it. It wasn't my fault. It was yours. You killed Rosie. Not me, but you.'

He paused and then smiled. 'All you had to do was pay me what was rightfully mine and then I would have left that precious animal of yours well alone. But you wouldn't, would you? You had to keep it all to yourself. Well, as far as I'm concerned, you got what you deserved. Every last bit of it. So,' he said, examining a nail, 'what was it like finding her strung up in the barn? Good was it?'

She watched him with a cold unflinching hatred. Let him talk; she didn't care. Let him dig his own grave.

He took a step towards her. 'Well, answer me, peasant. How did it feel to find your dog?'

She pulled the gun round and pointed it at him.

'You killed my dog.'

His shocked expression as he glanced from the gun to her, quickly dissolved into disbelief. He held up his hands in surrender. 'Okay, okay, that's enough, Claire. You've had your joke. It's gone far enough. Now put it down.'

She advanced closer towards him, the gun held tightly in her hands, her agonized eyes fixed on his face.

'You killed my dog,' she repeated. Her words were churchyard cold with menace.

He stepped back over the threshold. 'You don't really mean this, Claire,' he laughed nervously.

'Don't I, James? And what makes you say that?'

'Because . . .' He swallowed hard. 'Because you . . . you

could never kill me. You loved me remember, you still do. I know it.'

He was babbling. He knew he was, but he had to delay her.

'Listen to me, Claire.' He was walking backwards down the small hallway, his hands held up in front of him. 'Listen to me, I didn't mean to hurt her, really I didn't, but she attacked me first.'

'What crap!' she shouted, making him jump. 'My dog wouldn't attack anyone unless I told her to.'

'But she did, Claire, she did. I . . . I tried to open the kitchen door and,' he glanced over his shoulder, 'she went for me.'

'Well, you shouldn't have been there, should you, James? You had no right to poke around in my house while I was out. What were you doing anyway, trying to see where my money was?'

By now she had him cornered in the lounge. He was standing quivering next to the drinks table, holding on tightly to the back of a chair.

'I need a drink,' he muttered.

She let him pour one, a large one. As he drank, he pressed the wound on his back. She could see blood on his jumper but it didn't shake her resolve. She was calm and unwavering, and nothing he did or said was going to change her mind.

'Listen, Claire,' he said, bent slightly forward with pain, 'let me explain something to you.'

'What?'

He moved deeper into the room so that she had to come in if she were to keep the gun on him.

'That money you inherited,' he said quietly, watching the gun barrel with apprehension, 'it's all mine, you know. My uncle originally left it to me in his will and I was going to get it if there hadn't been a small misunderstanding.'

'So?'

She seemed weary of his ramblings but let him continue.

'He would have left it to me if he hadn't done some research and found out about you. Then I would have had my share, my hundred thousand pounds.'

Claire raised an eyebrow and started to smile. Then she laughed until her eyes began to run.

'What?. . . What's up?' he asked.

'A hundred thousand?' she laughed. 'Is that all, James?'

He nodded. 'Why?'

'Well, I've got some bad news for you.' She wiped her face dry. 'He left me over nine hundred thousand — so how about that?'

She watched him with amusement as he turned white and had to sit down, his legs buckling under him.

'Nearly a million pounds, James, and it's all mine,' she whispered, 'every last penny of it. So how about that, eh?'

The silence was palpable, the woman standing still with the gun and the man slowly shaking his head from side to side in disbelief. She viewed him with utter contempt and wondered how she had ever fallen for him.

James tottered weakly to his feet, clutching his back. He smiled vaguely at her. 'You're joking, of course, you have to be. I mean, why would a man like him, from such a good family, leave all that money to a complete stranger like you? He couldn't have,' he insisted, 'he just couldn't have.' He looked at her, furrows of puzzlement across his forehead. 'You're lying. You must be. I don't believe you.' He ran his hand through his lank hair. 'I mean, what have you, a rural upstart, got in common with a man like him? He kept racehorses and ran one of the biggest investment agencies in the City; he had breeding and tradition and a family heritage that stretched back generations.' He walked across to the window and stared out into the stormy blackness. 'How could he?' he added quietly, more to himself than her, 'have anything to do with you?'

And then suddenly he laughed, a loud raucous, ironic laugh. 'Of course!' he yelled, the light dawning. 'His dog!'

He finished his drink and walked back for another. 'Of course, of course,' he muttered. 'How silly of me. Ha! Little Tim.' He was speaking to himself now. 'A Yorkshire terrier. My uncle used to put a blue bow in his hair and feed him titbits from the table.' His face clouded over. 'That bloody little rat! Uncle loved him. He hated us, but he loved that little runt.'

Claire watched him puzzled. 'James?'

He turned to her, suddenly aware of her again. 'What?' he said tiredly. 'Go on then, shoot me, get it over and done with!'

She looked at the gun in her hands and then back at him. She was not so sure now.

'No,' he said, advancing towards her. 'I didn't think you could. You're not going to use that gun. Christ! You haven't even got the safety catch off.'

As she looked down, he flung his whisky in her face and pushed her to one side as she struggled to clear her vision. He bolted out and ran for the front door.

His first thought was his car. He had been about to leave when Claire arrived, so most of his luggage was already packed. It wouldn't matter about the few things left behind. All that concerned him now was putting as much distance between himself and her as possible, because he didn't trust her.

As he ran out, fumbling in his pocket for his keys, they flew out of his hand and into the mud by the side of the door.

'Shit!'

He got to his knees and started to look for them, his hands clawing wildly in the sodden earth, small sharp stones getting under his nails. He glanced, terrified, back over his shoulder. She would be coming to get him. Christ! Where were the fucking things?

Claire recovered almost immediately. When her eyes were clear, she picked up the gun, which had fallen to the

481

floor, and went to the door. This was it as far as she was concerned. He had done his worst and now she was going to get him.

She stepped into the corridor. By the light of the overhead bulb, she could see his frantic figure kneeling in the mud. He glanced at her, his eyes wide with terror, his hair streaming across his face.

As she raised the gun to her face and took aim, he stood up with all the delicacy of a poised ballet dancer. He held out his hands.

'No!. . . No . . .' he pleaded, his face riven with lines of extreme fear.

'Your turn now, James,' she whispered and pulled the trigger, feeling the smooth cold pressure tighten under her finger.

Nothing. The gun had jammed. James didn't need a second chance. In his abject terror he took off into the night, running as fast as he could.

Claire tried forcing the gun but it was hopeless. She couldn't open it or fire it so she threw it down and raced off after him.

'You bastard!' she screamed, the words whipped away from her by the wind. 'You bastard!'

His chest heaving and his back aching, James looked blindly from side to side as he ran. There had to be somewhere in this godforsaken place he could hide. There had to be. If only he could find somewhere then he would be safe. He couldn't see further than two feet in front of his nose, it was so dark. Stumbling and terrified, her screams coming closer, he raced blindly down the road. Where could he go? Where?

Then a gateway appeared and, thankful for an escape, he climbed over it and ran for his life across the wet grass.

Claire saw him disappear across the field and called out to warn him.

'James! James! The bull! The bull!' but he ignored her. By the time she reached the gate, she knew it was too late.

TWENTY-EIGHT

'Jack, oh please, Jack, help me!' She fell forward into his astonished arms, crying, 'I think he's dead, Jack. I think he's dead. It was horrible.'

The old man held her slim shivering body in his calloused hands.

'Who is Claire?'

She couldn't answer him. She was too distraught. He helped her into the warm kitchen and tried to sit her down next to the Aga. She perched on the edge of the chair like a frightened bird, sobbing hard. He held her shoulders to stop her shaking.

'Come on, Claire, calm down now. Shh, and tell me what's happened.'

When she looked at him with her stricken eyes, she could only shake her head.

He stood up bewildered. His wife appeared, wrapping her dressing-gown around her.

'What is it, Jack?'

He shrugged. 'Don't know.'

She saw Claire's dejected body. 'Oh my poor dear, what's happened to you?' She put her arms round Claire. 'Heavens! You're soaking and frozen solid. We've got to get these wet things off you.'

And without protest, she stood Claire up and started to undress her.

'My God!' she whispered, seeing the bloodstained shirt. She looked at Claire's still-crying face. 'What's been going on?'

She turned to her husband. Jack came and saw the mess. They gave each other a knowing look.

'I think you'd better ring Tom, Jack.'

'Right oh, Mother.'

As Jack went to call the police, his wife saw to Claire, removing her wet clothes and rubbing her down with a warm towel.

'It's all right,' she told Claire, who stood like a dumb animal, her eyes staring straight out in front of her with terror. 'We'll soon get things sorted out for you, dear. Don't you worry about it now. I'll just undo your jeans, dear.'

Nan pulled at the sodden trousers, covered in blood and bits of fur.

'Oh my God,' she whispered again. 'What has been going on?'

She looked at Claire and still the young woman's face stared across the room. Nan wrapped her in the towel and sat her down in front of the open oven.

'You sit down, dear, while I get you some of my daughter's things to wear.'

She walked over to Jack, who was waiting for PC Tom Wilson to answer his telephone.

'I don't know what's been going on, Jack,' she whispered, 'but something terrible's happened. There's blood all over her clothes.'

Jack pursed his lips and sighed heavily. 'I wish Tom would answer his bloody phone. Ah, hello, Tom, it's me, Jack Burrows. I think we've got a problem.'

Tom came in without knocking, removing his hat and wiping the rain off it. A large, corpulent man, he was the benign terror of the few hooligan elements that lived in Torhampton.

'Jack. Nan.' He nodded a sombre good evening, looking at Claire's hunched figure, which Nan was trying to comfort.

'What's going on then, Jack?'

Jack glanced towards Claire and said in a quiet voice: 'Don't know exactly, Tom. When she arrived here, covered in blood and crying her eyes out, she kept saying that someone was dead. She won't say who or where, though. Nan's been trying to get her to talk but,' he shook his head, 'damned if we can get anything out of her. She seems to be in a state of shock.'

The two men studied the bowed figure by the Aga. Slight, and her hair still wet from the rain, she looked truly pathetic. Nan was sitting on a chair next to her, holding her hands and making small soothing noises. Claire didn't seem to be listening.

'Mmm,' said the policeman. 'We'd better see if we can get any information from her. Any idea at all who she might be talking about?'

'Well, I don't know for sure, but she was having a bit of a thing with that bloke I rented Briar Cottage to. It could be him.'

Tom put on his hat.

'Well, maybe we'd better go and see this man first then. What's his name?'

'Lamont. James Lamont.'

On hearing his name, Claire looked up, her eyes staring wildly at them. 'I didn't meant it ... please ... I didn't mean ...' and she trailed off, crying again.

The two men stared at her.

'What didn't you mean, dear?' asked Nan, stroking Claire's frozen hands.

Claire turned to her, only just realizing who Nan was. 'James ...' she repeated. 'I didn't mean to kill him.' She glanced towards the two men who were now concentrating on her. 'The bull ... he ... James in the field ... Oh Nan, you've got to believe me!' she wailed. 'It wasn't me, I didn't mean it.'

Nan put her arms round Claire's shaking shoulders. 'Shh, shh, it's all right, my dear. Shh, shh. Of course you 'didn't mean it.' She looked at the two men.

'I think I'll have to ring Exeter, Jack,' said Tom. 'Can I use your phone?'

Jack nodded, not comprehending what Tom said. His bull, his prize Charolais bull. If he had killed someone . . .

Claire was rocking backwards and forwards, not listening to anything. Her cold hands were fiercely entwined with each other, going round and round in circles.

Nan offered her some tea. 'Here, my lover, drink this. It'll make you feel better.'

Claire turned her pallid face to Nan, streaks of tears rolling down her cheeks. 'I didn't mean it, Nan, honestly I didn't.'

'I know, dear, of course you didn't. Now drink this.'

Claire ignored the mug of tea.

Tom finished his call. 'Detective Inspector is coming from Exeter with a sergeant. They'll be here soon.'

The three of them watched Claire from the kitchen table as she kept muttering to herself.

'Do you think I ought to call the doctor?' asked Nan in a whisper.

'Wait till the others get here from Exeter, Nan, they'll know what to do. She does look bad, though, doesn't she?'

'Terrible.'

Claire kept rocking.

'Listen,' said Nan, 'she's saying something else.' She got up and went to Claire. 'What is it, my dear?'

'Alistair,' said the tremulous voice. 'Please. I want Alistair.'

'Of course, dear.'

Jack went straight to the telephone.

Alistair was asleep in his chair, gently rumbling in front of a dying fire and still switched-on TV, when the telephone woke him.

When he left five minutes later, his TV was still on.

By the time he had raced to Jack's farm, skidding along the rough lanes in the Saab, the police from Exeter had arrived. Nan met him at the door.

'Where is she?' he asked, brushing past her.

'In there.'

Alistair saw Claire and stopped dead in his tracks. He had never seen her look so awful. Her hair hung lifelessly over her white, white face and her eyes were huge orbs of dark green rimmed in red. Everything about her, from the way she sat curled up, to the way she ignored everyone in the room, spoke of her misery.

He went to her and, kneeling down so he could look into her eyes, he gently brushed strands of her hair away from her face.

When she recognized him, her eyes immediately filled with tears.

'Rosie!. . . She's dead . . . He killed her. Oh God!' she cried and fell forward into his arms, her wet face against his shoulder.

'Oh my darling, my poor, poor darling.'

When they drove down to the field, the ambulance had already arrived. Jack and his son, Robbie, led the now placid bull out of the field while the policemen and ambulancemen went in to remove the body. Alistair sat with Claire in his Saab. She was wrapped in a blanket that one of the ambulancemen had given her.

'What happened, Claire?'

She stared out of the car window. The storm had passed now.

'Rosie,' she answered, her voice dead and empty. 'He killed her.'

'I'm so sorry, Claire,' and she leant against him and cried. He held her tightly. The stretcher came out of the field, a red blanket covering the cold body of James. Claire got out of the car. Alistair tried to stop her, but she insisted.

'I must,' she said. 'I must see him. Just once more. Please, Ali, please understand.'

'All right, but I'm coming too.'

She walked over to the ambulancemen. 'Is he dead?'

They nodded.

'It's not a pretty sight,' warned Tom.

'Please,' she asked, 'let me see.'

Tom nodded to one of the men and the blanket was pulled back to reveal only the face. It was so very pale. His black hair had stuck to his forehead making his skin even whiter.

She stepped forward, unaware of the people watching her, and laid her hand gently against his cheek.

'Goodbye,' she whispered.

It was then that she collapsed.

The town grapevine worked in double-quick time.

Alistair was sitting in the corridor waiting for news about Claire, who was now in the operating theatre, when Ange arrived. Pink and breathless, she bustled up to Alistair.

'Oh my dear, how awful for you!' She kissed him on the cheek and sat down. 'And Claire! How dreadful!'

He wearily turned to her. 'How did you hear about it?'

'Nan Burrows rang me. She knows what a good friend I am of Claire's so she rang me to let me know what had happened. Is it true that Lamont chap is dead?'

He nodded. 'Yes. And his name isn't Lamont, it's Skerrett.'

He sat back in the uncomfortable plastic chair and folded his arms across his chest. 'He was a con man, Ange, an absolute first-class con man. I found out all about him after making a few discreet enquiries from a friend of mine in London. Apparently he was up to his eyeballs in debt and desperately needed the money. Claire, believe it or not, is, or should I say, was, a distant relative of his. She got all the money from a family inheritance instead of Skerrett. That's why he was down here – to get it back.' He sipped his cup of tea. It tasted foul and he placed it back on the chair next to him.

'So what happened last night?' asked Ange.

'Well, it seems Claire discovered something about him: God knows what, although I did tell her enough of the facts but not enough to change her mind about him. I presume she told him it was all off, he went berserk, so did she, and he ended up being flattened by Jack's bull.'

Ange's eyes were very round and blue. 'My goodness, Ali, how awful!'

'That wasn't the only thing.' Alistair stared blankly at the floor by his feet. 'Rosie's dead.'

'What!'

'Claire told me herself before she collapsed and was brought in here, Constable Wilson asked me to accompany him and the detective to Tor Heights.' He paused to collect himself. 'We found Rosie's body on the kitchen table. She was mutilated beyond recognition, Ange. It was terrible. Absolutely terrible. The detective said he'd never seen anything quite so horrific.'

Ange reached for his hand. 'Oh Alistair.'

'It's Claire that really matters, Ange. That bastard Skerrett killed Rosie.' He closed his eyes to wipe out the memory. 'No wonder she went after him like she did. I think even I would if I had discovered that.' His voice fell quiet. 'I never want to see anything like that again.'

'Poor Claire,' said Ange, squeezing Alistair's hand. 'She must have been under the most intense pressure.'

Alistair smiled weakly. 'Yes, insupportable. No wonder she collapsed.'

'What did you do with Rosie's body?'

'Buried her. In the back garden. I couldn't face leaving her on the table so I suggested there and then that I dispose of her. The police were very good about it. Very understanding. I found a spade in the greenhouse and dug a hole by the kitchen window. I wrapped her in a seed bag and covered her up. It wasn't a particularly enjoyable operation, but when Claire recovers, I think she'll appreciate it.'

'Yes, of course she will.' She paused. 'Claire worshipped that animal.'

They sat in companionable silence.

'And where is she now?' Ange asked.

Alistair looked straight at her. His voice had a hollow sound to it. 'She's miscarried. The doctor told me that at some time last night she was almost certainly sexually assaulted. That's what might have caused the miscarriage.'

Ange put her hands to her horrified mouth. 'Oh . . . my . . . God!' she whispered. 'That's appalling, Ali! Terrible. Oh dear, I can't believe it.' She blinked away her sudden tears. 'Are we allowed to smoke in here?'

'No.'

'In that case, I'm going outside. I've got to have a cigarette.'

They walked slowly about the hospital car park. The sky had cleared and a faint pink dawn was beginning to break.

'She wanted a baby so much. It's all she ever used to talk about when she was married to Matt.'

'I know.'

Ange dragged deeply on her cigarette. She had stopped crying. 'Poor Claire.'

When they returned, the doctor met them.

'How is she doctor?'

'Fine, Mr Kingston. She's lost a great deal of blood, but she's young. I'm sure there will be no problems and a full recovery shouldn't take too long. However,' and he glanced awkwardly to one side, 'I'm not so sure about her mental state. She's been through a very traumatic time and it may take far longer for her to recover mentally than physically.'

'Can I go and see her now?'

'Yes, but she's still asleep.'

'That's all right. I'll wait.'

'We . . .' The doctor hesitated. 'She doesn't yet know the full extent of her injuries. There wasn't time to tell her.' His eyes searched Alistair's face. 'It might help if you were there when I tell her.'

Alistair glanced at Ange. 'Certainly.'

Ange squeezed his arm. 'I'll pop in later, Ali. I've got to get the kids sorted out. I can't leave them with Colin otherwise all hell will break loose.'

'Thanks, Ange. I'll see you then.'

'Give my love to Claire, won't you, and tell her I'll be in to see her?'

'Yes, of course.'

Claire woke up to see Alistair sitting dozing on a chair next to her bed. His eyes were shut and his chest rose and fell evenly with each breath.

At first disorientated, she soon realized where she was: the Torhampton Cottage Hospital. She was in a small room by herself and for that she was thankful. The last thing she wanted was other people around her.

She had a terrible itch on her nose and scratching it, she found her hand bandaged up on a splint with a drip going into her arm. She was very thirsty.

'Alistair.' She nudged him and he woke up.

'Hello, Claire, how are you?'

'I . . . don't know.' The tears started to fall again. 'What am I doing here?'

He leant over and brushed them away with his finger. 'It's all right now, Claire, don't cry. Everything's all right.'

'But why am I here, Ali?' She held up her arm. 'And why have I got this in my arm?'

He smiled ruefully. He was exhausted himself. 'I'll go and get the doctor. He'll tell you what's happened.'

A few minutes later, a tall sandy-haired young man

with a scrubbed face and gentle demeanour came into her room and sat down on the side of her bed. He took hold of her hand in his cool one.

Claire looked towards Alistair but he couldn't face her. Instead, he fixed his gaze out of the window. She looked back at the doctor. He had a concerned expression and gentle voice.

'I'm sorry, Mrs Bromage,' he said quietly. 'But there was nothing we could do.'

She frowned. Nothing they could do about what? She looked to Alistair for an explanation, but he continued to look steadfastly out of the window.

'About what, doctor?'

The doctor faltered. 'Didn't you know?'

She shook her head. 'Know what? What's he talking about, Ali?'

The doctor sighed. It was going to be more difficult than he'd expected to explain this one.

'You were pregnant,' he began, 'not very far gone, maybe only six or seven weeks or so. I'm sorry, but you miscarried.'

She stared open-mouthed at him. 'Pregnant? I was pregnant?' she repeated.

'Yes. Had you no idea?'

She slowly shook her head. 'No; I didn't . . . I didn't notice anything.'

He patted her hand to comfort her. 'Don't worry, Mrs Bromage, plenty of ladies have miscarriages. It's very common. There'll be other times. I'm very sorry.'

He glanced from Claire's frozen face to Alistair's. 'Well, I'll leave you now.' He backed off towards the door. 'If you have any queries . . .'

Alistair came over to Claire and held her tightly.

'I'm so sorry, Claire.'

'Oh Alistair, what have I done?'

At that moment he couldn't answer her because he was almost crying himself.

TWENTY-NINE

Autumn. A muted decay filled the air with leaves turning brown and drifting down to pile up by the side of the lanes. The days were grey and damp but it wasn't cold yet. That came later, after Christmas, with hoar frost nights that carpeted the whole landscape in a blanket of frozen glistening dew.

Claire was sitting in her kitchen, staring at a magazine. She hadn't read anything for the last half-hour. She couldn't because she still found it difficult to concentrate. She had only been home for a few weeks and it still felt peculiar to be back in her familiar surroundings, looking after herself when someone had always been there to do it for her during the last six months.

The people in the hospital had been very kind. She couldn't recall their names, but they all had gentle voices and guided her through the endless days with patience and kindness. There were the pills as well. They helped her to sleep and kept the terrible nightmares at bay, but it took a long time to get better. It was only recently that she had begun to focus on what had happened.

Dr Kent, a giant of a man with a soft, lilting Scottish accent and grey curly hair, had spent hours with her, allowing her the time to talk and talk her way back to reality. It was an infinitely slow and painful process, but she had finally done it. She no longer required any therapy but she did wonder sometimes, when she sat by herself in her empty house, just what the future held. For the first time ever, she felt unsure.

She had been nervous about leaving the hospital. Alistair picked her up and drove her home. He tried hard to cheer her up, but he wasn't successful. She preferred to sit silently and watch the landscape go by. It was much easier than trying to talk.

For the first week a nurse came by each day to check on her. The hospital had given her a large supply of pills and the nurse had to make sure that she took her prescribed amount each morning. When she was satisfied that Claire had settled back in nicely, she left her to the capable ministrations of Nan. Nan, who was as practical and capable as her husband and as strong as the very moor she lived on, treated Claire as if nothing had happened. She arrived each morning and spent her time doing the chores and tidying up while all the time, keeping up a seamless monologue of local gossip.

Sometimes Claire remembered to smile and occasionally she would pass a comment but usually she said nothing. It was far easier to let Nan gently boss her about and take charge of things. Claire really appreciated her calling each day and looked forward to it. It gave her back her sense of being that she had lost somewhere in the last six months.

Jack didn't say much. Unlike his wife, he found it difficult to talk to Claire. A mental breakdown was something he was deeply suspicious of. In his world such things were unheard of unless a person were really odd. He thought Claire was just like the rest of them and her illness shocked him.

He knew about Rosie and her butchered death. Everyone did. The whole neighbourhood was very upset about that. And James; they made a meal of that too. The town and surrounding countryside really got talking when they read all about it in the local newspaper.

The truth was, Jack was frightened. He didn't understand and he didn't know if he ever could. He listened to his wife telling him about Claire's progress but it didn't add up to him. He was wary of her. To him, it was a madness and Claire being away in that special hospital for so long only heightened his disquiet. So he avoided her.

But together with his son, he looked after her farm.

Claire had a great deal to thank them for, which was why she was reading a copy of the *Farmers Weekly*. A nearby farmer was selling his herd of Charolais cattle, which included a prize-winning bull. It would be expensive, but Claire didn't mind. Bruno had been destroyed after James's death and she knew how much of a blow that had been to Jack. She felt it was the least she could do under the circumstances. She wanted to say thank you to the old man and this seemed the most practical way of doing it.

She sighed and rested her chin on her hand and pushed the magazine away from her. She would read it later when she wasn't so tired.

A car pulled up. As usual, Claire still waited to hear Rosie's deep bark, and was still surprised when it didn't happen.

On her first night back, she had wandered aimlessly about from room to room, unable to settle until she found something that had belonged to her dog. Nan had thrown away her blanket, thinking it would upset Claire, but she hadn't found Rosie's collar and lead. Claire had put those in one of the kitchen drawers the night Rosie got killed and safely locked it. The first night back she remembered it. As soon as she had the familiar soft and worn leather in her hands, she went back to bed and slept peacefully. There were no barks, no drooling for titbits and no walks on the moor. Claire missed all of it very much but at least she had her memories.

There was a knock at the door.

'May I come in?' It was Alistair.

'Of course.'

He took off his coat and sat down at the table, kissing her on the cheek.

'How are you?'

Her smile was faint. 'Okay, getting better.'

'Good. It's not too . . . too quiet for you?'

She looked away from him and picked at a stray thread on the tablecloth. 'No, not really. Rosie . . .' She glanced up at him. 'I mean it is very quiet but I'll get used to it. Tea?'

'Yes, please.'

She filled the kettle.

'Not a nice day is it?' he commented.

'No,' she said, staring out of the window. 'All damp mists and the evenings drawing in. Sad really. The landscape seems to pull in on itself. It's very melancholy.'

'Do you have any of those nice cakes?' he asked brightly, thinking it would be better to change the subject.

'Yes.' She went to the cupboard and took down an old battered tin. 'It's Nan. She helps me out with loads of things like that. She's a much better cook than me.'

She pushed the magazine over towards him. 'I've decided how I'll pay Jack back for everything he's done for me.' She pointed at the advertisement for the auction. He read it. 'What d'you think?'

'Good idea. I'm sure Jack would appreciate that very much, although you do realize' he said, stirring his tea, 'that the bull was insured?'

'Yes, but that's not the point. It's my fault the bull had to be destroyed and I feel I ought to do something about it.'

'All right, Claire, if that's what you want, but it wasn't your fault.' She looked away from him. They had had this conversation so many times.

'Listen,' he said gently, 'you're blaming yourself for all the wrong reasons and none of it makes any sense. It was Skerrett who ran into that field, not you. You tried to stop him remember?'

'I don't know, I can . . . I think I tried to stop him. I'm not sure. God, I would have run into that field if I thought someone was chasing me with a gun.'

'But you weren't,' he insisted. 'We established that long ago. You left the gun at Briar Cottage.'

She twisted her cup in the saucer. 'I know,' she said

quietly. 'But I did go there to kill him.'

They were silent, her words hanging in the air between them.

'Claire?'

'Yes?'

'It doesn't matter any more. Whatever reasons you had for going to Briar Cottage are now immaterial. That man committed the most hideous attack on your dog and when you look at the full circumstances surrounding the case, anyone can see you were under the most extreme duress and provocation. When it comes to court I shouldn't think there'll be a case to answer. You'll probably get off with just a caution for using an offensive weapon.'

In the afternoon light, dim now as the clouds grew thicker and the tops of the tors became hidden in the mist, he could see she wasn't concentrating.

'I didn't love him, you know,' she said quietly. 'It was an obsession, sexual obsession.' She smiled, embarrassed by her words. 'There you are,' she laughed awkwardly. 'I've said it. At long bloody last I've admitted it.' She looked up at him, her eyes deep wells of mystery.

Alistair said nothing.

'It's funny,' she continued, 'the ring he gave me, the engagement ring. One of the stones fell out. When I took it to the jewellers to be repaired, he told me it was made of paste. Needless to say the pearls were fake too. Sums it all up really, doesn't it?'

'I'm sorry, Claire.'

She tried to smile but her face couldn't manage it. 'Obsession, that's what it was.' She stared out of the window. 'I can't explain it, you know.'

'Then don't, darling, it doesn't matter, really it doesn't.'

And with sudden urgency she said, 'But it does, Alistair, it does to me! Why did I do it? I have to know. Why?'

'Claire, I don't know why, no one does. These things just happen sometimes.'

He didn't know what else to say. He had been trotting out the same argument for weeks now and she still wasn't convinced.

'Why me? Why did I have to be so bloody stupid?'

'Look, Claire, at risk of sounding clichéd, all I can say is . . . well, what is it that attracts two people together in any particular set of circumstances? What is it that drives us?' He paused. 'I don't know, and what's more, neither do you nor anyone else. It just happens and last spring it happened to you. But it's all over now and you've got to get on with your life.'

For a while only the sonorous ticking of the clock could be heard. Then she said: 'Real love is different, isn't it?' It wasn't a question and he let her carry on. 'Real love is much quieter. It's something that's there all the time, only you don't really know it. It's like the background of a painting; whatever the main picture is, it's the landscape or whatever's behind it that sets it in context.'

He waited. Her voice had a distant tone to it as she settled the old ghosts to rest.

'Real love is what most of us have day in, day out, only we don't really know it. It's . . . it's what I had with Matt. And Rosie.'

'And with someone else maybe,' he said, clasping her hands in his.

'Rosie . . .'

He held her hands tighter. She always cried when she spoke of Rosie.

'I loved her, Alistair, more than anything or anyone and James knew it. He knew that by destroying her, he had destroyed me.' She put her clenched fist next to her heart. 'He knew that by doing that, he had torn me apart at my very soul.'

He passed her his hanky. She wiped her face.

'I know, Claire, believe me, I know. It was a wicked, wicked thing to do and quite honestly, I don't think anyone around here regretted his passing.' He sighed. 'It's almost a poetic justice for the bull to have killed him when he had killed Rosie.'

She blew her nose. 'Yes, it was. I take it,' she said at last, 'that there was a funeral for him somewhere?'

'Yes, after the inquest. His sister arranged it all back in London. A small event that only the immediate family attended. I found out through my contacts up there that he was virtually penniless: no property, no business and no capital.'

Claire looked at him, puzzled. 'Are you sure?'

'Why do you ask?'

'Because I gave him fifteen thousand pounds for a deposit on a house he said he had found us.'

Alistair shook his head. 'No, there was nothing.'

'I wonder where it went then?'

'Probably gambling. He did a lot of that and from what I can gather, was singularly unsuccessful at it. It seems that he owed a very large sum of money and it wasn't to a bank either, although he was also wanted for questioning over some fraudulent deals, I gather. All in all, he was up to his eyeballs in more ways than one.'

She looked at her hands, so small in his.

'I'm sorry, Claire. Is all this upsetting you?'

'No, really it isn't.' She smiled weakly.

'Well, at least he didn't get his hands on any more of your legacy.'

'No, thank goodness.'

'I take it you have been to see Peter Collier since your return?'

'No, not yet,' and seeing his slight frown, she added, 'but don't worry, Ali, I will soon. After all this, do you really think I wouldn't?'

'No, of course not,' and his smile was one of relief.

They finished their tea, happier now than they had been for a long time. It seemed to Alistair that Claire had, in her

499

own way, turned a corner. She was definitely on the mend. Quieter perhaps and more wary, but she was coming back.

'So what are you going to do now?'

'About what?'

'About everything. Are you going to stay here?'

'Yes. Do you remember that Neale chap who wanted to buy me out? Heavens, I got him all wrong, he turned out to be all right really when before I had thought him to be a real pig.'

He smiled. 'We all make mistakes, Claire.'

'Well yes, I know, and some of us make them far more often than others.' They smiled at each other. 'Anyway, when he came with his family to look around, he said that he was going to rip out this and that wall, put in central heating, and totally revamp the place, and I've been thinking.'

'What?'

'Well, he gave me some ideas. I've decided,' she said, more animated than he had seen her look for months, 'that I'm going to spend whatever it takes doing the whole place up. I'll get it done professionally, hire an interior designer, the whole works. As Neale said, the place has potential and now that I'm back I can see what he meant. Yes,' she said, looking round the room, 'I'm going to have it all painted and redecorated, everything. Wipe out the past and start all over again.'

'That's great, Claire,' he enthused. 'So you won't be leaving here then?'

'No, of course not. This is my home. It's where I belong and I'll never leave it.'

'I can't tell you how pleased I am to hear that.'

'Well, it's only right, isn't it? Matt and I spent so much effort getting this place going as a farm, I mean, it just wouldn't be fair for me to walk out on it.' She looked at him. 'Who knows, Ali, you might even want to come here a bit more often if I put central heating in.'

'You won't need to ask twice, Claire.'

'You know, I didn't think I would. There are plenty of things round here that need to be done by someone who has muscles like yours. Chucking a few bales of hay around should be no problem for you.'

'I'd be only too happy to. Anyway,' he said, 'to change the subject, I have something for you.'

'You do?'

He held up a plastic carrier bag that he had brought in with him. 'It's a rose,' he said. 'A deep red one with the most gorgeous scent. I thought we could plant it on Rosie's grave.'

Her face broke out into a wreath of smiles.

'Oh Alistair, that's wonderful! How considerate of you,' and she leant over the table and kissed him. 'I really can't thank you enough for what you did for me, especially about Rosie. To tell the truth, I find it hard to picture what she looked like that night. I think I must have wiped it all away somehow. But then I have my photos and that's something.' She hesitated. 'Anyway, you came and buried her and that was exactly the right thing to do. Thank you.'

'Don't even think about it. It was the least I could do. You would have done exactly the same for me. Shall we go and plant it?'

They went out into the damp autumnal garden with its moist smells of slowly decaying vegetation. Weeds and grass had grown over Rosie's grave during Claire's absence but she didn't mind. There would always be a slight bump on the lawn and now that Alistair had got a beautiful rose to plant on it, there would be a continual reminder of her beautiful, beloved dog.

He dug out a sizeable hole and put in the rose. Claire pushed in the wet soil and stamped it down with her boot.

'There,' he said, 'that's better, isn't it? A fitting memorial for one who so richly deserves it. You wait, next summer

501

there will be flowers all over this bush. You'll be able to smell them from the kitchen if you have the window open.'

Claire smiled. The tears threatened but didn't fall. Her dog was gone and although she still missed her every day, the pain was lessening. She had even allowed herself to stroke Jack's new bitch the other day, something she never could have done a few weeks ago. The rain had started again. Claire didn't have her jacket on.

'Go inside,' he said. 'I'll be in in a minute. I've just got to get something from the car.'

She was making a fresh pot of tea when the door opened. She turned around expecting to see Alistair when in came a small black and tan puppy, wobbling on its sturdy legs and huge feet.

'Alistair! What is it?'

She fell to her knees and gathered up the pup who wriggled excitedly in her arms and tried to lick her face.

'Alistair! You so and so! You're wonderful! Oh thank you so much!'

This time they were tears of joy that fell down her face as she laughed. She kissed him. 'Thank you so much. She's beautiful, Ali, a real beauty.'

Alistair beamed. He had so wanted her to be happy with the dog. Initially he had hesitated about giving it to her, worried that she might find it all a bit too much and be unable to cope with it. He changed his mind, however, after seeing her doctor who said it would be an excellent idea.

'What is she, Ali?'

'German shepherd dog – an Alsatian; a long-haired one. My mother has kept GSDs for years and this was the best of the latest litter. Mother says she's a fine big specimen and will make a very good pet. She knows your circumstances,' he added more quietly, 'and all that happened with Rosie. She was really upset when I told her and it

502

was more her idea than mine that I should give you this puppy.'

'Well really thank her for me, won't you, Ali, because she's beautiful.'

'She's got a pedigree as long as your arm. Her dam does all kinds of work at home and I'm sure the puppy will be just as capable. Sheep dog or house pet, she'll work for her keep no matter what.'

Claire cuddled the puppy who was hell bent on trying to eat her fingers. 'Ow! My goodness, I'd forgotten what sharp teeth they have at this age.'

Alistair watched them both. He was overjoyed. 'What are you going to call her?'

'Not Rosie, if that's what you're asking.'

'I didn't think you would.'

'No, there was only one Rosie and no other dog could replace her.' She held up the wriggling puppy. 'I think I'll call her Polly,' and she put her on the floor.

'Polly,' repeated Alistair. 'That sounds like a very suitable name to me, and by the look of things, she's starting as she means to go on!'

The dog had made a puddle on the floor.

Claire picked her up. 'Little terror,' she said gently, 'I can see you're going to be a real handful for me.'

She put the pup to one side while she cleaned up the mess. Then she and Alistair sat down at the table watching the curious new arrival who began to explore the kitchen.

'She's beautiful, Ali, I can't thank you enough.'

He held her hands in his. 'Yes you can, Claire. There is a way that would more than make up for it.'

'How?'

'Don't you know?' he asked her, tenderly pushing a stray lock of hair to one side of her face. 'Can't you see what you mean to me? What you've always meant to me?'

She started to cry.

He put his arms around her shoulders and pulled her close to him.

'Why are you crying, Claire? You should be happy.'

'I know,' she sniffed, 'but . . . well, I've been so stupid, haven't I? I knew all along what you felt for me, but I couldn't face it. I feel so idiotic.'

'Rubbish,' he said, smiling and kissing each of her cheeks. 'It just took you a bit longer to realize that you felt the same way, that's all.'

'I know. I can't think what happened to me. Couldn't see the wood for the trees, I suppose.'

And then they kissed, the puppy chewing one of Alistair's shoelaces.

'I love you, Claire.'

'And I love you, Ali.'

THIRTY

'Well then, what do you think?' Saskia turned from side to side in front of the full-length mirror.

Terri watched her with apathy from the bed. She was far more interested in the apple she was eating than Saskia's dress.

'Terri! I asked you a question!'

Terri looked up. 'Very nice.'

'Do you mean that?'

'Yes I do. For a wedding dress, it looks fine. It's white, full-length, and nicely patterned with bits and bobs. So what else does it need?'

'Don't be like that, Terri,' she whined. 'You know how much this means to me.'

'What? Getting married to the dumb moron or getting married wearing that dress?'

Saskia turned round sharply.

Two years had passed since they had come to Australia – eventful ones for both of them. The Australian sun had bleached her hair even blonder and she had slimmed down considerably, finding it difficult to eat in the tropical heat of Queensland.

'Can't you show any enthusiasm, not even a little bit? And he's not a dumb moron. I happen to love him.'

Terri got off the bed and went over to the window. The view from the house was stunning: miles of unbroken sand and surf stretching along the coast for as far as the eye could see. It was beautiful. She squinted up her eyes in the bright sunshine. It was far too hot to go out yet.

'Of course I'm happy for you, Saskia, but I can't get all excited about weddings. It's impossible. As far as I'm concerned, it's one step away from white slavery. You might as well have a ring through your nose as on your finger.'

'Oh Terri, how silly can you get? Norman's not like that at all! For goodness' sake! Any man who is the only son of the most powerful family in the state is not going to treat me like his slave. He's got money enough to employ other people for that.'

'Okay, if you say so.' She went back to her magazine on the bed. 'Do I have to wear that bloody awful outfit you picked out for me?'

'Yes. You're my maid of honour, for heaven's sake, of course you've got to dress up for it.'

'Christ! I'll hate it. I know I will.'

'No you won't. There's going to be a huge buffet and dance afterwards. It'll be fantastic.'

'Is your father coming?'

Saskia's face fell. 'I don't know. Mum says she's finally got him to realize it wasn't my fault that the house in London got burnt down just after we left. The police convinced him it was arson but they never arrested anyone. God knows why anyone did it. Probably someone with a grudge against James.'

'Yes, you never did hear from him again, did you?'

'No. I wonder what happened to him?'

'Sharon! Sharon!'

'Oh God. What?'

'What the hell are you doing up there?'

'What does it look like, Patrick? I'm having my lunch.'

'Really? Large rum and soda eh? Call that lunch?'

'Don't snipe, Patrick, it doesn't suit you.'

'Well, dear, now that you're so comfortably ensconced on your trim behind, there's a customer for you.'

'Oh Patrick, do I have to?'

'Yes, otherwise you'll be pissed by the time you come downstairs again. It's a very important customer and given

506

you're my best stylist – heaven forbid – I want you to see to her.'

'Can't Sue or Lizzy do it?'

'No. I want you. So move it.'

'And what if I won't go?'

'Then, my dear, I'll have to think twice before getting your visa extended. So move your arse!'

'Bastard! By the way, Patrick, who is it?'

The man smiled, his white teeth very bright in his black face.

'A friend of yours, I believe.'

Sharon went downstairs, clicking on her high heels down the narrow dimly lit stairway. She went through a door marked 'Staff Only' and out into the hot fragrant salon.

All round her sat ladies, expensively dressed and pampered as they had their nails polished or their hair set. Sharon said hello to several of them as she walked past on the way to her station. She was well known now among the island's rich clientele and she liked to keep in with them.

Her work area was in the middle of the salon. It was her right as the best hairdresser to have the biggest, most prominent area. Everything there; all the equipment, her combs, brushes, sprays and shampoos, were used by her alone. She had fought hard for her recognition.

'Good morning, madam, and how may I help you today?'

She looked up and stopped dead in her tracks, a very familiar face looking back at her.

'Well, well, well. If it isn't good old Elyssa! I'd heard through the gossips that you'd gone to ground somewhere when the bank crashed, although I had no idea it was here. So how are you?'

Elyssa needed a drink. She avoided Claudia's eyes and looked down at the floor. She was so embarrassed.

'Fine,' she said, tight-lipped.

507

'Aren't you going to say anything else?' drawled Claudia. 'It's not like you to be so reticent.'

'I'm fine, Claudia, honestly.'

'Lady Myers to you if you don't mind, Elyssa. Rupert was knighted last year for services to British Industry. Or should I call you Sharon? I gather that's your real name. Kevin, your chauffeur, told me before he left you.'

Elyssa blanched under her tan. The treacherous bastard!

'Whatever you like, Lady Myers,' she sneered.

'Now now, Sharon, keep your nails covered. I'm sure your boss wouldn't like it if you misbehaved,' and she smiled again. 'My, how the mighty have fallen! Who would have thought that you'd end up working as a hairdresser! Ha! It's like some dreadful tabloid headline, isn't it? It must be so awful for you having to work for your living again.'

Elyssa took hold of a lock of Claudia's hair, rather too tightly. 'How would you like it, madam?' she said through clenched teeth.

'Aditha! Come and have a look at this!'

'What is it, Kevin?'

'Look! We've got a write-up.'

'What's that?'

'That man, the reporter bloke, who came in the other night — well, he says some really nice things here about us. "The food's delicious the atmosphere is delightful and the service prompt." He also says,' he added, his eyes shining, '"that the part owner, Mrs Aditha Smith, gives an authentic ambience and feel to the place." There,' he said proudly looking at his wife. 'How about that?'

She kissed him. 'That lovely, Kevin. Very good. I told you we could do it.'

'Yes you did and I'm bloody glad I listened to you. How's little 'un then?' and he swung his young daughter out of her mother's arms and up into the air so that she squealed with delight at her father's antics.

'She very good girl, Kevin, and don't throw her like that, she only just have her breakfast.'

He cuddled his wife and daughter, a smaller mop-headed version of her mother with the same brown almond-shaped eyes and wide, white smile.

'I'm so glad I met you, Aditha. You're the best thing that ever happened to me.'

'We love you too. Both of us.'

'Yeah, and there'll be more of us next week.'

'Oh Kevin. I so excited. A new house and my mother and son coming to live with us. I tell them all about King's Lynn. They very excited.'

'Good and I can't wait to meet them either.'

'Hello.'

Claire opened her eyes and the first thing she saw was a huge bouquet of flowers. Then Alistair's face appeared, smiling broadly. He kissed her.

'Did I wake you?'

She rubbed her eyes. 'No not really. I was just having a nap.'

'Flowers for you,' and he placed them on her hospital bed.

'They're beautiful, Ali, really nice, although,' she laughed, 'I don't know if the nurses will be able to find a vase big enough for them.'

'Oh I'm sure they will,' he said, sitting on the chair next to her bed. 'How are you? You look a bit better than when I saw you at 5.30 this morning.'

'I'm not surprised, Ali! All that effort. I was absolutely exhausted.'

'But you're feeling better now?'

'Yes. Much. A bit tired still, and a bit sore, but I'm getting better.'

'And where is she then?' He looked round the ward. The two other patients had their babies.

'She's in the nursery. The nurse took her down there to

change her because I was too tired to do it myself. She'll be back in a minute.'

'I'm so proud of you,' he said beaming. 'You did really well last night. It looked pretty dramatic from where I stood. I'm amazed I didn't pass out.'

'You were wonderful, Ali. I couldn't have done it without your help now, could I?'

The nurse arrived then, pushing a Perspex cot, a small blanket-wrapped bundle lying inside it.

'Mr Kingston, Mrs Kingston, your daughter.'

She brought the cot round to Alistair's side of the bed. He looked in, the nurse and Claire exchanging understanding maternal looks.

'My goodness!' he exclaimed. 'Look at the size of her. She's tiny!'

'Not really, Mr Kingston. She was eight pounds eight ounces and that's a good size for a first baby.'

He cautiously touched her hand and the miniature fingers grabbed hold tightly to his large one. He smiled with delight and astonishment.

'Heavens, she's gripping really hard.'

'They all do, Mr Kingston. It's part of the newborn reflexes.'

'Would you like to hold her, Ali?'

He abruptly turned round. 'I couldn't. She's too small. I'll drop her or something.'

'Not at all, Mr Kingston,' assured the nurse with experienced patience. 'Babies are much tougher than they look and you'll have to get used to her sometime.'

He looked at his wife. 'Are you sure?'

Claire laughed. 'Of course, Ali. Sit down here and hold out your arms.'

The nurse picked up the wrapped golden-haired bundle. He looked apprehensive.

'Put your arm like that and then you'll be supporting her head. Okay? There, you look as though you've been doing it all your life.'

'I don't feel like it.'

'Don't worry, Mr Kingston, all new fathers feel worried to start with. You'll soon get used to it. Right then, Mrs Kingston, I'll leave you to it,' and she smiled warmly as she walked away.

'I can't believe it, Claire. Look at her.'

The baby's face, pink and white and fast asleep, was surrounded by small silken tufts of hair.

'She's beautiful,' he whispered.

'She's going to be a redhead,' said Claire.

'Do you think so?'

'Oh yes, her hair's exactly the same colour as your moustache. Mind you,' she added, 'I hope she takes after me on the size front. It's all very well having a rugby playing husband, but I don't want a daughter who's that big.'

'Don't worry,' he said, rocking the baby gently, 'she looks every bit like you.'

They both admired their offspring.

'Has your mother arrived yet?'

'Yes. She took Polly out for a long walk this morning and told me to tell you she thinks you've done a marvellous job with her. And she really likes her new flat over the barn. Says the view is lovely.'

'High praise indeed coming from your Mum. And the cow?'

'Milked her myself, the miserable old bag. I don't think she likes me. She wouldn't let down at all to start with.'

'Poor Ali. Did she kick you?'

'No, but she upset the bucket. I'll have to buy some milk later.'

'Oh dear. Never mind, darling. I'll be home soon.'

'Not soon enough. Tor Heights isn't the same without you.'

'Thank you, Ali.'

He kissed her. 'Have we decided on a name for Miss Kingston?'

'Yes. Rose Alexandra.'

'Mmm,' he said, 'very nice. Very . . . English.'

'Of course,' she added, 'if I call her Rosie by mistake, you won't mind, will you?'

'Oh Claire, how could I, darling? I think it's a beautiful name.' He turned back to the baby. 'Rose Alexandra. Just beautiful.'